THE BILLIONAIRES COLLECTION

High-powered negotiations, exotic locales and lavish parties…marriages of convenience, surprise pregnancies and undeniable passions. This 2-in-1 collection will take you into the luxurious world of the rich and powerful, where all that you could ever desire is at your fingertips.…

But for these irresistible tycoons, the thing they want the most is the thing they'll have to work the hardest to attain.… Because the stakes are never higher for these passionate, jet-setting men than when they're fighting for the affection of the women they love.

LYNNE GRAHAM

lives in Northern Ireland and has been a keen romance reader since her teens. Happily married, Lynne has five children. Her eldest is her only natural child. Her other children, who are every bit as dear to her heart, are adopted. The family has a variety of pets, and Lynne loves gardening, cooking, collecting of all sorts and is crazy about every aspect of Christmas. Visit her online at her website at www.lynnegraham.com.

LYNNE GRAHAM

A Spanish Affair

 HARLEQUIN® THE BILLIONAIRES COLLECTION

Recycling programs
for this product may
not exist in your area.

ISBN-13: 978-0-373-60614-6

A SPANISH AFFAIR
Copyright © 2014 by Harlequin Books S.A.

The publisher acknowledges the copyright holder
of the individual works as follows:

NAIVE BRIDE, DEFIANT WIFE
Copyright © 2010 by Lynne Graham

FLORA'S DEFIANCE
Copyright © 2011 by Lynne Graham

HARLEQUIN®
www.Harlequin.com

Printed in U.S.A.

CONTENTS

NAIVE BRIDE, DEFIANT WIFE 7

FLORA'S DEFIANCE 171

NAIVE BRIDE,
DEFIANT WIFE

CHAPTER ONE

ALEJANDRO NAVARRO VASQUEZ, the Conde Olivares, sat on his superb black stallion in the shade of an orange grove and surveyed the valley that had belonged to his ancestors for over five hundred years. On this fine spring morning, below a clear blue sky, it was a gorgeous view encompassing thousands of acres of fertile earth and woodland. He owned the land as far as the eye could see, but his lean, darkly handsome features were grim as they had often been since the breakdown of his marriage almost two and a half years earlier.

He was a landowner and wealthy, but his family—which every Spaniard cherished far beyond material riches—had been ripped asunder by his imprudent marriage. For a male as strong, proud and successful as Alejandro, it was a bitter truth that undermined his every achievement. He had followed his heart and not his head and he had married the wrong woman, a very expensive mistake for which he was still paying the price. His half-brother, Marco, had taken a job in New York, cutting off all contact with his mother and siblings. Yet if Marco, whom Alejandro had helped to raise after their father's premature death, had appeared before him at that moment could he have forgiven the younger man and urged him back to his childhood home with sincerity and warm affection?

Alejandro swore under his breath as he pondered that merciless question and the less than acceptable negative answer that he would have had to give it. However, when it came to *Jemima*, there was no forgiveness in his heart, only outrage and aggression. He nursed a far from charitable desire for vengeance against the wife and the brother who had together betrayed his trust and his love. Ever since Jemima had walked out on their marriage and disappeared, defying his wishes to the last, Alejandro had burned with a desire for justice, even while his keen intelligence warned him that there was no such thing when it came to affairs of the heart.

His mobile phone vibrated and, suppressing a groan of impatience, for it was always a struggle to protect his rare moments of leisure, he tugged it out. His ebony brows rose when he learned that the private detective he had hired to find Jemima had arrived to see him. He rode swiftly back to the castle, wondering impatiently if Alonso Ortega had finally managed to track down his estranged wife.

'My apologies for coming to see you without an appointment, Your Excellency,' the older man murmured with punctilious good manners and a promising air of accomplishment. 'But I knew you would want to hear my news as soon as possible. I have found the Condesa.'

'In England?' Alejandro questioned and, having had that long-held suspicion confirmed, he listened while Ortega furnished further details. Then, unfortunately, at that point his mother, the dowager countess, entered the room. A formidable presence, Doña Hortencia settled acid black eyes on the private detective and demanded to know if he had finally fulfilled the purpose of his hire. At the news that he had, a rare smile of approval lightened her expression.

'There is one more fact I should add,' Ortega revealed in a reluctant tone of voice, evading the uncomfortably intense scrutiny of his noble hostess. 'The Condesa now has a child, a little boy of around two years of age.'

Alejandro froze and a yawning silence greeted the detective's startling announcement.

The door opened again and his older sister, Beatriz, entered with a quiet apology to her brother for the interruption. She was hushed into silence by her domineering mother, who said glacially, 'That wanton English witch who married your unlucky brother has given birth to a bastard.'

Horrified at such an announcement being made in front of Alonso Ortega, Beatriz shot her brother an appalled glance and hastened to offer the detective refreshments in an effort to change the subject to one less controversial. His discomfited sister, Alejandro appreciated, would quite happily sit and discuss the weather now while he, her more primitive brother, was strongly tempted to seize hold of Ortega's lapels and force every single fact from the man without further ado. But, possibly sensing his employer's impatience, the detective handed Alejandro a slim file and hastily excused himself.

'A...child?' Beatriz gasped in shock and consternation the instant the door had closed on the detective's departure. 'But *whose* child?'

His profile set like granite, Alejandro answered his sister only with a dismissive shrug. It was certainly not his child, but for him that had to be the biggest badge of ignominy he had ever endured. Yet another metaphorical nail in Jemima's coffin, he conceded bitterly. Jemima, he had learned the hard way, knew exactly how best to put a man through an emotional and physical wringer. *Dios mio*, another man's child!

'If only you had listened to me,' Doña Hortencia lamented. 'The instant I met that wicked young woman I knew she was wrong for you. You were one of the biggest matrimonial prizes in Spain and you could have married anyone—'

'I married Jemima,' Alejandro pointed out tersely, for he had never had much time for the older woman's melodrama.

'Only because she mesmerised you like the shameless hussy she is. One man was never going to be enough for her. Thanks to her, my poor Marco is living on the other side of the world. That she could have given birth to an illegitimate child while still bearing our name is the most disgusting thing I ever—'

'Enough!' Alejandro incised with crushing force to close out that carping voice. 'There is no point to such recriminations now. What is done is done.'

Doña Hortencia, her lined face full of anger and malice, rested accusing eyes on his lean strong visage. 'But it is *not* done yet, is it? You still haven't begun divorce proceedings.'

'I will travel to England and see Jemima as soon as the arrangements can be made,' Alejandro pronounced grittily.

'Send the family lawyer! There can be no need for you to make a personal trip to England,' his mother protested with vigour.

'There is every need,' Alejandro contradicted with all the quiet, unhesitating assurance of his rich, well-educated and extremely aristocratic background. 'Jemima is still my wife.'

As Doña Hortencia broke into another barrage of loud objections Alejandro lost patience. 'I inform you of my intentions only as a matter of courtesy. I do not require either your permission or your approval.'

Alejandro retired to the privacy of his study and poured himself a stiff brandy. A child? Jemima had had a child. He was still in shock at that revelation, not least because he could hardly forget that his wife had miscarried *his* baby shortly before she'd left him. That was how he knew beyond any shadow of doubt that this child, which she had given birth to since, then could not possibly be his. So, was the boy Marco's baby? Or some other man's? Such speculation was sordid, he acknowledged with a distaste that slivered through his lean powerful frame like a knife blade.

He leafed through the file but the facts were few. Jemima was now living in a Dorset village where she ran a florist's shop. For a moment as he allowed himself to think about his estranged wife memories threatened to overwhelm him, but he shut them out, utilising the fierce intelligence and self-discipline that were second nature to him. Yet where had either trait been when he got involved with Jemima Grey in the first place?

He could make no excuses for his behaviour because he had freely acknowledged the huge and irrefutable differences between them even before he married her. Of course, what had mesmerised him then—to borrow his mother's expression—was Jemima's superlative sex appeal. Like many men, he had been more vulnerable to that temptation than he had ever realised he might be. Possibly life prior to that point had spoiled him with too many easy female conquests. His failure to keep a lid on his fierce sexual desire to possess Jemima's pale slim body had proved to be his fatal weakness, he assured himself with grim conviction. Fortunately, however, the passage of time and the process of hard disillusionment he had experienced during his short-lived marriage had obliterated Jemima's desirability factor entirely.

His ill-judged marriage had, after all, virtually destroyed his family circle. But in the short term, Jemima had no family support of her own and she was still his legal wife; regardless of his feelings on that score she remained *his* responsibility. As did her child, whom the law would deem to be his child until a divorce was finalised, Alejandro conceded, irate at that demeaning fact. He had to go to England.

No Conde Olivares since the fifteenth century had ever been known to act as a coward or to shirk his duty, no matter how unpleasant it might be. Even in the most trying circumstances, Alejandro expected no less of himself. He reckoned that Jemima was fortunate to be a twenty-first-century woman, for his medieval ancestors would have locked an unfaithful wife up in a convent or killed her for inflicting such a stain on the family honour. Though at least his less civilised ancestors had possessed the power of retaliation, he reflected broodingly.

WHILE JEMIMA WRAPPED the bouquet in clear, decorative cellophane, Alfie peered round the corner of the shop counter, his big brown eyes dancing with mischief. ''Ello,' he said chirpily to the waiting customer, shyness not being one of Alfie's personality traits.

'Hello. He's a beautiful child,' the woman remarked, smiling down at Alfie as the toddler looked up at her with his irrepressible grin.

It was a compliment that often came Alfie's way, his mother conceded as she slotted the payment in the till, while wondering what age her son would reach before that particular description embarrassed him. But like father like son, she thought ruefully, and in looks Alfie was very much a product of his Spanish father's genes, with gorgeous dark brown eyes, olive-tinted skin and a shock of black silky hair. All he had inherited from his less exotic mother was her rampant curls. On the inside, however, Alfie had all the easy warmth of his mother's essentially optimistic nature and revealed only the occasional hint of his father's infinitely darker and more passionate temperament.

With a slight shiver, Jemima pushed that daunting thought back out of her mind again. With Alfie playing with his toy cars at her feet, she returned to fashioning a flower arrangement requested by a client who had photographed a similar piece of floral art at a horticultural show. Pure accident had brought Jemima to the village of Charlbury St Helens at a crisis point in her life and she had never regretted staying on and laying the foundations for her new future there.

The only work she'd been able to find locally while she'd been pregnant was as an assistant at a flower shop. She had needed to earn back her self-respect by keeping busy and positive. Discovering that she had a very real interest in floristry, she had found more than a job to focus on and had since studied part-time for formal qualifications. By the time her employer decided to retire, owing to ill health, Jemima had had the courage and vision to take over the business and expand it by taking on occasional private projects that encompassed small weddings and other functions.

She was so proud of running her own business that sometimes she had to pinch herself to believe that she could have come so far from her humble beginnings. Not bad for the daughter of a violent, criminal father who had never worked if he could help it, and a downtrodden, alcoholic mother, who had died when her husband crashed a stolen car. Jemima had never dared to develop any aspirations as a teenager. Nobody in her family tree had ever tried to climb the career or social ladders.

'Those kinds of ideas aren't for the likes of us. Jem needs to get a job to help out at home,' her mother had told the teacher who'd tried to persuade the older woman that her daughter should stay on at school to study for her A-level exams.

'You're like your mother—dumb as a rock and just about as useful!' her father had condemned often enough for that label to have troubled Jemima for many year afterwards.

With lunch eaten, she walked Alfie down to his session at the playgroup in the village hall, wincing when her son bounded boisterously through the door calling his friends' names at the top of his voice. Alfie, named for his great-grandfather on Jemima's mother's side of the family, was very sociable and full of energy after spending the morning cooped up at the shop with his mother. Although Jemima had created a play corner in the backstore room for her child, there really wasn't enough space to house a lively little boy for long. With the help of a childminder, she had often contrived to keep Alfie with her during working hours, but now that he was of an age to join the playgroup in the afternoons and she no longer attended floristry classes she needed a lot less childcare. Considering that her close friend and former childminder, Flora, was now often too busy with her bed-and-breakfast operation to help out as much, Jemima was grateful for that fact.

It was a pleasant surprise therefore when Flora came into the shop an hour later and asked Jemima if she had time for a coffee. Brewing up in the small kitchen, Jemima eyed her red-headed friend and read the other woman's uneasiness with a frown. 'What's up?'

'It's probably nothing. I meant to come over and tell you at the weekend, but a whole family booked in with me on Saturday and I was run off my feet,' Flora groaned. 'Apparently some guy in a hire car was hanging around the village last Thursday and someone saw him taking a picture of your shop. He was asking questions about you in the post office as well.'

Jemima stilled, dark blue eyes widening while her heart-shaped face paled below her cloud of wildly curling strawberry-blonde hair and the stance of her tiny slender figure screamed tension. Just an inch over five feet in height, she had reminded the more solidly built Flora of a delicate blown-glass angel ornament when they'd first met, but she had later appreciated that nobody as down-to-earth and quirky as Jemima could be seen for long in that improbable light. However, her friend was unquestionably beautiful in an ethereal way and if men could be equated to starving dogs, Jemima was the equivalent of a very juicy bone, for the male sex seemed to find her irresistible. Locals joked that the church choir had been on the brink of folding before Jemima had joined and a swell of young men had soon followed in her wake, not that any of them had since got anywhere with her, Flora reflected wryly. Badly burned by her failed marriage, Jemima preferred men as friends and concentrated her energies on her son and her business.

'What sort of questions?' Jemima prompted sickly, the cold chill of apprehension hollowing out her stomach.

'Whether or not you lived around here, and what age Alfie was. The guy asking the questions was young and good-looking. Maurice in the post office thought he was playing cupid...'

'Was the man Spanish?'

Flora shook her head and took over from her anxious friend at the kettle to speed up the arrival of the coffee. 'No, a Londoner according to Maurice. He probably just fancied trying his chances with you—'

'I don't remember *any* young good-looking men coming in here last week,' Jemima pointed out, her concern patent.

'Maybe he lost interest once he realised you were a mother.' Flora shrugged. 'I wouldn't have told you about him if I had known you would get wound up about it. Why don't you just get on the phone and tell...er...what's his name, your husband?'

'Alejandro,' Jemima supplied tautly. 'Tell him what?'

'That you want a clean break and a divorce.'

'Nobody gets away with telling Alejandro what to do.

He's the one who does the telling. It wouldn't be that simple once he found out about Alfie.'

'So you go to a solicitor and say what a lousy husband he was.'

'He didn't drink or beat me up.'

Flora grimaced. 'Why should such extremes be your only yardstick? There are other grounds for divorce, like mental abuse and neglect—and what about the way he left you at the mercy of his horrible family?'

'It was his mother who was horrible, not his brother or his sister,' Jemima pointed out, wanting as always to be fair. 'And I don't think it's right to say I was mentally abused.'

Flora, whose temper was as hot as her hair, regarded the younger woman with unimpressed eyes. 'Alejandro criticised everything you did, left you alone all the time and got you pregnant before you were ready to have a kid.'

Jemima reddened to the roots of her light-coloured hair and marvelled that she could have been so frank with Flora in the early weeks of their friendship, sharing secrets that she sometimes wished she had kept to herself, although not, mercifully, the worst secrets of all. Of course, back then, she had been as steamed up as a pressure cooker of emotions and in dire need of someone to talk to. 'I just wasn't good enough for him…' She spoke the truth as she saw it, as lightly as she could.

Growing up, Jemima had never been good enough for either of her parents and the ability to search out and focus on her own flaws was second nature to her. Her mother had entered her in juvenile beauty contests as a young child but Jemima, too shy to smile for the photos and too quiet to chatter when interviewed, had not shone. Bored out of her mind as she was as a daydreaming teenager, she had done equally poorly at the office-skills course her mother had sent her on, shattering her mother's second dream of her becoming a high-powered personal assistant to some millionaire who would some day fall madly in love with her daughter. Her mother had pretty much lived in a fantasy world, which, along with the alcohol, had provided her with her only escape from the drudgery and abuse of a bad marriage.

Jemima's father, whose only dreams related to making pots of money without ever getting up off the sofa, had wanted Jemima to become a model, but she failed to grow tall enough for fashion work and lacked the bountiful curves necessary for the other kind. After her mother's death, her father had urged her to become a dancer at a club run by his mate and had hit her and thrown her out of the family home when she'd refused to dress up in a skimpy outfit and attend an audition. It was years before she saw her father again and then in circumstances she preferred to forget. Yes, Jemima had learned at an early age that people always expected more from her than she ever seemed able to deliver and, sadly, her marriage had proved no different. It was for that reason that making her own way in life to set up and run her business had added greatly to her confidence; for once she had surpassed her own expectations.

Yet when she had first met Alejandro and he had swept her off her feet, he had seemed to be *her* every dream come true, which in retrospect seemed laughable to her. But love had snatched her up like a tornado and made her believe in the impossible before it flung her down again. Somehow, and she had no idea how, she had truly believed that she could marry a rich, educated foreigner with a pedigree as long as her arm and make a go of it. But in practice the challenges and the disparities had proved insurmountable. Her background had come back to seriously haunt her, but her biggest single mistake had been getting too friendly with her brother-in-law, Marco. Although, she reasoned defensively, had Alejandro been around more and made more effort to help her come to terms with her new life in Spain she wouldn't have been so lonely and wouldn't have jumped at the offer of Marco's company. And she had *adored* Marco, she acknowledged abstractedly, recalling how wounded she had felt when even after her marriage broke down he had made no attempt to get in touch with her again.

'You were *too* good for that husband of yours,' Flora told Jemima with strong emphasis. 'But you really should tell Alejandro about Alfie instead of staying in hiding as if you have something to be ashamed of.'

Jemima turned her head away, her cheeks colouring as she thought, *If only you knew...* Telling the whole unvarnished truth would probably turn her closest friend off her as well, she reckoned painfully.

'I honestly believe that if Alejandro found out about Alfie, he would go to any lengths to get custody of him and take him back to Spain to live,' she replied heavily. 'Alejandro takes his responsibilities towards the family very seriously.'

'Well, if you think there's a risk of Alfie being snatched by his father, you're wise keeping quiet about him,' Flora said, although there was an uncertain look on her face when she voiced that opinion. 'But you can't keep him quiet for ever.'

'Only, for now, it's the best option,' Jemima declared, setting down her coffee to attend to a customer as the shop bell on the door sounded.

Soon afterwards, she went out to deliver a floral arrangement for a dinner party to one of the big houses outside the village. On the way home she collected Alfie, his high energy dissipated by a couple of hours of horseplay. The tiny terraced cottage she rented on the outskirts of the village enjoyed a garden, which she had equipped with a swing and a sandpit. She was proud of her small living space. Although the little house was inexpertly painted and furnished cheaply with flat-pack furniture, it was the first place she had ever been able to make feel like her home since childhood.

Sometimes it seemed like a dim and unbelievable fairy tale to recall that after she had married Alejandro she had lived in a castle. *Castillo del Halcón,* the Castle of the Hawk, built by his warrior ancestors in a mix of Islamic and European styles and filled with history, luxury and priceless artefacts. Moving the furniture or the pictures around had been forbidden and redecorating equally frowned on because the dowager countess, Doña Hortencia, could not bear any woman to interfere in what she still essentially saw as her home. Living there, Jemima had often felt like a lodger who had outstayed her welcome, and the formal lifestyle of changing into evening clothes for dinner, dealing with servants and entertaining important guests had suited her even less.

Had there been any redeeming features to her miserable marriage? she asked herself, and instantly a picture of Alejandro popped up unbidden inside her head. Her spectacularly gorgeous husband had initially felt like a prize beyond any other she had ever received, yet she had never quite been able to stifle the feeling that she didn't deserve him and he deserved better than her. It crossed Jemima's mind that most of the best things that had happened to her in life had occurred seemingly because of blessed accidents of fate. That description best covered Alfie's unplanned conception, her car choosing to break down in Charlbury St Helens after she had run away from Spain, her marriage, and ironically it even covered her first meeting with Alejandro…

He had knocked her off her bike in a car park or, rather, his driver's overly assertive driving style had done so.

She had been on her day off from the hotel where she was working as a receptionist and riding a bicycle was a necessity when she was employed in a rural business and buses were scarcer than hens' teeth. The opulent Mercedes had ground to a halt and Alejandro and his chauffeur had emerged to check out the damage done while she was struggling to blink back tears from the pain of her skinned knees and bruised hip. Before she had known what was happening to her, her damaged bike was stacked in the local repair shop and she was ensconced in the luxury Mercedes, being swept off to the nearest hospital A and E department by the most gorgeous-looking guy she had ever met in her life. It was a shame that she really hadn't noticed that day just how domineering and deaf to all argument Alejandro could be, for he had refused to listen when she declared that she did not require any medical attention. No, she had been X-rayed, cleaned up, bandaged and bullied within an inch of her life all because Alejandro's dazzling smile had cast a spell over her.

Love at first sight, Jemima labelled with an instinctive frown of antipathy while she shifted about restlessly in her bed that night. She had never believed in love at first sight, indeed had grown up promising herself that she would never allow any man to wield the kind of power over her that her father had always exercised over her mother. But despite the hard lessons she had believed she had learned at her mother's knee, Jemima had taken one look at Alejandro Navarro Vasquez and fallen as hard and as destructively for him as a brick thrown from a major height. And the *real* lessons she had learned she had picked up from Alejandro himself, only she had failed to put what she learned to sensible use.

Long before Alejandro had shocked her with his proposal of marriage, he had put her through months of dating hell by not phoning when he said he would, by cancelling meetings last minute and by seeing other women and getting photographed with them. Even before she'd married him he had battered her heart and trodden her pride deep in the dirt. But she had understood even then why he was giving her the runaround. He was, after all, a Spanish count, while she worked for peanuts at a little hotel that he considered to be a dump. He had known she was not his equal on any level and the disparity had bothered him deeply from the outset of their acquaintance. Six months after that first encounter, however, Alejandro had seemed to shed that attitude…

'*Sol y sombre*…sun and shade, *querida mia*,' Alejandro had murmured then as he compared the pale skin of her slender arm to the bronzed vibrancy of his darker colouring. 'You cannot have one without the other—we belong together.'

But they had mingled as badly as oil and water, Jemima conceded with the dulled pain of acceptance that she had learned she had to live with, and she finally dropped off to sleep around two in the morning by dint of trying to forget the delivery she had to get up for the next morning.

There was hardly any floor space left in the shop once she had loaded the fresh blooms into the waiting containers. Her fingers numbed by the brisk spring morning temperature and too much contact with wet stems and water, Jemima rubbed her hands over her slim jeans-clad hips and tried not to shiver, because she knew that one shiver would only lead to another half-dozen and that in the end she would only feel colder. After all, winter or summer, the shop was always cool. It was an old building with poor insulation and she was always quick to remind herself that too much heat would only damage her stock. She went into the back room and dragged a black fleece jacket off the hook in the wall and put it on. Alfie was out in the little backyard playing on his trike while making loud motoring noises and she smiled at the sight of his innocent enjoyment, which took no account of the early hour he had been dug out of his cosy bed or the chilly air.

'Jemima…'

It was a voice she had hoped never to hear again: rich, melodic, dark and deep, and so full of accented earthy male sexiness it sent little quivers down her sensitive spine. She shut her eyes tight, refusing to turn round, telling herself wildly that her mind had somehow slipped dangerously back into the past and that she was imagining things…

Imagining waking up in bed with Alejandro, all tousled black hair, stubble and raw male sensual appeal… Alejandro, who could ignite her hunger with one indolent glance from his stunning black-fringed dark-as-the-night-sky eyes and seal it by simply saying her name… But even as a steamy burst of imagery momentarily clouded her brain and interfered with her breathing, she was instead recalling the emptiness of her bed once she had fallen pregnant and the wounding anguish of that physical lack of interest in her rapidly swelling body. As a chill slid through her slender length she spun round.

And there he was, Alejandro Navarro Vasquez, her husband, who had taught her to love him, taught her to need him and who had then proceeded to torture her with deprivation for her weakness. She was shocked, deeply, horribly shocked, her dazed violet-blue eyes widening to roam slowly over him as if she could not credit what she was seeing. Thick blue-black hair swept back from his brow, a fitting overture to the splendour of high patrician cheekbones bisected by a strong arrogant nose and punctuated by a sensually shaped and perfect masculine mouth. He was a staggeringly handsome man and fabulously well turned out in a dark business suit of faultless cut and polished handmade shoes. He always looked immaculate… except in bed, she recalled dully, when her hands had disarranged his hair and her nails had inflicted scratch marks down the long golden expanse of his flawless back. And she wanted to scream against the recollections that would not leave her alone, that were uniting with her sense of panic to destabilise her even more.

'What are you doing here?' she exclaimed breathlessly...

CHAPTER TWO

'WE HAVE UNFINISHED business,' Alejandro intoned softly, his keen gaze wandering slowly over her small figure.

And Jemima went from cold to hot as if he had turned a blowtorch on her. She flushed because she knew she looked less than her best with her hair loose round her to keep her ears warm and only a touch of mascara and lip gloss on her face, not to mention the worn jeans, fleece jacket and shabby low-heeled boots that completed her practical outfit. And even though it was bloody-minded— for she wanted nothing between them to be as it had once been, when she'd had no control over her responses—she deeply resented his cool stare and businesslike tone: it was the ultimate rejection. She leant against the door frame, her slender spine taking on an arch that enhanced the small firm curves below the neat fit of wool and denim, her head lifting so that the pale foaming ringlets of her eye-catching strawberry-blonde hair rippled back across her shoulders.

An almost infinitesimal tightening hardened Alejandro's darkly handsome features, his sculpted jaw line clenching, his brilliant gaze narrowing and brightening. Then Jemima knew he had felt the challenge from her as stridently and clearly as though she had used a loud hailer. Suddenly the atmosphere was seething with tension. At that point, she suffered a dismaying reduction in courage and veiled her gaze, drawing back a step while being terrifyingly aware of the swelling tightness of her nipples inside her bra and the twisting slide of sexual awareness low in her pelvis. It shocked her that a man she now hated as much as she had once loved him could still have such a powerful effect on her body.

'Always the temptress,' Alejandro drawled with a roughened edge to his dark deep voice that vibrated through her like a jamming wireless signal and made her rigidity give way to a trembling vulnerability. 'Do I really look that desperate?'

The fierce chill of his rejection might have cut her like a knife had she not been more aware of the way his strikingly beautiful eyes lingered on her. As she tore her attention from the lean, strong face that haunted her dreams and her gaze dropped she could not help noticing the distinctive masculine bulge that had disturbed the perfect fit of his trousers. Her cheeks flamed as hot as a kettle on the boil as she was both mollified by that reaction and burned by it at the same time.

'What are you doing here?' she demanded for the second time.

'I want a divorce. I need an address for you to obtain it,' Alejandro spelt out in a driven undertone. 'Or didn't that occur to you? Your staging a vanishing act was selfish and immature.'

That fast Jemima wanted to lift one of the buckets of flowers and upend it over him. 'You forced me to behave like that,' she told him heatedly.

'How?' Alejandro growled, striding forward to brace his lean, well-shaped hands on the counter, clearly more than ready for an argument.

'You wouldn't listen to a word I said. We had reached stalemate and there was nothing more I could do.'

'I told you that we would work it out,' Alejandro reminded her in a tone of galling condescension.

'But in the whole of our marriage you never did work anything out with me. How could you when you wouldn't talk to me? When I told you how unhappy I was what did you ever do to make anything better?' Jemima demanded, her violet eyes shimmering with pain and condemnation as she remembered the lavish gifts he had given her instead of more concrete and meaningful things like his time and his attention.

Straight away, anger flared in Alejandro, his stunning eyes flaming bright gold with heat just as the bell on the shop door rang to herald the arrival of Jemima's assistant, Sandy. The silence inside the shop was so deep and so tense it could have filled a bank vault and as she came in the dark-haired, neatly dressed older woman shot Jemima a look of dismay. 'Am I late? Were you expecting me to start early today?'

'No, no,' Jemima hastened to reassure her employee. 'But I'm afraid I have to go back home for an hour, so you'll be in charge.'

Without even looking in Alejandro's direction, Jemima went out to the backyard to retrieve Alfie, hoisting him into her arms and hurrying back indoors to say in a frazzled aside to Alejandro, 'I live a hundred yards down the road at number forty-two.'

But before she could reach the door a broad-shouldered young man with cropped fair hair strolled through it brandishing a bag. 'Fresh out of the bakery oven, Jemima!' he exclaimed with satisfaction. 'Cherry scones for our elevenses...'

'Oh, Charlie, I totally forgot you were coming today!' Jemima gasped in dismay. She had made the arrangement the previous week when she'd last seen Charlie at choir practice. 'Look, I have to go out for a little while, but first I'd better show you that electrical socket that's not working.'

Anchoring Alfie more firmly to her hip, Jemima dived

back behind the counter with Charlie close behind her and pointed out the socket that had failed the previous week.

Full of cheerful chatter, Charlie rested appreciative eyes on her delicate profile. 'If it would suit you better I can come back tomorrow when you're here.'

'No, that's fine, Charlie. Today is perfect,' Jemima insisted, turning back to head for the door where Alejandro waited in silence, his shrewd gaze pinned to the hovering electrician, who was making no attempt to hide his disappointment that she was leaving. 'Sandy will look after you.'

Jemima stepped out into the fresh air, hugely conscious of Alejandro's presence by her side but also perplexed, because if he had even looked at Alfie for ten seconds he had contrived to hide the fact from her. 'I'll see you at the house,' she said flatly, setting Alfie down and grasping his hand because he was too heavy for her to carry any further.

'I'll give you a lift,' Alejandro drawled.

'No, thanks.' Without any further ado, Jemima crossed the road and began to walk away fast with Alfie tottering along beside her. Outside working hours she used the van to get around, but when the shop was open it was needed to deliver orders.

She had only gone twenty yards before a neat, dark saloon car pulled in beside her and the driver's door opened. Then a tall man in a business suit climbed out. 'Going home?' Jeremy prompted. 'Get in. I'll drop you off.'

'Thank you, Jeremy, but I'm so close it's easier just to walk,' she declared breezily, though all her thoughts were miles away, lodged back on Alejandro and his assurance that he wanted a divorce.

Had he already met someone else? Some well born beauty from a moneyed background, much more suitable than she had been? She wondered how many other women he had been with since she had left him and it made a tiny shudder of agonising emotional pain arrow through her tender heart. She didn't want Alejandro back, no, she definitely didn't, but she didn't want any other woman to have him either. Where he was concerned, she was a real dog in the manger. But it would be foolish to imagine that he might have been celibate since her departure, for that high-voltage libido of his required frequent gratification…or at least it had until he was faced with her enlarged breasts and thickening waistline and it had become painfully, hurtfully obvious that he'd found his pregnant wife's body about as attractive as a mud bath. So how could she possibly care what he had done and with whom since then?

Jeremy yanked open the passenger door of his car. 'Get in,' he urged. 'You're both getting soaked.'

Belatedly appreciating that it had started raining while she'd stood there, Jemima scooped up her son and clambered in. Jeremy pulled in just ahead of the sleek sports car already waiting outside her home. He vented a low whistle of appreciation as he studied the opulent model. 'Who on earth does that beauty belong to?'

'An old friend of mine,' she replied as she stepped out of his car. 'Thanks.'

As she attempted to turn away Jeremy strode round the bonnet to rest a staying hand on her arm. 'Eat out with me tonight,' he urged, his blue eyes pinned hopefully to her face. 'No strings, no big deal, just a couple of friends getting together for a meal.'

Turning pink, Jemima stepped back from his proximity, awesomely conscious that just feet away from them Alejandro was listening to the exchange. 'I'm sorry, I can't,' she answered awkwardly.

'I'll keep on asking,' Jeremy warned her.

Jemima almost winced at that unnecessary assurance, as she had already discovered that Jeremy, the local estate agent and a divorcee in his early thirties, had the hide of a rhinoceros when it came to taking a polite hint that a woman wasn't interested. Since the day she had signed the rental agreement on her cottage, he must have asked her out at least a dozen times.

Aware of the glacial cool of Alejandro's scrutiny, Jemima hastened to slot her key into the lock on the front door.

'Why didn't you just tell him that you were married?'

'He already knows that. Everybody knows that,' Jemima fielded irritably, making a point of flexing the finger that bore her wedding ring as she pushed open the door. 'But he also knows that I'm separated from my husband.'

'There's nothing official about our separation,' Alejandro countered, crowding her with his presence in the tiny hall before he moved on into the small living room. 'But I am surprised that you're still wearing the ring.'

Jemima shrugged a slight shoulder and made no reply as she unbuttoned Alfie's jacket and hung it up beside her fleece.

'Juice.' Alfie tugged at her sleeve.

'Please,' Jemima reminded him.

'Peese,' Alfie said obediently.

'Do you want coffee?' Jemima asked Alejandro grudgingly. He had taken up a stance by the window and his height and wide shoulders were blocking out a good deal of the light.

'*Sí*,' Alejandro confirmed.

'Peese,' Alfie told him helpfully. 'Say peese.'

'*Gracias,*' Alejandro pronounced in his own tongue, stubborn to the last and barely sparing the attentive toddler a glance.

Once again Jemima was taken aback by that pronounced lack of interest in her child. She had expected Alejandro to be stunned by Alfie's existence and, at the very least, extremely curious. 'Haven't you got any questions to ask me about him?' she enquired, her attention resting pointedly on Alfie's dark curly head as he crouched down to take his beloved cars out of the toy box and line them up in a row.

Alfie liked things organised and tidy, everything in its place. She had a sudden disconcerting recollection of Alejandro's immaculately neat desktop at the castle and wondered if there were other similarities that she had simply refused to see.

'When the family lawyer engages a solicitor here to represent my interests, they can ask the questions,' Alejandro responded very drily.

'So, you're already convinced he's not yours,' Jemima breathed in a very quiet tone, her lips sealing over her gritted teeth like a steel trap.

Luxuriant black lashes swept up on Alejandro's gorgeous dark golden eyes, his handsome mouth taking on a sardonic cast. 'How could he be?'

Seething frustration filled Jemima. For a crazy instant, she wanted to jump on him and kick him and punch him, batter him into a state where he would be forced to listen to her. But she wasn't a violent woman and if he didn't listen to her, or believe in her, or even trust her, and he never had, at this stage of their relationship he probably never would. Wasn't that another good reason as to why she had walked out on their marriage? The conviction that she was beating her stupid head up against a brick wall? Not to mention the sheer impossibility of staying married to a man who was utterly convinced that she had had an affair with his brother?

While she waited on the kettle in the galley kitchen, she reached a sudden decision and lifted the wall phone to call Flora, asking her friend if it would be possible for her to look after Alfie for an hour. 'Alejandro is here,' she explained stiffly.

'Give me five minutes—I'll come down and pick Alfie up,' Flora promised.

Jemima set a china mug of coffee down near Alejandro. She knew what she had to do next but she just didn't want to. Been there, done that, got the T-shirt and the scars. Flora arrived very quickly, bridging the awkward silence with her chatter while Jemima fed Alfie into his coat again.

'Alejandro...Flora,' Jemima performed the introduction stiffly.

'I've heard so much about you,' Flora said brightly to Jemima's husband. 'None of it good.'

Alejandro sent Jemima a censorious look of hauteur and she reddened, wishing that the other woman had kept quiet rather than revealing how much she knew about her friend's marital problems.

The silence left after Flora's departure spread like a sheet of black ice waiting to entrap the unwary. Jemima straightened her slight shoulders, her blue eyes so dark with strain they had the glimmer of purple against her skin. 'I hate that I have to say this again, but you don't give me much choice—I did *not* sleep with your brother.'

Alejandro shot her a grim dark-eyed appraisal. 'At least he had the courage not to deny the charge—'

'Oh...right,' Jemima sliced in, rage bubbling and pounding through her like a waterfall that had been dammed up inside her. 'Marco didn't deny it, so therefore I have to be lying!'

'My brother has never lied to me but you have,' Alejandro pointed out levelly.

Jemima's hands clenched into fists. 'What lies? What are you talking about?'

'You went through thousands and thousands of pounds while we were still living together, yet you had nothing to show for your extravagance and could not even cover your own expenses in spite of the generous allowance I gave you. Somewhere in that financial mess, when I asked you for an explanation, there must have been lies,' he concluded.

Jemima had turned white as milk, for those were charges she could not deny. She *had* got through a terrifying amount of money, although she hadn't spent it on herself. Sadly, she had had nothing to show for it, however, and had found herself in the embarrassing position of not being able to pay bills during the last weeks of their marriage. All her sins had come home to roost by then, all because of the one seemingly harmless and seemingly even sensible little lie that she had told him when they'd first met.

'Did you give all that money to Marco?' Alejandro asked her abruptly, his voice harsh. 'He often overspent and I was afraid that he might have approached you for a loan.'

For a split second, Jemima was tempted to tell another lie to cover herself and then shame pierced her and she bent her head, refusing to look at him. Although, while on one level she was still angry with Alejandro's brother for dropping her in the mire by refusing to deny the allegations of an affair, she still retained enough fondness for the younger man not to seek revenge and to tell the truth. 'No, Marco never once asked me for money.'

Alejandro's lean, powerful body had tautened. He flicked her a narrowed glance so sharp that she was vaguely surprised it didn't actually cut her. 'I assume that you are still in contact with my brother?'

That comment startled her. 'No, I'm not. I haven't talked to Marco since I left Spain.'

Alejandro made no attempt to hide his surprise at that news. 'I'm amazed, when you were so intimate.'

Her teeth clenched at that crack. Not for the first time she was tempted to give way and simply tell him the truth. Unfortunately the repercussions threatened to be too great. Furthermore she had once faithfully promised Marco that she would never betray him. After all, she had seen for herself and on more than one occasion why the younger man was quite so determined to keep that particular secret from his family. Unfortunately, Marco's selfishness did not release her from her pledge of silence. In any case, she reminded herself ruefully, it was not solely Marco's fault that her marriage to his brother had broken down.

'Marco has been working in New York at our art gallery for the past couple of years. You haven't had any contact with him at all?' Alejandro persisted in a silky smooth tone, his accent growling along the edges of every syllable.

'But presumably he is supporting his child?'

'Alfie is not his bloody child!' Jemima raked at him furiously.

'There is no need to swear,' Alejandro murmured smooth as glass.

Jemima trembled and struggled to master a temper that was threatening to overwhelm her. Two years ago when she walked out on her marriage she had been exhausted and worn down to the bone by the weight of her secrets, but since then she had made a strong recovery. 'Alfie is not Marco's son,' she pronounced flatly.

'Your child is only the smallest bone of contention between us,' Alejandro intoned in a driven undertone, his stunning eyes full of condemnation bright as sunlight in his lean, saturnine face.

'Is that so?' Jemima asked tightly, ridiculously annoyed that he could so easily dismiss Alfie's existence as an unimportant element.

Alejandro bit out an unamused laugh. 'You know surprisingly little about men,' he breathed roughly. 'I'm much more interested in what you *did* in my bed with my brother and why you felt the need to do it.'

In one comprehensive sentence, he tore down the deceptive veil of civility and confronted her with the reality of his convictions and she was shocked into silence by that direct attack. The experience also reminded her that she had never found Alejandro's moods or actions easy to predict and had often failed to identify the whys and wherefores that drove that hot-blooded temperament of his.

'Did you *have* him in our bed?' Alejandro gritted, lean brown hands clenched so hard by his side that she could see the white of bone over his knuckles. Intimidated, she stepped away, which wasn't easy to do in that small room and her calves pressed back against the door of the pale modern cupboard unit behind her.

In the inflammable mood he was in she didn't want to engage in another round of vehement denials, which he had already heard and summarily dismissed two years earlier. 'Alejandro...' she murmured as quietly as she could, trying to ratchet down the tension in the explosive atmosphere.

He flung his dark head back, his brilliant gaze splintering over her so hard that she would not have been surprised to see a shower of sparks light up the air. For a timeless moment and without the smallest warning she was entrapped by his powerfully sexual charisma and it was like looking into the sun. She remembered the hum of arousal and anticipation that had once started on the rare nights he was home on time for dinner, when she knew he would join her in their bedroom and take her to a world of such joyous physical excitement that she would briefly forget her loneliness and unhappiness.

'Is my need to know such sordid details too raw for you? Did you ever once stop to think of what it might be like for me to be forced to picture my wife in my brother's arms?' Alejandro ground out wrathfully.

'No,' she admitted, and it was the truth because she had never been intimate with Marco in that way and had wasted little time wondering how Alejandro's offensive and unfounded suspicions might be making him feel.

Angry with her? Disillusioned? She had already been much too familiar with the knowledge that he had to be experiencing such responses while she failed to live up to the steep challenge of behaving like a Spanish countess.

'No, why should you have?' Alejandro growled, his accent thick as treacle on that rhetorical question. 'Marco was simply a sacrifice to your vanity and boredom, a destructive, trashy way of hitting back at me and my family—'

'That's absolute nonsense!' Jemima flailed back at him furiously.

'Then why did you ever let him touch you? Do you think I haven't wondered how it was between you?' Alejandro slung back bitterly. 'Do you think it didn't hurt to imagine you naked with him? Sobbing with gratification as he pleasured you? Crying out as you came?'

'Stop it!' Jemima launched at him pleadingly, her face hot with mortification at the pungent sexual images he was summoning up. 'Stop talking like that right now!'

'Does it strike too closely for you?' Alejandro hissed fiercely. 'You got off lightly for being a faithless, lying slut, so stop staring at me with those big shocked eyes. I won't fall for the little-fragile-girl act this time around— I *know* you for what you are.'

Disturbed by the implicit threat in those hard words, Jemima spun away and walked past him to the window, fighting to get a grip on the turmoil of her emotions. He had shocked her, he had shocked her very deeply, for it had not until that moment struck her that his belief in her infidelity could have inflicted that much damage. Two years back when he had confronted her about Marco, he had been cold, controlled, behaving almost as though he were indifferent to her. By then she had believed that Alejandro felt very little for her and might even be grateful for a good excuse to end their unhappy alliance. Only now did she recognise that she had been naïve to accept that surface show from a male as deep and emotional as he could be.

'I'm not a slut because I didn't have an affair with your brother,' Jemima muttered heavily, slowly turning back round to face him. 'And you should know now that my son, Alfie, is your son.'

'Is that supposed to be a joke?' Alejandro demanded with a look of angry bewilderment. 'I'm well aware that you suffered a miscarriage before you left Spain.'

'We *assumed* I had had a miscarriage,' Jemima corrected with curt emphasis. 'But when I finally went to see a doctor here in the UK, I discovered that I was still pregnant. He suggested that I might have initially been carrying twins and lost one of them, or that the bleeding I experienced was merely the threat of a miscarriage rather than an actual one. Whatever,' she continued doggedly, her slender hands clenching tightly in on themselves beneath his incredulous appraisal, 'I was still very much pregnant when I arrived in England and Alfie was born just five months later.'

Alejandro dealt her a seething appraisal, his disbelief palpable. 'That is not possible.'

Jemima yanked open a drawer in the sideboard and leafed through several documents to find Alfie's birth certificate. In one sense she could not credit what she was doing and yet in another she could not see how she could possibly do anything else. Her son was her husband's child and that was not something she could lie about or leave in doubt because she had to take into account how Alfie would feel about his parentage in the future. It was a question of telling the truth whether she liked it or not. Emerging with the certificate, she extended it to Alejandro.

'This has to be nonsense,' Alejandro asserted, snatching the piece of paper from her fingers with something less than his usual engrained good manners.

'Well, if you can find some other way of explaining how I managed to give birth to a living child by that date and it not be yours, I'd like to hear it,' Jemima challenged without hesitation.

Alejandro stared down at the certificate with fulminating force and then glanced up, golden eyes bright as blades and as dangerous. 'All this proves is that you must still have been pregnant when you walked out on our marriage. It does not automatically follow that the child is mine.'

Jemima shook her fair head and expelled her breath in a slow hiss. 'I know it doesn't suit you to hear this news now and I really didn't want to tell you. Too much water has gone under the bridge since we split up and now we lead separate lives. But the point is, I can't lie to you about it. Some day Alfie may want to look you up and get acquainted.'

Alejandro studied her with brooding dark ferocity. 'If what you have just told me is the truth, if that little boy does prove to be mine, it was vindictive and extremely selfish of you to leave me in ignorance!'

Jemima had paled. 'When I left you I had no idea that I was still pregnant,' she protested.

'Two years is a long period of time, yet you made no attempt to inform me that I might be a father,' he fielded harshly. 'I will want DNA tests to confirm your claim before I make any decision about what I want to do.'

Jemima compressed her lips hard at the reference to the testing. Once again Alejandro was insulting her with the assumption that she had been an unfaithful wife and that, for that reason, there could be doubt over who had fathered her child. 'Do as you like,' she told him curtly. '*I* know who Alfie's father is and there has never been any doubt of his identity.'

'I will make arrangements for the tests to be carried out and I will see you again when the result is available,'

Alejandro drawled, with lashings of dark Spanish masculine reserve emanating from his forbidding demeanour
and cool taut intonation.

'I'll contact a solicitor and start the divorce,' Jemima
proffered in turn, determined not to leave him with the
impression that he was the only one of them who could
act and make decisions.

Alejandro frowned, dark eyes unlit by gold narrow-
ing in a piercing scrutiny that made her uncomfortable.
'It would be foolish to do anything before we have that
DNA result.'

'I disagree,' Jemima flashed back at him angrily. 'I
should have applied for a divorce the minute I left you!'

Cool as ice water, Alejandro quirked an ebony brow.
'And why didn't you?'

Jemima dealt him a fulminating glance but said nothing,
merely moving past him to yank open her front door in a
blunt invitation for him to leave. She was shaken to register that she was trembling with temper. She had forgotten
just how angry and frustrated Alejandro could make her
feel with his arrogant need to take charge and do exactly
what he wanted, regardless of other opinions.

'I'll be in touch,' he delivered on the doorstep.

'I'd appreciate some warning the next time.' Jemima
lifted a business card off the table and gave it to him.
'Phone and tell me when you're coming.'

Anger shimmering through her, she slammed the door
in his wake and peered out from behind the shelter of the
curtains to watch him swing into his fancy car and drive
off.

Nothing had changed, she reflected unhappily. Even
being in the same room again as Alejandro revived all
the doubts, insecurities and regrets she had left behind
her when she gave up on being his wife…

CHAPTER THREE

JEMIMA LEFT HER teenaged babysitter in charge of the house and closed the front door as quietly as she could behind her. Thursday nights she and Flora went to choir practice and enjoyed a convivial evening in the company of friends. As a rule she looked forward to getting out. But, recently, Jemima had been in a thoroughly bad mood and indeed was still stiff with the angry resentment that she had been struggling to suppress for two long weeks.

'Cheer up,' Flora urged as the two women walked in the direction of the quaint little medieval stone church and village green that made Charlbury St Helens so pretty a village. 'You're letting this whole DNA-testing business eat you alive and it's not healthy for you.'

Jemima flung her friend an apologetic glance. 'I can't help feeling as though I've been publicly humiliated by it,' she confessed ruefully.

'Both the notary and the GP are bound by rules of confidentiality,' Flora reminded her with a reassuring glance. 'I seriously doubt that either will discuss your private business with anyone, particularly if it may end up in a civil courtroom.'

Unconvinced, but recognising her friend's generous attempt to offer comfort, Jemima compressed her lips, not wanting to be a bore on the subject, even though the DNA tests had proved to be an exercise in mortification in which she felt that her anonymity and privacy had been destroyed. When such tests were required for a case that might end up in a court they had to be done in a legal and formal manner. A snooty London solicitor acting on Alejandro's behalf had phoned her to spell out the requirements. Jemima had had to make an affidavit witnessed by a public notary as well as have photos taken to prove her identity before she could have the tests for her and Alfie done by her own GP. The actual tests had been swabs taken from the mouth and completed in seconds, but Jemima had writhed in mortification over the simple fact that both the notary and the doctor were being made aware of the fact that her husband doubted that Alfie was his child. She knew that she would never, ever forgive Alejandro for forcing her to undergo that demeaning process, all because he was convinced that she had broken her marriage vows.

Yet how could she have refused the tests when refusal would have been viewed as a virtual admission of wrongdoing? she asked herself as she moved into the comparative warmth of the church and greeted familiar faces with a wave and a determined smile. Common sense told her that it was essential that Alfie's father should know the truth; for Alfie's sake there should be absolutely no doubt on that score in anyone's mind. Those were the only reasons why she had agreed to the tests being carried out.

The effort of raising her voice in several rousing choruses and then singing a verse solo in her clear sweet soprano took Jemima's mind off her combative feelings. She was definitely feeling more relaxed by the time she helped to stack the chairs away. Fabian Burrows, one of the local doctors and a very attractive male in his mid-thirties, reached for her jacket before she did and extended it for her to put on.

'You have a really beautiful voice,' he told her.

'Thanks,' she said, her cheeks warming a little beneath his keen appraisal.

He fell into step beside her and Flora. 'Are you going

for a drink?' he asked, a supportive hand settling to her spine as she stumbled on the way down the church steps.

'Yes.'

'Fancy trying The Red Lion for a change?' he suggested, coming to a halt by the church gate while other members of the choir crossed the road to the usual hostelry.

'Thanks, but I'm with Flora,' Jemima told him lightly.

'You're both very welcome to keep me company,' he imparted while Jemima tried frantically to interpret the frowning meaningful expression on her friend's face. Did that look mean that Flora wanted to take up the invitation or that she didn't?

'I'm afraid this isn't a good night,' Flora remarked awkwardly, turning pointedly to look out onto the road.

Jemima saw the sports car parked there a split second before she saw the tall dark male sheathed in a cashmere overcoat leaning up against the bonnet and apparently waiting for her. Dismay gripped her and then temper ripped through her tiny frame like a storm warning. After all, she had specifically asked Alejandro to give her notice of his next intended visit. How dared he just turn up again without giving her proper notice of his plans?

But somehow the instant her attention settled on Alejandro an uninvited surge of heat shimmied over her entire skin surface and sexual awareness taunted her in tender places. His dangerous sensuality threatened her like the piercing tip of a knife. Scorching dark golden eyes set in a lean dark-angel face assailed her and suddenly it was very hard to breathe because, no matter how angry she was with him, Alejandro was still drop-dead gorgeous and sinfully sexy. Even the lean, well-balanced flow of his powerful body against his luxurious car was elegant, stylish and fluid with grace. She wanted to walk past him and act as if he were invisible while the compelling pull of his attraction angered her almost as much as his unexpected appearance.

'How did you know where I was?'

'The babysitter,' Alejandro told her softly. 'My apologies if I'm intruding on your evening.'

'Who is this?' Fabian demanded loftily.

'Oh, I'm just her husband,' Alejandro drawled in a long-suffering tone that made Jemima's teeth grind together in disbelief.

The other man stiffened in discomfiture and muttered something about seeing Jemima the following week at practice. Turning to address Flora, who was also hovering, Fabian escorted her away.

'How *dare* you say that and embarrass him?' Jemima hissed like a spitting cat at Alejandro.

Alejandro, very much in arrogant Conde Olivares mode, gazed broodingly down at his diminutive wife. 'It is the truth. Every time I come here you're knee-deep in drooling men and flirting like mad.'

'You don't have the right to tell me how to behave any more.' Jemima threw those angry words back at him in defiance of the manner in which he was looking down at her.

Alejandro closed lean, strong hands over her shoulders and, dark eyes glittering like polished jet in the moonlight, he hauled her close and his wide sensual mouth plunged down on hers in an explosion of passion that blew her defences to hell and back. She hadn't been prepared, hadn't even dreamt that he might touch her again, and she was so taken aback that she was totally vulnerable. Her legs wobbled below her as the fiery demand of his mouth sent a message that hurtled through her slight body like a shriek alarm and awakened the desire she had shut out and denied since Alfie's birth.

In an equally abrupt movement, Alejandro straightened, spun her round and pinned her between his hard muscular length and the car. A gasp of relief escaped her as he pressed against her for, at that moment, pressure was exactly what her body craved; indeed, in the grip of that craving she had no shame. Her breathing was as ragged as the crazy pulse pounding in her throat while he ground his hips into her pelvis and heat and moisture burned between her thighs.

'*Dios mio! Vamonos*…let's go,' Alejandro urged raggedly, pulling back from her to yank open the car door. He almost lifted her nerveless body into the leather passenger seat and with a sure hand he protected the crown of her head from a painful bump courtesy of the roof.

'Let's go,' he said. Let's go where? she almost shouted back in response. But she hid from that revealing question to which she already knew her own answer while being fully, painfully aware of what her body longed for. She shrank into the seat as he clasped the seat belt round her and then bent her buzzing head, her hands closing over her knees to prevent them from visibly shaking in his presence.

She had trained herself to forget what that desperate, yearning, wanting for him could feel like and she did not want to remember. But the taste of him was still on her lips, just as the phantom recall of his hands on her still felt current while the slow burn pain of his withdrawal of contact continued to shock-wave through her and leave her cold.

'We really shouldn't touch in public places,' Alejandro intoned soft and low.

Jemima clenched her teeth together, hating herself for not having pushed him away. How dared he just grab her like that? How dared he prove that he could still make her respond to him? Of course, had she known what he was about to do she would have rejected him as he deserved, yes, she definitely would have, she reasoned stormily. But back when she had still been living with him, she had *always* wanted him. Need had been like a clawing ache inside her whenever she looked at him and the only time she had felt secure was when she was in his arms and she could forget everything else. Hugging that daunting memory to her, she hauled a stony shell of composure round her disturbed emotions, determined not to let him see how much he had shaken her up.

'You still haven't told me what you're doing here,' Jemima complained as he followed her to her front door.

'We'll talk inside.'

Jemima had to swallow back a sharp-tongued comment. In every situation Alejandro assumed command and that he rarely got it wrong only annoyed her more. She went in to her babysitter and paid her. Audra lived only two doors down from her and the arrangement suited both of them.

'Do you make a habit of leaving a child in charge of a child?' Alejandro enquired.

'No, I don't,' Jemima countered curtly. 'And though Audra may look immature, she's eighteen years old and training to be a nurse.'

Alejandro did not apologise for his misapprehension. Jemima hung up her jacket and hovered, her face burning as she remembered the heat of that extravagant kiss.

'It's a little late for a social call,' she remarked flatly, avoiding any visual contact with him, refusing to knuckle down and play hostess.

'I wanted to see my son,' Alejandro confided in a roughened undertone.

The import of that admission engulfed her like a tidal wave. So the DNA testing had delivered its expected result and backed up her claims, and thanks to that he now had to accept that she had not been lying to him yet he had not opened the subject with the fervent apology that he owed her. Her chin came up at a truculent angle. 'Alfie's asleep.'

'I don't mind looking at him while he sleeps,' Alejandro confessed in a not quite steady rush, his excitement at even that prospect unconcealed.

For a split second that look on his face softened something inside her but she fought it. 'But you didn't believe me when I told you he was yours—'

'Let's not get into that. I know the truth now. I know he is my child. I only got the news this morning. This is the soonest I could get here.'

His eagerness to see Alfie dismayed her, even while she tried to tell herself that his reaction was only to be expected. He had just found out that he was a father. Naturally he was much more interested in Alfie than he had been when he had assumed that her son was some other man's. 'I'll take you upstairs,' she offered, striving to take control of the situation.

Alejandro moved quietly into the bedroom in Jemima's wake and studied the sleeping child in the wooden cot. Black curls tousled, with his little sleep-flushed face, Alfie looked peaceful and utterly adorable to his besotted mother's eyes. Alejandro closed a strong hand over the cot rail and stared down, spiky black lashes screening his gaze from her.

Without warning Alejandro looked across the cot at her, brilliant dark eyes brandishing a fierce challenge. 'I want to take him home to Spain.'

That announcement hit her like a bucket of icy water, shocking her and filling her with fear for the future. She backed away to the door and watched Alejandro award his son an undeniably tender last glance. Yes, he could be tender when he wanted to be but it wasn't a notion that took him very often, she conceded painfully. He had looked at her the same way the day they learned that she had conceived and his initial unconcealed pleasure in the discovery that she was pregnant had made her swallow back and conceal her own very different feelings on the same score. Yet how could she recall those confusing reactions now when Alfie had since become the very centre of her world? Given the chance she would never have turned the clock back to emerge childless from her failed marriage, but it was already beginning to occur to her that a child-free marriage would have been easier to dissolve.

I want to take him home to Spain. That frank declaration raced back and forth inside her head as she led the way back downstairs. It was only natural that Alejandro would want to show Alfie off to his family while ensuring that Alfie learnt about the magnificent heritage and ancestry that he had been born into on his father's side, she reasoned, eager not to overreact to his announcement.

'What did you mean when you said you wanted to take him back to Spain?' Jemima heard herself ask abruptly.

Alejandro took off his heavy cashmere overcoat and draped it on a dining chair by the table that filled the small bay window in the living room. His elegant charcoal-grey business suit accentuated his height. His classic profile was cool and uninformative when he turned back to her but his stunning dark eyes were bright gold chips of challenge.

'I cannot allow you to have full custody of my son,' Alejandro spelt out without apology. 'I don't believe that you can offer him what he needs to thrive in this environment. I wish I could say otherwise. I have no desire to fight you for custody of our child but I do not see how I can do anything else without betraying my duty to him.'

'How...*dare*...you?' Jemima threw back at him in a fiery temper of disbelief, her heart racing as if she were running a marathon. 'I gave birth to your precious son alone and unsupported and I've been on my own ever since. Alfie is a very happy and well-adjusted little boy and you know nothing about him, yet the minute you find out he exists you assume that I am an unfit parent!'

'Does he even know he has a father or a family in Spain?

Is he learning to speak Spanish? What kind of stability can
you give him? You are not a responsible person.'

'What gives you the right to say that to me?' Jemima
interrupted thinly, her hands clenching into defensive fists
by her side.

His lean, darkly handsome face tautened into censorious lines. 'Look at the way you dealt with our marriage,
your debts, your affair with my brother—'

'For the last time, I did not have an affair with your
brother!'

'You don't deal with problems, you run away,' Alejandro condemned without hesitation. 'How could you possibly raise our child properly and teach him what he needs
to know?'

'I don't have to stand here putting up with being criticised by you any more. We're separated,' Jemima rattled
out, her voice brittle. 'I want you to leave.'

Alejandro grabbed up his coat. 'It's impossible to talk
to you,' he vented in a driven undertone of frustration.

'You call threatening to take my child away from me
talking?' Jemima exclaimed with incredulous force. 'How
did you expect me to respond to a threat?'

'A threat is something that may not happen, but I will
most assuredly fight you for custody of my son,' Alejandro extended grittily, refusing to back down.

Jemima breathed in deep and slow to calm her jangling
emotions and studied him with angry, anxious eyes. 'What
can I do or say to convince you that I am a good mother?'

Having donned his coat, Alejandro shrugged a broad
shoulder as if she was asking him the unanswerable.

Jemima's thoughts were already ploughing ahead to
reach several fear-inducing conclusions. If a custody battle
went to court, Alejandro had the wealth to hire the very
best lawyers and nobody representing her interests would
be able to compete. The very fact that she had kept quiet

about Alfie's existence for the first two years of his life would weigh against her. And how much importance might a judge lay on the truth that Alfie would one day be an influential member of the Spanish aristocracy in charge of a massive country estate and a very successful string of international family businesses? Such a background and his father's ability to prepare his son for those responsibilities could not be easily ignored.

'You can't do this to me,' Jemima protested. 'I love Alfie and he loves and needs me.'

'Perhaps it is my turn to be a parent for a change,' Alejandro said drily, tugging open the front door to facilitate his departure with an alacrity that was ironically no longer welcome to her. 'When it comes to sharing one little boy a divorce will leave few, if any, equitable solutions possible. We will both have to compromise.'

Jemima reached out in an ill-considered movement to thrust the door he had opened closed again before sliding between it and him like an eel. Violet eyes dark with strain in her pale heart-shaped face, she stared up at him and muttered tightly, 'We need to discuss this *now*!'

Alejandro sent her a sardonic glance. '*Madre mia*, you change direction with the wind. You told me to leave…'

Jemima gritted her teeth. 'Possibly I was a little hasty. I wasn't expecting you to already be making plans for Alfie. You annoyed me earlier. Why did you kiss me?'

Alejandro took a small step forward that trapped her between the wooden door and his lean, powerful body. 'Because I wanted to, *mi dulzura*.'

He called her 'sweetness' and she ran out of breath and rationality in the same instant. Awareness ran like a river of red-hot lava through her trembling length, her nipples swelling and blossoming like fire flowers while the tender flesh at the very heart of her burned and ached. The atmosphere was explosive and she couldn't fight the hunger stabbing at her. She studied the full curve of his sensual lower lip, reliving the taste of him, and slowly tipped her head back to meet hot golden eyes.

'Ask me to stay the night,' Alejandro urged thickly, pushing her back against the door, letting her feel the hard, promising power of his erection through his well-cut trousers. Air scissored through her lungs in a breathless surge, sexual heat uniting with dismay to hold her there.

'You want to stay?' Jemima whispered, already visualising closing a hand into the expensive fabric of his overcoat to haul him down to her, already imagining the taste and passion of him that drew her like a fire on a winter day. Desire had her in the fiercest of holds.

A long brown finger skimmed along the quivering line of her white throat, pausing to flick the tiny pulse flickering wildly above her collarbone. 'It's what you want too—'

'No,' Jemima gasped strickenly, feeling her self-discipline shatter like glass in the ambience and below it the roar of need she had resisted for so long.

'Liar,' Alejandro countered without hesitation, his confidence in his own powers of seduction absolute.

Her slender body vibrating with awareness, she still managed to tear free of him and step back. It hurt like hell. She couldn't think; she could only fight the craving that she recognised as a dangerous weakness. 'Leave,' she urged again, wanting to hug herself in consolation for the rush of cold and disappointment enveloping her.

'Call me when you come to your senses,' Alejandro drawled, hooded dark golden eyes undimmed by rejection as he tossed a business card down on the little shelf in the hallway.

And in a moment he was gone and she was left in a disturbing mess of conflicting emotions and regrets. She was furious with herself because she hadn't sorted out anything. Sex had got in the way and had only exacerbated the tensions between them. But she should have risen above the challenge to concentrate on Alfie and on Alejandro's threats. He had wanted to stay the night with her. He had wanted to share a bed with her again. The blood ran hot below her fair skin. For just a moment he had been as vulnerable as she to the powerful attraction that could still flare between them. She adjusted that thought the instant she thought it. No, Alejandro had *not* been vulnerable. If she had let him he would have slept with her again but it wouldn't have meant anything to him or led anywhere. He believed she had slept with Marco and he hated her for it. She lifted his business card and threw it down on the dining table in a fever of self-loathing. Alejandro was calling the shots again and she didn't like that at all.

Yet over three years earlier when they were dating she had liked the way Alejandro had automatically taken charge and looked after her and had revelled in his masculine protective instincts. Looking back with hindsight, she marvelled at the way he had made her feel and how much maturity had changed her. Of course, she had been a virgin when they'd first met. As a result she had been far too quick to idealise Alejandro and believe that they had something special together. She had not even recognised him for the womaniser he was until one of the hotel maids had slid an old newspaper beneath her nose, pointed to a photo and said, 'Isn't that that Spanish guy you're seeing?'

And there Alejandro had been, pictured at some snobby London party with a beautiful blonde in an evening dress. The accompanying prose had made it clear that he enjoyed the reputation of a heartbreaker who always had more than one woman in tow. She hadn't wanted to believe the evidence even though Alejandro had already proved to be anything but a devoted boyfriend, cancelling dates as he did at the last minute and rarely phoning when he said he would. When she'd questioned him, however, Alejandro had been commendably frank.

'I'm not looking for a serious relationship,' he had told her without apology. 'I'm not interested in being tied down.'

Feeling stupid and hurt over the assumptions she had made and grateful that she had, at that stage, stayed out of his bed, Jemima had put the brakes on her feelings for him and had begun going out socialising again with her friends. Before very long she too was dating someone else, a local accountant who was flatteringly keen to offer her an exclusive relationship. But when Alejandro had realised that she was seeing another man, he had had a furious row with her, which had made it perfectly clear that, while he expected her to share him, he was not prepared to share her. For a few weeks they had split up and, although she was heartbroken at losing him at the time, she had thought it was the only option left.

Barely a month later, though, Alejandro had come back to her and had said that he would stop seeing other women. Jemima had been overjoyed and their relationship had entered a far more intense second phase. Head over heels in love with him as she had been, she had plunged straight into a passionate affair. He had rented a house not far from the hotel where she worked and they had spent every spare minute there together. In her entire life she had never known such happiness as she had known then, during the romantic weekends he'd shared with her. The demands of business and family, not to mention the fact that he lived in Spain, had often kept them apart when they wanted to be together, and on her twentieth birthday Alejandro had asked her to marry him. He had not said he loved her; he had *never* told her he loved her. He had merely said that he could not continue spending so much time in England with her. He had made marriage sound like a natural progression.

But he had not invited her to meet his family before they took that crucial final step. No doubt he had known how much his relatives would disapprove of his ordinary English bride, who had so little to offer on their terms. Within weeks of his proposal they had married in a London church with only a couple of witnesses present. She had had no idea at all of what his life in Spain would be like. In fact she had been a lamb to the slaughter in her ignorance.

Dragging herself free of wounding memories that still rankled, Jemima lifted her head high. That silly infatuated and insecure girl was dead and gone. This time around she was in control of her own destiny and, with that in mind, she snatched up her phone and rang Alejandro.

'We have to meet to talk about Alfie,' she told him urgently.

'Couldn't you have decided that while I was still with you?' Alejandro enquired drily.

'I'm not like you. I don't plan everything,' she reasoned defensively.

He suggested that she and Alfie meet him the following afternoon at his London apartment.

'I know you want to see Alfie again, but he would be better left out of it tomorrow—we'll probably argue.'

Having agreed a time and won his agreement on the score of Alfie, Jemima put down the phone again and wondered anxiously what rabbit she could possibly pull out of the hat that might persuade him that their son was better off living with his mother in England...

CHAPTER FOUR

THE LONDON APARTMENT was not the same one that Jemima remembered. The new one was bigger, more centrally located and sleek and contemporary in style, while the previous accommodation had been knee deep in opulent antiques and heavy drapes, a home-from-home backdrop for a family accustomed to life in a medieval castle.

A manservant showed her into a huge elegant reception room with the stark lines and striking impact of a modern artwork, again a very appropriate look for a family that owned a famous chain of art galleries.

She caught her reflection in the glass of an interior window and decided that, even though she was wearing the smartest outfit in her wardrobe, she looked juvenile in her knee-length black boots, short black skirt and red sweater. But her lifestyle no longer required dressy clothing and she preferred to plough her profits either back into the shop or into her savings. Having survived a childhood in which cash was often in very short supply, Jemima only felt truly safe now when she had a healthy balance in her rainy day account.

In the act of putting away a mobile phone, Alejandro emerged from an adjacent room to join her. His elegant black pinstripe suit and blue shirt fitted him with the expensive fidelity of the very best tailoring and the finest cloth, outlining broad shoulders, narrow masculine hips and long, long, powerful legs. Her attention locked to his lean dark features, noting the blue-black shadow round his handsome jaw line, and for a split second she was lost in the memory of the rasp of stubble against her skin in the mornings. She could feel a guilty blush envelop her from her brow to her toes. His black hair still damp and spiky from the shower, Alejandro was the most absolutely beautiful man she had ever seen and her heart was jumping inside her as if the ground had suddenly fallen away beneath her feet.

'Is your friend looking after Alfie?' he enquired.

'Yes, but he attends a playgroup in the afternoons,' she explained.

She turned down an offer of refreshments and hovered while Alejandro helped himself to strong black coffee that scented the air with its unmistakeable aroma. Memories she didn't want were bombarding her again. He had taught her to grind coffee beans and make what he called 'proper' coffee. There had been so many things she didn't know about that he took for granted. He had even been a better cook than she was and right from the start she had been captivated by his knowledge and sophistication. But before their marriage—when things had gone wrong between them—he had scooped her up into his arms and swept her off to bed and she had been so ecstatic that she wouldn't have cared if the roof had fallen in afterwards. But once their sex life had ground to a halt, they'd had no means of communication at all and it had seemed natural to her that their marriage had then fallen apart. He had just lost interest in her, a development she had seen as being only a matter of time from the outset of their acquaintance.

'I couldn't sleep last night,' Jemima admitted in a sudden nervous rush, her eyes violet as pansies in the sunlit room. 'I was worrying about what you said about Alfie.'

'You named him Alfonso after my father. That was a pleasant surprise,' Alejandro remarked.

'He was named in memory of my grandfather, Alfred,

as well,' Jemima advanced, not choosing to admit that the kindly vegetable-growing maternal grandfather she recalled had probably been the only presentable member of her former family circle, in that he had worked for a living and had stayed on the right side of the law. 'That's why I call him Alfie, because that was how my grandpa was known.'

Alejandro studied her with stunning dark golden eyes ringed and enhanced by black inky lashes. His charismatic appeal was so powerful that she couldn't take her attention off him and her mouth ran dry.

'We can't reasonably hope to share a child when we're living in different countries,' he told her.

Jemima tensed and smoothed her skirt down over her slight hips with moist palms. 'Other people manage it—'

'I want my son to grow up in Spain—'

'Well, you can't always have what you want,' Jemima pointed out flatly.

Alejandro set down his empty cup and strolled across the floor towards her. 'I too gave this matter serious thought last night. I can give you a choice...'

Her spine went rigid, her eyes flying wide with uncertainty. 'What sort of a choice?'

'Option one: you return to Spain and give our marriage another chance. Or, option two: I take you to court over Alfie and we fight for him.' As Jemima lost colour and a look of disbelief tautened her delicate pointed features Alejandro surveyed her with unblemished cool. 'From my point of view it's a very fair offer and more than you deserve.'

As an incendiary response leapt onto Jemima's tongue she swallowed it back and welded her lips closed, determined not to say anything before she had thought it through. But sheer shock was ricocheting through her in wave after wave. Alejandro was asking her to go back to him and live with him as his wife again? She was totally stunned by that proposition and had never dreamt that he would consider making it. 'That's a crazy idea,' she said weakly.

'If you take into account our son's needs, it's a very practical idea,' Alejandro contradicted levelly.

Jemima breathed in slowly and tried to concentrate her mind solely on her son's best interests, even though her brain was in a total fog at what he had just suggested. Many children might be more contented with two parents rather than one but that wasn't the end of the story. 'If we're not happy together, how could Alfie possibly be happy? I don't understand why you're even discussing the idea of us living together again.'

'Are you really that naïve?' His intent gaze was semi-screened by lush sooty lashes to a hot glitter of gold while the muscles in his strong jaw line clenched hard. 'I still want you. If I didn't I wouldn't be offering you this alternative.'

The heat of that look welded Jemima to where she stood and colour ran in scarlet ribbons into her cheeks. Once again he had taken her by surprise. 'Are you saying that you're able to forgive me for the past?'

Alejandro loosed a harsh laugh of disagreement. 'No, I couldn't go that far. I'm saying that if I get you back into my bed, I will make the effort to overlook your past transgressions.'

Her bosom swelled with wounded pride and resentment as she drew in a very deep and steadying breath. 'Fortunately for me, I haven't the slightest desire to be married to you again. You may have considered it an honour the first time around, but for me it was more like living in purgatory.'

Alejandro dealt her a stony look that chilled her to freezing point and she knew that she had angered him. She

recognised that he believed that he was making an enor-
mously generous concession in offering her—an unfaithful wife—the opportunity to live with him again. She even
recognised that lots of women would bite off his hand in
their eagerness to accept such an offer. After all, he was
drop-dead gorgeous, amazing in bed and open-handed
with money…as long as you could tell him what you'd done
with it, she completed inwardly and suppressed a shiver,
flinching from her bad memories. But at heart Alejandro
was as flint-hard and unyielding as his centuries-old castle. He believed she had betrayed him and he was not the
forgiving type and would never come round to seeing or
understanding her side of the story. He thought she was
a slut and even if she lived with him for another twenty
years he would die thinking that she was a slut.

'I've made a life for myself now in the village and I
enjoy my life there,' Jemima responded in a stiff tone of
restraint that did not come naturally to her. 'I was miserable in Spain and you didn't seem any happier with me as
a wife. Why would you want to revisit the past?'

'Only because we have a son.' Alejandro gave her a sardonic appraisal. 'And this time around life could be much
more straightforward.'

'How?' Jemima prompted baldly, wanting every detail
of his thoughts even though she had no intention of accepting his offer.

'I know you for who you are now. I would have no false
expectations, no sentimental ideas. Our marriage would
merely be a convenient agreement for Alfie's benefit. All I
would require from you would be the superficial show—'

'And sex,' Jemima added in a tight-mouthed undertone, because she felt demeaned that he had dared to include that aspect.

'Be grateful that you still have that much appeal, *mi*

dulzura. Without the pull of that angle, I wouldn't even have considered taking you back.'

Clashing unwarily with hot golden eyes, Jemima experienced a deeply mortifying sliding sensation low in her pelvis. It infuriated her that she could still react to him that way when so much else was wrong between them. Her body took not the smallest account of her brain or even of common sense, for being attracted to Alejandro was destructive and stupid and likely to get her into serious trouble. It occurred to her that maybe he felt the same way about her and that was such a novel suspicion that she stared at him, wondering if he too could be fighting the same rearguard action against his own natural inclinations.

'You don't like the fact that you still find me attractive,' Jemima commented, daringly taking a stab in the dark.

'But I can handle it. Familiarity breeds contempt—isn't that what they say?' His brilliant eyes were lit by a sensual golden glimmer that as his gaze wandered over her seemed to burn over her skin like a tiny point of flame. 'I believe that this arrangement will give me a healthy chance of working you right out of my system.'

Jemima could not resist the sensual temptation of imagining what it would be like to be put to that kind of work in the marital bedroom. The more responsive parts of her treacherous body hummed with enthusiasm until shame and pride combined to suppress her facetious thoughts. She had never been able to escape the fear that wanting and loving any man as much as she had once loved and wanted Alejandro was weak and pathetic. It had inspired her into making numerous attempts to play it cool with him, most of which had blown up in her silly face as she had lacked both subtlety and good timing. She had acted all cool, for instance, once he'd stopped sleeping with her while she was pregnant; rather a case of closing the barn door after the horse had already bolted, she recalled impatiently. Those final weeks of their marriage he hadn't seemed to notice her at all and his increasing indifference and long working days had made her feel invisible and insignificant.

'I couldn't just go back to Spain,' she told him again. 'I've worked hard to build up my business. I don't want to lose it—'

'I'm willing to cover the cost of a manager for several months. That would give you the time and space to come up with a more permanent solution.'

Cut off at the knees by that unexpectedly practical proposal, Jemima muttered, 'I couldn't live with you again.'

'That decision is yours to make.' Alejandro shifted a broad shoulder in a fluid and fatalistic shrug, his lean, strong face full of brooding dark Spanish reserve and pride. 'But I've already missed out on two years of my son's life and I don't want to waste any more time. My English lawyer is waiting to hear whether or not I wish to proceed with a custody claim.'

That assurance hit Jemima like a bucket of snow thrown across unprotected skin. Every anxious cell in her body plunged into overload. 'Are you simply expecting me to make up my mind about this here and now?' she gasped.

Alejandro quirked an ebony brow. 'Why not? I'm not in the mood to be patient or understanding. I doubt that you suffered many sleepless nights while you were denying me the chance to get to know my son.'

In receipt of that shrewd comment on her attitude, Jemima turned almost as red as her sweater. It was true. She had pretty much celebrated her escape from Spain. She had regretted her failed marriage and cried herself to sleep many nights but she had blamed him entirely for that failure. Now sufficient time had passed for her to be willing to acknowledge that she, too, had made serious mistakes that had undoubtedly contributed to their break-up.

She had certainly kept far too many secrets from him, had spent a lot of money, but that did not mean that she was prepared to have another go at their marriage. But she did, however, love her son very much and she did appreciate how much she had denied Alejandro when she chose not to inform him that he was a father.

'I could come and stay in Spain for a few weeks,' she suggested limply as an alternative.

'A temporary fix of that nature would be pointless.'

'I couldn't possibly sign up to return to our marriage for the rest of my life. That's an appalling idea. Even convicts get time lopped off their sentences for good behaviour!' Jemima pointed out helplessly. 'Maybe I could consider coming out to Spain for a trial period, like, say…three months.'

Alejandro frowned. 'And what would that achieve?' he derided.

'Well, by then we would know if such an extraordinary arrangement was sustainable and I would still have a life to return to in the village if it wasn't working,' she argued vehemently. 'I'm not saying I will do it, but you would also have to give me a legal undertaking that you would not try to claim custody of Alfie while he was still in Spain because that would give you an unfair advantage.'

'The exact same advantage that you would have as an Englishwoman applying for custody in an English court,' Alejandro traded drily.

Her eyes fell before his at that response. 'But we just couldn't do it…*live* together again,' she protested in an enervated rush, folding her arms and walking round the room in a restive circle.

'There has never been a divorce in my family!'

'That's nothing to boast about. We're not living in the Dark Ages any more. People don't have to live with a mistake for ever.'

'But you think it's all right for our son to suffer all the disadvantages of coming from a broken home?'

Jemima groaned out loud in frustration, all shaken up at the very idea of reliving any part of their brief marriage. 'We can't make everything perfect for Alfie.'

'No, but it is our responsibility to give him the best of ourselves, even if that means making personal sacrifices. I respect that,' Alejandro intoned with insistent bite.

'You're always so superior. I want the best for Alfie too.'

'Yet you didn't see a problem bringing him up without a father,' Alejandro lashed back soft and low.

Her face flamed.

'If you truly do want the best for our son, come back to Spain.'

It was blackmail whichever way she looked at it: emotional blackmail, moral blackmail. He knew which buttons to push. He knew how to make her conscience writhe. He was too clever for her, she thought worriedly. If her best hadn't been good enough two years back, how much worse would she fare now with him? But had she ever really given him her best? a little voice asked her doggedly and the abstracted look in her gaze deepened. She was older and wiser and more confident, she reminded herself fiercely. Would it do her so much harm to give their marriage another shot? Of course it went without saying that it wouldn't work out and that both the trial and the subsequent break-up would hurt her again, but wouldn't agreeing give her the satisfaction of knowing that she had tried every option and made the best effort she could?

In the heat of that last inspiring thought, Jemima turned back to focus on her tall, darkly handsome husband. 'All right. I'll come back to Spain but initially I'm only agreeing to stay for three months,' she extended, nervous tension rippling through her in a quivering wave as she realised what she was giving her consent to.

Alejandro stared back at her with brooding dark eyes, revealing neither satisfaction nor surprise at her surrender. 'I will accept that.'

Jemima gazed back at him, suddenly horrified at what she had allowed herself to be persuaded into. He had the silver tongue of the devil, she decided wildly. He had made her feel that any decent mother would have another go at being married for her child's sake. He had studied her with those smouldering dark golden eyes and told her that he *still* wanted her. Not only had she liked that news very much but her body had burned and her brain had shrivelled while she'd thought that truth through to its natural conclusion.

'Have you had lunch?' Alejandro asked.

Jemima backed away a step like a drug addict being offered a banned substance. 'No, but I'm not hungry. I think I should get back to the shop.'

'Of course, you'll have a lot of arrangements to put in place. I'll instruct a recruitment agency to find you a manager,' Alejandro imparted smooth as ice, gleaming dark golden eyes raking over her with a subdued heat that she felt as deep as the marrow of her bones. 'I don't want this to take too long. I also want to see Alfie.'

'Will you still be here over the weekend?' At his nod of assent, Jemima added breathlessly, 'Then come down and see him tomorrow.'

'How soon will you come to Spain?' he prompted.

'Just as soon as I can get it organised.'

'I should take you home,' Alejandro murmured before she got as far as the hall.

'No. I'm used to getting the train…'

'I'll take you to the station, *mi dulzura*.'

The immediate change in his attitude to her made a big impression on Jemima. All of a sudden he believed it was his job to look after her again and it felt seriously strange to have someone expressing concern on her behalf. She accompanied him down to the basement car park and climbed into his shiny car. As she clasped the seat belt Alejandro reached for her, a lean hand tugging up her chin so that his beautiful mouth could crash down on hers without anything getting in the way. It was like plugging her fingers into an electric socket or walking out unprepared into a hurricane. As he plundered her readily parted lips her hand rose and her fingers speared into his luxuriant black hair, holding him to her. The passionate pressure of his mouth on hers was a glorious invitation to feel things she hadn't felt in too long and the plunge of his tongue stoked a hunger she had never managed to forget.

'Dios mio! Te deseo.' He told her he wanted her in a voice hoarse with desire and it sparked a flame at the heart of her and made her shiver with shock. That fast, he had contrived to turn the clock back.

As Jemima drew back from him, breathless with longing and self-loathing, his brilliant gaze scanned her flushed face. 'If you stayed, I would give you so much pleasure.'

Jemima tore her stricken eyes from his, shame sitting inside her like a heavy rock because she was tempted. 'I'll see you on Saturday,' she said tightly.

All the way home on the train she was picturing his lean, strong features inside her head and tearing herself apart over what she had agreed to do. He might as well have hypnotised her! Sandy picked her up in the shop van and dropped her at Flora's cottage.

Twenty minutes later, Jemima was sitting at the island in her friend's kitchen with Alfie cradled half asleep on her lap from his afternoon exertions. Flora was studying her with wide and incredulous green eyes. 'Tell me you're not serious…I thought you hated your ex.'

Jemima shifted her hands in an effort to explain a decision that felt almost inexplicable even to her. 'What Alejan-

dro said about giving our marriage another go for Alfie's
sake made sense to me,' she confided ruefully. 'When I
walked out on him I didn't know I was still pregnant and
I'm not sure I would've gone if I'd known.'

Her friend's face was troubled. 'You were a bag of
nerves when I first met you and you had no self-esteem.
It's not my place to criticise your husband but if that's
what being married to him did to you, something was
badly wrong.'

'Several things were badly wrong then, but not everything was his fault.' Alfie snuggled into his mother's shoulder with a little snuffle of contentment and she rearranged
his solid little body for greater comfort. 'Marco's living
in New York now and another…er…problem I had, well,
it's gone too,' she continued, her expressive eyes veiled as
she thought back reluctantly to those last stressful months
in Spain, which had been, without a doubt, the most distressing and nerve-racking period of her life.

'You want to give your marriage another chance,' Flora
registered in a tone of quiet comprehension. 'If that's what
you really do want, I hope it works out the way you hope.
But if it doesn't, I'll still be here to offer support…'

CHAPTER FIVE

FROM HER STANCE on the edge of the small adventure playground, Jemima watched Alejandro park his sumptuous vehicle. Halston Manor estate lay a few miles outside the village and its grounds were open to the public the year round and much used by locals. Jemima had arranged their meeting with care, choosing an outdoor location where Alfie could let off steam and where all interaction between his parents would have to be circumspect.

Alejandro was dressed with unusual informality in a heavy dark jacket, sweater and jeans. Black hair ruffled by the breeze and blowing back from his classic bronzed features, he looked totally amazing and every woman in the vicinity awarded his tall, well-built figure a lingering look. Jemima tried very hard not to stare and, shivering a little in the cool spring air, she dug her hands into the pockets of her red coat and focused on Alfie, who was climbing the steps to the slide, his big dark eyes sparkling with enjoyment.

'The family resemblance is obvious,' Alejandro remarked with husky satisfaction. 'He is very much a Vasquez, though he has your curls and there is a look of you about his eyes and mouth.'

'I've told him about you,' Jemima informed him.

'How did he take it?'

'He's quite excited about the idea of having a father,' she confided. 'But he doesn't really understand what a father is or what one does.'

In receipt of that news, Alejandro gave both Jemima and Alfie an immediate demonstration, striding forward to intervene when a bigger boy pushed his way past Alfie on the slide steps and the toddler nearly fell. Jemima watched as Alejandro grabbed her son and steadied him. Alfie laughed and smiled up at Alejandro, who spoke to him before stepping back to applaud Alfie's energetic descent of the slide.

Her attention glued to man and child, Jemima hovered. Father and son did look almost ludicrously alike from their black hair and olive-tinted skin to their dark eyes and the brilliance of their smiles. Alfie shouted at her to join them at the swings and she went over, her small face taut, her eyes wary. She could barely speak to Alejandro, yet they'd had a child together: it was an unsettling thought. She pushed Alfie on the swing and watched him show off for his father's benefit. Then her son jumped off the swing before it came to a halt and fell, bursting into tears of over-excitement.

Alejandro scooped him up and took him straight over to another piece of equipment to distract him and Alfie quickly stopped crying. Jemima hadn't expected Alejandro to be as assured at handling a young child as he so obviously was. She watched him crouch down to wipe Alfie's tear-wet face, and tensed as Alfie suddenly flung his arms round Alejandro and hugged him with the easy affection that was so much a part of him. She saw Alejandro's expression as well: the sudden blossoming warmth in his dark eyes, the tightening of his fabulous bone structure that suggested that he was struggling to hold back his emotions and the manner in which he vaulted upright to unashamedly hug Alfie back.

Set down again and in high spirits, Alfie scampered over to his mother and grabbed her hand. 'Ducks...ducks,' he urged and, turning his head, he called, *'Papa...Papa!'* in Spanish as if he had been calling Alejandro that all his life.

'Now we go and feed the ducks,' Jemima explained to Alejandro.

Alfie tearing ahead of them, they walked along the wide path by the lake.

'He's a wonderful little boy,' Alejandro commented abruptly, his dark, deep accented drawl low pitched and husky. 'You've done well with him.'

Jemima shot him a surprised glance and met gleaming dark golden eyes with an inner quiver. 'Thanks.'

'Only a happy, confident child could accept a stranger so easily.'

Warmed by that approval, Jemima felt less defensive and she leant back against a tree and relaxed while Alfie fed the ducks and talked to Alejandro about them. A lot of what the little boy said was nonsense-talk because he only had a small vocabulary, but Alejandro played along. Alfie stretched out a trusting hand to hold his father's and Alejandro began to tell his son about the lake at the Castillo del Halcón and the ducks that lived there.

'The recruitment agency got in touch yesterday and have promised to send me a couple of CVs by midweek,' she told him.

'*Estupendo!* Marvellous,' Alejandro pronounced, studying her from below the dense black fringe of his lashes, eyes a glinting gold provocation that sent colour winging into her cheeks.

He looked at her and she could barely catch her breath. Her nipples were taut, distended buds beneath her clothing and her thighs pressed together as though to contain the rise of the hot, sensitised heat there. She swallowed hard, struggling to shut out the fierce sexual awareness that was racing through her veins like an adrenalin rush.

'Tell me,' Alejandro murmured in a lazy undertone as he towered over her, one lean brown hand braced against the tree, and there was absolutely no forewarning of what he was about to say. 'What did you get from Marco that you couldn't get from me?'

Jemima recoiled from him as though he had stuck a knife in her and moved away several steps, her face flushing, her eyes evasive and full of discomfiture.

'Naturally I want to know,' Alejandro added curtly. *So beautiful and so treacherous*, he reflected darkly. It was a fact he could not afford to forget.

Jemima threw her head up, her eyes purple with strong emotion. 'He talked to me, he took me places, he introduced me to his friends… He wanted my opinions and my company, which is more than you ever did!'

In receipt of that recitation of his brother's deceptive talents, Alejandro dealt her a forbidding appraisal. 'Primarily, Marco used you to get at me. He's a player and you found that out for yourself, didn't you? Did you or did you not tell me that you hadn't heard from my brother since you left Spain?'

At that retaliatory crack, furious mortification gripped Jemima for, of course, he was correct in that assumption. Put under pressure, Marco's friendship had lacked strength, permanence and true affection. Refusing to respond in kind, however, she set her teeth together and for what remained of Alejandro's visit she spoke mainly to Alfie and only when forced to his father.

A MONTH LATER, a four-wheel-drive driven by an estate worker collected Jemima and Alfie from their flight to Spain. Jemima had hoped that Alejandro might pick them up personally but she was not surprised when he failed to appear. As she had learned when they were first married, Alejandro was always very much in demand and, as his wife, she was usually at the foot of his priorities list.

It was a recollection that could only annoy Jemima on the day that she had had to leave behind both the home and the business that she cherished. An excellent manager had taken over the shop. Jemima had put most of her possessions in storage so that the older woman could also rent her house. But all the work she had put into training as a florist, growing her client base for the shop and decorating her home now seemed pointless. On the other hand, she *had* only agreed to a three-month sojourn in Spain, Jemima reminded herself bracingly. Surrendering to Alejandro's blackmail had cost her dear but retaining custody of the little boy securely strapped in the car seat beside her was much, *much* more important to her.

The Castle of the Hawk sat on rocky heights above a lush wooded valley in the remote Las Alpujarras mountains, the last outpost of the Moors in Spain. Little villages with white flat-roofed houses and steep roads adorned the mountainsides while olive, orange and almond groves, grapevines and crops grown for biofuels flourished in the fertile soil. The Vasquez family had ruled their hidden valley like feudal lords for centuries and anyone seeing Alejandro, the current Conde Olivares, being greeted by deferential locals soon appreciated just how much weight that heritage still carried.

Agriculture alone, however, had proved insufficient to keep Alejandro's family in the style to which they had long been accustomed. His father had opened an art gallery in Madrid, but it had taken Alejandro—an astute businessman with the guts to take risks and an infinitely more ruthless edge—to turn that initial purchase into a hugely profitable and influential chain of international galleries. A hotel group and several financial enterprises had also been acquired by Alejandro and between the demands of his business empire and the running of the family estate Alejandro had very little time to spare.

He had always tried to maintain a low profile with the media at home and abroad. However, not only was he very photogenic and the bearer of an ancient title, but he had also, prior to his marriage, enjoyed a love life that was very newsworthy. Those facts, allied with his growing visibility in the business world, had ensured that he could no longer pass undetected and both their wedding and their break-up had, to Alejandro's intense annoyance, attracted newspaper coverage. For that reason, Jemima felt she should have been better prepared when she'd found cameras waiting at the airport earlier that day to record their departure for Spain, but she had been out of the limelight for so long that the appearance of the paparazzi had taken her completely by surprise.

Jemima would also have liked to have known how on earth word of her apparent reconciliation with her Spanish Count and the fact that they now had a child had reached the public domain. She did have very good reason to dread renewed media exposure. Indeed, just thinking about how those photos might cause trouble for her again made Jemima feel sick with apprehension. She was praying that the bad luck that had overtaken her some years earlier and trapped her between a rock and a hard place would not reappear to cause her and those connected with her even more damage and distress.

Endeavouring to bury her worries and control her nerves, Jemima drank in the beauty of the picturesque landscape while the heavy vehicle climbed a familiar road girded by a forest of oaks and chestnuts. The car finally pulled into a courtyard ringed by ornamental trees in giant pots that bore the family coat of arms. Alfie stared out with rounded eyes at the towering thirteenth century stone fortress that now surrounded them on three sides. Her youthful figure slender in casual jeans and a tangerine T-shirt, Jemima left Alfie in the car and rattled the knocker on the giant studded front door.

The door was opened by the middle-aged housekeeper,

Maria, but she stepped back to give precedence to a stout older woman with greying hair who carried herself with a ramrod straight spine, her hard black eyes glinting with outrage.

'How dare you come back to my home?' Doña Hortencia erupted, barring the doorway.

Her daughter, Beatriz, hurried into view and twisted her hands together in an ineffectual protest. 'Jemima, how lovely to see you again… *Mamá*, please, *please*…we must respect Alejandro's wishes.'

Her sister-in-law's anxious, embarrassed face was painful to behold. That her loyalties were tearing her in two was obvious.

The driver carted over two suitcases while Beatriz stared out at the child she could see peering through the window of the estate vehicle. 'Oh, is that Alfie, Jemima? May I go and see him?'

For once impervious to her mother's mood, Beatriz hurried out to the car. The driver hefted up the luggage and stepped past Doña Hortencia with a subservient dip of his head.

'Good afternoon, Doña Hortencia,' Jemima said stoically, following the driver indoors with her flight bag on her shoulder. She was determined not to react in any way to the dirty looks she was receiving and believed that she was a good deal less likely to be bullied than she had been two years earlier. The older woman would certainly make the attempt but Jemima had learned to care less about the impression she made.

Aglow with satisfaction, Beatriz returned holding Alfie's little hand in hers. '*Mamá*, look at him,' she urged with enthusiasm.

Doña Hortencia gazed down at her first grandchild and her forbidding stare softened for an instant before she shot a grim glance at her daughter-in-law. 'This little boy, Alejandro's son and heir, is the one and only thing you have got right.'

Swallowing back the urge to retaliate in kind, Jemima said nothing. What was there to say? Alejandro's mother would never like her or accept her as an equal. Her son had married an ordinary working woman and a foreigner, rather than the wealthy Spanish aristocrat whom the older woman had thought his due, and Doña Hortencia was too stubborn, arrogant and prejudiced to revise her attitude. When Jemima had first come to the castillo, the Spanish woman had done everything possible to ensure that her daughter-in-law's daily life was as miserable as she could make it. This time around, however, Jemima had no plans to accept victimhood.

Beatriz accompanied Jemima up the carved staircase and made small talk as if her life depended on it. Dark gloomy oil portraits of Alejandro's ancestors lined the hall and landing walls. Serious though Alejandro so often was, Jemima reflected helplessly, he was a positive barrel of laughs when she compared him to his predecessors.

'Alejandro has engaged a nanny to help you with Alfie,' Beatriz announced.

'How very thoughtful of your brother,' Jemima remarked after a noticeable pause.

'Placida is the daughter of one of our tenants and a very able girl,' her companion extended anxiously.

Jemima did not want to make Beatriz feel uncomfortable. 'I'm sure she's perfect for the job.'

'This is the room I chose for Alfie,' Beatriz announced with pride, throwing wide the door on a fully furnished nursery complete with a cot, a junior bed and piles of toys. 'Of course, you may prefer to choose another.'

'This is lovely. Did you organise all the toys?'

Beatriz laughed. 'No, that was my brother. Can you believe that Alejandro went shopping for his son?'

'I wouldn't have believed it if you hadn't told me,' Jemima admitted, as Alejandro's dislike of shopping was well known. Bitter as she was about finding herself back in Spain, she could only be touched by the effort he had made on Alfie's behalf. Equally quickly, however, her thoughts travelled in the opposite direction. Of course, wouldn't Alejandro's actual presence mean more than the purchase of expensive toys? In fact wasn't Alfie receiving his first dose of the same benign neglect that Jemima had once endured as Alejandro's wife?

Undisturbed by such deep and troubled mental ruminations, Alfie pelted across the room to grab a toy car with an eager hand. His aunt watched him, entranced. 'You must be so proud,' Beatriz remarked.

Not for the first time, Jemima felt sorry for Beatriz, who was only thirty-five years old but very much on the shelf of her mother's making, for no young man capable of winning Doña Hortencia's approval had ever come along. A dutiful daughter to the last, Alejandro's older sister lived the sedate life of a much older woman.

Placida, the small dark-haired nanny, came to be introduced. After chatting for a while, Jemima left Alfie with Placida and Beatriz and crossed the corridor. The elaborate suite of tower rooms in which she had lived with Alejandro before her pregnancy had brought all sharing to an end was unrecognisable to Jemima at first glance. All the furniture had been changed and a pale yellow colour scheme had banished the dark ornate wallpaper that she had once hated, but that Doña Hortencia had informed her was hand-painted, exceedingly rare and there for eternity. A maid was already busily unpacking her cases and putting her clothes away in the dressing room.

A weird and worrying sense of déjà vu was now settling over Jemima. Alejandro's non-appearance at the airport had first ignited the suspicion that she was about to discover that nothing had changed in the marriage she had left behind. He had also just demonstrated his engrained habit of taking authoritarian charge of anything and everything that came within his radius. In hiring Placida over her head, Alejandro had shown that only his opinion mattered and Jemima did not appreciate being made to feel superfluous in her child's life.

Once the maid had gone, Jemima went for a shower and padded through to the dressing room to extract fresh clothes. It was a shock to open the closets and find that they were already stuffed full of brand-new garments and the drawers packed with equally new lingerie, all of it in her size. Her own small collection of clothes looked shabby in comparison. Evidently, Alejandro, the guy who hated to shop even for himself, had ordered her a new wardrobe. Such generosity was very much his trademark but it made Jemima feel uncomfortable. Perhaps he didn't trust her to dress smartly enough. Perhaps her lack of formal fashion sense had once embarrassed him. Maybe that was why he had gone shopping for her…

Yet the prospect of dining with her haughty mother-in-law garbed like a poor relation in more humble clothing had surprisingly little appeal and Jemima succumbed to the temptation of the new clothes. She selected an elegant sapphire blue dress and slid her feet into delicate sandals before hurriedly going to check on Alfie. He was playing happily in the bath while Placida watched over him. Using her slightly rusty Spanish, Jemima established that Alfie had already eaten his evening meal and she returned to the bedroom.

While she was combing her rebellious hair into a less tumbled style the door opened and she froze. Alejandro, already in the act of removing his tie, appeared. His immaculate grooming was, for once, absent. Indeed, in the bright light of the sunset flooding into the room through the windows, his tailored suit looked crumpled and almost dusty, his black hair tousled, while a dark shadow of stubble heavily accentuated his angular jaw line. But, even with all those flaws taken into consideration, he *still* looked spectacular, awesomely masculine and awesomely sexy. As she studied him, her body reacting with treacherous enthusiasm even as her pride rejected those earthy responses, hot, heady anger threatened to consume her.

'I told Maria we would dine alone next door tonight. Give me ten minutes for a shower,' Alejandro urged her carelessly, but the scorching golden eyes that raked over the mane of strawberry-blonde curls framing her heart-shaped face, before roaming down to the pouting curves defined by the fine fabric of her dress, were in no way casual. That appraisal was so hot she was vaguely surprised that her body didn't start smoking and if anything that bold, sensually appreciative appraisal only increased her resentment.

'Where do you get the nerve to look at me like that?' Jemima launched at him in furious condemnation of that familiarity and the evident plan for a romantic meal for two. It would take a great deal more than that one tiny effort to turn her into the compliant wife he so obviously wanted and expected.

His well-shaped ebony brows drew together as he shed his jacket and embarked on the buttons of his shirt. 'You're too eye-catching to ignore,' he told her teasingly

Jemima was fighting to hang onto her temper. She didn't need a crystal ball to tell her that it was never cool to rail at a man for keeping his distance and even less cool to complain of a lack of attention. So she spun away and glowered at her own frustrated reflection in a tall cheval mirror. Why should she give him the satisfaction of knowing that she had been disappointed when he failed to show up at the airport? Or when he didn't even take the trouble to phone to make a polite excuse for his absence from home? Yet that lack of consideration for her feelings was so familiar from the past that she couldn't help wanting to scream and shout in complaint.

'I'm such an idiot!' she suddenly exclaimed, unable to hold back her seething emotions and keep her tongue glued to the roof of her mouth any longer. 'Somehow I thought it would be different…that you'd make more of an effort to make this work this time—'

'What are you talking about?' Alejandro demanded in the act of shedding the shirt to reveal a superb bronzed muscular chest sprinkled with dark curling hair and a hard, flat stomach that easily met the attributes of the proverbial six-pack.

Jemima spun back to face him. A pulse was beating so fast at the foot of her throat that it was a challenge to find her voice. With every fibre in her body she was blocking out and refusing to respond to his mesmeric physical appeal. 'I arrived here a couple of hours ago. What did you think it would be like for me to be confronted with your mother before I even saw you again? Obviously it didn't occur to you that for once in your life you should have been here for me!'

'I left a message with my mother for you. Are you saying that you didn't receive it?' Alejandro prompted in a tone of hauteur that only set her teeth on edge more.

'Your mother hates me like poison. Are you still so naïve that you think she would take the trouble to pass on a message to me?' Jemima fired back at him.

'If you didn't get the message, I can only apologise for the oversight,' Alejandro drawled smooth as glass, casting off the remainder of his clothes with incredible cool and strolling into the bathroom as lithe and strikingly naked as a sleek bronzed god.

That non-committal and reserved response made

Jemima so mad, she was vaguely surprised that the top of her head didn't blow off. 'Don't pull that aristocratic indifference act on me to try and embarrass me into silence!' she hissed, stalking after him into the bathroom.

'Since when has it been possible to embarrass you into silence?' And with that cutting comeback Alejandro switched on the shower and forced her to swallow back her ire as she assumed that he could no longer hear her above the noise of the water beating down on the tiles.

But Jemima was so irate she still couldn't shut up. The suave assurance with which Alejandro had stripped off in front of her and calmly entered the shower had acted like an electric shock on an already raw temper. 'I hate you when you treat me like this!' she yelled.

While Alejandro showered, Jemima paced in the doorway, all recollection of her past unhappiness as his wife returning then and there to haunt her. Not for anyone would she go through that experience again! And yet hadn't she just signed up again for a rerun on Alfie's behalf? How could it benefit Alfie that she wanted to kill his father in cold blood?

The water switched off and the fleecy white towel on the tiled wall was snatched off the rail. Jemima was trembling and she wrapped her arms round herself. Alejandro reappeared with the towel knotted round his narrow hips, his damp black hair slicked back from his brow and his big powerful body still beaded with drops of moisture. He surveyed her with infuriating, deeply offensive assurance.

'You don't hate me. Of course you don't,' he told her drily.

'And how do you make that out? By the time that I walked out on our marriage, I couldn't *stand* you!'

Alejandro moved towards her and she backed into the bedroom. 'But why?' he queried in the most reasonable of voices. 'Because I had realised what you were up to with

Marco? Because I asked you to explain what happened to all that money? Any man would have demanded answers from you.'

'First and foremost I left you because you wouldn't believe a word I said, but I *did* have lots of other good reasons,' Jemima flung, her eyes bright as violet stars below her fine brows as she challenged him.

Alejandro frowned darkly. 'I'm hungry. I want to get dressed and eat. I don't want to get into a big scene right now.'

Such a surge of rage shot through Jemima's tiny frame that she genuinely felt as though she had grown physically taller. 'Alejandro...there's never a right time with you. But I suggest that for once you look at what you did to contribute to the breakdown of our marriage and stop blaming me for everything that went wrong—'

'Leave the past behind us.'

'Don't you dare say that to me when you continually throw everything I did back at me!' Jemima hissed.

Alejandro groaned out loud. 'So, say what you have to say in as few words as you can manage.'

'You forced me to live under the same roof as your mother—'

'The castle is very large. Such living arrangements are common in Spain—'

'It was never that simple. Doña Hortencia loathes me and she made my life a misery the last time I was here. What did you ever do to stop her?' she condemned fiercely.

'You always exaggerate. How was your life made a misery?' Alejandro countered in a discouraging tone of disbelief.

'If I asked any of the staff to do anything they had to run it by your mother first because she insisted that she was still the mistress of this household. Usually, whatever I wanted I didn't get and I found that humiliating. She criticised everything I did, refused to speak to me at meal-times when you weren't there and insulted me to my face in front of visitors. Ask your sister. Beatriz avoids trouble like the plague but she won't tell you any lies if you ask the right questions.'

Alejandro had screened his brilliant gaze and his wide sensual mouth was compressed by the time she had finished speaking. 'I'll check it out.'

Jemima knotted her hands into fists. 'So, you can't take my word on that either?'

'Since it looks as though I am destined to go hungry tonight, what else do I stand accused of?' Alejandro enquired with sardonic bite.

His derisive intonation made Jemima's teeth grind together. She was shivering with temper and her gaze locked accusingly to his. 'It's your fault that I fell pregnant with Alfie!'

Alejandro studied her in obvious bewilderment. 'You love our son. You can scarcely hold his conception against me.'

'I did when I first discovered that I was pregnant. You chose to be careless with contraception but I paid the price for it,' she challenged, flushing as she recalled the passionate bout of lovemaking in the shower that had led to her unplanned pregnancy. 'We had only been married a few months and I was still quite young for motherhood. I didn't feel ready for a baby and being so sick while I was carrying him didn't help. It made me feel more trapped than ever here but you didn't understand how I felt, did you?'

'No, I didn't, but then you didn't tell me at the time,' Alejandro countered levelly. 'Naturally I realised that you were unhappy but I assumed that was because you were unwell. I would've thought that by now you would have put any bitterness behind you on that score.'

Jemima regarded him with seething resentment. 'So

you get a clean slate while *I* get reminded of my every mistake?'

'Alfie is *not* a mistake, Jemima. He is most probably the best thing that ever happened to either of us,' Alejandro proclaimed in an undertone of driven emotion that was rare for him, his stunning golden eyes unusually eloquent.

Her eyes suddenly stung with prickling tears. 'I didn't mean that *he* was a mistake…'

'Then what *did* you mean?'

'You see, there you go again…thinking the very worst of me!' Jemima launched accusingly, the swimming moisture in her eyes overflowing.

'No, I don't.' Alejandro reached for her slim shoulders in a sudden movement that took her by surprise and he pulled her up against his lean, powerful body. 'But it's hard for me to understand how you can love Alfie but still regret his conception.'

Jemima quivered with awareness as the heat of him penetrated her dress. 'I don't regret it any more.'

'Yet you're still blaming me for a moment's forgetfulness when you could equally well blame yourself.' His stunning dark golden eyes flamed over her upturned face.

As she met his gaze head-on a kind of crazy lethargy gripped Jemima. She could feel the slow pound of her blood through her veins, the racing beat of her heart in her ears and in the pit of her stomach the pull of that electrifying, shockingly strong craving that only he could ignite. He lowered his head and kissed her with unashamed hunger, his lips demanding, his tongue probing with ravishing skill, his teeth nipping at the soft underside of her generous lower lip in a way that made her release a long, shuddering moan of helpless response.

He kissed her until her heart hammered, until she was breathless and hot and no longer thinking straight. She *felt* the zip of her dress going down. She felt the garment shimmy down her arms and simply slide to her feet. As he lifted her up she kicked off her shoes and let him bring her down on the bed. She loved his strength, his unhesitating self-assurance. She knew that she couldn't pretend that she was being seduced against her will. She knew she wouldn't be able to tell herself that he had caught her in a weak moment. What was driving her was the almost painful clawing heat of sheer sexual hunger and the awareness shocked her.

'We shouldn't,' she told him weakly, even as her hand rose to his face and her fingers traced the splendid angle of one high cheekbone, her thumb stroking along the edge of his beautiful mouth, which was capable of giving her so much pleasure.

'Let's not go back to the games we used to play before we got married, *mi dulzura*,' Alejandro husked in sensual reproof.

Utterly bewildered by that comment, Jemima dropped her hand and stared up at him. 'What are you trying to imply...?'

CHAPTER SIX

'No COMMITMENT, NO sex,' Alejandro paraphrased huskily. 'You utilised the most basic feminine weapon of all.'

'That wasn't a game or a weapon!' Jemima protested in a pained voice, wounded that he could even think that of her. From the moment she'd realised just how strong a hold Alejandro had on her heart, she had tried her best to protect herself. Saying no to sex while he still had other women in his bed had seemed to be common sense rather than a form of manipulation.

'Why pretend?' Alejandro murmured, lowering his handsome dark head and letting his jaw line rasp softly along the extended line of her throat before he followed that trail with his mouth, lingering in places that became erogenous just through his touch and laughing when she squirmed beneath him. 'It was highly effective. In the end I wanted you, *only* you. I wanted you so much that having you began to seem like winning the top prize. And I have to admit, you more than lived up to your promise in my bed.'

Her cheeks flushed. 'But it wasn't a game. It might've been for you, it wasn't for me. I was a virgin, for goodness' sake!'

'And I was duly appreciative of the fact. I married you,' Alejandro reminded her doggedly.

But Jemima had just had an unsettling glimpse into how he viewed those months prior to their marriage. Evidently he had always believed that it was the power of lust for her long-withheld body that had stoked his desire to the point where he offered her a wedding ring so that she was always around, always available. With that shallow basis, was it any wonder that their relationship had failed? There was nothing lasting about lust, she told herself, even as she lifted her hips in a helpless circling motion beneath the pressure of his weight on hers, every skin cell singing with eagerness.

Alejandro shimmied down her body to let his mouth travel across the pale hillocks of her breasts encased in turquoise silk and lace cups. He released the catch on her bra and tugged her up against him to enjoy the warm soft weight of the sensitive flesh that spilled into his hands. She gasped as he entrapped the straining peaks between thumb and finger, rubbing the swollen pink tips until she leant back into him with an uninhibited moan of response.

'I love your breasts,' he husked. 'Such a delightfully lush surprise on that tiny frame of yours.'

Jemima strained back against him, her spine arching as the feeling of pressure and awareness low in her pelvis increased. He twisted her round and down again and found the delicate rosy buds he had already massaged into prominence with his devouring mouth. It was as though her breasts were a hotline to her groin, for the surge of heat and moisture between her thighs was instantaneous. A finger stroked along the taut damp band of fabric at her crotch and she flinched, letting her head fall back as a low moan of encouragement was wrenched from her throat. She wanted him so much it hurt to wait.

'Have you any idea how often I've fantasised about this moment in the last few weeks?' Alejandro asked her thickly, peeling off her panties and using a knee to part her legs. His dark golden eyes glowed with sexual heat over the naked expanse of her delicate curves.

Jemima was trembling. The temptation to revel in the

depth of his desire had died on the reflection that lust had no longevity and lying willingly naked for his appraisal only made her all the more conscious of the things she didn't like about her body. She had always thought that her legs were too short and the extra weight she carried at breast and hip too much for her height. As she began to curl away from him he bent down and crushed her lips under his with a passionate urgency that burned through her like a flaming brand. The plunge of his tongue affected her like a chain of firecrackers sparking through her taut length and her hips rose pleadingly, her whole body singing with sharp urgent need.

'Oh, *please*,' she said shakily, impatient, needy, wanting more than she could bear.

'I want to enjoy you first...I want to wait,' Alejandro framed with ragged ardour, playing with the delicate pearly folds between her thighs while he worked his skilful passage down over her quivering body, watching her expressive face as she fought to stay in control.

'Don't watch me,' she urged unevenly, suffering sweet torment from the hunger he was stoking.

He touched her with such infinite finesse, knowing the perfect spot, the exact amount of pressure, the ideal pace. She cried out loud, eyelashes sliding down to screen her eyes as the pleasure raced and screamed through her twisting length. He licked the skin of her inner thigh, following the trail to a more intimate place and dallying there with sensual expertise until she thought she might pass out with the intensity of her response. Her climax took her like a roaring storm, demanding every ounce of her energy and throwing her up to a breathless height of excruciating pleasure as she writhed in sobbing satisfaction.

He pulled back from her when she wanted him to hold her close. The world was a thousand miles away from her at that moment when she was still lost in the cocoon of all that breathtaking pleasure. Then she heard the slide of a drawer, the sound of foil tearing and a moment later he was back with her. After what she said earlier, she registered that he would not risk her falling pregnant again.

Jemima felt wanton, because when he came back to her he was hugely aroused and her body thrilled anew for she could hardly wait for that final act of possession. Orgasm hadn't satisfied that deep driving need to be with him again in the most basic way of all. He slid over her and she lifted to him at the first probing thrust of his bold shaft. He felt so big, so good when he plunged into her long and hard and deep and she gasped, violet eyes flying wide, raw excitement licking through her like flames.

'You *really* want me,' Alejandro growled with all-male satisfaction, surging into her receptive body with sudden driving urgency.

It was like being caught in the eye of a hurricane. A kind of stormy wildness pulsed through her to stoke the rising rush of crazy excitement already leaping high with her anticipation. Alejandro settled on a potent pagan rhythm. He was rampant, irresistible and her heartbeat thumped faster and faster in tune with his strong movements. Gasping, she rose under him, her body moving of its own accord as the feverish, hot, stimulating delight of his possession gave her ever-increasing pleasure. Somewhere towards the end of that ravenous ride she screamed, writhing as the ecstatic convulsions of a second climax seized hold of her. The sheer intensity of the experience almost made her black out and she lay shell shocked in the aftermath.

'*Dios mio.* That was amazing,' Alejandro husked above her head, his arms still anchored round her to keep her close. 'To think that I was afraid I might not be able to get it up with you because of Marco. You deliver such an erotic buzz I would have to be made of stone to resist you.'

Jemima tensed and stiffened defensively. Her lips parted

and almost simultaneously a long brown forefinger nudged
against her mouth.

'No more denials, *querida*. Every time you deny what
you did I get angry again and it has been a very long and
difficult day,' Alejandro admitted heavily.

Prevented from stating her case by his wall of en-
trenched disbelief and distrust, Jemima suffered an immediate sense of alienation and she pulled free of his embrace
to roll over into a cooler spot in the bed. She lay on her
side and looked back at him, her violet eyes bright with
antagonism below her wildly tumbled strawberry-blonde
curls. He looked so relaxed, black hair tousled by her fingers above his bold bronzed profile. Her fair skin was tingling and probably pink from the burn of the stubble he
hadn't got to shave off before taking her to bed, but deep
down inside her there was a well of indescribable physical
satisfaction that had been running on empty ever since she
had left Spain previously. Their marriage had always been
a blazing success in the bedroom. But she knew it would
be a long time before she got over the embarrassment of
having revealed just how much she had craved his touch.

Alejandro turned his handsome head on the pillow to
look at her with spectacular dark brown eyes semi-veiled
by lush ebony lashes. 'Surely you can see that we cannot
make a success of living together again without an honest
acceptance of the past?'

Her generous mouth took on a mutinous slant. He had
already travelled from refusing to believe her to refusing
even to *listen* to her denials so what hope of exoneration
did that give her for the future? His belief in her infidelity was unshakable.

'Shower, then dinner,' Alejandro instructed arrogantly
in the smouldering silence, closing a stubborn hand over
hers to drag her across to his side of the bed while he tossed
back the sheet and vaulted upright.

'Where were you today? What happened that you had to leave a message for me?' Jemima asked abruptly as he propelled her into the spacious bathroom with him.

'Pepe, one of the vineyard workers, had a tractor accident. He was badly hurt,' Alejandro told her, his mouth compressing into a bleak line. 'I stayed at the hospital to support his wife. Their only child lives abroad and the other relatives are elderly. I'm afraid Pepe didn't make it and by the time I got his wife home again and offered my condolences to the rest of the family...'

Jemima was aghast at what he was telling her. 'Yes, I can imagine how awful it must have been. I'm sorry, if I'd known I wouldn't have said anything—'

'But you didn't know so you were entitled to complain.' The speed with which he dismissed the matter told her that he didn't want to discuss it further. He had not exaggerated when he had said what a difficult day he'd had.

In the spacious tiled shower with the water streaming down over his big bronzed body he leant back against the wall for a moment or two, his eyes closing, and she finally appreciated just how tired he was. Her conscience smote her and she resented that feeling because when they were first married Alejandro had often contrived to make her feel that way. So often he'd had something more important, serious or meaningful to do with his time than be with her. She had often felt guilty, undeserving or selfish for just wanting to see more of him. Pepe's wife and family, however, would have found his presence a source of great comfort and support because he was that kind of a guy: strong and reliable in times of crisis.

Knowing that, she had often wondered why he had let her down so badly when she needed him. Or as his unsuitable and unhappy wife had she simply been yet another burden and source of worry for him, one he'd been relieved to be free of again? It would be foolish for her to forget that he had only taken her back so that he could have his son living with him in his home in Spain.

She didn't bother getting dressed again. Clad in a blue nightdress and satin wrap, she joined Alejandro in the reception room adjoining their bedroom where a meal was served in spite of the late hour. Casually clad in jeans and a black T-shirt, he looked younger and more approachable as well as heart-stoppingly handsome. A big vase of fresh white daisies adorned the round table and she remembered how his mother had once summarily dumped one of Jemima's own amateur floral arrangements. In those days she had been naïve, easily hurt and upset. She had barely had the maturity to be a wife, never mind a mother, and she had made more than one stupid decision, opting for the wrong choices and what had seemed like the easy way out when life got tough.

Alejandro studied his reclaimed wife intently across the table. Even with her pale hair in an untidy riot of curls and without a scrap of make-up, she was so beautiful with her fragile features, flawless skin and unusually coloured eyes that she commanded and held his full attention. The sex might be even more amazing than he recalled but he wasn't yet fully convinced that he had her where he wanted and needed her to be. The memory of her three-month proviso outraged his sense of justice. His polar opposite, she was impulsive, capricious and, as he had cause to know, wildly extravagant. It would be a challenge to predict her next move.

Once again he was at war with himself, Alejandro recognised angrily. It was a familiar predicament where Jemima was concerned. How could he have so compromised his convictions that he took back an unfaithful wife? Moreover, an unfaithful wife who still refused to admit her guilt? And an unrepentant gold-digger who had undoubtedly only survived in England for so long without his financial support because she had already carefully bled him dry of thousands of euros before she'd left him. Her escape fund? What else? It was a galling suspicion for a male once accustomed to female adulation and pursuit. Only his wife had run in the other direction.

But what right had he to the moral high ground? He had used their toddler son as a weapon and blackmailed her into returning yet, amazingly, he didn't feel guilty about what he had done. Had he not acted in his son's best interests? Dealing with such a woman demanded extraordinary measures.

He sipped his wine, savouring the vintage while his keen intelligence continued to present him with truths he would have preferred to ignore. Jemima might make him burn with desire but she was bad news for him. A man should aspire to a decent woman with standards, not stoop to the level of a dishonourable and deceitful one. But the instant he'd been subjected to the sight of the men panting after her skirts in that little English village his libido and territorial instincts had flamed to unmanageable heights. The prospect of leaving her free to take such men to her bed in his place had sentenced him to sleepless nights and repeated cold showers, for his blood ran hot.

Jemima was *his* and, undeniably, a weakness. Every man could afford an indulgence as long as he practised damage control, Alejandro ruminated, his lean, strong face hard with self-discipline. And she couldn't hurt him because he didn't love her. He had never been in love and was proud of the fact, he reminded himself with innate pride. Men in love were fools with women while a man in lust knew exactly what he was doing and why he was doing it.

Uncomfortable with the lingering silence, Jemima finally spoke up. 'There were reporters and cameras at the airport when I arrived for my flight out here today. They seemed to be waiting for Alfie and me, expecting us…'

Alejandro was frowning with annoyance. 'Someone must have tipped them off. How else would they have known you would be there?'

'Well, it wasn't me—'

'Are you sure of that?' Alejandro prompted cynically.

Her eyes widened in surprise and consternation. 'But why would I tip off the paparazzi?'

'Either because you were paid for the information or because you revel in the attention of the press.' Alejandro tossed his napkin down and rose to his full impressive height. His devastatingly handsome features were grave. 'Whichever it is, be warned: I don't like that kind of publicity.'

'Where are you going?' Jemima pressed tautly, already reeling from the accusation he had just made.

'To bed. I'll look in on Alfie first. *Buenas noches, querida.*'

A faint surge of pink illuminated her delicate bone structure. Her hands clenched into fists of restraint below the level of the table but she passed no further comment. After their passionate lovemaking in what had once been the marital bed his departure for the night to a separate room was like a slap in the face. It was a reminder that appearances were deceptive and that neither the expensive gift of a new wardrobe nor the meal eaten *à deux* meant that they were engaged in a genuine reconciliation.

'I didn't tell the paps that we were getting back together,' Jemima declared loudly.

'Someone did.' Unimpressed dark golden eyes clashed with hers, his strong jaw line at an aggressive angle.

'You know, I didn't appreciate you taking on a nanny without discussing it with me first,' she confided abruptly, deciding that she might as well confront that issue.

'We can discuss that tomorrow,' Alejandro fielded impatiently and a moment later he was gone, leaving her still seated with her dessert sitting untouched in front of her.

Minutes later, the maid arrived with a trolley to clear the table and Jemima went to check on her son, finding him sound asleep in his cot. For a moment she envied the contentment etched in Alfie's peaceful little face. A strange cot in an unfamiliar room and new faces all around him? No problem. Alejandro's son had rolled with the punches and he saw no reason to stay awake and on guard. And why shouldn't her son feel that way? There could be no comparison between his childhood and the one his mother had endured, which had marked her all her life with fear and anxiety. Alfie's world had always been safe and his needs had always been met. He had never been denied love. He had never known violence or malice. And Jemima was quietly proud of the fact that she had done much more for him than her parents had ever done for her.

Back in the bedroom she slid into bed and put on the television, finally tuning into a music channel before resting back against the pillows.

She had no idea what time it was when a sound wakened her and she half sat up, pushing her hair out of her eyes and blinking as Alejandro flicked the remote control at the television to switch it off. The bedside lamp was still lit. 'I must've fallen asleep,' she mumbled drowsily, wondering if the noise from the set had disturbed him, for he was barefoot and wearing only his jeans with the top button undone. A silky black furrow of hair ran down over his stomach and disappeared below the waistband. Suddenly she felt hot.

Alejandro sent her a brooding look from glittering dark eyes. 'I'm sleeping here tonight,' he informed her with a hostile stare-you-down cool stamped on his lean dark features as though he expected her to argue with him.

Jemima was startled by that announcement. After all, it

was already three in the morning according to the digital display on the clock by the bed. Lips parting slowly in surprise, Jemima watched as he shed his jeans. A lean, powerfully muscular silhouette—he was wearing, it transpired, not a stitch below the denim and he was…well, he *was* sporting a rampant erection. There was really no avoiding that fact. Hot colour washed her face and a melted-honey sensation curled low in her pelvis. She was his object of desire and he couldn't hide it and she liked that. The separate-bedroom concept had bitten the dust at remarkable speed.

'I should be too tired for this, *querida*,' Alejandro growled as he came down on the bed beside her, his every fluid movement full of virile masculine promise. 'But I can't sleep for wanting you.'

Jemima lay back like Cleopatra reclining on a ceremonial barge, ever ready to be admired. She gazed up at him in sultry invitation and with hot golden eyes he crushed her soft full mouth under his with an erotic savagery that sent desire lancing through her slim length in an arrow of fire. She closed her hand round him and he shifted against her with a guttural sound while she teased the silky sleek heat of his sex over its iron-hard core. With an eagerness that thrilled her, he wrenched her free of the nightdress, his hands finding the white globes of her breasts and then the swollen damp flesh between her thighs. Every sense on high alert, her body went wild as the pounding throb of heat and hunger pulsed through her tender body, racking her with a stark storm of need.

'*Por Dios*, I can't wait,' Alejandro framed hungrily through a welter of passionate and devouring kisses that only left her gasping for more.

And dimly Jemima wondered what was happening to her because, somehow, even though she had been satiated he had set her alight again and the balance of power was no longer hers. Alejandro had never felt more necessary to her as he turned her on her side and plunged into her tight hot core, stretching her, filling her with a sweet, dominant force she could not resist. Delirious excitement powered through her quivering body in wave after wave when he rubbed her swollen nipples and teased the tiny bud of pleasure below her mound. He pounded into her at an enthralling pace until the ache and the burn combined into a fiery explosion. She reached a shattering release, convulsive spasms of delight roaring through her sobbing, shaking length until at last she lay still in his arms, weak and utterly spent.

Alejandro turned her round and pressed a kiss to her cheek before stretching up to douse the lights. 'Nobody but you has ever given me pleasure like that.'

And in receipt of that accolade, Jemima went from warm and reassured into a place of wounding self-doubt. Nothing had changed. It was always all about sex as far as Alejandro was concerned. He had never loved her yet, even though she had never believed she was the wife he really wanted, he had still married her. That had never made sense to her. But even so, Jemima was all too used to not making the grade with those she loved. Her mother would have loved and valued her daughter more had Jemima been the baby boy she had wanted to please her husband. Her father had never loved her, nor had he ever pretended to. There had been boyfriends but no one serious before Alejandro and she had fallen so hard for him that the sheer pain of having once loved and lost him still had the power to wound her.

She lay awake in the darkness, reassured by his continuing presence. It might only be sex that kept him there but that was better than nothing, wasn't it? She could walk away from him again without getting hurt, she told herself soothingly. She didn't love him any more; she had got over that nonsense. Once she had believed that Marco's obvious pleasure in her company might magically make his big brother view his wife with newly appreciative eyes. Instead Alejandro had simply assumed that her close friendship with Marco was based on sex. When that was the only tie he himself acknowledged with her, how could he have understood that she and Marco had bonded on quite another level?

Suppressing a regretful sigh over her tangled and unhappy past, Jemima finally drifted off to sleep...

CHAPTER SEVEN

JEMIMA ONLY AWOKE when china rattled on a tray and the curtains were trailed noisily back. Sunlight drenched the bed in a shower of warm golden brilliance and she sat up with a sleepy sigh. She was immediately conscious of the stiffness of her limbs and the intimate ache at the heart of her. X-rated memories of how she had celebrated the breaking of the dawn assailed her. It was little wonder she had slept like a log afterwards, not even stirring when Alejandro got up.

She stared in disbelief at her watch, for the day was in full swing and it was comfortably past noon. The maid set down the tray on a side table and settled Jemima's wrap down on the bed for her use while asking her whether she wanted to eat in the room next door or outside on the roof terrace. Self-conscious at being naked, with her nightdress lying in a heap in the middle of the floor where Alejandro had hurled it, Jemima fought her way into the wrap while contriving to stay mostly covered by the sheet.

'Thanks. I'll eat outside,' she said, sliding out of bed and pushing her feet into mules to follow the maid through the door and up the little narrow curving staircase in the corner and out onto the roof terrace of the tower. Once it had been her favourite place in the castle, safe from all intruders and prying eyes. Warm, all-encompassing heat curled round her lightly clad frame when she stepped out into the fresh air to enjoy the magnificent view she remem-

bered. It stretched as far as the eye could see right up to
the snow-capped Sierra Mountains that girded the valley.

Far below in the gardens she heard a child's laughter and
she stood at the battlements from where she espied Alfie,
who was playing ball on an immaculate green lawn with
a small figure she assumed to be Placida. Some mother
she had proved to be since her arrival at the castle, she reflected ruefully. Resolving to spend the rest of the day with
him, Jemima sat down at the shaded table and quickly embarked on the delicious lunch on the tray. She was really
hungry and ate with appetite before taking the tray back
downstairs, laying out white cropped knee-length trousers
and a green T-shirt from her own store to wear and heading straight for the shower.

Her hair in damp ringlets, she was coming down the
main staircase when she heard a female voice raised in
shrill argument. Indeed the voice might almost have been
described as being at screaming pitch and it was matched
by the deep bass notes of a clipped male voice. The racket
was emanating from the imposing salon on the ground
floor. In the main hall two of the domestic staff were stationed outside the service door to the kitchens and clearly
engaged in eavesdropping. Her face flushed and miserable, Beatriz emerged abruptly from the room and the staff
slipped hurriedly through the service door and out of sight.

'What's going on?' Jemima asked baldly.

'*Mamá* is very offended with Alejandro,' Beatriz told
her uncomfortably.

'Oh…' Stifling her curiosity because she thought
it wiser not to get involved in a family matter, Jemima
walked right past the door of the salon. 'I'm going out to
the garden to join Alfie and Placida.'

Alejandro's sister accompanied her, clearly keen to escape the bad feeling on the domestic front. 'Alejandro has

asked Doña Hortencia to move into a house on the estate,' she revealed.

Startled by that news, Jemima turned to look at her companion with wide eyes of enquiry. 'My goodness, that's very sudden!'

'Her belongings are already being packed,' Beatriz declared in a dazed undertone. '*Mamá* is very shocked. I have never seen Alejandro so angry or so resolute. She is to move into a hotel until the house is fully prepared for her.'

'That must have been some argument.' Jemima did not have the hypocrisy to pretend regret at the prospect of Doña Hortencia moving out of the castle, but she was very much surprised by the development.

'I will miss my nephew,' Alejandro's sister admitted heavily.

'But surely you're not moving out as well?' Jemima exclaimed.

'*Mamá* will expect me to accompany her.'

'But I don't and I'm sure Alejandro won't either,' Jemima stated, because she knew that Alejandro was very fond of his sister and troubled by the restricted life she led with their mother. 'This has always been your home, Beatriz.'

The tall, full-figured brunette lifted worried eyes to hers. 'Are you sure that you and Alejandro wouldn't mind if I stayed on?'

'Of course, we wouldn't. I would be glad of your company, particularly when Alejandro is away on business.'

'My stepmother would never forgive me for deserting her...' Beatriz looked shocked at the concept of the new way of life she was clearly envisaging. 'I'm not sure I *could* go against her wishes and do it—'

Her brow pleating, Jemima had come to a sudden halt. 'Did you just refer to Doña Hortencia as your "stepmother"? Or did I get that wrong?'

In her turn, Beatriz frowned uncertainly at the smaller blonde woman. 'Didn't you know?' she queried somewhat abstractedly, her mind clearly still focused on her future living arrangements. 'Of course we have always had to call her *Mamá*. I was only three years old and Alejandro a newborn baby when our own mother died.'

Jemima stifled the curious questions ready to spring to her lips. It was typical that Alejandro had not chosen to enlighten her as to that salient fact. It did at least explain why Doña Hortencia had always seemed very cold towards her elder son while seeming almost dotingly fond of his younger brother, Marco. 'But Marco is?'

'Marco was born four years after Doña Hortencia married our father,' Beatriz confirmed quietly. '*Mamá* was very upset when she realised that Marco could not inherit a larger portion of what our father left in his will because it would have meant splitting up and selling the estate.'

Alfie ran across the lawn to throw himself at his mother when he saw her approaching. Laughing and cuddling his solid little body, Jemima hugged her son close and urged his nanny to take a break. Beatriz played ball with her nephew and Jemima found herself hoping that her sister-in-law would have the courage to break free of her stepmother's suffocating control and stay on at the castle.

Almost an hour later, Alejandro strolled out to join them. Sheathed in lightweight khaki chinos with the sleek lines of a designer fit and a short-sleeved shirt, he looked gorgeous. When his spectacular black spiky-lashed golden gaze sought hers, Jemima went pink as she recalled the intimacies they had shared so freely during the night hours. Alfie beamed at his father and gave him the ball while Beatriz excused herself, saying that she ought to go and see if she could assist Doña Hortencia.

Jemima stood by containing her intense curiosity while Alejandro and Alfie fooled about with the ball. When they had both had enough, Alejandro suggested taking Alfie down to the lake and loaded them into an estate vehicle.

'I didn't realise until Beatriz mentioned it that Doña Hortencia was actually your stepmother.'

Alejandro compressed his lips. 'She's the only mother I can remember. My own died from eclampsia within hours of my birth.'

'That was a tragic loss for all of you,' Jemima remarked.

'My father remarried months after her death. Hortencia, not my mother, was the true love of his life,' Alejandro explained flatly. 'He worshipped the ground she walked on and he came close to bankrupting the estate in his determination to give her the very best of everything.'

Jemima was suddenly beginning to revise her once sunny assumptions about Alejandro's childhood. 'Was it a happy marriage?'

'*He* was happy, but I don't think she has ever been satisfied in her life with what she had. When my father was dying, however, he became very concerned about Hortencia's future—I believe she had shared her fears with him—and he begged me to always treat her as though she was my birth mother. It was his last wish. I gave my word and I have respected it ever since. Until today it did not occur to me that in tolerating her excesses I had been unfair to you.'

'Why?' Jemima questioned. 'What happened today?'

'Had you let me know how my stepmother was treating you when we were first married I would have stopped it then. You should have been honest with me,' Alejandro murmured in a tone of reproach rather than censure, his striking eyes troubled. 'This was your home and as my wife it is your right to take charge of the castle and the staff—'

'I'm not sure I could have coped with the responsibility in those days,' Jemima cut in lightly, realising that for some inexplicable reason all she wanted to do at that moment was make him feel better rather than add another weight to his conscience.

His lean, strong face clenched hard. 'But you never had the opportunity to *try*. Had you not been hampered by Hortencia's spite you would have managed perfectly well. You are a capable young woman.'

'Did your sister say that she was spiteful?' Jemima prompted in surprise, for Beatriz virtually never had a bad word to say about anyone. They were walking down towards the lake that gleamed through a grove of silvery olive trees like a reflective mirror on the valley floor.

A brooding expression darkened Alejandro's features. 'There was no need for her to do so. The manner in which my stepmother spoke of you today was sufficient for me to appreciate the level of malice which I was dealing with. The only possible solution was for her to move out—'

'Do you regret that?'

'How could I?' Alejandro confided with a harsh laugh that acknowledged the older woman's challenging temperament. 'Although Beatriz and I had no choice but to treat her as our mother, she had no maternal love to give us. She sent both of us off to boarding school as soon as she could. And after Marco was born, she resented my position as the eldest son and ensured that I had little contact with my father.'

'Then you were kinder to her than she deserved,' Jemima pronounced feelingly.

'But I can't forgive myself for not appreciating how she was treating you when I first made this your home.' Alejandro stared down at her with intent eyes and reached for her hand in a warm gesture of encouragement that took her by surprise. 'I hope you can move past that bad beginning now and learn to love this place and its people as I do, *querida*.'

That he wanted things to change for her benefit and that he had already made a bold first move towards that end pleased Jemima a great deal. But it was the eloquent expression in those beautiful eyes the colour of rich malt whisky in sunlight that affected her the most. He really did want their marriage to work this time around and, even though that might be primarily because they now had a child to consider, his determination and his caring about what it would take to make her happy in Spain impressed her. It was a beginning, and a better beginning than they had made together when they first married…

A SLIGHT FIGURE in an emerald-green silk skirt suit that was bright against her fair complexion and wealth of straw-berry-blonde hair, Jemima stepped up to the podium with a heart beating as fast as a drum. She set her little prompt card down where it could catch her eye if she forgot what she had to say. As this was her first ever public speech, she had kept it short and succinct and had rehearsed it thoroughly with Beatriz beforehand.

In spite of those precautions, though, perspiration still dampened her short upper lip and her nerves were bouncing about like jumping beans. At a nod of readiness from the charity director, Jemima began to speak about the need for the sanctuary for female victims of domestic violence being provided by the shelter. The fund-raising benefit was aimed at providing new purpose-built premises where women and children could stay in safety and begin to re-build their lives.

At the back of the function room, she was conscious of Alejandro watching her. Beatriz was by her brother's side and smiling encouragement, but it was less easy to tell what Alejandro was thinking. She was pleased enough that he had rescheduled a business trip so that he could accompany her to the evening event. Jemima returned to

their table, quietly content that she had contrived to control
her nerves. It was thanks to Beatriz, who had long had an
interest in the charity, that Jemima had got involved. Although it was not a fact that she would have shared with
her husband, she had felt a great sense of empathy with
the frightened women and children she had met and talked
to at the shelter.

'You were terrific, *esposa mia.*' Alejandro regarded
her with frank approbation and she reached for his hand
to squeeze it. He had just called her his wife in a tone of
pride and affection that went a long way towards healing
the still raw wounds inflicted in the past.

But then, over the past couple of months Jemima had
seen a different side to Alejandro's brooding temperament. As he turned his handsome head and stood up to
politely acknowledge the greeting of a local businessman
she was wearing a warm smile. Somehow they had put
the past away, although sometimes she feared that putting
those troubles untouched into a locked box was more of a
shortcut than a long term solution. Marco was never, ever
mentioned and neither, fortunately, she felt, was the disturbing question of all the money she had once contrived
to run through.

On the other hand, she and Alejandro were enjoying an
accord that they had never had in the past when he worked
such long hours that she was constantly left to her own
devices and deprived of a social life. It was that isolation
that had made her so grateful for Marco's friendliness. But
over two years on Alejandro had learned how to make time
for her and Alfie and he had made the effort to introduce
them to his world. He had taken them over every inch of
the valley, showing them over his various businesses and
introducing them to the tenants and the employees, so that
for the first time Jemima felt as though the estate and the
castle were her home as well.

An opening day for the public to view the castle had given Jemima the excuse to do several floral arrangements. Family, friends and relations, who had attended a dinner party that same evening, had been hugely impressed and Jemima had already received several requests to act as a floral consultant at local events. Having acted as an advisor at a couple now, she wasn't yet sure that she wanted to embark on what promised to be another business. No longer subject to Doña Hortencia's withering asides and cutting put-downs, Jemima was comfortable entertaining guests at the castle and had discovered that just being herself was sufficient.

Day by day, Alfie was blossoming; his days were much more active and varied than they had been in Charlbury St Helens and there were far more people around to give him attention. In fact, for a while, all that admiring attention had rather gone to Alfie's head and he had become too demanding; a solid week of toddler tantrums had ensued whenever he'd been subjected to the word no. Jemima had been amused by the discovery that Alejandro, so tough in other ways, had had to steel himself to be firm with his son when the little boy had thrown himself on the ground and sobbed with a drama that she was convinced came from his father's side of the family. It was a new relationship for Alejandro, who had never been allowed to enjoy the same close ties with his own father as a boy.

And so far Alejandro had shown every sign of being a brilliant dad. He had put a lot of effort into building a good relationship with his little son. Alfie adored him and raced to greet him the minute he heard his footsteps or his voice. Jemima had been impressed by the time and trouble Alejandro had taken to get to know Alfie and find out what he enjoyed. She had only to see father and son together to know that she had made the right decision in coming back to Spain.

Jemima was also happy in a way she had never thought she could be again, although sometimes she felt as if she were floating in a deceptively calm sea while wilfully ignoring the dangerous undertow and the concealed rocks. The next day, Alejandro took her on a long drive through the mountains to a sleepy town with an amazing little restaurant that served astonishingly good food. As they were getting back into the car Alejandro asked without the smallest warning, 'Did Marco ever bring you up here?'

And caught unawares with her defences down, she felt her face freeze, wasn't able to help that strong reaction to a name that was never voiced. 'No, he didn't. I would have said,' she murmured stiffly.

Clearly unimpressed by that claim, Alejandro gave her a hard dark appraisal, which warned her that though the body of her supposed infidelity might have been buried it was still at great risk of being disinterred. He hadn't forgotten or forgiven her imaginary betrayal and, for several taut seconds while she gazed stonily back at him, she bristled with an amount of resentment and rancour that would go a fair way to destroying any marital reconciliation. It was a struggle to keep the lid on her emotions.

'I shouldn't have asked,' Alejandro conceded tautly, the two of them momentarily enclosed by the suffocating sweaty heat of the car before the air conditioning could kick in and cool the interior.

'I'm surprised you did—Marco has urban tastes. He prefers clubs and culture to the countryside,' Jemima reminded him, staring fixedly out through the windscreen but seeing nothing, wondering why she had said that, why she had extended the dialogue instead of dropping it cold.

'And you always did like dancing,' Alejandro quipped, his intonation stinging like a sharp needle jabbed in the arm.

'After we were married, when did you ever take me?'

Jemima countered defiantly, ready and looking for a fight now, all patience at an end.

Brilliant dark golden eyes alight with scorching rebuke at that tart gibe, Alejandro closed long brown fingers round her hand to tug her closer and he brought his mouth hotly and hungrily down on hers in retribution. For an instant her hand skimmed down over one high olive cheekbone in an unintended caress and then she dropped her hand and her fingers closed into the front of his jacket and clenched there instead, because the burning stream of desire he had unleashed fired her up as fiercely as her disturbed emotions. Her breasts were taut nubs below her clothing, the tender flesh between her thighs warm and moist and ready. Swearing only half under his breath at the intensity of her response, Alejandro thrust her back from him and started up the car.

'You shouldn't begin anything you can't finish,' she whispered helplessly, her body stabbing her with jagged regret over the loss of that so necessary physical contact with him.

Without warning Alejandro laughed and shot her a wicked long-lashed glance, his wide sensual mouth curling with amusement. 'I have every intention of finishing what I began, *tesora mia.*'

'It will take us well over an hour just to get home,' Jemima reminded him.

But only a few minutes later, Alejandro turned his Ferrari off the road and drew up outside a country hotel. She turned startled eyes on him. 'You can't be serious?'

'Only an acrobat could have good sex in this car,' Alejandro fielded, vaulting out and striding round the bonnet to open the passenger seat door and extract her.

'But we've got no luggage!' she protested in a panicked undertone, colouring hotly with self-consciousness when he strode over to the reception desk, his dark head held high, and asked for a room without the smallest hint of discomfiture.

'Your face is too well known. People will get to know about this,' she muttered ruefully when the door closed behind the porter and left them alone in a well-appointed room. Yet even as she sounded that note of caution she was excited by his audacity and his single-minded pursuit of satisfaction.

An unholy grin lit Alejandro's lean, darkly handsome features as he reached for her again. 'After imbibing a little too freely of the wine we had with lunch I was falling asleep at the wheel and rather than risk continuing our journey I did the sensible thing and took a break,' he mocked.

'The famous Spanish siesta, much written about but more rarely found in practice these days,' she teased.

'I promise that you will enjoy every moment of our siesta, *querida*,' Alejandro swore with a husky growl of anticipation edging his deep dark drawl.

And then he kissed her, and the heat and the craving gripped her again with even greater power. He stripped off her clothes between passionate breathless kisses and she fought with his shirt buttons and his belt, already wildly, feverishly aware of the rigid fullness of his erection. She sank down on her knees and used her mouth on him until his hands closed tightly into her hair to restrain her and he was trembling against her.

He hauled her back up to him and tumbled her down on the crisp white linen sheets that awaited them. There was no need of further foreplay for either of them. He sank into her long and slow and deep and she quivered on a sexual high of intense response and so it continued until she hit a soul-shattering climax and her body convulsed in sweet spasms of delight around him.

'You can go to sleep now if you like,' Jemima whispered generously with a voluptuous stretch in the aftermath.

Laughing, Alejandro cradled her close and claimed another kiss. 'I have a much better idea.'

Jemima smiled, loving that physical closeness and relaxation and the charismatic smile tugging at the corners of his mouth as he gazed down at her. And suddenly new awareness of her emotions struck like an electric shock pulsing through her brain. Her eyes veiled when she registered that she could no longer imagine returning to England to live and work, could not picture herself ever leaving him again, indeed could not face the prospect of such a separation. Yet hadn't they both agreed to a three-month trial, which would very soon be up?

Although she had only been back in Spain with Alejandro for a brief period it had taken him a remarkably short time to break through her defensive barriers. She had started looking for him whenever he wasn't there, counting the hours when he was away from her until he was back again and within reach. She was falling for him all over again, she reflected worriedly, falling back in love with a guy who could only be programmed to hurt her for as long as he still believed that she had slept with his kid brother.

'What's up?' Alejandro queried, feeling her tension and lifting his tousled dark head to look down into her face with a frown.

'Nothing,' she swore, pushing close again, turning her lips up to his again and offering sex as a means of distraction.

And because Alejandro was and always had been a very passionate man, it worked a treat. There were no more awkward questions and there was an astounding amount of lovemaking until eventually they both drifted off to sleep exhausted. After dining at the hotel, they arrived back at the castle at quite a late hour. Maria, the housekeeper, greeted Jemima with the news that an Englishman had rung twice asking for her but had not left his name for her to call back.

Jemima had no idea who could have been calling her, for virtually all her connections back in England were female. 'Are you sure it was a man?' And at Maria's nod of confirmation, she shrugged and remarked, 'If it's important he'll ring back again.'

While she talked to the older woman, Beatriz had emerged from the salon and was speaking to her brother. Her sister-in-law's usual ready smile was absent and before Jemima's eyes Alejandro's stance transformed from relaxed to tense.

'Did something happen while we were out?' Jemima enquired when Beatriz hurried away again.

Alejandro settled his forbidding dark gaze on her, his lean bronzed face all Renaissance Man angles and hollows in the shadows cast by the wall lights, his jaw line as set as though it were carved from stone. 'Marco's come home for a visit. He's staying with his mother.'

And having dropped that bombshell, Alejandro said something flat about having work to do and, before she could part her lips, he was gone and she was standing alone in the echoing stone hall...

CHAPTER EIGHT

MARCO WAS BACK! It seemed a surprising coincidence that Alejandro's brother should choose to make his first visit home in years so soon after her own return to Spain. Jemima tossed and turned in her bed, unable to sleep while her thoughts ran on at a mad frantic pitch and refused to give her peace. She wondered too where Alejandro was and if he was really working.

Alejandro was less than pleased by news of his brother's arrival. Guilt squirmed through Jemima as she could remember when Alejandro was very fond of his younger brother and, whether she liked it or not, she had played an unwitting part in their estrangement. With hindsight, however, she recognised that Marco's feelings for his elder brother had always been less clear-cut. Idolised and spoiled by both parents as the baby of the family, Marco had nonetheless competed all his life within Alejandro's shadow and had never equalled or surpassed his sibling's achievements. Athletically gifted and academically brilliant, Alejandro had outshone Marco without effort and had set a bar that Marco could not reach. Even in business, Alejandro had triumphed while Marco had failed as an independent businessman and had eventually settled for a tailor-made position running one of the art galleries in his brother's empire.

But, those facts notwithstanding, Jemima had got on like a house on fire with Marco from the moment she had met him. Not that back then Marco had had much competition, since although Alejandro had been a brand-new husband at the time he had also been a workaholic and Jemima had been lonely, bored and unhappy. In the stiflingly formal household that Doña Hortencia had insisted on then, Marco had seemed like a breath of fresh air and Jemima had quickly warmed to her brother-in-law's light-hearted charm. In those days she had been blind to the reality that Marco might have a darker side to his nature than he had ever shown her.

How else could Marco have sacrificed a friendship with Jemima that he had once sworn meant a great deal to him? How else could he have allowed Alejandro to go on believing that his wife had slept with his brother? Why on earth had Marco done that? How could he have been so cruel and callous towards his brother and his former friend? She still didn't understand and *needed* to know the answer to those questions. What she did know was that Marco had gone to New York and embarked on a new life there, seemingly indifferent to the chaos and unhappiness he had left in his wake.

But while Jemima lay there ruminating on the past anger began to smoulder deep down inside her. Why was she feeling guilty about someone else's lies and another person's refusal to believe in her word? Marco was the one who had lied, at the very least by omission, and as a result Alejandro was convinced that his wife had been unfaithful. Alejandro had disbelieved and rejected Jemima's pleas of innocence. So why did she still feel as though she had done something she shouldn't have done? Why was she shouldering the blame when she was the victim of Marco's lies and her husband's distrust?

In a sudden movement, Jemima scrambled out of bed and at the speed of light she pulled on her long silky aquamarine wrap before heading downstairs in search of Alejandro. Acting like the guilty party would win her no prizes and, recalling Alejandro's coldness earlier in the day just saying his brother's name, she knew that forgiveness wasn't even on the cards.

Alejandro wasn't at work in his study. He was outside on the terrace, his classic profile hard as iron as he leant up against a stone pillar and stared out at a midnight-blue night sky studded with twinkling stars. Jemima came to an uncertain halt in the doorway, the electric light framing her curling mane of silvery pale hair to give it rosy highlights while darkening the violet hue of her eyes and accentuating the soft vulnerable pink of her mouth.

'I thought you would be asleep by now,' Alejandro confessed, awarding her a single studied glance that was cool and unreadable.

'I'm not quite that thick-skinned,' she fenced back. 'I don't like being made to feel bad when I haven't done anything wrong.'

'Let's not go digging, *mi dulzura*.'

'Marco's pulled quite some number on you,' she condemned, her slight shoulders rigid with resentment, her spine ramrod straight. 'In choosing to believe your brother rather than your wife you've given him the power to torment you—'

Alejandro spun round in a fast fluid motion that took her by surprise. His lean, strong face was taut with suppressed emotion but his eyes were as golden, dazzling and aggressive in their fiery heat as the sun. '*Porque Demonios!* Nobody torments me,' he declared, his lean, powerful body poised like a panther's, about to leap on its prey.

'All right—*I'm* being tormented by this!' Jemima proclaimed, willing to bend the point and take the hit if it persuaded him to listen to her. She took a hurried step out into the warm night air. 'It's like a big chasm is opening up between us again.'

A sardonic ebony brow quirked. 'And you're *surprised*?'

Her cheeks flamed with embarrassment. She felt angry

and bitter, hurt and fearful, all at one and the same time. It was not a good recipe for tact. Her temper on a razor edge, she resisted a needling, worrying urge to move closer to him because for the first time since she had returned to Spain she was afraid of rejection. 'Don't do this to us,' she muttered in urgent appeal.

His attention lingered on her, sliding from the full pout of her lips down to her slender, elegant throat and the dim white sloping valley of her breasts interrupted by the ribboned edge of her nightgown. 'Go back to bed before we say things that we won't be able to forget,' Alejandro urged with curt emphasis.

Jemima recognised the reserve that restrained him from matching her candour and feared the damage such diffidence might do. In her opinion, bottling things up only made problems fester. 'I'm not scared. I'm not running away. I *want* to be with you.'

'But possibly I don't want to be with you right now,' Alejandro murmured smooth as silk.

That admission hit Jemima like a brick and momentarily she felt stunned and reeled dizzily from that rebuff. He had once told her that when she was cornered she reacted like an alley cat, eager to scratch and bite. 'Only because you won't let yourself want me,' she challenged, padding nearer him on bare feet cooled by the worn granite tiling.

'You can be such a baby sometimes.' His beautiful obsidian gaze had a lethal gleam in the moonlight, the anger and rawness tamped down out of her sight, patently too private for her viewing. 'If I could put it all behind me and no longer think about it, I would have done so by now.'

In comparison, a cascade of happy images gleaned from recent weeks was flooding Jemima's thoughts. Everything she valued, not just happiness, was at risk and it terrified her. She cursed Marco and wished she had never befriended him and she hovered within reach of Alejandro, wanting to be needed, needing to be wanted if that was all she could have.

'Come to bed,' she whispered soft and low, despising herself for sinking low enough to play that card.

'I'm not up for that either tonight,' Alejandro asserted with chilling bite.

Talking to him in such a mood was like death by a thousand tiny cuts, Jemima reflected wildly. He was too controlled to shout at her. He wouldn't tell her what he was thinking, but then he didn't really need to, did he? Not when his derision could seep through the cracks to show on the surface and burn her like acid sprinkled on tender skin.

'Why did you ask me to give our marriage another chance if you were planning to behave like this?' Jemima slung at him accusingly.

'I never pretended I could give you a clean slate but I believe I've done reasonably well in the circumstances—'

'Well, I disagree!' Jemima shot at him furiously, temper clawing up through her with such speed and ferocity that the strength of her anger almost took *her* by surprise. 'In fact I think you are screwing our relationship up this time just the way you did last time.'

Alejandro viewed her with cold dark eyes that reflected the silvery moonlight. If she was an alley cat in a fight, he was the equivalent of a deadly rapier blade flashing without warning. '*I* screwed it up?' he traded very drily.

'When you are finally forced to accept that I *never* had an affair with your brother, who are you going to blame then?' Jemima demanded between gritted teeth. 'But at the rate you're going now, we won't last that long. You might not be forgiving, Alejandro, but neither am I and I'm beginning to think that I've wasted enough of my youth on a dead relationship—'

His stunning bone structure was now visible below his

bronzed skin, his potent tension patent in his set jaw line and the stillness of his tall muscular body. 'It's not dead—'

'Right at this minute it feels like it's as dead as a dodo,' Jemima pronounced, spelling out that comparison in defiant disagreement. 'I shouldn't be wasting time here on you. I should be getting a divorce and looking for a man who *really* wants me...not some guy tearing us both apart over an affair that never happened!'

'I *really* want you,' Alejandro bit out in raw dissent. 'I won't agree to a divorce.'

'Can't live with me, can't live without me,' Jemima parried shakily, fighting to get a grip on her flailing emotions. 'But I *can* get by without you. I've proved it. I had a good life in Charlbury St Helen's...'

His well-shaped mouth curled into a sardonic smile. 'But not so good that you weren't prepared to walk away from all of it to come back to a life of luxury with me!'

Turning pale with rage at that taunt, Jemima trembled. 'I only came back here to try again for Alfie's benefit. Don't you dare try to make out that I'm some sort of gold-digger!'

Silence fell like a blanket and it seemed to use up all the available oxygen as Jemima waited impatiently for him to take back that final taunt. He stared steadily back at her as if she had got what she deserved in that exchange and, in a way, she supposed she had. Her refusal to embrace the role of the disgraced wife caught out in adultery lay between them, an obstacle neither of them could overcome. Alejandro was very proud, but he might have managed to come to terms with what he believed she had done had she enabled him to believe that she was truly sorry. In the absence of that development there was no natural way forward and both of them were stuck in their respective opposite corners.

Her small face stiff, Jemima threw him a look of angry reproach. 'I never wanted you for your money,' she told him heatedly. 'I may have got in a bit of a mess and spent more money than I should have done when we were first married, but it wasn't done out of greed and there was never any plan to rip you off.'

His brilliant gaze was intent but wary and locked to her every changing expression. 'I can believe that,' he said, surprising her with that declaration of faith.

'I am really sorry about the money—I was stupid,' Jemima admitted, warming to a topic that she could be honest about on at least one level. She had indeed been stupid: she had thrown away thousands and thousands of pounds and yet she still could not bring herself to tell him what she had done with it.

Alejandro took a jerky step forward. 'It was a case of bad timing. My business enterprises were over-extended. The winds of recession were howling around us and I was struggling to just hold onto what I had. It was the worst possible moment for you to go mad with money...but then I shouldn't have left you access to so much of it.'

Jemima was breathing rapidly and by the time he had finished speaking her lower lip had dropped fully away from the upper while she gaped at him in unconcealed astonishment. 'Are you saying that you had financial problems a couple of years ago when we were still living together?' she gasped in disbelief. 'But why didn't you tell me?'

Alejandro's handsome mouth compressed into a wry line. 'I didn't want to worry you...'

Her wide eyes prickled with a sudden hot rush of spontaneous tears. 'But I thought you were *so* rich,' she framed before she could think better of using that immature phraseology.

'I know. I knew you hadn't a clue there was anything to worry about,' Alejandro murmured ruefully. 'But the truth is that my father left so much money to my stepmother and

Marco when he died that up until quite recently it was a struggle for me just to keep the estate afloat.'

Jemima was shaking her head slowly back and forth in a negative motion. She could not hide how shocked she was by what he had confessed. 'I had no idea. You really should have told me, Alejandro. In fact, not only did you not tell me there was a problem, you seemed to go out of your way to throw loads of money and expensive gifts at me,' she reminded him tautly. 'Why the heck did you do that?'

'You wanted the whole fairy tale along with the castle and I very much wanted you to have it as well,' Alejandro admitted with a wry twist of his mouth. 'How could I tell you that I was in danger of losing it all?'

'All the hours you were working, turning night into day…you were never at home,' she muttered unsteadily, fighting to hold the tears back with all her might. 'You were trying to keep your businesses afloat?'

'Yes, and the extra work did pay off in one regard. I secured new contracts and in the end the financial tide turned, but by then it was too late: I had lost my wife,' Alejandro intoned bleakly.

Her generous mouth wobbled at that reminder. She wanted to hug him, but at the same time she wanted to slap him really hard for keeping secrets from her. He had treated her like a fragile little girl who couldn't cope with the grown up stuff when, in actuality, she had never been that naïve even as a child. She was appalled to appreciate that he had undertaken such a struggle and worked such long thankless hours while she went out on endless shopping trips and went out at night clubbing with Marco.

'Alejandro…if you had told me the truth, shared the bad stuff with me instead of leaving me in ignorance, things would have been so very different,' Jemima breathed unevenly, tears rolling down her cheeks unchecked until she dashed a hand across her face in an embarrassed gesture and sniffed furiously. 'I would've understood. I would have made allowances.'

Alejandro braced a hand to her slender spine and pressed her back indoors where he handed her a tissue. 'I'm not sure anything would have been different. You were very young and naïve and you were already pregnant and unhappy and at the time I don't think you could have coped with any more stress.'

He was wrong, but she didn't argue with him because she was too choked up to do so. She knew that as much as anything else his fierce pride would have prevented him from telling her that he had financial problems. He was an old-fashioned guy and he had always seen it as solely his role to provide for her needs. He had loved to spoil her with unexpected gifts and treats, to give her the frills he knew she had never had before she met him. She could have cried her heart out in that instant for all she had truly wanted from him two years earlier were his precious time and attention, not his wealth or what it could buy her.

'I didn't expect you to be my superhero all the time,' Jemima told him awkwardly, her voice hoarse as she dabbed at her damp cheeks. 'If you'd confided in me, I would never have spent so much time with your brother. I felt neglected. I thought you regretted marrying me and you were bored and that that's why you never came home.'

'It never would have occurred to me that telling you I was on the brink of losing everything, including our home, might save my marriage,' Alejandro confided, his cynical doubt in that likelihood unconcealed.

'Well, that just goes to show how very little you know about me. I'm very loyal and I would have stuck by you through thick and thin!' Jemima claimed proudly.

'But in those days I think you had much more in common with my fun-loving brother,' Alejandro murmured with a derisive edge to his dark deep drawl.

'I wasn't that shallow.' Although she was back in control of her emotions and composed again, Jemima's fingers still bit into the damp tissue clutched between her fingers. She had really, really loved him two years earlier and she wished he could at least accept that the love had been genuine and real, even if it hadn't proved strong enough to withstand the misfortunes that had engulfed them both. 'But you didn't give me the chance to be anything else.'

Casting a last lingering look at his breathtakingly handsome features from below damp feathery lashes, Jemima walked back up to bed without another word. Her mobile phone was flashing on the dressing table and she lifted it. She had missed one phone call and there were two text messages. One was from Beatriz, saying that she hoped that Jemima didn't mind her having given her brother her phone number. The second text and the missed call were from Marco and she jerked in shock when she realised that he had actually dared to get in touch with her again.

Must see you to talk. Urgent, ran his message.

Jemima deleted the text with stabbing fingers and tossed the phone down again. Marco had to be joking. In the current climate she was not prepared to take the risk of seeing him again even if she did have questions of her own to ask. My goodness, wouldn't Alejandro just love that? The last thing her marriage needed was more fuel for the same fire.

The door opened, startling her. She froze when she saw Alejandro and then she slid out of bed like an eel and sped over to him, wrapping her arms round his neck and letting her head fall back as he meshed one strong hand into the depths of her pale hair and kissed her breathless.

'I thought you wouldn't come,' she confided, heart thrumming like a plucked string on a violin, the full effect pulsing through her entire body along with her intense relief that he had not stayed away from her.

'*Dios mio!* Living apart won't help us. Been there, done that, *querida*,' he reminded her darkly. 'We might as well have been living in different houses while you were pregnant with Alfie. It made everything worse.'

Her generous mouth swollen from the onslaught of his, Jemima got back into bed. His arrival had already made her feel two hundred per cent happier. 'Well, that was your choice, not mine,' she traded cheekily.

His ebony brows pleated as he shed his suit. 'It wasn't anyone's choice, it was a necessity.'

'How was it a necessity?' she questioned once he had emerged from the bathroom and joined her in bed.

'Right from the start, Dr Santos was afraid you would miscarry. He was quite frank with me. You are very small and slightly built and it was obvious early on that what we thought was one baby was going to be big. I didn't stay happy that you were pregnant for very long,' Alejandro admitted heavily, his arm tightening round her to pull her closer. 'I felt hugely guilty for putting you at risk.'

'I wasn't at risk.'

'I felt that you were and with my own mother having died from complications in childbirth it was not a matter I could ever take lightly.'

Jemima mulled that over, registering that her obstetrician had been more honest with her husband than he had been with her. Or had he been? Her Spanish had been less fluent in those days and it was perfectly possible that she had misunderstood some of what he told her, picking up only the gist rather than the full meaning of his advice. That he had shared his apprehension with Alejandro, however, was news to her and that Alejandro had been seriously worried about her was also a surprise. Suddenly she frowned as she made another deduction.

'Are you saying that you stopped making love to me because Dr Santos warned you off?'

'Why else would I have stopped?' Alejandro growled soft and low in her ear, tugging her back into the heat of his long, hard body. Her nostrils flared on the husky scent of his skin and she quivered with awareness. 'I used another bedroom, not only because I was keeping late hours and didn't want to waken you but also because I didn't trust myself in the same bed with you any more.'

'You should've explained—I had no idea.'

'I was present when the doctor warned you that you would have to be very careful indeed if you wanted the pregnancy to go to term. You had already had some bleeding,' he reminded her grimly. 'I know I didn't discuss it with you but what was there to say? We didn't have a choice.'

She pressed her mouth in silent apology against a bare bronzed shoulder. Consternation had a strong grip on her. She was shaken by how badly she had misjudged his past behaviour. She had viewed everything through the distorting prism of her unhappiness and insecurity and two and two had seemed to make four but she had added up the facts incorrectly. Alejandro had not been bored with her. He had not deliberately neglected her either. At a difficult time he had simply done the best that he could for the two of them, while her behaviour had only added to their problems. That acknowledgement shamed her and made her appreciate just how much she had grown up since then.

'Let's make an agreement,' Alejandro breathed in a measured undertone above her head. 'You stay away from Marco. You don't speak to him, you don't see him. That will keep the peace.'

Jemima had stiffened, taken aback by that proposition coming at her out of the blue. She drew in a quivering breath. 'All right...if that's what you want.'

'That's how it *has* to be,' Alejandro countered in a tone of finality.

'I'm not arguing. I couldn't care less. It's not a problem,' she muttered in a small voice.

The tension in his big powerful frame eased and he smoothed a soothing hand over her hair. 'Go to sleep,' he intoned huskily. 'If you don't, you'll be too tired to join me for breakfast in the morning. I'm leaving early for a board meeting in Seville.'

That he was already planning breakfast in her company made her smile. She was remembering the hot sexual passion of the afternoon in the hotel room, but lying in his arms there in their own bed felt so much more intimate and significant. Even after news that neither one of them had wanted to hear, they were still together. The agreement Alejandro had demanded warned her that she would be walking a knife edge if she defied him, but she had no such intention. Marco might be home, but she was not prepared to allow him to damage her marriage a second time.

The following morning, Alejandro left her enjoying her coffee on the roof and Alfie went downstairs with Placida so that their son could watch his father's helicopter take off from the front lawn. Jemima was still sitting outside, lightly clad in a cotton sundress, when Beatriz came up to join her. Her sister-in-law looked strained.

'Was I wrong to give Marco your cell-phone number last night?' the brunette prompted anxiously. 'He was so eager for the chance to speak to you that when he pressed me, I didn't know what to do for best.'

'I'm afraid I don't want to speak to him,' Jemima admitted quietly.

'But if you and Marco talked and then you talked to Alejandro, maybe all this bad feeling could be put away,' Beatriz suggested with unconcealed hope. 'The way things are now is very awkward for all of us and it's only going to get more difficult once word gets out that Marco is home again. Our relatives and neighbours will soon start including him in their invitations. Nobody outside these walls is aware that my brothers are at odds with each other—'

'How can that be? I assumed your stepmother would have told tales about me everywhere after I left Spain to go home,' Jemima admitted with an expressive shudder.

'Not when she believed her son might have been involved with you. Doña Hortencia is very proud of the family name and her goal was to protect Marco's reputation, rather than yours,' Beatriz told her ruefully. 'She's hoping that now he's home he'll find a girl to marry.'

Jemima stiffened at that comment. 'Your stepmother might have quite a long wait.'

Was that an answering glint of amusement in her sister-in-law's dark eyes? It was there and then it was gone and Jemima wondered if she had imagined it. Not for the first time Jemima wondered just how much Beatriz might know about her younger brother's life. The habit of silence, however, kept her quiet for she could not credit that Beatriz might know what Alejandro did not even appear to suspect. It was never easy to tell with Beatriz, though, because the brunette was always very discreet and cautious even with her own family. Beatriz liked to mind her own business and steer clear of trouble, but lately it had come to light that she could also stand up for herself when she had to. She had helped her stepmother move into her very comfortable house on the estate and had withstood the storm of being accused of ingratitude and selfishness when she'd revealed that she was planning to stay on below her brother's roof. Jemima valued the other woman's friendship and wished that she could have confided in her. She missed Flora's company and chatter, she acknowledged ruefully, and wondered if her friend would be able to come out to Spain for a visit any time soon.

The following week, Jemima spent some time reorganising rooms with the housekeeper, Maria. She was keeping

busy because Alejandro had spent several days working
in Seville. A room was being set up for use as a smaller,
cosier dining room in place of the huge banqueting space
and even vaster pieces of antique furniture, which Doña
Hortencia had considered necessary to her dignity. Jemima
wondered if she should have discussed the change with
Alejandro first, and then wrinkled her nose and decided
to follow her own preferences. When she mentioned anything to do with the interior workings of the household
Alejandro generally looked blank and hastened to dis-
claim either interest or authority. When Maria spoke to
someone behind her, she was fixing some flowers for the
table in an effort to give the room a touch of the feudal
magnificence that the Vasquez family pretty much took
for granted in their daily life.

'Jemima…'

Violet eyes wide, Jemima flipped round and focused on
the tall broad-shouldered male in the doorway. She paled.
With his coal black curls he was a very good-looking,
younger version of his big brother, although he was not so
tall nor so powerfully built. He was also so well dressed
that he closely resembled a model who had stepped out of
a glossy magazine.

'Marco?' she whispered in dismay. 'I didn't want to
see you.'

'That's not very friendly, is it?' Marco said in reproach.
'We are family, after all.'

CHAPTER NINE

JEMIMA REACHED A sudden decision and told Maria that she would finish the room on her own. As the housekeeper departed Jemima closed the door behind her, leant back against it and focused on Marco.

'I can't believe you've got the nerve to come anywhere near me,' she admitted, her bright eyes sparkling with angry hostility.

Marco frowned. 'I don't understand why you are so angry with me.'

Registering that Alejandro's brother had decided to act as if he were ignorant of what he had done, Jemima tensed up like a racehorse at the start line. 'You're not stupid. You know very well why I'm angry. How *could* you allow Alejandro to believe that we had had an affair?'

'You had already left the country. Your marriage was over. What difference did it make to you what he thought?' he questioned, treating her to a level look that implied that he still had no real grasp of what the problem was.

'Doesn't it make a difference to you? It *should* do. Don't you have any affection for your brother that you could let him believe such a thing of us both?' Jemima slung back at him furiously.

Marco breathed in deep. 'All right, I'll try to be honest with you. I didn't really care what anyone thought if it gave me a good reason to leave home and move to New York. Dario and I needed the privacy to lead our own lives. As I honestly believed that you and Alejandro were all washed up as a couple, I didn't think it mattered.'

'You're not that innocent,' Jemima countered between compressed lips, any patience she had left fast shredding in the face of Marco's brazen refusal to express an ounce of regret, particularly when he was tossing his own relationship in her teeth and pointing out that he had wanted and needed it to prosper. 'You could have gone to New York with Dario and without hurting and humiliating your brother with that filthy lie!'

His smooth brow furrowed. 'I didn't actually tell any lies,' he retorted with an infuriating air of condescension. 'I didn't have to. Alejandro was convinced that you and I had had an affair and I didn't deny it. As far as I was concerned, if he wanted to believe something so ridiculous, that was his business and nothing to do with me—'

'It had everything to do with you!' Jemima yelled back at him. 'You didn't care who got hurt. You used our supposed relationship as an excuse—'

'Your marriage was over,' Marco reminded her afresh. 'I didn't know you were still pregnant—'

'I didn't know either at the time I left Spain,' Jemima conceded unwillingly.

'Naturally if I had known there was going to be a child it would have made a difference to what I allowed my brother to believe,' Marco argued. 'But I had no idea.'

'Well, you know now and I'm back with Alejandro and we're trying to make a go of our marriage again,' Jemima pointed out. 'Only that's not very easy when he still thinks that I slept with you...'

'My brother has always had an easy ride through life. Everything always fell perfectly into place for him, at school, in business, with women,' Marco enumerated with a bitter resentment that he could not hide. 'A little bit of suffering over you and his marriage probably did wonders for his character.'

At that unfeeling crack, Jemima had to struggle to hang onto her temper because she had already decided that telling Marco exactly what she thought of him would be a counterproductive rather than positive act when she needed him to redress the wrong that he had done. Now she marvelled that she had not previously appreciated just how much Marco envied his brother's success in every field. Had she known what was really in Marco's heart she would never have made him her confidant or trusted him as much as she had. Just how much had his unrelenting negativity about her marriage influenced her when it came to making the decision to leave her husband? She did not want to think about that.

'You *have* to tell Alejandro the truth.'

Marco shook his handsome head, his eyes guarded. 'No can do.'

'Well, that's your decision,' Jemima said tightly in the tense silence, her teeth gritting on an urge to be a good deal more aggressive. 'But you can't expect me to stay quiet. If you won't tell Alejandro the truth, I *will*.'

Apprehension now tightening his boyish features, Marco strode forward. 'But you promised to keep my secret.'

Jemima lifted her chin, the anger in her clear gaze an open challenge. 'I didn't know then how much damage keeping your secret was likely to do to my marriage. Surely you can be honest now with your family?' she said forcefully. 'It may not be what they want for you, or expect, but families have got over worse revelations.'

'As far as my mother is concerned, there could be no *worse* revelation than the news that the love of my life is a boy and not a girl,' Marco declared in scornful disagreement. 'Have you ever heard her talking about gay people?'

Jemima grimaced and nodded confirmation. 'She is prejudiced but that could well change if you talked to her and gave her the chance to understand who you really are.'

'You've got to be joking!' Marco snapped back at her, angry colour edging his cheekbones. 'She'd throw me out of the house and cut off my allowance!'

Jemima's brows knitted and she studied him with narrowed eyes. 'I wasn't aware that you received an allowance from your mother.'

Marco released his breath in a weary groan. 'Do you really think that I could afford to live as comfortably as I do on an employee's salary?'

Stepping away from the door, Jemima stiffened. 'Your financial arrangements are none of my business, Marco. Whether you tell your mother or not is nothing to do with me either. But Alejandro is my business and I *do* expect you to tell him that you're gay so that he, at least, can appreciate that we did not have an affair.'

Marco sent her a furious look of umbrage. 'I'm certainly not telling Alejandro. He sacked the only gay man on his staff—did he tell you that?'

'Yes, but I believe the guy in question was also a bully and had had several warnings about the way he'd treated other staff before he was fired. I have never seen or heard Alejandro do or say anything which would lead me to believe that he has homophobic views. He doesn't share your mother's religious outlook on the issue either,' Jemima reasoned levelly. 'I'm not asking you to do this, Marco, I'm telling you that if you don't tell your brother, I will do it for you. I don't have to keep your secret when it's threatening to wreck my happiness and my child's.'

'You're blackmailing me,' Marco accused her angrily.

'I don't owe you any explanations or apologies after what you did to Alejandro,' Jemima contended, lifting her chin in challenge. 'I don't owe you anything.'

Registering that she was serious and not about to back down, Marco lost his temper. Throwing her a furious look of hostility, he swore at her. Then he yanked open the door with an impatient hand, stalked past the astonished housekeeper in the hall and straight back out of the castle. Jemima breathed in deep and slow and returned to the flower arrangement she had been doing. Beatriz joined her and admired the room, remarking that its more comfortable proportions would be a great deal warmer and more pleasant during the cooler months of the year when the fires were lit. For just a few minutes in the other woman's soothing company, it seemed to Jemima that the raw, distressing little scene with Marco had only taken place within her own imagination.

She couldn't help but think back to their former friendship. She had also just learned something from Marco that shed a rather different light on the past. Marco was financially dependent on his mother's continuing goodwill and, if Doña Hortencia's past pronouncements were anything to go by, it was very possible that Marco's admission that he was gay would lead to the kind of ructions that might well hit him hard in the pocket. Was that why Marco had always gone to such lengths to conceal his sexuality? Had money always been the primary reason for his silence on that issue? It occurred to Jemima that she had once been incredibly naïve and trusting when it came to Marco.

Retaining her brother-in-law's friendship, she acknowledged sadly, had come at a high cost, for she had been forced to conceal more and more from her husband. Marco had used her as an alibi and a front when he went places where he preferred not to be seen without female company. His Italian boyfriend, Dario, had often accompanied them on those nights out. What had happened to the open and honest nature that she had once prided herself on having?

Almost from the start of her marriage she had begun to keep secrets from Alejandro.

That thought made her heart sink and her mind return to a place she didn't want to revisit. The past was best left untouched, she reckoned uneasily. There would be no advantage to digging everything up. Alejandro would be grateful for all of five minutes when she told him the truth of what she had done with the large sums of money that she had taken from their joint account over two years earlier. But five minutes after that he would wish she had kept quiet and he would see her in yet another unflattering light. Once again she would be shown up as his less than perfect match. She didn't think their marriage could withstand a second blow of that type.

'Marco can be very volatile,' his sister, Beatriz, remarked gingerly, her attention locked to Jemima's troubled and expressive face.

'Yes,' Jemima agreed.

'But if you ignore his moods, I've found that he soon gets over them,' Beatriz added comfortably. 'Doña Hortencia indulged him too much when he was a child.'

The housekeeper came to the door to pass on a message from Alejandro. He had phoned to say that he would be spending the night at the family apartment in Seville. Jemima's slim shoulders sagged. Only when she learned that he wasn't coming back did she realise how much she had been looking forward to seeing him that evening. In addition she was a little hurt that he had not thought to speak to her personally about his change of plan.

'Jemima…go to Seville and be with my brother,' Beatriz urged, causing Jemima's violet eyes to fly to her in shock. 'You want to be with Alejandro and why shouldn't you be? I'll ensure that Alfie has his bath and his bedtime story. In fact if you wouldn't mind I'm planning to visit my friend, Serafina, this afternoon and I'd like to take Alfie with me. Serafina has a toddler as well.'

All concerns laid to rest by Beatriz's willingness to entertain her nephew, Jemima went upstairs to change. She was delighted by the idea of surprising Alejandro, for she had never done anything like that before, indeed had always shrunk from putting her feelings for him on the line, but the connection they had formed since her return to Spain really did feel much deeper and stronger. There was nothing wrong with being confident and optimistic, she told herself urgently. Once Marco did what he had to do the dark shadow that her brother-in-law had cast over her marriage would soon disappear.

She was in her bedroom when the phone call came. Engaged in checking her reflection in a raspberry-coloured dress with a draped neckline that clung to the curve of her breasts, outlined her tiny waist and bared a good deal of her legs, she snatched up the receiver by the bed to answer it.

'Jem…is that you?' a rough-edged male voice demanded. 'The woman said she'd put me straight through to you.'

Jemima froze, the animated colour in her face fading fast to leave her white as milk. Her heart sank to the soles of her feet and she almost tottered back against the bed for support on legs that felt too woolly to keep her standing upright. She had hoped never, ever to hear that voice again but fate, it seemed, was too cruel to grant her that escape from the memory of past connections and mistakes. Too late did she remember the phone calls from the unnamed male that Maria had mentioned that she had missed.

'How did you know where to find me?' she asked tautly.

'Your cousin, Ellie, saw a picture of you in a magazine and showed it to me. My little Jem in an evening dress mixing with all the toffs like she's one of them!' the older man jeered. 'So you went back to live with that high and mighty Spanish count of yours and you never even got in touch to tell me.'

'Why would I have?' Jemima asked her father sickly.

'The magazine mentioned that you have a kiddy as well now—my grandson and I've not even seen him,' Stephen Grey complained. 'Maybe I should pay you a visit. If I was to come out of the woodwork now and embarrass you, you'd have a lot to lose, Jem.'

'I haven't got any money…I'm not giving you anything,' Jemima protested feverishly. 'You can't threaten me any more. Just leave me alone!'

Without waiting for a response, Jemima cut off the call and stood there clutching the receiver so hard in her hand that it hurt her fingers. She wouldn't let it start up again. She wouldn't be a pushover this time around. She would stand up for herself and refuse to be alarmed and intimidated by his threats. But in the back of her mind she was already wondering how much of the money in her bank account it would take to keep her father quiet.

He was an evil, frightening man, who had abused both his wife and his daughter with his nasty tongue and his brutal fists, finally throwing Jemima out onto the street as a teenager and washing his hands of responsibility for her. She had made her own way in life no thanks to Stephen Grey. He had no right to demand money from her, no right to terrorize her. He would phone back, she *knew* he would phone back, or worse…come and pay her a visit as he had once before. She had paid him to keep his distance and keep his mouth shut two years ago and his hopes would be riding high that she would crumble and make the same mistake again.

And she was in this position all because early on in her relationship with Alejandro she had told a little white lie that had seemed harmless, she thought in anguish. In fact at the time it had felt like simple common sense to conceal the ugly truth. Conscious that Alejandro came from a much more privileged and respectable background than she did, she had seen no reason to trail out all the dirty washing that accompanied her own more humble beginnings. Indeed she had cringed from the prospect of telling Alejandro that her father had been imprisoned repeatedly, never mind broaching the reality that he'd also regularly beaten up her mother. She had lived a sad, grubby life as a child with a mother who drank herself into a stupor daily to escape the world and the husband she couldn't cope with.

In Seville, Jemima parked below the large office building that housed Alejandro's headquarters. When she arrived on the top floor she learned that he was in a meeting and thought that perhaps it had been a bad idea to spring a surprise on him when he was clearly so busy. She was just getting comfortable in Reception when two of Alejandro's executives passed by and, recognising her, stopped to chat.

A very profitable contract renegotiated and agreed, Alejandro saw his business colleagues and their lawyers off the premises before he discovered his wife surrounded by a little ring of admiring men in Reception. She was like a small but very powerful magnet, he conceded bleakly, watching her violet eyes sparkle with natural enticement as she laughed. Her jacket was hanging open, her slender but curvy little body on display. His handsome mouth compressed into a hard, ruthless line.

Jemima's gaze fell on Alejandro and she scrambled upright with a sunny smile to greet him. He looked outrageously handsome although even at a glance she recognised his leashed tension and assumed he was tired after a stressful day. 'Are you too busy for me?' she asked.

'I doubt if there is a man in the building who would be too busy for you, *querida*,' he murmured, nodding as his executives acknowledged him and went on about their business. 'You look irresistible in that dress.'

But Jemima noticed that his brilliant answering smile didn't reach the cool darkness of his eyes and an odd little stab of alarm ran through her. As he guided her towards the lift with a firm hand at her spine that made her nerve-endings tingle she shot a glance at his hard bronzed profile. The dense screen of his black lashes cloaked his gaze even as an electrifying surge of awareness shimmied through her slender length. Within a heartbeat she was recalling the way his lean, powerful body had shuddered over hers in release around dawn and the all-consuming love that had overwhelmed her in his arms. She had never been a morning person but Alejandro had changed that. There was something intensely sexy about waking up next to his hot, hungry body. The merest touch made her ready for him and the reflection plunged her into a cascade of erotic imagery. By the time she emerged from that colourful daydream she was trembling and conscious that he had yet to break the heavy silence.

'Were you finished for the day?' she asked anxiously then. 'I mean, I didn't intend to just show up and force your hand.'

The lift doors whirred back to reveal the basement car park. 'I was ready to leave. Are you parked here?'

'Yes.'

'What brought you to Seville?' Alejandro enquired as his driver pulled in to pick them up a few yards from the lift.

Jemima went pink. 'You...I wanted to see you.'

Alejandro lifted a sardonic dark brow.

'Yes, I *did*!' Jemima proclaimed in the face of that disbelief.

'*Dios mio*—is it possible that you have something to tell me?' Alejandro enquired silkily.

Aware of the undertones of tension pulling at her,

Jemima shifted uneasily and wondered why he was ask-ing her that. 'No—what would I have to tell you?'

'Only you can answer that question,' Alejandro breathed icily.

Jemima shot him an enervated look and decided that while he always went for subtle she was more at home with being blunt. 'I'm no good at trick questions. Just tell me what's wrong.'

His lean dark features were taut, his eyes shielded. He said nothing. In the humming quiet, she stared out of the window at the crowded streets and waited in vain for his response.

'Well, this will certainly teach me a lesson. Don't go surprising you at the office...you're keeping such a dis-tance from me I feel like Typhoid Mary!' she declared in flippant continuance, struggling to hide her hurt and mor-tification at the chilly welcome she had so far received from him.

'Exactly what did you expect from me?' Alejandro shot at her with dark eyes that flashed as golden as the heart of a fire.

As her bewilderment increased the limo came to a halt. They would walk the remaining distance through the pe-destrian zone in the oldest part of Seville. The Vasquez apartment was in a gracious old building that had consid-erable character.

The anger that Alejandro could no longer hide was like a blast of heat on her unprotected skin. His driver opened the car door and they climbed out to walk down narrow streets past tall eighteenth-century houses and fi-nally through a familiar flower-filled courtyard. By then her heart was beating as fast and loud as a jungle drum and a sheen of nervous perspiration had dampened her skin. They walked through tall gates and across the cobblestones towards an elegant building. She felt sick with apprehension.

'Why are you angry with me?' she prompted finally.

'Because you're a liar and I can't stay married to a woman I can't trust out of my sight!'

That thunderous aside punched through Jemima's defences like a hard physical blow. As she stepped into the old-fashioned lift fashioned of ornate wrought-iron folding gates she was in shock. She was a liar and he couldn't trust her? All of a sudden he was threatening to end their marriage? She could think of only one possible explanation for his behaviour.

Entering the cool, spacious apartment that spanned the equivalent of two buildings, Jemima stole an enervated glance at her tall, well-built husband and said abruptly, 'You know I've seen Marco, don't you? How?'

'When I phoned to speak to you, Maria mentioned that you were with him.'

Alejandro strode on into the airy drawing room where the shadows cast by the palm tree in the front courtyard were dancing in flickering spears of ghostly foliage across the pale walls. Once again the décor was new to her, the old darker, richer colours banished and replaced by shades that were light and new. The silence dragged horribly.

'Marco just came up to the castle to speak to me,' Jemima told him jerkily, giving way first to the dreadful tension. 'Probably because he texted me and called last night and I didn't respond in any way.'

Alejandro rested unimpressed eyes on her, his wide sensual mouth taking on a contemptuous twist. 'And you didn't mention that fact to me, either.'

'Be fair,' Jemima urged in desperation. 'I didn't want a stupid text message and a missed call from Marco to cause more trouble between us.'

Alejandro turned blistering dark golden eyes on her. His

fabulous bone structure was set in hard lines of restraint. 'Without trust I can't live with you,' he breathed with a suppressed savagery that raised gooseflesh on her exposed skin. 'How could it be otherwise? I believed that we were getting somewhere and then today I learned that you were with Marco, in *spite* of your promise to me.'

Jemima was trembling, nausea stirring in the pit of her stomach. She had never felt as alone or scared since childhood as she did at that moment. She could feel his strength, his force of will and his immovable resolve. If he decided that walking away from her was the right thing to do, he would do it, no matter what the cost. Unhappily for her she had promised not to see Marco and she had broken her promise. How could she defend herself from that charge?

It was not the moment, she sensed, to tell him that he was being unreasonable, and that, for as long as Marco was a family member with automatic access to their home, avoiding the younger man would be a challenge. Alejandro was not in a cool, rational state of mind, she conceded inwardly. Indeed he was containing so many powerful emotions that he radiated glowing energy. But she could feel the distance in him, the wall he was already erecting between them. She had wounded him and he had taken a mental step back from her and their marriage. She was so appalled by the awareness that he was talking about a divorce that she could barely think straight. She could not bear to have got Alejandro back, to have tasted that happiness and then lose it and him again; it would be too cruel to bear.

Too late she saw where she had gone wrong. She had seriously underestimated the damage being done by Alejandro's conviction that she had been unfaithful. And she had made that cardinal error because she had known that she was innocent and had loftily dismissed the likely fallout from his destructive belief that she was not to be trusted.

But she could also be a fast learner. When she feared losing Alejandro, no other loyalty had the power to hold her and she broke the silence in haste.

'There's never been anything between your brother and me and he will be speaking to you about that by the end of the week,' Jemima told Alejandro in a feverish rush, too worked up to stop and plan what she had to say before she spoke.

Alejandro was frowning at her. 'What are you talking about?'

'Marco informed me that he never actually told you that we had had an affair—he just didn't deny your accusation. But, by the start of the weekend, you'll know the truth because either he or I will tell you why there was never any possibility of an affair...'

'Porque demonios!' Alejandro exclaimed in frustration at that tangled explanation. 'Stop talking to me in riddles!'

'I gave my word to Marco that I would let him talk to you before I did.'

Outrage flared in Alejandro's brooding scrutiny. 'If there is something that I should know, I demand that you tell me now!'

The silence closed round them, thick and heavy as treacle.

'Marco is gay.' Jemima almost whispered the words, conscious of the pledge she had given and even while she refused to be bound by it she felt the bite of guilt and regret all the same. 'So there was never any question of anything intimate between us.'

Alejandro studied her in irate consternation. 'Are you trying to come up with a good cover story now? That's a despicable lie to tell me about my brother.'

'I appreciate that what I've just told you may come as a shock to you, but I'm not lying or trying to come up with a story,' Jemima protested fiercely.

'My brother has been dating…very extensively…since he was sixteen years old. I think we would know by now if he were gay,' Alejandro proclaimed very drily, his lean, strong face hard with denial.

'Marco has done everything possible to hide his true nature and he was at university before he reached the conclusion that he was gay. The girlfriends were just part of the pretence he put up. Didn't you ever wonder why he never hung onto any of them for longer than a couple of weeks?'

'Not many young men in his age group want a serious relationship.'

An uncertain laugh fell from Jemima's lips. 'I'm not getting anywhere with you, am I? You just don't believe me but I am telling you the truth. Marco didn't want anyone to know, not you and particularly not his mother. I know Doña Hortencia's outlook and Marco was afraid she would cut off the allowance she gives him.'

'As there is no question of my brother being gay, we will not discuss the matter further,' Alejandro pronounced with derision, his sensual mouth curling with disdain. 'But I would not have believed that even you would sink as low as to tell such lies.'

Having paled, Jemima took another tack in the hope of convincing him. 'From what I can understand Marco is still with Dario Ortini,' she remarked gingerly.

'What has that to do with anything? They were students together. They're old friends.'

'*No*, they are much more than that to each other.' Jemima shook her head slowly, her pale cloud of hair shifting round her strained face as she voiced that confident assurance. 'They're a couple, Alejandro. And pretty much inseparable. Didn't you think it strange that Dario went to New York as well?'

Alejandro parted his lips as if he was going to speak again to argue with her, and then suddenly he frowned and slowly closed his mouth again. She could literally see him thinking over what she had told him, making the connections, and while the uneasy silence stretched she watched him travel gradually from a state of incomprehension and angry disbelief to one of troubled and stunned acceptance.

'I can hardly believe it,' Alejandro muttered. 'Dario, now, he is less of a surprise. But their continuing friendship does stretch credulity too far.'

Jemima studied Alejandro fixedly, recognising that he was still fighting his astonishment.

'Evidently my brother has been leading a double life for years,' he intoned between compressed lips. '*Dios mio.* Why couldn't he just tell me? Did he believe I would think less of him? It doesn't matter a damn to me—he is still my brother. But why the hell did Marco allow me to go on believing that you and he had had an affair?'

Jemima brushed her hair off her damp brow with an impatient hand. 'He's jealous of you, well, *very* jealous of everything you've achieved in life,' she divulged reluctantly.

'It is true that he has always been very competitive with me,' Alejandro acknowledged.

'I don't know how he could let you go on believing there had been an affair, but that's something you need to discuss with him rather than me.'

'Right now, what I need is a strong drink,' Alejandro admitted in a raw undertone, striding over to the drinks cabinet and asking her what she would like.

She closed a damp palm round the moisture-beaded tumbler he handed to her and pressed the glass against the overheated skin below her collarbone, all the while watching Alejandro, noticing how pale he was beneath his bronzed complexion and how prominent his hard bone structure seemed. His hands weren't quite steady either: he was really uptight.

'Are you all right?' she whispered worriedly.

'No,' he admitted flatly. 'I'm shattered, absolutely bloody shattered. My brother is gay and I never even suspected the fact.'

'That was how Marco wanted it. He didn't want his family to know.'

'My stepmother will throw a fit.' Alejandro scored long brown fingers through his luxuriant black hair, tousling it into disorder and turning his handsome head to study Jemima again with intense dark eyes. 'But, right at this moment, it is more important that I concentrate on what I've done to you and our marriage. I condemned you, misjudged you, refused to accept your word.'

Jemima gave an awkward shrug. 'I'm just grateful that you finally know and accept the truth. I can understand that when Marco didn't deny the affair you found it hard to believe that nothing had ever happened between us.'

'He used you to get at me. I should have had more faith in you.' Alejandro drained his glass and set it down in a hasty movement. 'Let's go out to eat.'

The abrupt change of mood and focus took her aback but it was very much Alejandro's way to reclaim his space and self-discipline. She had broken through his reserve with her revelation and he wanted the breathing space to put all those messy emotions back again where she couldn't see them. He continually frustrated her with his refusal to share what he thought and felt, she thought ruefully. She wanted to throw herself in his arms and tell him that she loved him enough to forgive him, but she sensed that that would not be a comfort. Alejandro was very proud. He had such high standards and, unhappily for him, he had just failed those standards. He had to come to terms with that and deal with it in his own way.

They dined only a few streets away in a tiny restaurant where the food melted in her mouth to be washed down by the finest wine. Alejandro had reinstated his iron self-control, for not a single reference to his brother passed his lips. In the candlelight she reached for his hand once and he gripped her fingers so tightly he almost crushed them.

'Don't say anything,' he urged in a roughened growl that was as much a plea as a command. 'I would rather have your anger than your pity, *tesora mia*.'

Sensing that a change of subject would be timely Jemima asked him when he had had the apartment re-decorated.

'Soon after you left Spain, I still imagined you were waiting for me every time I walked through the door. I didn't like it,' he confessed, his dark, deep accented drawl as clipped as if he were talking business.

'And when you went into our bedroom at the castle?'

'The same.' He shrugged a broad shoulder in dismissal, subject closed.

He was more sensitive than she had ever appreciated, she conceded, and it was a discovery that troubled her more than it pleased her, for it made her think about the trauma he must have suffered when he'd believed she had betrayed him in his brother's arms. He hadn't needed to love her to be hurt. Marco had struck at the very roots of his sibling's pride and possessiveness, and his strong and protective family instincts, and it had been a devastating blow on all fronts.

Later, she slid naked and alone between the white linen sheets of the king-sized bed in the master bedroom. Alejandro had said he had work to catch up on before morning when they were to fly back home. Work, or a preference for his own company? She tossed and turned, wanting to be with him, refusing out of pride to make that move. He wasn't weak; why should she be? Giving into love was a weakness when it was for a man who did not love her back and who would despise any attempt to offer him re-assurance. Eventually she fell into an uneasy doze, waking again with a jerk. She put on the light to check her watch and the empty bed. It was three in the morning and her resistance to natural promptings was at its lowest ebb. She thrust back the sheet and padded off in search of her missing husband.

And when she did, she discovered that Alejandro still had the power to surprise her...

CHAPTER TEN

JEMIMA KNEW DRUNK when she saw it. An awareness of the
signs was etched deep in her psyche after a childhood in
which a man's stumbling steps or a mother's shrill slurred
complaints could make her turn cold with fear or insecurity. And with them went an out-of-control sensation that
Jemima herself did not like, which was why she never,
ever drank and why she had been happy to marry a man
of abstemious habits.

But undeniably and disturbingly, Alejandro was the
worse for wear because of alcohol. He was in the lounge,
bathed only in moonlight as the curtains were still open
wide. He was barefoot, his jeans unbuttoned at his narrow
waist and his white shirt hung open on his bronzed muscular chest. But as he lurched upright to acknowledge her
entrance he swayed and almost lost his footing. He steadied himself with a timely hand on a carved lamp table. His
ebony hair was dishevelled, his stubborn jaw line rough
with stubble and his midnight-dark eyes had a wild glitter unfamiliar to her.

'Alejandro?' Her violet eyes were full of concern; it was
a question as much as a greeting.

She watched him struggle to focus and regroup. 'I can't
talk to you right now—'

'You're going to talk to me whether you want to or
not. Anything is better than you sitting drinking alone!'
Jemima pronounced, a small hand pouncing on the bot-

tle of spirits on the coffee table before he could reach for it again.

For a split second, outrage flashed over his lean dark features because he had been prevented from doing what he wanted to do. Then he froze as if he was registering that he had been caught in a less than presentable state and wasn't quite sure how to handle that exposure.

'You've been drinking and I want to know why,' Jemima spelt out.

With a visible effort, Alejandro squared his broad shoulders, muscles rippling across his flat, hard stomach as he sucked in a shuddering breath. 'Not now...'

Her violet eyes softened. 'I *need* to understand why,' she rephrased gently.

'Isn't that obvious? I got everything in our marriage wrong!' he launched at her with an explosive wrath that had finally escaped his containment. *'Everything!'*

Jemima sighed. 'It happens. You just have to live with it.'

'No sympathy?' A black brow lifted.

'You put me through hell. You don't deserve it,' she told him bluntly.

'You have the power to drive me mad with jealousy—you always did,' he confided harshly, his lean bronzed profile bleak. 'I saw you with another man once and I never forgot the way it made me feel.'

Jemima's brow had pleated. 'When?' she cut in.

'Long before we were married. That time you decided that if I was seeing other women you would see another man,' he specified.

Undaunted by the reminder, Jemima tilted her chin. 'That was fair enough,' she commented.

'You were in the street, smiling at him the same way you smiled at me and he was holding your hand,' Alejandro recalled, his dark eyes brooding with remembered hostility and recoil. 'I couldn't stand it. There is nothing I wouldn't have done to get him out of your life! But that predilection for jealousy stayed with me. It's in my nature.'

She remembered how fast their relationship had become exclusive once Alejandro had realised that the agreement had to cut both ways. But it was news to her that his demon jealousy had continued to dog him.

In the simmering silence, Alejandro clenched his hands into powerful fists. He sent her a burning look of condemnation from below the fringe of his lush black lashes. 'If you want honesty, I'll give it to you. I hated you spending so much time with my brother three years ago. I tried very hard to be reasonable about it. I knew I was working too many hours. I knew you were bored and unhappy, but you and Marco got on too well. You seemed so close. Of course it bothered me at a time when our marriage was under strain. I thought I was losing you. Naturally I began to believe that you had more than a platonic friendship going with my brother.'

'Even though I was pregnant with Alfie and was as sick as a dog for weeks on end?' Jemima pressed, keen to bring him to an awareness of how far-fetched his fears had been in the circumstances.

'Your friendship with Marco started months before that. He was always seeking you out, phoning you, sharing secret jokes with you…'

'I suppose we were too close for comfort. He told me his big secret that he was gay and it made me feel privileged,' she muttered ruefully. 'I just didn't realise that you could be jealous of me because you never let me see it.'

'I was too proud to show you my Achilles' heel. But the jealousy tortured me and twisted the way I saw everything,' he revealed in a roughened admission. 'I thought you were taunting me with your preference for Marco's company.'

Jemima swallowed and then spoke up even though she didn't want to speak up on that angle. 'There was an element of that in my attitude. I so wanted your attention. I thought that if you saw how much Marco liked being with me it might make you want to spend more time with me,' she confessed unhappily. 'I didn't know that you were working so hard because you were trying to keep your businesses afloat. I thought you were bored with me.'

'I felt many things when we were first married but boredom never featured for even five minutes,' Alejandro revealed with a look of sardonic amusement marking his lean, darkly handsome features.

In the moonlight, which silvered his bronzed skin and accentuated the angles and hollows of his sculptured face, his sheer masculine beauty took her breath away. It crossed her mind that she now loved him much more deeply than she had when she first married him. She saw the man and his flaws. He wasn't perfect but it didn't matter because neither was she. But all that truly mattered to her just then was that he had never stopped wanting her before or after their marriage. Jealousy, assuming he could keep it within bounds, well, she could live with it by understanding that all that deep dark emotion of his had to occasionally find the wrong outlet.

'Why were you drinking?' she asked him worriedly.

Alejandro released a bleak laugh that was like a cold hand trailing down her spine. He settled haunted dark eyes on her, his tension unrelieved by their discussion. 'I let you down. I let you down in every way that mattered. You were my wife and, instead of supporting you and caring for you, I accused you of sleeping with my brother. Then I drove you away.'

'But now you know the truth.'

'And like many truths, it's not one I will enjoy living with.' Lean, powerful face grim, he yanked off his shirt in a physical move that startled her and strode past her, his steps even, his head high as though the very act of having had to talk to her had sobered him up. 'I need a shower.'

And Jemima went back to bed and lay awake waiting for him, but wherever he went to wash it wasn't in the en suite bathroom that adjoined the master bedroom. And wherever he slept it was not with her.

The next morning, however, it was business as usual for Alejandro. There was not a hint of the night's excesses visible in his crackling vitality and immaculately dressed appearance or, indeed, in his light and courteous conversation over breakfast. He'd made arrangements for the car she had driven to Seville to be returned to the estate and they left for the airfield and the short flight home. Alfie came running out into the garden to greet his parents and Alejandro snatched his son off his feet and hugged him close with an unashamed affection that touched Jemima's heart while making her crave the same treatment. Why were pride and perfection so important to Alejandro? Why could she accept his faults and live with them so much more easily than he could hers? She hadn't expected a perfect man and she hadn't got one. A more enlightened husband willing to accept that there was a learning curve in their marriage was the very best she could reasonably hope for. The difference between them was that she was already happy with the balance they had achieved now that he knew the truth about her supposed 'affair'.

It was the very next day that she received her second phone call from her father. She was with Alejandro when the call arrived and she excused herself to take it.

'It's normal for a man to expect his daughter to help him out,' Stephen Grey told her in a self-pitying whine. 'I'm not long out of prison, times are tough...'

'Have you tried to find work?' Jemima enquired flatly.

'It's not that easy.'

'You've never worked, never tried to keep yourself honestly. I'm not giving you any money this time.'

'How can you be so selfish? You're married to a very rich man. I've done my homework on him. You can afford to be generous—'

'I don't intend to spend the rest of my life being blackmailed by you. I've said no. You're out of luck. I'm not giving you a single euro of my husband's hard-earned cash. For a start, it's not mine to give,' Jemima asserted with cold clarity, and she replaced the phone receiver the instant she heard the warning rumble of her father's abusive response beginning.

She felt hot with shame when she recalled how she had first given way to her father's threats almost three years earlier, recklessly and fearfully handing over cash that she now knew Alejandro had not been able to afford just to keep the older man silent. Now she was calling Stephen Grey's bluff while dreading the prospect that he might go to the newspapers to reveal their relationship. The sleazy tale of her father's criminality and her unsavoury background and upbringing could only embarrass Alejandro and his family.

'Who was that on the phone?' Alejandro asked when she joined him and her son in the swimming pool, her slender body fetchingly clad in a ruffled apricot bikini.

'Oh, just someone from home.' Jemima struggled to telegraph casualness and lifted and dropped a thin shoulder while feeling the stiff discomfiture of virtually lying to him handicapping her pretence. 'Nobody important.'

It seemed to her that Alejandro's dark golden eyes rested on her a little longer than they need have done but, mercifully, he said nothing and went back to the task of teaching Alfie to swim. Very much a water baby, her son paddled over to her and giggled as he splashed her. The movement of the water was like cool silk lapping against Jemima's overheated skin. She rested back against the side and took in the sweeping view of the lush valley encircled by the snow-capped peaks. Her marriage had a horizon and a future again. She was not about to let go of that without a fight.

In the week that followed, Alejandro went out of his way to spend time with her and Alfie but, even though he returned to the marital bed, he didn't make love to her again. They dined out twice and on the second occasion he gave her a fabulous diamond ring just before they went out.

'What is this for?' she asked helplessly over dinner, watching the light flash blindingly on the glittering jewel and knowing that such magnificence must have cost at least two arms and a leg.

His ebony brows drew together, his dark golden eyes level. 'You're my wife. It's natural for me to want to give you gifts.'

'As long as it's not your guilty conscience talking,' Jemima cut in uncomfortably. 'You don't need to buy me, Alejandro. You already have me.'

'Do I? That's not something I would like to take for granted. You like pretty things,' he drawled softly. 'And I like giving them to you. I always did.'

Jemima turned a guilty pink. 'I had a fairly dismal childhood and I suppose I'm still making up for what I didn't get then.'

'You never talk about your childhood.'

Jemima tensed and shrugged, fixing a bright smile to her full mouth that felt hopelessly false. 'There's not much to talk about. We were always short of money and my parents didn't get on very well. It certainly wasn't a marriage made in heaven.'

'I seem to recall you telling me that your mother died in a car crash.'

'Yes. It was a sad time,' she said quickly, striving to

steer him away from further discussion in that line because she did not want to be forced to tell him any more untruths. Somehow lies told in the past when they had seemed to have no relevance bothered her less than the prospect of having to tell more in the present.

After a stressful week, her nerves were still on a cliff edge of doubt, fear and uncertainty with regard to the future. Her father had phoned twice more, one call arriving when she was out and the second proving to be more or less a repeat of the first one she had received, in which he bemoaned his financial state, urged her to be generous and threatened to come and visit her in Spain. The last time Stephen Grey had insisted on being paid in untraceable cash, and although Jemima had sworn she would not pay blackmail money again, she knew to the last pound sterling how much money she had in her bank account, and also had a very good idea of how much of a breathing space it would buy her from her father's persistent demands.

'I've decided to meet up with Marco this weekend,' Alejandro told her. 'I don't think he's going to speak to me of his own free will, but I did want to give him the opportunity to make the first approach.'

'Give him some more time,' Jemima suggested.

'I can't, *tesora mia*,' Alejandro countered, his lean, strong face shadowing. 'I have to deal with him. This feud has gone on long enough, though I can see that it suited Marco to keep us all at a distance. By the way, Beatriz knows.'

'I suspected that she might,' Jemima confided.

'She knew for a fact that Dario was gay and worked it out from there. But, being Beatriz, she said nothing to anyone for fear of causing offence,' Alejandro remarked wryly. 'I could wish she had been less scrupulous. Is it the prospect of my confronting Marco which is making you so jumpy?'

Jemima tensed, violet eyes veiling. 'Jumpy?'

'This past week I've often had the feeling that you're worrying about something. I assure you that I have no plans to have a huge messy row with my brother. It's a little late for that.'

Taken aback that he had noticed that she was living on her nerves, Jemima nodded and tried to look unconcerned.

'For the sake of the family I'll keep it under control, but I don't think I could ever forgive him for what he allowed me to believe,' he admitted squarely.

'Let it go with Marco. It's all in the past and over and done with,' Jemima pointed out just before she climbed out of the car outside the castle.

Alejandro closed a possessive arm round her on the stairs. The tangy scent of his citrus-based aftershave flared her nostrils and sent a flood of helpless awareness travelling to the more sensitive parts of her body. Unfortunately that was as close as he came to instigating a more intimate connection. Later she lay in bed about a foot away from him and wondered why he was still keeping his distance. Of course she could have bridged the gap, but why risk rocking the boat when she was already so stressed and feeling far from daring? Even during the night hours she was always somehow waiting for another phone call to destroy her peace of mind.

On the surface, though, most things were now fine in their marriage and she was determined to accept that without looking for pitfalls and pressures that might not exist. After all, her one and only real problem was Stephen Grey and what he might do. She told herself that if she continued to stand up to her father, he would eventually give up and leave her alone.

So, Alejandro had never said that he loved her and he probably never would, she reflected ruefully. Well, that was life. You couldn't have everything and what you did get was rarely perfect. He was making a real effort to make her happy and he was also proving to be a terrific father. It didn't get much better than that, she bargained with herself, determined not to succumb to taking for granted what she did have in favour of craving the one thing she couldn't have. She had always loved him, had learned to get by without him when their marriage failed, but now she was older and wiser and she knew that no other man could make her feel as good about herself or as happy as Alejandro did without even trying very hard.

In the week that followed it seemed to Jemima that Alejandro was angling at winning some 'perfect husband' award. Even though he disliked nightclubs, he took her out in Seville and they stayed over in the apartment there. They had a picnic down by the castle lake in the shelter of the trees with Alfie on what felt like the hottest day of the year and she paddled at the water's edge with her son chuckling in her arms. In the cool of the evening they dined out on the terrace, a practice that Doña Hortencia had once dismissed as too common and undignified to even be considered.

At a family party held at Alejandro's uncle's home on the occasion of his seventieth birthday, Marco and Dario put in an appearance as a couple and Doña Hortencia claimed that she was ill and left early, while everyone else pretended not to have noticed anything in the least bit unusual. Jemima was asked if she would do the flowers for a cousin's wedding and Marco let it be known that he and his partner were heading back to New York that weekend. Doña Hortencia was popularly held to be prostrate with relief at the news that the closet door could be closed again. Marco, on the other hand, informed Jemima that his mother had taken the news without comment; she was certainly annoyed with him but was still giving him his allowance. He also confessed that he was surprised by his older brother's continuing coolness towards him, an admission that made Dario Ortini, who was more sensitive, glance at Jemima in some embarrassment.

The next morning, Jemima was making some notes of her ideas for the flowers for the family wedding when Maria announced a visitor in an unusually anxious and apologetic tone.

Even while she was frowning in surprise at the sound of the housekeeper's strained voice, Jemima was truly appalled to scramble upright and see her father walking into the huge salon as bold as brass. While not tall, he was a broadly built man. With his shaven head and diamond ear studs, not to mention a purple and pink striped sports shirt, Stephen Grey was quite a sight to his daughter's dismayed eyes.

'This place is in the back of beyond. I had to pay a taxi a fortune to get up here!' he complained, sweeping the beautifully furnished room with assessing eyes that were striving to tot up the price of everything he could see. 'I hope you're planning to make coming out to Spain worth my while!'

Mastering her consternation at the older man's appearance, Jemima sucked in a deep steadying breath. She was grateful that Alejandro was out on the estate and unlikely to return before evening. 'What are you doing here? I asked you to leave me alone.'

His bloodshot blue eyes hardened. 'You've got no business talking to me like that, Jem!' he retorted furiously, his voice rising steeply. 'I brought you into the world and raised you and I expect you to treat me with proper respect.'

Jemima was very pale but she didn't back off, even though he was too close and too loud for comfort. 'After the way you treated me and my mother, I don't owe you the time of day,' she argued with an anger she couldn't hide. 'You washed your hands of me when I was only a teenager. My son and I have a good life here and I'm not about to let you ruin it for me.'

'Aw...will your fancy-pants Spanish Count be too much of a snob to keep you, once he knows what stock you're from?' Stephen Grey sneered, strolling over to the fireplace to lift a miniature portrait off the wall beside it and give the delicate gold and pearl-studded frame an intent scrutiny.

Alarm ran through Jemima as she watched. 'Please put that back. It's very old...'

The older man sent her a knowing look. 'It must be worth a packet on the antique market, then. If you can't help me with some cash like the last time, you can at least close your eyes while I help myself to a few little items that I can sell.'

'No!' Jemima shot back at him, crossing the pastel embroidered rug to stand in front of him. 'You can't have it. Give it back to me!'

The older man slid the portrait into his pocket and studied her with scorn. 'Mind your own business, why don't you? Either I take some stuff now or I come back some night with a few mates and we help ourselves to a good deal more.'

'If there's ever a burglary here, I will tell Alejandro about you.'

Stephen Grey loosed a derisive laugh. 'You won't! You'll do anything to keep that husband of yours in ignorance. You're the one who set a price on keeping the truth from him.'

'Yes, and I was very wrong. I understand that now,' Jemima conceded painfully. 'Now give me that miniature back before I call the police—'

'You wouldn't dare call the police!' he bit out with smug assurance.

In a complete panic because she was afraid that he might be right on that score and its potential for extreme embarrassment, Jemima tried to slide a hand into his pocket to retrieve the miniature portrait from him. He struck her shoulder with a big clenched fist to push her out of his way and she went flying off her feet and fell backwards across the coffee table. A startled yelp escaped her as she struck her head against a wooden chair leg and she lay in a heap, momentarily in a daze, one hand flying up to the bump at the back of her head.

There was a loud noise as the door burst open and then an outburst of strident Spanish. An instant later, Alejandro was lifting Jemima bodily up off the floor, settling her down with care on a sofa and demanding to know how she had got hurt.

'He's my father and he's threatening me,' Jemima whispered dizzily, way beyond trying to cover up the sordid scene and present it other than how it was. 'He has one of the portrait miniatures in his pocket and he hit me when I tried to get it back off him.'

'Now you listen 'ere,' her parent began loudly.

'The portrait first,' Alejandro murmured flatly, extending an authoritative hand.

Scowling, the older man dug the item out and passed it over. Blinking, her head pounding less from the blow she had sustained than from the thud of the unbearable tension, Jemima watched her husband return it to the wall. She saw her father lean close and say something to Alejandro and a split second later, and to her intense shock, Alejandro swung round and punched her father hard. The older man reeled back with a gasp of pain while Alejandro flung open the door and told him to get out before he brought the police in. Two vineyard workers were waiting outside and, at a word from Alejandro, they marched in and propelled Stephen Grey, struggling and vociferously complaining, out of the room.

'How on earth did you know what was happening in here?' Jemima demanded shakily.

'He frightened Maria by forcing his way in to see you. She didn't like the look of him or the way he spoke to her. I was at the vineyard and she phoned me immediately to warn me that there might be trouble.'

'I suppose you'll never forgive me now for not telling you the truth,' Jemima mumbled shakily as Alejandro sank down beside her to turn her head and gently examine the slight swelling at the back of her head. 'But when we first met I no longer had any contact with my father and I pretended he was dead rather than tell you about his history.'

Alejandro released his breath on a slow hiss. 'I think I can understand why.'

'He has a criminal record as long as your arm,' Jemima confided. And then she stopped trying to pick her words and the whole sorry story of her childhood came tumbling out: her father's violence and long stays in prison, her mother's alcoholism and the toxic atmosphere in their home.

'That you had found a decent job for yourself and were fully independent when we first met says much more about your character than the accident of birth that gave you your parents,' Alejandro told her with quiet confidence. 'I'm not stupid. I always knew that there were things you were choosing not to talk about and I wish I had dug deeper but it never seemed important enough to me. I wanted you as my wife whoever you were and regardless of what background you came from...'

Jemima looked at him through tear-filled eyes, her emotions swelling and overflowing in the aftermath of that nasty, distressing confrontation with her father. 'Honestly?'

'Walking away was never an option for me. I met you and that was that—it was a done deal. Do you remember the weekends we spent together at the house I rented near the hotel where you worked?' Alejandro queried, dark eyes intent on her troubled face as she nodded uncertainly. 'Those weekends were some of the happiest of my life and I could never have let you go after that.'

'But when we were first seeing each other you kept on breaking dates or not phoning when you said you would.'

Alejandro groaned. 'I regret the way I behaved but, right from the start, I was fighting what I felt for you. It was unnerving to want you so much. I wasn't ready to settle down. After what I'd suffered through my father's obsession with his second wife, I was determined not to fall in love either.'

'The differences between us bothered you.'

'Until I began to see that those differences meant that we complemented each other. After that month when we were broken up, when we were first dating, I knew just how necessary you were to my peace of mind,' Alejandro admitted tautly, his lean, strong face grave. 'You were like no other woman I had ever met and I was fascinated.'

'I thought…' Jemima breathed in deep and went ahead and said it anyway. 'I thought that for you it was just sex.'

'Just sex would have been easier to deal with,' Alejandro quipped. 'I didn't know at the time that you were my soul mate, I only knew that I wanted you in my life every day and not just on the weekends I could travel to England. When I was away from you I missed you so much that the only option left was to make you my wife.'

'It didn't seem like that then. You never mentioned needing me that much.'

'Of course, I didn't, *preciosa mia*. I was trying to play it cool and I never will be into sharing my every waking thought,' he pointed out wryly. 'But the point is that I stopped seeing other women so that I could have you all to myself, and the more I saw of you, the more I wanted you to be mine. It's my fault that you didn't feel you could tell me about your background—obviously I didn't make you feel secure enough.'

'Even before I met you I was telling people when they asked that both my parents were dead—it was easier than telling the truth,' she admitted. 'That's where some of the money I ran through went two years ago. Dad was threatening to go to the newspapers and tell all to embarrass you.'

'It won't embarrass me. Let him do his worst if he must,' Alejandro responded with immense assurance. 'And don't be upset if he carries out his threats. Most people will only have a passing interest in the fact that your father is a jailbird. So, you allowed him to blackmail you when we were first married?'

'Yes. I thought you'd be ashamed of me if you found out the truth of the kind of home I was from. You'd have to go back a generation to find any respectable relatives.'

Alejandro closed two hands over hers and held her fast. 'I just wish that you'd told me that you were being threatened and that you'd given me the chance to sort him out for you. Your father is like most bullies—once he saw that I wasn't afraid of him or what he might do, he was weak.'

'You must hate me, though, for giving all that money to him and wasting it,' Jemima reasoned, pale with shame and discomfiture.

'You were foolish. You could have trusted me even then.' Alejandro gazed down at her with dark eyes filled with regret. 'But I do appreciate that I wasn't a good enough husband in those days to inspire you with that trust. Without it, you were lost and your father got a stranglehold on you instead.'

'He's the other reason why I walked out then,' Jemima

confided abruptly. 'It wasn't just your suspicions about my relationship with Marco, it was the fact that I also couldn't see an end to my father's demands for money. I just felt our marriage was cursed and that the best thing I could do was walk away from it.'

'The best thing you could have done was confide in me. I wouldn't let anyone harm you ever again,' Alejandro swore with conviction. 'But I made too much of a habit of feeling and thinking things that I didn't then share with you and that's one very good reason why our marriage broke down.'

Jemima looked up into his somber, darkly handsome face and stretched up to kiss him. For an instant he stiffened and then he kissed her back with such passionate fervour that she gasped beneath the onslaught. Her heart thumping like a piston, she pressed her hot face against his shoulder and struggled to catch her breath again. 'I was starting to think that you were never going to kiss me again.'

'I was playing safe by making no demands.'

Jemima looked blank. 'What on earth are you talking about?'

'Our agreement that we give our marriage a three-month trial,' Alejandro reminded her grimly. 'The three months were up this week and there you were acting strangely. Naturally, I thought that you were on edge because you were thinking of leaving me again and were worrying about how to go about it and retain custody of Alfie.'

Jemima was frowning. 'My word, I totally forgot about the three-month thing!'

'You *forgot*?' Alejandro exclaimed with incredulous emphasis. 'How could you forget an agreement like that? It's been haunting me ever since I was stupid enough to say yes to it.'

'Oh, so that's why you took me dancing,' Jemima guessed with a sudden giggle of appreciation.

'I got so much wrong in my relationship with you I had to make an effort to get some things right,' Alejandro pointed out darkly, his dignity clearly under threat from her growing amusement. 'I was scared that you had decided to return to England.'

Jemima rested a hand on his shirtfront, spreading her fingers to feel the solid pound of his heart and the heat of his muscular torso through the fine cotton. 'I want you for ever,' she told him without hesitation.

His hand covered hers. 'For ever?' he questioned with a frown.

'Like the castle in the fairy tale. For ever and ever… I'm greedy, I want it *all*.'

'All I want is you,' Alejandro confided in a roughened undertone. 'All I've ever wanted is you. I love you very much.'

Her heart leapt but so did her eyebrows. 'Since when?' she asked, initially suspicious of the claim.

'Since very soon after I met you, only I didn't want to admit it even to myself because it made me feel so powerless, *querida*,' he confided heavily.

'But you never told me that you loved me then.'

'I was stingy with the words,' Alejandro admitted ruefully. 'But why do you think I married you? We were dynamite in bed together, but I wouldn't have married you if I hadn't felt a great deal more for you. I was crushed when you walked out on our marriage.'

'Maybe it was for the best.' Jemima sighed, her violet eyes pools of deep reflective emotion. 'I needed to grow up a lot. I was too immature for you.'

'I knew you were too young to get married, but I couldn't face waiting any longer for you. I wouldn't even wait long enough for my stepmother to organise a wedding for us,' he pointed out.

'I didn't even know that that was ever an option.'

'It wasn't once I realised how long the arrangements would take. I was counting the days until I could bring you back to Spain. That's why I opted for a quick ceremony in England.'

For the first time she began believing in what he was telling her and a wondering smile lit up her face. 'We rushed into getting married...'

'But with the very best of intentions,' he traded. 'Don't ever walk out on me again.'

'I won't.' Jemima hesitated as a long-suppressed thought occurred to her and then spoke up. 'After I left were there other women...affairs?'

'No. I told myself I would wait until I was divorced,' Alejandro extended. 'But I didn't want anyone else. I still wanted you.'

'There wasn't anyone else for me either,' Jemima volunteered.

He framed her cheekbones with long brown fingers and regarded her intently. 'Don't ever leave me again.'

'I'm not going anywhere,' she declared, and then she blushed. 'Apart from, well, if you should feel like it, our bedroom.'

It took a moment for Alejandro to grasp that invitation and then he wasted no time in vaulting upright and grasping her hand. 'Shouldn't I take you to a doctor to get that bruise on your head checked?'

'It's a bump and I saw stars for an instant, that's all. What I *really* want...'

'I'm more than ready to give you, *preciosa mia,*' Alejandro intoned with raging enthusiasm, pausing only to bundle her into his arms and mount the stairs with her clasped to his chest like a valued gift.

But Jemima had yet to forgive him for those nights she had lain awake wondering. 'I was worried that, maybe, as far as you were concerned, the passion had gone off the boil…'

'I'm on the boil round the clock!' Alejandro contradicted with a feeling groan, shouldering open the bedroom door and tumbling her down on the bed with an impressive amount of energy. 'I always want you.'

And he discarded her clothes and his in an untidy heap while he stole hot, hungry kisses from her willing mouth. His hands found her swollen breasts, the tender peaks and the moist heat between her legs. Seconds later he plunged into her and the intensity of her response hit fever pitch. Her orgasm roared up through her like an unstoppable fountain of burning sparks. She came apart in his arms, crying out her wild hot pleasure.

'Is this the optimum moment to tell you that I forgot to use a condom, *mi corazón*?' Alejandro drawled, his chest rising and falling rapidly as he struggled to catch his breath in the aftermath.

Jemima froze, thought about the possible consequences and then gave him a great big sunny smile because he had called her, 'my heart'. 'I suppose it must be because I forgot as well.'

'I would love to have another baby with you,' Alejandro husked, his dark golden eyes full of tenderness as he kissed her and held her close with possessive arms. 'I would like it very much indeed.'

'We could always try.'

Alejandro lifted his dark head and looked down at her with a heart stopping grin that made her feel all warm and squashy inside. 'I would like trying to get you pregnant very much as well, *preciosa mia*.'

'And if at first you don't succeed, try, try again,' Jemima reminded him with dancing eyes of amusement.

'That strikes me as the perfect blueprint for a second honeymoon. We'll go to the coast—Alfie will love the beach,' Alejandro forecast with satisfaction.

'I love you, Alejandro Navarro Vasquez,' Jemima told him, hugging him tightly to her.

'But not as much as I love you, *mi vide*,' Alejandro countered. 'You and Alfie are my whole world. Without you I would have nothing.'

Afloat on a wonderful cloud of happy contentment with all her worries and fears laid to rest, Jemima kissed him with tender loving appreciation.

A YEAR LATER, Jemima gave birth to her daughter, Candice, a blue-eyed, black-haired little darling, who charmed both her parents and her big brother long before she gave them her first smile.

Jemima had sold her florist's shop in the village of Charlbury St Helens and had decided against opening a similar business in Spain because to make it a viable full-time enterprise she would have had to base it in Seville. Besides, decorating houses with flowers was less of a tradition in her adopted country. She did act as a floral consultant for several smart weddings and events in the extended family circle and once she learned that she was carrying her second child she was no longer concerned about how she would fill her time. Her fear that her pregnancy would be as difficult as the first proved unfounded and she suffered very little sickness and, when the time came, enjoyed a straightforward delivery. Raising her children, acting as Alejandro's hostess when they entertained at the castle, and continuing to take a strong interest in the charity that supported the women's shelter and enshrined the cause of battered women kept Jemima more than sufficiently busy.

Flora flew out every three months or so for a visit. Beatriz met an architect at a family christening and was mar-

ried to him within six months. Currently expecting her
first child, Beatriz was a good deal more confident than
she had once been and remained Jemima's closest friend
in Spain. Of all of them, Doña Hortencia had changed the
least. Although Marco still visited his mother, relations
were often strained between them because it remained a
challenge for her to accept him as he was. On the other
hand, her strong desire to retain her ties with the castle
had ensured that the older woman had become much more
polite to Jemima.

Alejandro and Marco had repaired their brotherly bond
to some extent but past history ensured that Alejandro remained wary. Marco, however, was flourishing at the art
gallery in New York and, having found his true métier,
was steadily climbing the career ladder. In the field of
business, the brothers shared a very strong bond indeed.

Alfie was thriving and had recently started pre-school,
which was improving his grasp of Spanish by leaps and
bounds. Stephen Grey had sold a story about his wealthy
daughter and son-in-law to a downmarket British tabloid
but the article hadn't amounted to much and had attracted
little attention. Since then Jemima had heard nothing from
her father, although Alejandro had established that the
older man had recently lost his freedom, having been returned to jail for committing an offence.

Jemima remained exuberantly happy with her life and
never allowed herself to forget how close she had come
to losing Alejandro and the marriage that had become the
centre of her world. She told him just about everything
and hid almost nothing from him and, in turn, he tried
to talk more to her and share his deeper concerns. If he
was working very long hours, Jemima stayed in Seville
so that they saw more of each other. With a little compromise and mutual respect on both sides, they had ensured
that they were closer than ever by the time that they cel-

ebrated the first anniversary of their reconciliation with
a holiday in England.

Three months on from that, Jemima was in the Seville
apartment, awaiting the sound of Alejandro's key in the
lock on the front door. When she heard it, she flew out
of bed and raced out to the hall, a slight figure in a black
silk nightdress.

Alejandro leant back against the door to shut it, all the
while studying her with appreciative dark golden eyes and
a charismatic smile that made her tummy flip. 'You make
coming home such an event, *esposa mia*,' he told her huskily.

'You've already eaten, haven't you?' she checked, moving forward to trail his jacket off his shoulders and lock
flirtatious fingers round his tie to ease it slowly out from
below his collar.

'I ordered in food once I knew that the talks would run
late.' Keen to be of help, Alejandro jerked his shirt out of
the waistband of his trousers and kicked off his shoes. He
knew their housekeeper would find a trail of clothes leading down to the bedroom in the morning but he didn't care.
He was delighted when his wife pounced on him. His shirt
drifted down to the floor.

Jemima settled big violet eyes on his superb bronzed
torso and uttered an appreciative sigh, which made him feel
ten feet tall. On the threshold of the bedroom, he stepped
out of his trousers and a step later paused to shed his socks.

'I really love being married to you,' Alejandro confessed raggedly as he came down on the bed.

Surveying Alejandro in his boxer shorts, Jemima had
no complaints to make either. Indeed she was dizzily conscious of the sheer happiness bubbling through her. 'I love
you too—more every day...'

He leant forward and kissed her and she quivered with
pleasure and anticipation, revelling in the reality that it

was a Friday and they had the whole night to enjoy each other. Much as they loved Alfie, it would be relaxing not to have a lively toddler sneaking into their bed at first light and ensuring that any fun had to be clean fun. The pressure of her handsome husband's mouth on hers was unbearably sexy.

'I love you…more than I have words to describe,' Alejandro told her thickly.

'I've got plenty of words,' she broke free to tell him.

'Shush,' he urged, kissing her again until she forgot what she had been talking about and settled up against his lean powerful body like an extra layer of skin. The silence that ensued was broken only by revealing little gasps, moans and sighs while Alfie and Candice's parents got thoroughly acquainted again after a day spent apart…

* * * * *

FLORA'S DEFIANCE

CHAPTER ONE

ANGELO VAN ZAAL studied the nine-month-old child that the nurse had brought to him. The little girl was golden-haired with the wide, pansy-blue eyes of a china doll, and the minute she saw him she smiled in happy recognition. The innocence of that trusting smile cut Angelo as sharply as a knife, for few children could have been subjected to a tougher start in life than little Mariska. Only a dark bruise and a scratch on one cheek bore witness to the fact that she had been miraculously thrown clear in her special car seat from the accident in which both of her parents had died.

'I understand that you are not related by blood to Mariska,' the female doctor by his side remarked.

'Her father, Willem, was my stepbrother, but I thought of him as my brother and I treated him as such,' Angelo stated with the clarity for which he was famed in the business world. 'I consider Mariska to be part of my family and I'm keen to adopt her.'

'The social worker in charge of her case did mention that you have been involved in Mariska's life since she was born—'

'I did what I could to support Willem and his wife, Julie. I only wish it had been enough,' he imparted with a wry twist of his mouth, as he knew that the medical staff would be well aware of the state in which Mariska's parents had been at the time of the crash. He was merely grateful that the sordid truth had not appeared in the newspapers.

Angelo van Zaal was an extraordinarily handsome man,

the doctor reflected with an appreciative glance. He was also extremely wealthy, the bearer of a name famous for its benevolence in the field of philanthropy. Nevertheless, the steel magnate was equally well known for his ruthless cutting edge and success as a businessman. According to the press, a procession of international fashion models entertained him outside working hours. In looks, he had inherited his Spanish mother's black hair and darker skin tone rather than his Dutch father's fair colouring. But his eyes were a bright burning blue, as lucid as a flawless sapphire and enhanced by a frame of lush ebony lashes that gave his gaze spectacular impact. Tall, at several inches over six feet, and well built, he had attracted a good deal of notice from female staff and patients alike as they walked through the hospital to the children's ward. He was also, as far as the doctor was aware, still a single man.

'The hospital has had several enquiries about Mariska's welfare from her aunt, Flora Bennett. I understand that she is Julie's older sister.'

Angelo's superb bone structure took on a forbidding aspect. At the same time, he had a mental flash of eyes the colour of emeralds, skin as impossibly white as milk and the sort of lush full pink mouth that could plunge a man into an erotic daydream. Flora was a tall, feisty redhead with the kind of sensual appeal that would have entrapped a less wary and experienced male. As he had on previous occasions, Angelo crushed that provocative thought and shook himself free of it in exasperation. 'A half-sister,' he pronounced quietly. 'She and Julie had the same father.'

Angelo could have said a great deal more but he compressed his lips, reluctant to voice his hostility towards the other side of Mariska's family because that was a private matter. He'd had the then pregnant Englishwoman Julie Bennett and her connections investigated when Willem had decided to marry her, and his strong reservations about Julie had proved prophetic.

Had it not been for Julie's inclinations, Angelo was convinced that Willem would still be alive and, from what he had learned about Julie's elder sister at the same time, she was not to be trusted either. The same investigation had revealed that lurid scandal laced Flora's background; some years earlier she had used sleazy tactics in an attempt to advance and enrich herself in the workplace. While Flora was considerably more memorable in looks and personality than her rather more ordinary sister, she was an already proven gold-digger and Angelo knew he would go to any lengths to ensure that Willem's daughter, Mariska, was protected from her influence. Mariska would, after all, inherit her father's trust fund. As Willem had died before he'd reached the age where he could gain access to the money, his daughter would some day be a rich young woman.

Indeed, if Angelo had anything to do with the matter, Mariska would lead a very different life from that of either of her feckless parents. His wide sensual mouth hardened. He might have failed to rescue Willem from his demons, but doing the very best he could for his stepbrother's daughter would help him to sleep a little more peacefully at night.

The doctor cleared her throat as Mariska lay in Angelo's arms; he had been granted temporary custody of the child. 'Have you any plans to marry?' she enquired, unable to stifle her curiosity on that score.

Brilliant blue eyes flew straight to her blushing face. Angelo was too much of a player to reveal his thoughts but tension held him fast. 'It is possible,' he responded. 'Where this little girl is concerned, I still have much to think through.'

His acknowledgement that there might be some grounds

for concern over his suitability as a single parent made the doctor give him an approving appraisal. Someone had once called Angelo van Zaal chilly but, although she would never have called him an emotional personality, he was innately practical and reliable. Many men would have shrugged off the problems of so troublesome a set of relatives, but Angelo had stood his ground and done what he could to help until the inevitable tragic end was reached. In the doctor's book, that not only made him a force to be reckoned with but also a very suitable guardian for a vulnerable child.

FLORA SAT RIGID-BACKED in the taxi that had collected her from her flight into Schipol airport. Every step of her journey to Amsterdam had been organised without any input from her and, although those arrangements had made the trip easier for her, she was not only ungrateful for that assistance, but also as tense as a bowstring.

At five feet eleven inches tall, she was a long-limbed coltish beauty with slender curves in elegant keeping with her height and graceful carriage. But Flora had never seen herself in that favourable light because from an early age she had been made to feel excessively large and gawky beside her dainty, diminutive mother who had often bemoaned her daughter's size.

Her thick auburn hair, which when loose fell well past her shoulders since she had decided to grow it again, was tied back with a black ribbon at her nape. Her apple-green eyes shone clear against her flawless skin, but the swollen reddened state of her eyelids betrayed the physical signs of her grief.

The knowledge that she would soon have to thank Angelo van Zaal for arranging her trip to Amsterdam for the double funeral made Flora grimace. She loathed him: he was such a controlling seven-letter-word of a man! His word was law within his family circle, at his offices and even beyond those boundaries, for such wealth as his carried considerable power and influence in every sphere. Flora, of course, had never liked being told what to do. She had learned to put up with it when she was an employee. She had also learned to keep her temper around bossy guests at her guest house, to nod and smile and let their arrogance wash off her again like a light rain shower.

But Angelo van Zaal could put Flora's back up without even trying. He had not even had the courtesy to phone her personally when her sister and his stepbrother had died within hours of crashing their car, she reflected bitterly. Instead he had instructed his family lawyer to ring and break the news for him. It was a dispassionate decision that was typical of his determination to keep her at arms length from events, thereby underlining his own authority and the absence of a true familial connection between them.

But if she was honest—and Flora always liked to be honest with herself—her primary objection to Angelo van Zaal was that, at first glance, he had turned her head as easily as if she were a dizzy adolescent. Even though eighteen months had passed since that debilitating first encounter, her cheeks could still burn at the mere memory of the effect he had on her—in spite of the fact that a man like Angelo van Zaal would never give her so much as a second glance.

Angelo was undeniably drop-dead gorgeous and Flora found it a terrible challenge not to stare at him and just float off into fantasy land. He flustered her and made her blush and stammer and, no matter how hard she tried to suppress her responses, she was already on the edge of her seat with anticipation at just the thought of seeing him again. There was no rhyme or reason to sexual attraction, she reminded herself impatiently. But all the same it exasperated her that even after her past unhappy experiences with men she could still succumb to a meaningless physical reaction. In truth, she was convinced that if sexual weakness could be inborn she had undoubtedly inherited that dangerous flaw from her womanising father. The acknowledgement that she could be drawn to someone she didn't even like shocked and affronted her, but she would have chewed off her own arm sooner than give Angelo van Zaal reason to suspect her weakness for him.

Furthermore, Angelo was severely underestimating her if he imagined that she might be willing to stand back and just allow him to claim full custody of her niece. Flora was ready to fight for the right to take Mariska back to England with her so that she could raise Julie's child as her daughter. Why should Angelo automatically assume that he would make the most appropriate guardian for a baby girl?

After all, Flora owned a comfortable detached house with a garden in the English village of Charlbury St Helens and was in a position to offer her niece her care and attention. At present, Flora, who also had a childcare qualification, ran a successful bed and breakfast business from her home. But, if need be, she could stop taking in paying guests until Mariska was of an age to attend school. Financially she could handle that temporary sacrifice of earnings because she had a good deal of money sitting untouched in the bank. She might not like to think about where that money had come from and what she'd had to go through to get it, but the very fact of its existence surely had to improve her chances of being considered a suitable adoptive parent.

As Flora detached herself from the disturbing memories of the very different life she had led as a city career woman before she'd settled into her former great-aunt's home in the village, she was painfully conscious of the ache of loss in her heart. Julie was gone and, sadly, Flora had seen all too little of her vivacious younger sister since she'd moved to the Netherlands. She had only seen Willem and Julie when they'd come over to the UK. Only once had Flora contrived to visit them in Amsterdam, for Willem and Julie had led very busy lives and it had quickly become apparent to her that they'd preferred to be guests rather than hosts.

Yet once upon a time Flora and the sibling five years her junior had been very close, although nobody who'd known the background from which both young women had come would ever have forecast that development. Flora had grown up as an only child in an unhappy marriage. Her father had been a chronic womaniser and she had few childhood memories that did not include a background of raised voices and the sound of her mother sobbing. Her emotionally fragile parent had often intimated that she would leave her unfaithful husband if only she could afford to do so, a lament that had ensured that her daughter set out to gain the highest possible educational qualifications in the hope of ensuring that she never had to rely on a man to keep a roof over her head.

Flora's parents had finally divorced while she'd been at university and she had then withstood the shock discovery that her father already had a second family, living only a few streets away from her childhood home! Evidently he had carried on an affair with Julie's mother, Sarah, almost from the outset of his marriage to Flora's mother. Her father had married Sarah straight after the divorce and there had been a huge family row when he'd insisted on introducing his daughters to each other. Even when that second marriage had also broken down in a welter of accusations of infidelity, Flora and Julie had stayed in touch, and when Julie's mother had died and Julie started college she'd moved into Flora's apartment in London. During the following two years, which had encompassed a period of great upheaval and unhappiness for Flora at work and in her personal life, the sisters had become close.

Flora's eyes swam with tears while she allowed herself to picture her late sister as she had last seen her. A small pretty blonde, Julie had been bubbly and chatty. Within months of meeting Willem, who had spent his gap year working in London, Julie had decided to abandon her studies so that she could live on a houseboat in Amsterdam with the handsome young Dutchman. Rejecting all Flora's cautious advice to the contrary, Julie had put love first with the wholehearted determination of the very young. Within weeks she had announced her pregnancy and soon afterwards a rather hasty marriage had taken place.

Angelo van Zaal had paid for the civil wedding and the small reception that had been held in London. Flora had only met him for the first time that day and, already warned what to expect from him by her sister, she had not been impressed by his chilly disapproval.

'I'm too common for Angelo's taste, not well enough educated and too cheeky for a woman,' Julie had told her with a scornful toss of her pretty blonde head. 'Catch me standing saying, "Yes, sir, no, sir, three bags full, sir" like Willem does! Willem is terrified of him because he's never managed to measure up to Angelo's expectations.'

And to be fair to Angelo van Zaal, he had made no attempt to pretend that he approved of her sister's relationship with his stepbrother. 'They're far too young and immature to be parents. This is a disaster,' he had pronounced with grim insensitivity after the ceremony, staring down at Flora with cold-as-ice blue eyes.

'It's a little late now,' Flora had countered, being of a naturally more optimistic bent, while marvelling at the unearthly beauty and unusual hue of those eyes of his. 'They do love each other and, thank goodness, they'll have Willem's trust fund to help them along—'

Angelo's lean bronzed face had frozen. 'Where did you get that idea from? Willem won't come into his trust fund for another three years.'

Flora had felt her face flood with mortified colour and wished she had kept her mouth shut. Was it wrong of her to have assumed that early access to the bridegroom's nest egg would provide much-needed help to the young couple in setting up their first home? The disdain on Angelo's handsome face had warned her that, as far as he was concerned, she had grossly overstepped her boundaries in referring to Willem's future prospects.

'I understand that they're both hoping that in the circumstances—Julie expecting their first child,' Flora had extended uncomfortably, 'they can challenge the provisions of the fund—'

'It would be insanity. I will not allow it,' Angelo had decreed in a tone of sardonic finality as though his opinion was the only one that counted. 'Willem and his wife will have to work for a living. Clearly that was not your sister's plan.'

Flora had bridled at the insinuation that her sister might have married Willem in the hope of sharing his handsome trust fund. 'Of course Julie is willing to get a job.'

'She's not qualified to do anything other than the most menial work,' Angelo had pointed out drily. 'And Willem will have to complete his business degree before he can aspire to a well-paid career.'

Ultimately the trust fund had been kept safe but what Flora had most feared from the outset had come to pass instead: Willem had dropped out of university to seek employment when Julie had become too sick to work during her pregnancy. Flora had blamed Angelo van Zaal entirely for that development, believing that as one of the trustees for the fund he had probably still patted himself on the back for having kept that precious money intact. She was

not at all surprised that the steel billionaire had put the con-
servation of cash ahead of family concern and kindness.

The taxi waited for her while she checked into her hotel
and then whisked her on to the funeral home. By the time
she arrived there she was truly dreading her approaching
encounter with Angelo van Zaal. There was a large gathering of mourners, many of them young people. But in
spite of the crowd the only person Flora was really aware
of strode across the room towards her and his very presence in the same airspace made her light up inside like a
secret firework display. Her spine rigid with shame and
denial, she blanked him out as though he weren't there,
evading any form of eye contact while warm colour began
to infiltrate her pallor.

Angelo spoke the conventional words of regret with
perfect courtesy, awaited her response and escorted her
round the room to meet some of Willem's relatives. When
it came to public behaviour his manners were always letter
perfect. But, so close to him, Flora could hardly breathe
for tension and she hated him for the effect he was having
on her, hated him for the lethal combination of looks and
hormones that had entrapped her from their first meeting. Even the faint evocative aroma of his citrus-based
cologne was familiar to her and she had to resist a powerful urge to lean closer to him. No man, even the one she
had once planned to marry, had ever made such a strong
impression on her.

Indeed, sex had never been a driving need for her and
she was still a virgin. She had always been level-headed
and reserved with men. She had seen too much unhappiness growing up to want to rush into any relationship. She
had also once suffered badly from the harassment of a bullying sex-pest in the workplace. And the discovery of the
potent physical attraction that Angelo, a man she didn't

even like, could exude had merely underlined her caution and disenchantment with that aspect of life.

'How is Mariska doing?' Flora asked the moment she had the chance to speak to Angelo van Zaal without an audience.

'Children are resilient. She was all smiles over breakfast this morning,' Angelo recalled, staring down at her with his electrifyingly blue eyes, eyes unfairly surrounded by lashes as dense and enhancing as thick black lace.

'You saw her that early at the hospital today?' Flora pressed in surprise, thinking that he must have called in to see the little girl on his way to the funeral.

Angelo gazed down at her in an unnervingly steady appraisal and it was as if pure energy were dancing over her skin with silken taunting fingers. Tensing, alarmingly conscious that her nipples were tightening beneath her clothing, she coloured accordingly, stilled a shiver of awareness and stared fixedly at the knot on his silk tie.

'Mariska is no longer in hospital,' Angelo revealed. 'She was released into my care yesterday.'

That was news to Flora and she lifted her chin. 'You pulled that off very quickly. Who's looking after her?'

'Her nanny, Anke.'

Flora was unimpressed. 'When she's already lost her parents the company of a stranger can't be much of a consolation.'

'Anke is not a stranger. She has been taking care of Mariska on a part-time basis for several months now...'

'Willem and Julie employed a nanny?' Flora was taken aback, as she had not thought that the financial problems Julie had often mentioned during their phone calls would have stretched to such a luxury as one-to-one care for Mariska. And, certainly, Julie had never once hinted that her daughter enjoyed the attentions of Anke.

'I took care of the expense.' His wide sensual mouth

compressed, Angelo dealt her a tough uncompromising
look as though daring her to say more on yet another subject that he clearly considered to be none of her business.

'How very generous of you…as you have been in shell-
ing out for my travel costs,' Flora commented stiffly.
'Thanks, but it wasn't necessary, though it did save me a
lot of hassle and got me here much faster, which I do appreciate. I can't stay for long though, and I would like to
spend what time I do have in Amsterdam with—'

'Your niece. Of course,' he incised smoothly. 'When
this is over, everyone is invited back to my home for coffee and you'll see her then.'

Flora flushed, for she had not expected him to make
seeing Mariska so easy and had somehow expected ob-
stacles to be put in her path. The wind taken from her sails
before she even got airborne, she nodded relieved acceptance of his assurance.

'I should mention…' She hesitated and then pressed on,
guided by her streak of innate honesty, which preferred all
the facts to be out in the open. 'I have an interview with
a solicitor here tomorrow and after that with Social Ser-
vices. I intend to apply to adopt Mariska.'

All of a sudden, those impossibly blue eyes briefly resembled chips of indigo-tinted ice, but then she wondered
if that was the result of her fertile imagination because he
merely nodded his acceptance. 'Of course, that is your
prerogative.'

The funeral did not last long. Someone had told her
that the Dutch were partial to giving eulogies at funerals,
but the tributes paid to Willem and Julie were short and
sweet. Tears continually flooded Flora's eyes because it
seemed so wrong that two such young people with everything to live for should be dead and she struggled to get
a grip on emotions that still felt exceedingly raw. Apart
from Mariska, Flora no longer had any surviving relatives

and that made her feel very alone in the world. Her best friend, Jemima, had recently returned to her husband in Spain and that had left another hole in her life.

When the talking was over, Flora accepted a lift with Willem's aunt and uncle to Angelo's home. He lived in an imposing historic building, a literal mansion, which Julie had once described to Flora in the most fulsome of terms as a 'palace'. The house, which had belonged to several generations of van Zaals, was very traditional inside and out, featuring high ceilings, polished wooden floors, gleaming antique furniture and walls covered with huge splendid paintings. Coffee was served in the very elegant drawing room by the plump, smiling housekeeper whom Angelo addressed as Therese.

Under cover of a conversation with a business colleague, Angelo found himself discreetly watching Flora, noting her every tiny move and change of expression and the faint silvery sheen of tears still marking her cheeks. Even at a glance he could see that she seethed with emotion, messy dangerous stuff that it was, he acknowledged grimly, for she was the sort of woman he had always avoided getting involved with. More than a year had passed since their last meeting. He approved of the fact that her hair was no longer short and he could not resist picturing those luxuriant coppery tresses freed from the restraint of their ribbon. *And trailing across a pillow?* a sarcastic little inner voice enquired. As irritation with his male predictability gripped Angelo, there was a tightening heaviness at his groin, his libido reacting all too enthusiastically to Flora Bennett's presence and the allure of an erotic fantasy.

He sensed the passion in her and it drew him like the sun on a cold wintry day. Brilliant eyes cloaked, he studied her fixedly and, just as he had from their very first encounter, fought the magnetic pull of her with all his considerable force of will. Control and lucidity were everything to Angelo, who demanded more of himself than he ever had from anyone else. After all, nobody knew better than Angelo that an affair with the wrong woman could lead to disaster and it was the one risk he would not take.

Flora dragged her attention from a superb painting of an ancestral family group, striving not to seek Angelo's resemblance to some of its members with his clear good-looking features, though he would be like a sleek dark avenging angel set amongst those fair rosy-cheeked faces, she thought absently. She turned round to see where he was and collided headlong with his burning appraisal. An arrow of pure burning heat slivered through her slim length, kicking every nerve-ending into almost painful sensitivity. Her full lips pressed together tightly as she walked towards him, suppressing her responses with furious resolve.

Angelo inclined his handsome dark head to his house-keeper and summoned her to his side. 'Therese will take you upstairs now to see Mariska.'

Flora was introduced to the pretty dark-haired nanny, Anke, but she really only had eyes for her niece, who sat in a child seat playing with a selection of toys. With her slightly turned-up nose and dimples, blue eyes and golden hair, the little girl bore a startling likeness to Julie. Flora's eyes stung and she got down on her knees beside the chair to get reacquainted with her niece, once again deeply regretting the truth that she was almost a stranger to Mariska.

Mariska studied Flora with big blue eyes and laughed when her aunt tickled her chubby little hand. A cheerful, affectionate child, she played happily with Flora and she was the perfect comfort for her aunt after the highly stressful week she had endured. When the little girl became sleepy, Flora checked her watch and was surprised by how much time she had spent with her niece, for the afternoon was over. Descending the stairs, she saw Angelo in the hall below. He was so tall and dark and his glossy black cropped hair shone beneath the lights. He had the bronzed profile of a Greek god and the body of one as well, her rebellious thoughts added defiantly.

'I wondered if it would be possible for me to visit the houseboat where Willem and Julie lived tomorrow afternoon,' she asked tautly.

'Yes. A cleaning crew is currently sorting the vessel out for a handover back to the landlord,' Angelo revealed. 'There may be some of your sister's things which you wish to take home with you.'

There was a thickness in Flora's throat. Julie had always travelled light so she doubted that there would be many keepsakes. She forced a rather watery smile and took her leave to walk out into the cool evening air.

Watching her departure from the window, Angelo had the cold comfort of knowing that he was behaving badly. Flora was on her own in a foreign city and she had just buried her sister and her brother-in-law. Yet he was leaving her to return to an anonymous hotel for the evening. His handsome mouth clenched hard. Even as he watched her he noticed the enticing feminine sway of her hips in the dark suit she wore, the pouting curve of her bottom that stretched the skirt's fabric and the shapely turn of her calves and narrow ankles. She had terrific legs. He imagined inching up that skirt and as his body reacted with full blown arousal he released his breath in a sudden sharp hiss. He knew that he could not trust himself if he offered dinner and so left it at that.

Exhaustion engulfed Flora by the time she reached her room as she had barely slept since receiving the news of the double tragedy. She kicked off her shoes and lay down on the bed, where she fell asleep almost instantly. The chirrup of the phone by the bed wakened her. 'Hello?' she mumbled drowsily.

'It's Angelo.' It was an unnecessary announcement because Flora knew only one male possessed of a dark deep drawl as rich and potentially sinful as chocolate melting on her taste buds. 'Have you dined yet?'

Flora froze in surprise and wondered if he could hear the sound of her jaw dropping in shock. 'Er...'

'If you haven't I would be happy to take you out to eat this evening,' Angelo murmured, smooth as silk.

His voice actually set up a chain-reaction quiver down her taut spine and she sat up with a start. She could not credit the invitation and it unnerved her. 'Thanks, but I've already eaten,' she lied without hesitation. 'But it was kind of you to offer.'

'I wasn't being kind,' Angelo countered, a rougher edge filtering through his unforgettable drawl.

'Oh...' Dry-mouthed and flushed, Flora could not think of a single thing to say and he filled in the silence with complete cool and bid her goodnight. He didn't like her, she *knew* he didn't like her, for the cool censure when he looked at her with those amazing eyes of his was unmistakeable, even if she didn't know what she had done to deserve that attitude. So why on earth had he suddenly decided to invite her out to dinner? Had he felt sorry for her? The very suspicion made Flora bridle because she had never sought out any man for comfort.

She ordered a snack from Room Service and then went for a quick shower. She ate perched cross-legged on the bed with a book propped open and just knew that Angelo would disapprove. But she had said no and she should be proud of herself, although if she was honest panic and surprise had together combined to ensure her negative response. In addition she had nothing to wear but the suit she had worn to the funeral, since she had only packed casual jeans and a top for her short stay. She could not even imagine dining out in some fancy restaurant in Angelo's company. On her final visit to Charlbury St Helens, Julie had shown her sister a magazine article featuring a couple of Angelo's lady friends, beautiful women dressed in cutting-edge fashion, who could match his sophistication and cool.

Regardless of those reflections, Flora could not help wondering what it would have been like to be the sole focus of Angelo's attention for a couple of hours. Heat bubbled like excitement low in her pelvis and she tensed and suppressed that disturbing line of thought. It was a very long time before she contrived to drift off to sleep again that night...

CHAPTER TWO

THE FOLLOWING DAY, Angelo was in a business meeting in Rotterdam. But for all the attention he was giving to the exchange of views, he might as well have stayed at home. He was proud of his cool logic and intelligence and could not understand why both had proved insufficient to forecast Flora Bennett's most recent move. The dinner invitation had offered him a valid way of bringing Flora up to speed on events in her late sister's life before she got the bad news from the professionals she was consulting that very morning. It would have been tasteless for him to pass on that information at the funeral. But she had, most unexpectedly, turned him down.

Handsome mouth tightening and quite unaware of the attention his unusually long silence was attracting, Angelo shrugged a broad shoulder sheathed in the finest silk and wool mix. He was willing to admit that he had no prior experience of hearing the word 'no' from a woman's lips. It was a fact that the females he met fell over themselves to say yes. Yes to every invite, yes to sex, yes to just about any damned thing he wanted. Women in Angelo's world were very predictable and he had never had the smallest urge, he told himself fiercely, to walk on the wilder side of life. He had never forgotten the years of misery that had resulted from his late father's desire to do exactly that with Willem's mother, a beautiful volatile widow.

But would Flora have slept with him last night? That question came out of nowhere at him before he was even aware of having thought about such a possibility. He was impervious to the covert looks he was receiving as his brilliant blue eyes became even more abstracted. He wanted her. He was even willing to admit that there was just something about Flora Bennett that grabbed him every time he saw her. Yet last night his intentions had been pure.

Of course it was entirely possible that Flora Bennett knew a great deal more about Willem and Julie's lifestyle than he had had cause to suspect. His lean strong features darkened at that idea. Flora had seen little of her sister since her wedding to Willem, but she could well have decided to give Julie and her problems a wide berth. Angelo had never had that option because the overwhelming need to protect Mariska from her parents' folly had repeatedly forced him to intervene. Unfortunately taking care of Mariska's needs would entail building some kind of an ongoing connection with the other side of her family. He might distrust Mariska's aunt but she was still the only blood relative the little girl had left alive. He could not ignore that bond or the fact that Flora had spent over two hours happily entertaining her niece and had inspired her nanny to remark that Mariska's English aunt was wonderfully natural with children.

How much weight would the professionals put on that bond or on so admirably maternal a demonstration? Was he prepared to get married just to improve his own claim to the little girl? Angelo shifted uneasily in his seat. The prospect of only sleeping with one woman for the rest of his life appealed to him as much as a dose of poison. Of course he could make marriage more of a business arrangement and retain a certain amount of freedom, he reasoned bleakly. Many women would accept such conditions simply to become a van Zaal with access to a fleet of private jets, a luxurious array of international homes and a huge allowance to spend on designer clothes and jewellery. Angelo had learned very young that it was possible to buy virtually anything he wanted and he was prepared to pay handsomely over the odds to acquire the perfect wife.

A perfect wife who would naturally be blonde, educated, classy and from the Netherlands. Dutch women were wonderfully practical and resilient, he thought appreciatively. He needed a sensible woman from a respectable background who would accept his challenging work schedule without complaint and who would embellish his social and domestic life while still essentially allowing him his privacy. A woman content to enjoy the lifestyle he could give her and make no further demands of him. He decided that as long as the controversial subjects of fidelity or romance were kept off the menu he could face the prospect of marriage for Mariska's sake. He had become very fond of the little girl.

Emerging from that lengthy and very sobering thought process, Angelo checked his watch and made one of the lightning-fast decisions that he was famous for. After a working lunch to make up for his non-participation in the meeting, he would meet Flora Bennett at the houseboat and tie up the loose ends between them before she left Amsterdam and returned to England. It was the rational thing to do and he was not being influenced by his attraction to her, he assured himself with considerable satisfaction. He was far too level-headed to stray into such hazardous territory with a woman of dubious morals.

AROUND THE SAME time as Angelo was travelling from his head office in Rotterdam back to Amsterdam, Flora was literally reeling out of the public building where she had met with Mariska's social work team: she was in deep shock from what she had learned during that encounter.

Shock that she'd had not the slightest idea of what really had gone on in Willem and Julie's lives, shock that Julie had managed to convince her during their weekly phone calls that they were leading a perfectly ordinary life when, in fact, the very opposite was true. Indeed, both Willem and her sister had resorted to petty crime in an effort to satisfy their addiction to drugs. Her half-sister and her husband had been *thieves and drug addicts*. Hopelessly addicted, so that despite all pleas and offers of counselling that had been offered to them they had continued on their dogged path to self-destruction. Indeed Willem and Julie had been high when Willem had crashed their car and then he and his wife had died. Flora remained amazed by the stroke of fate that had kept Mariska alive.

Although every attempt had been made to shield Angelo's privacy it had slowly become abundantly clear to Flora that Willem's stepbrother had been heavily involved from the outset in all attempts to persuade the young couple to enter a rehabilitation programme. He had also done everything that he could to protect his stepbrother's child from harm.

In recent months, Mariska had virtually never been left to rely on parental care alone. Either she had been in day care or in her nanny's care, and when Willem and Julie had partied and Anke had deemed her charge to be at risk she had taken Mariska to Angelo's home. Yet, even with all those safeguards in place, Flora's niece could still easily have been killed along with her parents when Julie had chosen to take her daughter out of day care early one afternoon without telling anyone and had got into Willem's car with her. Mariska's very survival was a small miracle.

A stiff late spring breeze gusted down the street of tall, narrow and highly ornamental buildings that bordered the canal Flora was walking alongside and her tears chilled on her cheeks. She stepped hurriedly out of the way of a cyclist riding past and sucked in a steadying breath while she paused to consult the map she had bought to help her negotiate the maze of streets.

It was an effort to think straight while she was being eaten alive by a great burst of angry resentment and regret. But her half-sister was gone and nothing could bring Julie back. Yet on whose say-so had Flora been excluded from knowing about and *trying* to help the young couple? Flora had a very strong suspicion about the identity of that culprit. While the social workers had been bound by rules of confidentiality, only Angelo van Zaal would have dared to leave Julie's one close relative in ignorance of her plight.

When she'd first moved to Amsterdam, Julie had sent her sister loads of photos, so now Flora had little difficulty picking out the bright blue-and-white-painted houseboat from the others moored on a quiet stretch of water overlooked by a picturesque terrace of gabled houses. After all, she had a framed sunlit picture of that same evocative scene sitting in her home. She stepped onto the deck and as she did so the door of the cabin opened, framing the tall black-haired male whose inexcusable silence over the past year had stoked her umbrage.

For an instant, Flora froze, her wide green eyes locking onto Angelo van Zaal. He looked strikingly elegant if out of place in his formality in a dark grey business suit and silk tie. The suit had the exclusive fit of a tailored designer garment, framing wide strong masculine shoulders and hugging lean hips and long muscular thighs. As he stepped outside the breeze ruffled his luxuriant black hair above his lean, darkly handsome features. The sheer impact of his physical charisma hit her like a sudden blow to the head, leaving her dizzy. She collided with sapphire-blue eyes and her tummy shimmied like a jelly while her breath feathered in her throat.

'What on earth are you doing here?' she demanded tautly.

'This seemed to be an opportune time and place to talk to you.'

'It's a little late for that now, isn't it?' Green eyes flashing as emerald as jewels in sunlight, Flora stalked past his tall still figure into the saloon of the houseboat. The spacious interior had a bare look, for all the surfaces were clear and a stack of cardboard boxes spread out from one corner. 'In fact I would say that talk of any kind between us now would be a waste of your valuable time.'

Unaccustomed to such a bold unapologetic attack, and with his handsome mouth in a sardonic line, Angelo studied her. Colourful copper-coloured hair falling in a lavish windblown cloud round her shoulders, Flora wore a short black trench coat, jeans and a green sweater, and even in that casual garb she looked amazing, he acknowledged with distinct reluctance. She had the transparent alabaster skin of the true redhead and soft pink self-conscious colour defined her cheekbones while he studied her, quietly marvelling at the amount of emotion she contrived to emanate even when she was silent. Trembling with the force of her fury, Flora undid her coat, dropped it down on a seat and spun back to face him.

'How could you not tell me what was going on here?' she demanded in ringing reproach. 'Willem and Julie were *my* family as well. At the very least I had a right to know that Julie was taking drugs!'

'She was an adult of twenty-one, Flora. She made her own choice, which was that under no circumstances were you to be told about their problems.'

Flora lifted her chin in challenge. 'Meaning?'

'Exactly what I said. I did speak to her and I know for a fact that her social worker urged her to confide in you, but your sister didn't want you to know that she had got caught up in drugs and I was not in a position to go against her wishes.'

'I don't believe that.' Flora dealt him a furious unimpressed look, convinced that he was simply trying to palm her off with excuses. 'You always do as you like, Angelo. You're a strong man. You're no one's whipping boy!'

'Believe me when I tell you that it was a huge struggle to keep the communication lines between me and Willem and Julie open. Their lifestyle was abhorrent to me but for their daughter's sake it was imperative that I still retained access to them,' Angelo retorted grimly. 'Had I gone against your sister's wishes they would no longer have trusted me and Mariska would have suffered...'

'So you got involved and I was left on the outside, kept in ignorance of what was happening in Willem and Julie's lives until it was too late,' Flora condemned with unconcealed bitterness.

'I made Mariska's needs my priority,' Angelo countered without apology. 'I did the best I could in a very difficult situation.'

'Well, the best you could wasn't good enough, was it?' Flora threw at him fierily, her temper rising again like steam inside a kettle as the sheer awfulness of what she had learned that morning bit into her like painful claws on tender flesh. 'Less than a year after Mariska's birth, your stepbrother and my sister are both dead and their child is an orphan!'

His superb bone structure rigid, Angelo surveyed her with cool ice-blue, astonishingly clear eyes set above the smooth olive planes of his handsome face. His eyes had the shockingly vivid clarity of a glacier lake she had once seen in the Alps, she thought absently. It struck her that so far nothing she had said had moved him in the slightest and his rigorous self-control seemed to mock her emotional state.

'Willem and Julie were a fatal combination,' Angelo murmured in a tone of flat finality. 'Willem was weak and troubled, and before they even met Julie was a habitual drug user.'

As the ramifications of that accusation sank in, shocking Flora all over again, she released a jagged laugh of disbelief. 'How dare you try to blame Julie for what happened to them? How dare you insinuate that she was the prime instigator?'

'I am telling you what I know to be the truth. I have no desire to malign your memory of your sister.'

Flora shot him an enraged glance, green eyes luminous as green glass on the seashore. 'Then don't do it.'

'I did not hurl the first stone,' Angelo countered levelly, his attention wandering to the way the fine wool sweater lovingly moulded the small pouting curves of her breasts and defined the slight bump of her prominent nipples. He suspected that she wasn't wearing a bra and the full taut sensation of heaviness at his groin increased as he imagined peeling off that sweater. It took enormous self-discipline to wrench his mind back from that erotic reverie and her ability to distract him without even trying to do so infuriated him.

'You could have told me that Willem and Julie had got involved in drugs!' Flora slung at him in a seething undertone, her eyes bright with antagonism and accusation. The growing tension in the atmosphere only put her more on edge. 'And you could have told me that I had to conceal where I got that information from.'

'As I've already said, when I was unable to persuade either Willem or his wife to stop using drugs or even to enter counselling, my main goal was to protect Mariska from their excesses.'

Flora snatched in an audible breath in an effort to calm her teeming emotions down to a more controllable level. She folded her arms tightly and crossed the floor, her slender spine stiff as a pencil. The dreadful compulsion to stare at him had her in its hold, though, for when she looked once she always had to look back at him again and admire his amazing bone structure, dazzling eyes and tall, powerful physique. That he could stun her even in the midst of a bitter argument outraged her sense of what was decent. In measured rejection she fixed her eyes on the view of the quiet canal beyond the window. 'It's so unfair that you're trying to foist the blame on Julie.'

'I am not trying to do that,' Angelo rebutted, his attention jerking away from the snug fit of her jeans over her heart-shaped derrière, for his imagination had really not required that added stimulus in her radius. His susceptibility to her every move around him galled him and gave him a disturbingly unfamiliar sense of being out of control. 'But I must be honest with you, even if you find that honesty offensive.'

'It is deeply offensive that you should accuse my sister of having been an habitual substance abuser,' Flora pointed out thinly, turning back to him for emphasis while her tongue slid out to moisten the dry curve of her lower lip.

'Even if I know that to be true?' Instantly engaged in picturing the effect of that small pink tongue tip on a highly sensitive part of his own anatomy, Angelo surveyed the sultry raspberry-tinted fullness of her mouth with driven concentration. She was making him feel ridiculously like a sex-starved adolescent boy and his hands clenched into defensive fists by his side.

'How could you possibly *know* such a thing to be true?' Flora flung in angry, scornful dismissal of that claim. She clashed head-on with his electrifyingly blue eyes, which might as well have been lit by tiny blue flames for she had the sensation of heat dancing over her entire skin surface. She flushed and her nipples tingled almost painfully while a scratchy sensation of warmth and awareness settled be-

tween her legs. In an uneasy movement, she shifted position off one foot on to the other.

'I know because I had Julie privately investigated before
she married Willem,' Angelo admitted with unapologetic
gravity. 'As a student in London your sister was running
with a druggie crowd and regularly took ecstasy and co-
caine. Even though she was pregnant she brought those
habits to Amsterdam with her and it wasn't long before
my stepbrother joined her and the two of them began to
experiment with heroin.'

As Angelo spoke Flora had fallen very still and her eyes
were very wide and dark with dismay. 'You had Julie investigated? There must be some mistake?'

'There was no mistake,' Angelo told her steadily, noticing how pale she had become, noting too how that pallor merely accentuated her bright copper hair and lustrous
green eyes. Even her prickly argumentative nature could
not detract from her considerable appeal. 'The report was
done by a reputable firm and it was very detailed. I'm
afraid that even as a teenager your sister was a heavy user
of recreational drugs—'

'It's not possible. When Julie was a student, she was living with me,' Flora confided, and her voice slowly trailed
away as she took that thought to its natural conclusion and
looked back in time, a sinking sensation forming in the
pit of her stomach.

Unfortunately, Julie had moved into Flora's flat and
started college during what was a very fraught period in
her older sister's life. Flora had had to put in very long
hours at work while being harassed by a bullying boss.
She had also been struggling to keep a demanding fiancé
happy and she had not been able to give her half-sister the
time and attention that she would have liked. Even so, she
valued her memories of their time together back then and
had seen nothing in Julie's behaviour that might have sug-

gested that there was anything seriously amiss in her life.
Certainly Julie had enjoyed a very active social calendar,
but then so did most students, Flora reasoned ruefully.
She did recall the very late hours the younger woman had
kept and Flora, who'd had to be at work early, had usually
been asleep by the time her sister came home. Julie had
also been very prone to changeable moods and staying in
bed all day at weekends, but that kind of behaviour could
surely be ascribed to many teenagers?

'If Julie took drugs in those days, and I'm not sure I
can accept that that could be true,' Flora breathed abruptly
and without warning discovered that her eyes were prickling with tears, 'I hadn't the slightest idea of what she was
up to.'

Angelo, who had a conscience as tough as the steel
his factories manufactured, saw moisture shimmer in her
beautiful green eyes and he closed the distance between
them without even being aware of a prompting to do so.
Bare inches away from her, he faltered to a halt and hovered, suddenly uncharacteristically uncertain of what to
do next because he was a man who had always walked the
other way or turned a blind eye when women got upset.
But he stared down into her tear-wet face and in an action
that felt ridiculously natural to him, but which was actually not at all his style, he reached for both her hands to
hold them firmly within his.

'Don't cry,' he told her urgently. 'Don't blame yourself
for this fiasco. Many well-intentioned and experienced
professionals tried and failed to help Willem and Julie.
Sometimes no matter what you do you can't change things.
What happened to them is in no way your fault.'

And Flora recognised his sincerity and finally accepted
that the sad tale he was telling her was indeed the truth as
he knew it. Guilt cut through her, though, like a knife as
her first thought was that she had failed her sister when

Julie had needed her most. While they'd been living together, she should have realised that Julie had problems
and watched over her more closely. She should have refused to accept the seemingly little white lies and excuses
that, even then, she had suspected her sibling was prone
to hiding behind and probed more deeply, asking the awkward prying questions that she had swallowed back for the
sake of peace. In those days, Flora had been afraid to tax
their new sibling bond by acting too much like a pseudo-
parental figure. And tragically that dangerous desire to
be liked and to seem younger and more hip had evidently
ensured that Julie had been free to take the first fatal steps
towards becoming a drug addict.

'Julie had such a h-horrible childhood!' Flora stammered chokily, unable to silence the words brimming to
her lips in her need to defend her late sister from the bad
opinion he must have formed of her. 'She used to see my
father out shopping in town with Mum and I and she had
to pretend she didn't know him, even though he was her
father as well. His affair with her mother, Sarah, was a
big secret and it meant that for years and years while Julie
was growing up she had to live a lie. That background left
scars, of course it did. She lived to be noticed, she craved
love and attention—'

'It's not your fault, *querida*. You were not her mother.
You had no control over her. What, realistically, could you
have done to change anything?' Angelo replied soothingly,
his dark deep drawl fracturing as he stared down into her
tear-bright green eyes.

That close to his lean, powerful body, Flora could smell
the distinctive scent of his skin, an intoxicating mixture
of citrus overlaying husky male, and as she drank in that
aroma it made her tremble. A little inner voice whispered
caution, warned her to step back and keep her distance
from him, but her feet might as well have been nailed to

the floor. She could feel herself beginning to lean forward, her attention locked to those unforgettable features of his, memorising the high line of his patrician cheekbones, the stubborn strength of his jaw and the arrogant jut of his classic nose. He drew her like a rock in a violent storm at sea.

He bent his proud dark head and parted her lips with his wide sensual mouth and it was as if she had been waiting all her life for that one kiss as it ran through her like a depth charge and struck deep in a sensual and potent explosion. Her hands flew up and clenched into his wide strong shoulders. It couldn't be him, she thought momentarily in wonderment, it couldn't *possibly* be Angelo van Zaal who was making her feel as though she were racing with her heart pounding on a wild roller-coaster ride. The pall of apprehensive isolation and loss that had dogged her since she had flown out to Amsterdam was suddenly banished.

One kiss led straight into the next and her fingers dug into his jacket for support to keep herself upright. Shaking, she felt a shudder rack his big powerful body against hers and she exulted in the hand he closed to her hip to press her into provocative contact with the hard swell of his erection. Something that had turned her off other men turned her on with him. The very knowledge that she aroused him went to Flora's head and because of what had happened in the past she gloried in that intoxicating proof of his masculine response to her. She was dizzy, exchanging feverish kisses while the passion exploded through her like a shot of brandy on an icy day. Heat sizzled through her veins and pooled low in her tummy. She discovered that she couldn't make herself let him go for long enough to catch her breath.

'You're wearing far too many clothes,' Angelo said thickly.

Flora looked up at him, revelling in the temperamental glimmer of stormy blue visible below his dense black lashes. She was amazed by the discovery that he was not one half as calm, cool and controlled as she had always believed. There was a wild hunger in that appraisal that gripped her imagination like a key to a locked door, promising her a glimpse of the unknown. Angelo was gorgeous, absolutely gorgeous, but until that heady moment of recognition he had always been a closed and forbidding book to her. Just then seeing him look at her as though she were the most desirable woman alive was balm to a self-esteem that had once been battered to pulp when the man she loved rejected her.

Her fingers slid from his shoulder down onto his shirt front, spreading starfish fashion on the muscular heat of his powerful chest. With a gruff sound in his throat his mouth swooped down on hers again with a dominant force that sent a primitive shiver of delight darting through her slender length. He pulled her back against him and eased a hand below her sweater to cup a small pouting mound topped by a swollen pink nipple. A gasp parted her lips below the marauding pressure of his mouth and his tongue darted deep in the moist interior. The effect of that driving passionate kiss, added to the effects of the blunt masculine fingers toying with the peaks of her breasts was more than she could bear and she sagged against him, her legs refusing to hold her up.

'Come here, *querida mia*,' Angelo growled, hauling her up into his arms without further ado and kissing her with passionate fervour...

CHAPTER THREE

THIRTY SECONDS LATER, Flora's lashes lifted. She was lying on a bed in a compact cabin. Her sweater had gone and, mortified by the sight of her bared breasts, she raised herself on her elbows ready to call time on the extraordinary event that was unfolding when she focused on Angelo.

He had already shed jacket and tie and his shirt hung open on a bronzed hair-roughened torso and the flat corrugated planes of his stomach. He looked amazing, every inch a male pin-up worthy of a centrefold. The oxygen Flora needed just vanished from her lungs without warning.

'How did this happen? We shouldn't be doing this...' she gasped breathlessly, suddenly thinking about the sister she had lost and mentally squirming away from that painful reminder to take refuge in the present again.

'*Dios mio*...don't ask me to stop, *querida*,' Angelo urged, blue eyes electrifyingly hot and hungry as they collided head-on with hers. 'I've never wanted any woman as much as I want you at this moment.'

Cheeks burning with self-consciousness, Flora hunched her shoulders and crossed her hands over her naked chest, embarrassed by the insubstantial size of her womanly curves, while her bemused thoughts were already replaying what he had just said. It shook her how good she felt being Angelo's object of desire and how much she liked the fact that he was unzipping his well-cut trousers with more haste than cool while seemingly unable to drag his gaze from her where she lay on the bed. In truth, she acknowledged in an instant of pure insight, any form of human contact and comfort eased the terrible bleak pain of the realization that she would never see her little sister again.

'You are so beautiful,' Angelo murmured in a dark deep voice that had a wonderfully distracting effect on her because she was desperate to avoid the desolate thoughts hovering on the horizon of her mind. 'I've wanted you for so long.'

'If you did you hid it well from me,' she pointed out helplessly.

'I've surrendered... I can't hide it any more.' Angelo stepped clear of the trousers and her mouth ran dry. Clad in silk boxers that defined more than they concealed, Angelo was an intimidating sight for a woman who was still a virgin. Of course that was not a truth that Flora was eager to brandish. Her lack of experience was more an accident of fate than a deliberate choice, for she had not got close enough to consider intimacy with anyone since her engagement had been broken off three years earlier.

'I'm not beautiful,' she told him almost defiantly, unwilling to trust him or any man.

Angelo suddenly smiled and his lean dark face lit up with a brilliance that made her heartbeat pick up speed as he came down beside her on the bed. 'I think you are and I'm only interested in my own opinion.'

When he smiled she felt as if she could fly, but Flora had no time for such fanciful thoughts and she was bone-deep stubborn, shrugging off the way he could make her feel to add in a tone of distinct challenge, 'I'm much too tall for a woman—'

'I'm tall and you're the perfect size for me,' Angelo countered, undaunted by her comeback as he joined her with predatory grace.

Men had always tended to find Flora too bluntly spoken for comfort but Angelo appeared to take that candour very much in his stride. He captured her hands in his so that she could no longer hide her body from him.

For a timeless moment she lay there while he caressed her wrists with his thumbs, his attention hotly pinned to the stiff crests of her prominent nipples. 'You have very pretty breasts,' he husked, intense blue eyes embellished by lush black lashes.

Embarrassment claimed her. She could not be comfortable lying there half naked in broad daylight. She shut her eyes tight and wondered what insanity had come over her and then he kissed her again and the insanity came back with a vengeance, blurring all rational thought and inhibition. Nothing had ever felt so sweet or so necessary to her as his mouth. His tongue plunged into the tender responsive interior of her mouth and lit her up inside like a fire. She had not known that much pleasure could exist in mere kissing.

Her hands sank into his black hair as he nibbled down the cord of her slender neck and began to centre his attentions on her swollen sensitive breasts. His tongue lashed over the tender tips before the graze of his teeth on her delicate flesh made her cry out and tremble while the burn of excitement travelled straight to the moist heat gathering at the heart of her body. He pressed the heel of his hand against the apex of her thighs and she writhed, helpless beneath that pleasure inflicted on the most sensitive part of her. She felt the zip give on her jeans, her hands falling from him as he sat up to remove the garment.

'This is crazy,' she muttered jaggedly, 'out of control.'

'I've never been out of control in bed before. It's exciting,' Angelo confided, pushing up her face with an impatient hand to steal another explosive kiss.

And when his hard, hungry mouth was sealed to hers, nothing mattered and nothing else existed. He cupped the damp crotch of her knickers and then whisked them off to explore the slick wet folds between her thighs. She was hyper-sensitive there and she dug her hips into the mattress beneath her and little sounds escaped her lips without her volition. Teasing the delicate entrance, he rubbed the tiny bud where all her nerve-endings centred. Drenched in exquisite waves of pleasure beyond any she had ever experienced, she became ever more frantic. A sense of pressure was building in her tummy and a pulsing ache stirred between her legs, making her feel unbearably taut and needy.

Angelo slid between her thighs. She looked up at him with apprehensive green eyes, reacting to the probing feel of him against her most intimate place. He shifted and sank into her, stretching her hot tight channel with his girth and length. His hungry growl of pleasure masked her hastily swallowed huff of pain as he thrust past her resisting flesh and filled her to the hilt.

'You're so tight you feel incredible,' Angelo groaned, blue eyes radiating deep sensual satisfaction as he gripped her hips in hard hands and moved slowly and erotically, acquainting her with the full extent of his power.

Instinct made her arch her spine and rise up as he withdrew and slammed back into her in a pagan rhythm that made her every sense sing. Her body wasn't her own any more. Invaded and controlled by his driving urgency and her own need to answer its demands, she was overwhelmed by the thunderously exciting rise of pleasure. The pressure built and built to a nerve-racking high inside her. She squirmed and writhed in the last seconds before an explosive orgasm ripped through her trembling body like an earthquake, sending sweet shards of ecstatic pleasure shooting through every limb.

Afterwards she was drained and wrapped in a cocoon of exhaustion. He gazed down at her, blue eyes shimmering, and he kissed her again, slow and deep and hungry.

Hungry? He was ready to do *it* again. She wasn't and was taken aback by his energy. Animation was returning to her brain and suddenly she wanted a magic lamp to rub so that she could leap fully clothed onto the quay beyond the window and run away as fast as her cowardly legs could carry her. What was she doing? Oh, what had she done, *what... had...she...done?* Bewilderment and shame drenched her in a tidal wave of regret. Her arms were wrapped tightly round him and she whipped them off him at supersonic speed and jerked free of his embrace.

'I've got to go,' she told him shakily. 'Places to go, people to see.'

Wincing at that airhead announcement even as it fell from her lips, Flora scrambled off the bed with a haste she couldn't hide.

Startled by her abrupt flight from his arms, Angelo pushed himself up on his elbows and rested frowning dark blue eyes on her. 'What's up?'

Stark naked, wreathed in blushes and with not the smallest idea where the bathroom was, Flora hovered in horrible confusion. What's up? she almost screeched back at him. Are you that insensitive that you think this situation, this appalling misstep, could possibly be acceptable?

'This should never, ever have happened. I'm embarrassed!' Flora gasped, reckoning he needed it all spelled out in simple words so that he could understand normal human reactions.

'Why should you be embarrassed? What we just shared was amazingly good sex,' Angelo commented thickly, pushing his powerful bronzed shoulders back against the tossed pillows and surveying her with deeply appreciative sapphire-blue eyes. 'Come back to bed.'

Every bit of Flora that wasn't already blushing took on a scarlet hue. *Come back to bed?* Whoever had said that men had a one-track mind had not been joking! Through an open door she espied something that looked reassuringly like a plumbing fixture and she sped towards it without further ado, only to discover that she was in what appeared to be a closet lined with pipes.

The door opened. Angelo looked in at her, alarmingly tall and broad and graphic in the nude. 'The bathroom is across the passage.'

Her hands knotted into fists. She was so upset she marvelled that she wasn't having a heart attack. On the way past the bed again she bent to scoop up her discarded clothes, trying not to wince at the soreness lingering between her thighs. Her first sex ever and she wanted to forget it, she thought in anguish. In the tiny bathroom she washed as best she could. There were no towels, just as there had been no bedding. She had rolled about on a bare mattress with Angelo van Zaal like a cheap slut and the mortification of that unacceptable fact bit deep.

A knock sounded on the door and she opened it a reluctant crack. 'Yes?'

'I have a country house. I'd like you to spend the weekend there with me,' Angelo suggested smoothly.

'Was the sex *that* good?' Flora enquired in a frozen voice that would have chilled a polar bear.

'I don't do one-night stands,' Angelo drawled softly.

Flora was getting desperate. 'Why don't you just go back to your office or whatever and leave me here?'

'We'll talk when you come out.' There was just the hint of a rougher edge to his tone as if he was finally accepting that she didn't even want to speak to him, never mind look at him, after the intimacy they had shared.

At least Angelo hadn't guessed that she had been a virgin until he touched her, Flora reflected wretchedly as she struggled back into her crumpled clothing in the confined space. Somehow the thought of Angelo van Zaal, with his stable of glossy, sophisticated supermodel girlfriends, learning that she had been a sad twenty-six-year-old virgin struck her as the final humiliation. He would think she had been desperate for a man to show an interest in her and that wasn't how she was at all. Flora just didn't have a very high opinion of men and didn't think that a man was always necessary to a happy life. After her broken engagement she had stopped dating and had concentrated her energy on rebuilding her life.

As she emerged from the compartment Angelo appeared in the bedroom doorway to direct her back upstairs. She recalled him carrying her to bed and kissing her every step of the way and her pale skin flushed a deep rosy pink. How on earth could she have behaved that way? She was a very private person and she had standards, strict standards. Casual sex was anathema to her and what for him had probably just featured as an excitingly unexpected roll between the sheets with an almost stranger meant a great deal more to her in terms of pride and self-respect.

Angelo watched Flora dig her feet into her shoes and reach for her coat. She was behaving as if she could not get away from him quickly enough, a reaction very far removed from what he usually received from women in the aftermath of intimacy, and her unashamedly dismissive attitude set his even white teeth on edge.

At the same time an unusual sense of dislocation was assailing Angelo, as if his world had suddenly been turned upside down and everything felt wrong and out of place. In the circumstances, it was hardly surprising that Angelo, always so in control of events and of himself, was in deep shock. He had, after all, just engaged in unprotected sex for the first time in his life. Even the awareness that he did not have a condom had failed to stop him in his tracks. He had gone way beyond the age when he always carried protection, for not since he'd been a teenager had he engaged in an impetuous sexual encounter. Yet he had knowingly accepted the risk he was running and had found Flora so irresistible that he had taken her regardless of all common sense. Those acknowledgements shattered many of the convictions Angelo had long held about his own character. What the hell had come over him?

'Are you using any form of contraception?' Angelo asked flatly.

Flora's head flew up, green eyes unguarded and full of dismay as she frowned, following that question back to its logical source only to register that neither of them had considered that possibility at the time. 'No, I'm not… Are you saying that—?'

'This—what just transpired between us,' Angelo extended with a shift of fluid brown hands that was very Mediterranean and non-verbally eloquent, reminding Flora that her sister had once mentioned that he had had a Spanish mother. 'It was out of character for me.'

'And for me,' Flora muttered numbly, tying the belt on her coat and pulling it tighter than was comfortable, desperately needing to keep her hands busy.

'I didn't stop to think of consequences. We had sex without protection, which was very foolish of both of us. However, I have regular health checks and you need have no fear of disease. *But*—'

Flora was already settling aghast eyes on him and she said shakily before he could continue, 'Obviously there's still a risk that you might have got me pregnant.'

'Let's try to be optimistic. We only had sex once and for all that we know one of us could even be infertile. We'll have to hope that the odds are in our favour,' Angelo breathed with deliberate cool, convinced that since he had never before tempted fate he would surely get away with it. He refused to even consider the alternative because messy situations like unplanned pregnancies had no place in his perfectly organised life.

Flora was stunned by his optimistic outlook, for she was much more prone to worrying that any moral mistake automatically attracted a punishment.

'As it's obvious that you don't want me to stay,' Angelo remarked silkily, one lean brown hand resting on the door, 'I'll leave you here to sort through those boxes.'

Flora had dug her hands into her pockets. 'Right. Okay,' she said awkwardly. 'I'd like to see Mariska again before I leave Amsterdam.'

Cool blue eyes rested on her anxious face. 'You're welcome to visit her whenever you like.' He reached into his pocket to withdraw a pen and write on the back of a business card. 'This is my home telephone number if you want to make arrangements with Anke.'

Flora studied the card he handed her with fixed attention, reluctant to look at him again. The atmosphere was so raw with unspoken tension that it squeezed at her nerves and her ability to breathe normally.

'I'll be in touch,' Angelo drawled.

Immediately, Flora braved her demons to glance up at him. 'That's not necessary,' she told him woodenly.

'We need to stay in contact for Mariska's sake,' Angelo contradicted. 'I will also seek reassurance that you are not pregnant. When will you know?'

Flora reddened at that very personal question. 'Mind your own business!'

Angelo dealt her a stony look shot through with reinforced steel. 'If you conceive my child, it will be very much my business, *querida*.'

As soon as he was gone, having told her where to leave the key when she was finished, Flora shed her coat again and embarked on the first box. Mariska in mind, she set Julie's diaries and photographs to one side along with a rather battered teddy that her sister had once kept on her bed. There was not much else to be conserved aside from a few cards exchanged between Willem and Julie and some inexpensive costume jewellery that she thought her niece might one day like to look at. She studied the photo of Willem and Julie on their wedding day, so young, so happy and full of innocent hope, and a flood of tears overwhelmed her. She wept until she was empty, and although her throat was sore afterwards, she felt much better for having vented her emotions. She then made use of the phone number that Angelo had given her and organised a time to visit that afternoon and see Mariska.

In the little bathroom she splashed her swollen eyes with cold water and thought she looked an absolute sight. She still could barely credit that she had had sex with Angelo van Zaal. Were there more of her sexually adventurous father's genes in her than she had ever realised? She would not let herself use the euphemism 'making love', for she was still hard pressed to explain exactly how she had ended up on that bed with Angelo, engaging in the intimacies she had avoided sharing with other men. While she had always experienced a strong buzz of attraction in Angelo's radius, it had never occurred to her that it might have the power to get so out of hand. Evidently all it had taken was for her emotions to get equally out of kilter for the proverbial weak moment to have made nonsense of her moral outlook on life.

She had dropped her guard while she had sought forgetfulness from the unhappy present. Even worse, she had become intimate with a man she didn't even like, a man who had always held her at arm's length and treated her with cool indifference. No matter how she looked at what had happened she felt that she had let herself down badly and could not imagine ever meeting Angelo van Zaal again without suffering severe embarrassment.

Clutching a laden bag of keepsakes, she climbed on board a tram and found a seat. The busy streets whirred past while she tried not to think about how different Angelo had seemed once he brought the barriers crashing down by kissing her. So open, so apparently honest. *So, you're really beautiful, are you?* an unimpressed little voice jeered in her head and she went pink and laced her fingers defensively together. It would be much wiser just to put all those inappropriate memories in a mental box and put them firmly away, she decided with a hearty sense of relief at having seen that obvious solution to her mental discomfiture.

How great a risk was there, though, that she might fall pregnant? Flora did the little sums with the menstrual dates that she had refused to share with Angelo and suppressed a troubled sigh of concern, for there was no comfort to be found in those figures. Their accident, if accident it could be called, had occurred squarely in the middle of her most fertile phase. She could only pray that she would not conceive, although even that thought felt strange to a woman already engaged in an application to adopt her baby niece.

But what were her chances of success on that score? Her reddened mouth curved down. She had embarked on her adoption plans with high hopes, secure in the knowledge that she was Mariska's only surviving relative and ignorant of the fact that Angelo might also cherish a desire to adopt Willem and Julie's daughter. And Angelo, she reckoned unhappily, was going to be much stiffer competition in the adoption stakes than she had ever dreamt, because he had been engaged in looking out for Mariska ever since she was born and had already established a record of consistent care where the little girl was concerned. Nobody seemed the least bit worried that he was an unmarried single man, which she supposed was only fair considering that she was an unmarried single woman with only her time as a qualified childminder to back her application.

Furthermore it would take months for her adoption application to be properly checked out and considered and, in the meantime, Angelo had custody of her niece. Mariska would naturally become more settled in his home and more attached to him. Flora did not think her chances of winning custody of the tot from Angelo were good and the acknowledgement filled her with deep sadness. Unaware of Angelo's claim previously, she had naively believed that there would be no barrier to her bringing little Mariska straight back home to Charlbury St Helens with her.

Mariska greeted her aunt with smiles and chuckles and lifted her mood. What remained of the afternoon passed away and Anke suggested that Flora join them for their evening meal and remain until the little girl's bedtime. Once she realised that she would not be eating with Angelo as well, Flora was grateful for the invitation to extend her stay. They had a light meal in the nursery and Flora had a lot of fun helping to bath her niece and prepare her for bed. At one stage as she towelled Mariska dry and the little girl succumbed to helpless giggles she looked down into her little face and saw her sister's delicate blonde, blue-eyed prettiness replicated there. For an instant her eyes filled with tears again and as she carefully got her emotions back under control she finally appreciated how terribly tired she was. Once the little girl was tucked up in her cot, Flora put her coat on and headed for the stairs.

'Good evening, Flora. I didn't realise that you were still in the house,' Angelo imparted, emerging from a door off the imposing landing and taking her uncomfortably by surprise. Garbed in an elegant dinner jacket, black hair spiky and damp above his lean, darkly handsome face, he looked stunningly handsome and well groomed.

Hugely disturbed by the unexpected encounter, Flora met his brilliant blue dark-lashed eyes and felt as though she had fallen on an electric fence to be fried. Disquiet ricocheted through her slim length, her cheeks hollowing, her soft full lips compressing with tension. 'I'm afraid I stayed as long as I could with Mariska because I'm leaving tomorrow, but now I'm absolutely bushed.'

'My driver will take you back to your hotel,' Angelo cut in smoothly.

'But I don't need...'

'I *insist*,' Angelo incised without hesitation. 'You look exhausted.'

Flora was not best pleased to be told that she looked less than her best. It did not have quite the same flattering ring as the 'beautiful' compliment had had, she reflected wryly. Nor did she like Angelo insisting anything in that dominant tone of voice that seemed to come so naturally to him. But as she parted her lips to argue the point, she belatedly realised that they were not alone.

A platinum-blonde dark-eyed woman in a very smart sleeveless white cocktail frock with a glittering diamond pendant at her throat was standing in the hall and clearly waiting on Angelo. He introduced Flora to the other woman with effortless courtesy, and Flora wondered what it would actually take to embarrass him for as far as she could see he was not even slightly ruffled by the need to make that introduction. Was Bregitta Etten his current girlfriend? When Angelo had slept with Flora earlier that day had he been unfaithful to this other woman? Or was Bregitta merely one of the endless parade of eager females in Angelo's life whom Julie had scornfully mentioned? Her sister had made it clear that Angelo was an unabashed womaniser who made the most of his freedom and Flora could only wish now that she had paid more heed to the warning and learned to be more cautious around him.

While Angelo organised Flora's lift back to the hotel, the very beautiful blonde rested possessive stroking fingers on his arm. Flora discovered that she would very much have liked to slap that hand away from him and was horribly shocked by that instant in which she reacted like a jealous cat who wanted to scratch. Frozen several feet away from the couple, she avoided making eye contact and left the house at speed when a sleek four-wheel-drive car drew up at the front steps and the driver climbed out to open the passenger door.

'I'll phone you,' Angelo informed her calmly.

Flora turned mutinous eyes to his lean strong face and the challenge she saw there, but she was all too conscious of Bregitta's curious gaze and she forced a casual smile and a nod before climbing into the waiting car...

CHAPTER FOUR

FLORA ARRIVED HOME the following afternoon and barely paused for breath before she headed round to Charlbury St Helens' veterinary surgery, which also accommodated a small boarding kennels, to pick up her pets.

Jess Martin, the youngest and newest vet to join the practice, who also lived on the premises, greeted her in the reception area. A small curvaceous brunette, Jess organised Flora's bill while the nurse went to fetch the animals from the kennels at the back. Skipper, a tiny black and white Jack Russell with more personality than size, raced out, his lead trailing, and hurled his stocky little body frantically at Flora's legs. Mango the cat, a magnificent black tom of imposing size, was in his box and steadfastly ignoring his mistress. He always sulked when she returned after leaving him.

'All present and correct,' Jess remarked, and then with a concerned look in her unusually light grey eyes, for she knew why Flora had had to board her pets at such short notice, she added, 'How are you? How was it over there?'

Flora grimaced and for a moment in receipt of that sympathetic look she did not trust herself to speak. 'I managed.'

'And your niece?' Jess asked eagerly. 'Have you got her out in the car?'

'I'm afraid it's not going to be that simple. There are quite a few legal formalities to be got through first,' Flora confided ruefully. '*And* Willem's brother, Angelo, has custody of Mariska at the minute and he's applying to adopt her as well…'

Jess looked surprised. 'But isn't he single?'

'So am I,' Flora pointed out wryly. 'And he's had a lot more contact with my niece than I've had.'

'But you'd make a terrific mother.' Jess chose to concentrate on the most positive angle. 'I've been told you were sadly missed locally when you stopped childminding and went into the bed-and-breakfast business instead.'

Her detached house, which Flora had inherited from the great-aunt she had been named after, was set back well from the road and was sheltered from the pretty village green by mature trees. Tourists loved the village of Charlbury St Helens and Flora's guest-house business kept her very busy indeed. When her rooms were fully booked she often employed Jess Martin's mother, Sharon, to help her out. As Skipper raced down the back garden to acquaint himself with all his favourite places and Mango the cat stalked out to settle on the patio to sunbathe, Flora tried not to think about whether or not she was ever going to get the chance to bring Mariska home to England with her.

And what if you have fallen pregnant? an anxious little voice whispered at the back of her mind and all the worry that she had tried to suppress shot through her taut length like a gunshot piercing tender flesh. It would be ten days at least before she would know either way, so there was no point working herself up into a state over the issue, she told herself firmly. But Flora was still so angry with herself about what had happened in Amsterdam that she was unable to shake free of her inner turmoil.

Once she had believed that sex should be very much part of love and that it should never be separate from it; that conviction had happily guided her through the five years she had spent dating Peter, whom she had met at university and planned to marry. When Peter had dumped her after the employment tribunal, without ever having slept with her, everything that Flora had once believed in had begun to fall apart. She had wanted to believe that she and Peter were the perfect couple but had learnt the hard way that they were not. Over time, his indisputable lack of sexual interest had battered her self-esteem almost beyond hope of recall and she had switched off as far as men were concerned, too scared of being hurt and humiliated again to take a second chance on finding love.

But, in many ways, Flora had been scarred almost as much by her own childhood as by Peter, for she had never been able to forget her mother's heartbreak or her father's constant self-serving lies and deceptions. Love had almost destroyed her mother, who had suffered several episodes of serious depression before she could finally work up the strength to build a new life without her unfaithful husband. And sadly, Flora recalled wistfully, her loving mother had only lived eighteen short months after embarking on that valiant fresh start.

Yet her mother had never stopped believing in true love and commitment. So, *how*, Flora asked herself painfully, could she have contrived to have lost her virginity to Angelo van Zaal? He hadn't even realised he was her first lover either. She had nothing in common with him. He was a man who had yet to take any woman seriously and he had offered her no promises or reassurances. Yet neither of those very sensible points had mattered once he kissed her. His kisses had burned through her like a forest fire, reducing her long-cherished convictions to ashes.

She had reached the mature age of twenty-six without realising just how vulnerable she might be with the wrong man. And Angelo was decidedly the wrong man. He was a very wealthy and sophisticated tycoon and at heart he was as cold as ice. But if that was true why was he offering to give Willem's daughter a home? Mariska was not even related to him by blood, Flora conceded ruefully, torn in opposing directions and disturbed by the bits that didn't add up in her view of him. To be fair to him he had looked out for the little girl's interests from birth. Seemingly he had also done his utmost to help Willem and Julie. Evidently Angelo had a strong streak of family loyalty and an active social conscience but neither trait made her feel any more comfortable about having shared the greatest act of intimacy there was with him.

FOUR DAYS LATER, Angelo phoned Flora.

'Why are you calling?' she demanded sharply.

'You're phoning my house daily but contriving not to speak to me,' Angelo returned in a mocking reminder.

Flora went pink because when she rang Amsterdam she always asked to speak to Anke. 'I didn't think you'd want to be personally involved in giving me regular bulletins on Mariska.'

'Are you always this prickly with men?' Angelo drawled silkily.

'I'm *not* prickly!' Flora snapped, her knuckles showing white as she gripped the phone tight with angry fingers, her stretched-tight control snapping at that fire-raising crack. Even his intonation set her teeth on edge. 'I assume you're calling to ask if I have any news yet on the pregnancy front and the answer is, sorry, no. I'll have a better idea by the end of next week.'

'So, we're only allowed to talk if there's bad news?'

At her end of the phone, Flora pulled a face. 'You said it—'

'For the benefit of your niece in the future, it would be sensible for us to establish a cordial relationship.'

Flora stiffened and reddened as if he had slapped her on the wrist for bad behaviour. Her teeth gritted because it was far from being the first time that Angelo van Zaal had managed to make her feel like a disruptive and rude child. Nor did she relish the obvious fact that Angelo remained confident that he would win the adoption competition. 'You should have thought of that in Amsterdam and kept your hands off me!' she snapped before she could think better of being that honest with him.

'Pot...kettle...black,' Angelo pronounced, deadpan.

And Flora was downright amazed that the violent jolt of rage that rocked her at that ruthless retaliation didn't send her screaming into orbit. A lengthy silence stretched at her end of the line as she struggled with her temper. 'I don't think we have anything more to say to each other right now,' she breathed shakily, before she set the phone down hastily lest she forget herself entirely and screech back at him like a virago.

Please, please, *please* don't let me be pregnant by him, she prayed in a frantic, feverish surge. Although at least he had been frank enough to admit that such an announcement would be 'bad news'. Yet that fact ironically only made Flora's heart sink, for she knew that if she conceived he would be anything but pleased and in even thinking that thought she felt that she was being unfair to him. After all, what rational man or woman wanted to conceive a child outside the bounds of a serious relationship? But, equally, how could she have put herself in the position of waiting to see whether or not she would fall pregnant from a casual sexual encounter? That very acknowledgement drenched her in hot shame.

Yet she could not possibly explain why her mind should immediately leap from that thought to a stirring recollection of her hands sweeping up over Angelo's muscular hair-roughened torso. Yes, he had had strong grounds for his retaliation, for she *had* found it equally impossible to keep her hands off him that afternoon.

The week that followed was very stressful for Flora.

Local education colleges were staging open days and all the accommodation for miles around was filled with parents and would-be students. Flora's five rooms were fully booked and Sharon came in every day to help with the cleaning and changing of bedding as well as the breakfast rush. Every night Flora fell into bed much too tired to lie awake worrying. But when the end of the week arrived she was suddenly fiercely and anxiously aware that unusually her menstrual cycle was exhibiting definite signs of being disrupted. She wondered if stress could be making her late. The next day, she woke at noon on the decision that, without further ado, she would head for the nearest pharmacy to purchase a pregnancy test. That decided, however, she was barefoot and still in her pyjamas when her doorbell rang in a shrill burst.

Having assumed it was the lady who delivered the mail, Flora flung open the door with scant ceremony and with a piece of jam-spread toast still clutched in one hand. She was aghast to see Angelo and stared at him much as she might have stared at an alien had he dropped out of the sky onto her doorstep.

Angelo studied her with narrowed shimmering blue eyes. The faded blue cotton pyjamas and bare feet made her look very young and, taken by surprise, her eyes shone green as precious jade against her rosy complexion.

'What on earth are you doing here?' Flora questioned in a rush of dismay. 'Oh, my goodness, Mariska is all right, isn't she?'

'Mariska is fine,' Angelo murmured quietly. 'I'm more concerned right now about you.'

'I'm concerned about me too…but you didn't need to come all the way from the Netherlands to check up on me,' Flora assured him in a surge of disbelief.

'I was already coming to the UK on business. I had a meeting in London early this morning,' Angelo responded deflatingly. 'Are you planning to invite me into your home?'

Flora hesitated, reluctant to bring him into her private space, much preferring to keep him outside.

Angelo dealt her a shrewd appraisal and murmured with silken derision, 'What age are you? Twenty-six years old, or sixteen?'

'Is it my fault that you get on my nerves? I mean, at the very least you might have warned me that you were planning to visit!' Flora complained heatedly, making no attempt to hide her resentment as she stepped back reluctantly to allow him into the hall.

A little black and white terrier barked frantically at Angelo from a doorway. He wasn't accustomed to indoor animals in any of his phenomenally clean and smoothly run homes, so he ignored it. Even though the dog made an attempt to nip at his trouser legs, Flora patted it soothingly and rewarded the little animal with the toast in her hand. While idly wondering if a successful bite that drew blood would have won a second piece of toast and an all-out hug, Angelo frowned until he noted the way her clingy top rose to expose the smooth white skin of her hip and the curve of her bottom when she bent down. He had a sudden startling recollection of her pale slender body spread across that mattress on the houseboat and his big hands clenched in defiance of that image as he fought off the insidious arousal tugging at him.

'Would you like coffee?' Flora enquired, striving to employ the good manners she had been raised with.

'We haven't got time for that. You need to get dressed… and quickly,' Angelo asserted, shrugging back his cuff to check the slim gold watch on his wrist.

Flora frowned, alarmingly conscious of the manner in which his beautiful sapphire-blue eyes lingered on her and of the lack of clothing she wore. She had never met any other man with such a powerfully sexual aura and she seriously hoped that she never did again. 'What the heck are you talking about? We haven't got time for...*what*?'

'A conversation or an argument,' Angelo responded drily. 'I've made an appointment for you with a London obstetrician and getting there on time will be a challenge.'

Her wide green eyes rounded in sheer disbelief. 'You've done *what*?' she gasped. 'Made an appointment for *me* with an *obstetrician*?'

'I'm done with hanging around waiting to find out whether or not you're pregnant,' Angelo spelt out with forthright cool, his stubborn jaw line squaring in emphasis. 'I'm assured that testing can safely be done at the earliest stage.'

Flora's lower lip had parted company from her upper because she was still shell shocked by his announcement. 'I can't believe you've got the nerve to do this to me!'

'*Por Dios,* I was waiting for you to take care of the issue and so far you haven't. Clearly it was time for me to step in.'

'No, it wasn't, you interfering...louse!' Flora clenched her teeth and swallowed a worse word while her eyes glowed with angry condemnation. 'For your information, I was planning to go out and buy a pregnancy test today...'

'I would prefer medical personnel to carry out the testing. There'll be a smaller margin for error,' Angelo pronounced stonily, standing his ground, black-lashed stunning blue eyes bright with challenge. 'If you've conceived, the sooner we know it, the better.'

Colour had already suffused Flora's cheeks. 'I'm not volunteering to be examined by some strange medic.'

'Natalie is an excellent doctor and she will be discreet. We need to know where we stand without any further delay.'

'How *dare* you meddle in my life like this?' Flora

launched at him fierily and she stalked past him to take the stairs two at a time. 'I really can't stand you, Angelo!'

'But you still wouldn't kick me out of bed, *enamorada mia*,' Angelo murmured silkily.

Flora spun back to look at him, outrage roaring through her while on another level she wondered what those Spanish words meant.

'The truth hurts, doesn't it?' Angelo breathed with raw-edged confidence, reading her resentful expression with alarming accuracy. 'It's good to know that I'm not the only one suffering.'

Flora stiffened and veiled her gaze in a defensive move, but it was too late for self-protection because his lean bronzed features were already etched in her mind's eye to ensure that every inch of her was insanely aware of him. Whether waking or sleeping, she saw Angelo van Zaal in her dreams. And it seemed that even when they were arguing the hunger he could invoke stayed in the ascendant, for her breasts were swelling, the tender nipples tightening while the heat of sexual response was simmering low in her pelvis.

'We need to know what we're dealing with,' Angelo reasoned with scantily suppressed impatience.

'But this is my body,' Flora pointed out.

'I would very much appreciate it if you would consent to see the doctor today,' Angelo intoned between audibly gritted teeth.

'You are so unspeakably bossy!' Flora complained as she turned on her heel to complete her passage upstairs to her bedroom. She was furious that she was too sensible to refuse to attend the appointment just to make a point.

Angelo stepped back into the living room and realised that what he had taken for a giant furry and rather messy cushion was an obese black cat. The animal got up to prowl round his feet and then nudged up against him in a clumsy bid for attention. Already ill at ease in a cramped room overfilled with furniture and now under assault from the suddenly excessively affectionate cat, Angelo swore impatiently under his breath. The undersized dog was growling and baring its teeth at him from below the coffee table. Not a heroic beast, it was carefully maintaining cover and a safe distance from him.

Why did Flora Bennett have to argue with everything he did and said? She was intelligent enough to know that his having organised that appointment for her made sound sense, but still she would insist on forcing a confrontation over it. As for him being bossy? His lean, strong face hardened, his wide, sensual mouth twisting. It was his nature to take charge, and a wise move when he was very often the most intelligent and decisive individual in the vicinity. Naturally he needed to know whether or not she had conceived his child.

And if she had? That was one question that Angelo refused to tackle in advance. After all, she was not at all the sort of woman whom he would have chosen to bring his first child into the world. No, she was very far from being the *right* sort, he reflected grimly, his lean, darkly handsome face settling into forbidding lines of censure. Having had a sleazy affair with her married boss three years ago, Flora Bennett had then proceeded to try and blackmail her lover into giving her an undeserved financial bonus. No revelation in her history could have filled Angelo with greater contempt, for he too had been targeted in the office by ambitious female employees keen to advance their careers by offering him sexual favours. In his experience it was clever women like Flora who were often the most calculating and greedy as well as being the most dangerous.

FLORA GOT DRESSED in a hurry. She picked out a simple denim miniskirt to wear with a striped top and a cotton cardigan and slid her feet into high-heeled sandals. She ran a brush through her hair to fluff it up and steadfastly ignored Angelo's shout up the stairs while she utilised her brown eyeliner and mascara and skimmed a sultry cherry colour over her lips.

'I'm on my way!' she yelled, speeding down the stairs.

Fuming at the amount of time she had wasted, Angelo paced in the hall and then, hearing her descent, swung fluidly round, only to tense at the sight of those endless long legs and slender thighs. 'That's a very short skirt,' he heard himself remark stiffly.

'No, it's not. I don't wear *very* short skirts—I just happen to have *very* long legs!' Flora snapped defensively.

Angelo found that unnecessary information, for he was already imagining those limbs wrapped round his waist again and his all-too-male body was reacting accordingly. So hard and full of repressed lust that he physically hurt, he swallowed back a curse and yanked open the front door. 'Come on,' he urged curtly.

Flora was taken aback to find a chauffeur-driven limo awaiting them on the street. She climbed into the very spacious interior and watched without surprise as Angelo flipped out a laptop to work on and proceeded to ignore her. Telling herself that she was relieved by his business-like attitude, she lifted the English newspaper lying on the seat and proceeded to read it. As she read Angelo proved what a dynamo of business energy he was while he made and received calls in more than one language and rapped out commands and advice to various underlings. Listening to the level of innate authority and conviction with which he spoke, Flora was not at all surprised that she was seated in his limo speeding towards an appointment that he had arranged for her. It would take a very tough and obstinate woman to stand up to a male as determined as Angelo van

Zaal, but she was convinced that she had the backbone if he pushed her hard enough.

It was late afternoon by the time they arrived at Dr Natalie Ellwood's smart private surgery in an upmarket part of central London. Flora sat edgily in the waiting room while Angelo continued to do business, just as he had during the journey. If someone had warned her that there was about to be a flood she would have left him to drown with his mobile phone still clutched in his hand. She had met some obsessively hard workers in her time, but Angelo van Zaal was in a class of his own. Mariska's would-be adoptive father was an unashamed workaholic.

'Angelo!' An elegant brunette in a beautifully cut trouser suit emerged wreathed in smiles and swam up to Angelo to kiss him effusively on both cheeks.

'Flora. This is Dr Ellwood. Natalie, your new patient,' Angelo drawled smoothly.

'Have you known Angelo for long?' Natalie asked Flora as she showed her into her surgery.

'No, not for long. You?' Flora could not resist asking, although she had noticed that the brunette wore a wedding ring.

'Oh, for ever. We went to university together. He's one of my oldest friends,' Natalie carolled with enthusiasm, her brown eyes resting on Flora with a bright questioning curiosity that she couldn't hide.

During the period that followed, Flora was examined and subjected to several tests. Natalie and her nurse were very pleasant. Finally, Flora sat down to face the doctor across her desk. 'Well?' she pressed nervously.

'Yes, I can confirm that you are pregnant.'

Flora lost colour. 'Are you absolutely certain?'

'Yes, I am. Is this an unintentional conception?' the brunette doctor asked delicately.

Flora was too much in shock to do anything other than

nod like a rather vacant puppet. *Pregnant!* And by Angelo van Zaal! Dry-mouthed and on wobbly legs, she indicated that she did not wish to discuss the matter further and she returned to the waiting area where Angelo was engaged on yet another phone call, this time in French. Snatches of dialogue about defective materials and an inefficient supplier buzzed in and out of her head while her dazed green gaze sought out his. She encountered brilliant blue eyes of cool enquiry and stared at him with some of the shocked disbelief she was experiencing. She registered the exact moment that he realised what news she had just received because he said something curiously indistinct for a change and, lowering his phone and ending the call, he sprang restively upright.

Every time they met she forgot how tall Angelo was until he stood beside her and she was forced to look up at him, a necessity that rarely came her way, particularly not when she was sporting high heels. For a split second her mind wandered and she recalled how Peter, who had been the same height as her, had hated her to wear heels and stand taller than him.

'You're so tall for a woman,' his mother had once re-marked with a raised brow, as if a woman being so tall was somehow in the poorest possible taste.

But then so many men preferred their women to be petite and delicate in stature, Flora reflected helplessly, thinking of how popular her sister, Julie, and her friend, Jemima, had invariably been with men. Being little was generally seen as cute and appealing. Being tall was some-how viewed as being less feminine and desirable.

'Let's go,' Angelo urged, his hand curving to Flora's rigid spine. His beautiful sapphire-blue eyes had a stunned quality before he lowered his ridiculously lush black lashes to conceal his expression.

'So you're not quite as lucky as you think you are and,

apparently, neither of us is infertile,' Flora remarked drolly on the way out onto the street.

'We'll discuss this in private,' Angelo pronounced crushingly.

'It's all right to be shocked,' Flora told him helplessly. 'I'm shocked as well.'

But unlike Flora, Angelo wasn't used to being shocked or put into a situation in which he was not in control of events. Suddenly, he appreciated, his life was yoked to Flora Bennett's whether he liked it or not. That was, assuming she planned to *have* his child. He swallowed back his questions and chose silence while he marshalled his thoughts.

In a world of her own, Flora sat in the limousine, struggling to adjust to the startling concept that in nine months' time she would become a mother. Her brain reminded her that there were other options that ranged from adoption to termination. The prospect of having to make either tough choice filled Flora with instinctive recoil. Eighteen months earlier, her sister had refused to consider any option other than giving birth to and keeping her child. But then Julie had been in love with Willem and he had been very much involved in that decision.

Yet Flora even now felt able to reflect that her own baby was already a part of her and, like little Mariska, would be her only other relative and the promising start to a new family circle. The very word 'family' warmed the chill of shock that still held Flora taut.

All right, admittedly, the baby wasn't planned, but life was all about rolling with the punches, wasn't it? And just as she was prepared to reorganise her life to become Mariska's mother she could hardly consider doing less when it came to her own child's future. She had money in the bank, a comfortable home and a viable business. Those acknowledgements gradually sent greater calm spilling

through Flora, a calm that soothed her ragged nerves and
fears while she reasoned that she could have found herself
pregnant in a much worse situation.

Essentially it didn't matter how Angelo felt about her
being pregnant with his child, she ruminated, and having
recognised that truth it was as though a heavy weight fell
from her shoulders. She sat a little straighter in her seat
and felt a good deal less awkward. She was convinced that
she didn't need Angelo for support and that belief acted
like a shot of reassurance in her veins, for not needing a
man for *anything* was a cause that lay very close to Flora's
securely guarded heart...

CHAPTER FIVE

'WHERE ARE WE?' Flora asked in dismay, lashes fluttering in bemusement as she appreciated that—unbelievably— she had actually followed Angelo blindly out of his limo into a building and, from there, into a lift.

'On the way up to my apartment. We have to talk,' Angelo informed her, his wide sensual mouth set in a deadly serious line.

At that point, Flora discovered that she had a deeply inappropriate desire to giggle. Angelo was poker-faced, the smooth, darkly handsome planes of his lean visage taut with self-discipline. He was determined not to put any real emotion on show, she realised with regret. Yet he was pure volatile male below that cool, calculated front that he showed to the world, she reasoned ruefully. She could not resist recalling the shockingly hot and explosive surge of the passion he had unleashed in Amsterdam. Heat slowly crept up from low in her tummy to the responsive peaks of her breasts, stiffening her nipples into tight dagger points below her clothing.

'Don't look at me like that, *enamorada mia*,' Angelo purred, his rich drawl low and rough-edged in pitch while he surveyed her with his amazing royal-blue eyes, the dark pupils as dilated as no doubt her own were.

Suddenly the atmosphere was thick as wet cement and the breath rattled in her throat. 'What does *enamor*—whatever—mean?'

'My lover,' Angelo supplied huskily.

'No, I'm not, not really,' she reasoned jerkily, fighting the compulsive pull of his charismatic masculinity with all her might, for every skin cell and nerve-ending she possessed was urging her to walk right into his arms.

His stunning eyes, accentuated by the ebony luxuriance of his lashes, narrowed to become even more devouring and magnetic. 'Then, what are you?'

Denying her vulnerability, Flora deliberately dropped her attention to study the floor at their feet. 'A mistake?'

'That is not how this feels,' Angelo growled, reaching out a hand to close long brown fingers round her wrist and tug her closer. But he knew he was lying, because that same word was flashing on and off like a warning neon sign at the back of his brain. Yet, as his attention slid from the pouting cherry-tinted invitation of her luscious mouth to the telling indentation of her prominent nipples below her top he had never been further from intellectual control; he was hard and erect and hungry for the tight sheath of her body and that was all that mattered to him.

As Angelo drew her to him dismay sent Flora's lashes skyward, green eyes flaring bright as jewels as she looked up at his bronzed sculpted features, scanning the slash of his high cheekbones, the jut of his arrogant masculine nose and his obstinate jaw line. This late in the day his golden-toned skin was steadily darkening with a shadow of stubble that simply highlighted his beautifully shaped mouth. Colliding with his startlingly blue eyes, she was utterly transfixed: he truly was gorgeous.

'Mistake,' she told him again unevenly. 'We're a mistake—'

Her voice died beneath the passionate onslaught of his sensual lips plunging down on hers and it was as if cautionary buzzers went off throughout her taut, quivering body. She craved him like a woman starved of oxygen, stretching up to kiss him back with fervour, needing and revelling in that heady taste of him with every fibre of her being.

She heard the whirr as the doors opened and he backed her out of the lift without breaking their connection. She stumbled in her heels until her spine was braced against a solid wall and she felt his hands splay to her hips, tilting her pelvis into provocative collision with the urgent thrust of his erection. A split second later, she was free again and reeling dizzily back against the wall for support with her body still greedily humming while she struggled to rescue her wits.

A mere step away, expelling his breath in an audible roughened hiss, Angelo thrust wide the door of his apartment for her entry. It was an effort for him to be that controlled. In fact it was a wonder that he wasn't still trying to take Flora out on the landing, he acknowledged with derision, resenting and distrusting her sexual power over him. She roused the hot-headed all-consuming sexuality he had believed he had left behind him. With Flora sex was elemental and as fierce and basic in its energy as a hurricane. Still hugely aroused, he was fighting a driving instinct to haul her back into his arms and carry her off to his bed. As a cascade of erotic imagery engulfed the imagination he had not known he had he almost groaned out loud in frustration. She was pregnant, she was carrying his child, he reminded himself doggedly. Rampant sex would only cloud that serious issue and add to the complexities of their dealings.

Flora could not look at Angelo as she preceded him into a very large modern reception room with a polished floor, sleek contemporary furniture and a wall of full height windows that offered breathtaking views of the river Thames. A deep inner trembling was still afflicting her and she was uncomfortably aware of the damp ache between her thighs and the stinging tightness of her nipples. When he touched her he turned her inside out and she hated it, for her earlier sense of keeping herself together was now entirely destroyed.

Angelo focused on her slender, graceful figure, noticing how the silky strands of her copper hair shone in the sunshine. Renewed desire pierced his tough hide like the point of a dagger sliding between his ribs. 'Obviously you'll come back to Amsterdam with me,' he heard himself say before he even knew he was going to say it, which was for him a most unnerving experience.

Wide-eyed, Flora spun back to look at his lean strong face, which, at every viewing, wreaked such havoc with her thoughts. 'Why on earth would I do that?'

'Primarily because you'll need my support now that you're pregnant.'

'I don't see why—I'm pregnant and healthy, not suffering from some dreadful disease,' Flora pointed out tartly.

Angelo rested piercing blue eyes on her. 'Are you planning to have this baby? Or is it too soon for me to ask you that question?'

Flora had frozen, her facial muscles pulling tight as she wondered if he was harbouring hopes that she might ultimately choose not to go through with the pregnancy. She lifted her chin. 'I already know what I want to do and I intend to have my baby,' she told him squarely.

Just as quickly Angelo was marvelling that he had ever cherished the smallest doubt on that score. Having a baby with a rich father was a lucrative passport to a more comfortable lifestyle for a scheming woman. And from the instant he had read Flora's history in that private detective's report two years earlier he had known how ambitious and grasping she really was. But he had chosen to take a risk without contraception and he could only blame himself for giving her the opportunity to hold him to ransom with a child for at least the next two decades.

His handsome mouth forming a cynical line, he said flatly, 'Naturally, I will support you in that decision in every way possible. But it would be easier for me to follow through on that promise if you moved to Amsterdam.'

'I don't need your support,' Flora proclaimed with pride.

'You're not thinking of the wider issues at stake here,' Angelo told her coolly. 'Mariska is in Amsterdam as well.'

Flora stilled, because in the first fine flush of discovering that she was pregnant she had indeed overlooked that connection and all its possibilities. 'You mean…we could share her care between us?'

'What other course would make sense now that you're also carrying my baby?' Angelo murmured drily. 'We could raise both children together.'

'Are you suggesting that we live together as well?' Flora pressed uncomfortably, colour flaring over her cheekbones as she had not grasped that more intimate aspect of his suggestion when he first mentioned the idea of her moving to the city where he lived.

'It would be the easiest solution,' Angelo pointed out with a profound lack of emotion that struck her as very nearly an insult. 'And the simplest solution is usually the best.'

In similar circumstances, Willem had once asked Julie to marry him. No, Flora had not expected Angelo to bite down on that sacrificial bullet, but the prospect of living under his roof and being forced to depend on him for all her needs filled her with consternation. In such a set-up she would lose her independence and become horribly reliant on her relationship with him working out. But if, in return, she would gain the much-desired right to be Mariska's mother…?

'Yes, I can see that my living in Amsterdam would have definite benefits from the children's point of view,' Flora conceded grudgingly. 'I would certainly like to be able to see Mariska every day and be a real part of her life rather than an occasional visitor—'

'*But?*' Angelo cut in, impatient for the objection he sensed coming and frustrated by her inexplicable reluctance to embrace the rich and privileged lifestyle that he had just offered her. He wondered if he needed to spell out the material advantages with greater clarity.

'I'm very independent. I like my own corner, my own way of life.'

'Yet you insist that you want to adopt Mariska.'

'I do, but you're not being frank enough to tell me what I need to know,' Flora condemned, lifting her bright head high with a glint of challenge in her clear green eyes. 'Exactly what kind of relationship are you offering me? Do you expect me to be a parenting partner and friend?'

'A lover.' That very frank contradiction slammed back at Flora like a crack of thunder, although he had not raised his voice in the slightest.

Flora was shaken. 'A l-lover?' she stammered uncertainly, taken aback by an angle she had not foreseen. 'I assumed you were talking about us coming to some platonic arrangement.'

Angelo's brilliant gaze was hot electric blue as amusement and sexual heat combined in his compelling appraisal, while a wolfish smile tugged at the corners of his handsome mouth. 'I don't think that platonic would work very well for us. I am very powerfully attracted to you, *enamorada mia.*'

The unashamed fire in that steady look sent wicked heat and anticipation hurtling straight to the most sensitive places on Flora's body. Uneasy at that rush of physical response and bemused by his bold statement of desire, Flora shifted position, her face burning pink as she struggled to think clearly. 'So, you're actually proposing that we live together in a relationship that would go much further than simply making a home for Mariska and the baby I'm expecting?'

This time it was Angelo who stilled to shoot her a questioning narrowed glance, his lean, darkly handsome features annoyingly unforthcoming. 'How much further?'

Flora recognised his tension and wariness. 'Have you really thought this proposition through, Angelo?'

'If I had not, I would scarcely have suggested it,' he fielded with cutting assurance.

But Flora was not easily cut off in full flow and an intense need to know exactly what he was offering her was now driving her. 'But you're being much too casual for something so serious,' she objected with a toss of her head, copper-coloured hair dancing back from her cheekbones. 'You're asking me to move in with you and I'm asking you on what terms would I be living with you?'

An ebony brow elevated, his stubborn jaw line clenching hard, his tone clipped and discouraging. 'Terms?'

If anything his reluctance to spell out the boundaries only made Flora more suspicious of his motives. 'Terms,' she repeated unapologetically.

'Obviously I would take care of all your expenses and you would have access to every material thing that a woman wants.'

'I can take care of my own expenses, Angelo. I don't need financial assistance and I don't need to be spoiled either. You said we would be lovers,' she reminded him uncomfortably.

Angelo shifted a broad shoulder. 'What more can you possibly want?'

Flora ground her teeth together and momentarily looked away from him, her hands clenching in aggravation. Just then, she would have loved to pour a bucket of cold water over him in punishment for his unwillingness to clarify his proposition. Did he not trust any woman or was it just her? He behaved as if words were handcuffs and chains that might come back to imprison him. 'Most people expect certain guarantees before they give up their own home and move into someone else's—particularly when there are children involved. Upheaval is very bad for children,' she spelt out loftily. 'And Mariska has already suffered quite enough change in her life.'

His beautiful eyes semi-screened by luxuriant lashes, Angelo released his breath in a slow measured hiss. 'What sort of guarantees are you asking for?'

'The obvious: stop acting like you're thick as a brick!' Flora launched back at him in growing anger. 'You know what I'm asking! How committed would you be to making this relationship work?'

'I'm not into discussing the finer points of relationships,' Angelo declared, slamming yet another door closed in her face.

'So, end of that conversation. I'm not moving to Amsterdam to live with a guy who's so immature he can't even talk about what he wants and expects from me or himself!' Flora shot back at him wrathfully.

'I am not immature, merely experienced enough to know that the instant a list of rules is drawn up in an affair I will most probably feel the need to break those rules,' Angelo drawled smooth as silk.

'Well, thanks, too, for that opportune warning. I definitely won't be moving to Amsterdam on those terms!' Flora tossed back at him in a tone sharp with scorn and antagonism that masked the painful sense of disappointment that she was experiencing. She was as hurt as she was annoyed. 'I don't think that you entertaining yourself with other women would help us to make a happy home for young children. I grew up in a divided home and I know exactly what I'm talking about, Angelo!'

'You're being unrealistic. None of us can see into the

future. What guarantees can I possibly give you?' Angelo countered levelly.

'Before I abandon my home and way of life to take a chance on depending on you in another country? At the very least, your commitment to offering me an exclusive relationship. But I can see that you're unwilling to promise fidelity,' Flora contended flatly, clashing with his stunningly blue eyes without flinching, even as another sharp little pain slivered through her at that wounding knowledge. 'And I'm afraid that I won't settle for anything less.'

'Now you're being unreasonable,' Angelo breathed curtly. 'I've never given any woman such a pledge.'

Flora grimaced, for she now knew her true value in his eyes. He might want her but evidently he already knew that he didn't want her enough to make sacrifices or promises that might offer her any hope of a viable future with him. He wanted her only for the moment and he wasn't prepared to make a longer-term commitment that would reduce his sexual options. 'Which really says all I need to know about you.'

'But what about Mariska's needs? What about the child you're carrying? Don't they deserve that we should at least *try* to live together?' Angelo demanded rawly, outraged by her inflexible outlook. He had made what he deemed to be a very generous offer. He had never asked a woman to live with him before. Nor had any woman ever boldly confronted him with an in-your-face demand for exclusivity. He had certainly been in receipt of plenty of hints and persuasive moves on that score, but he had always set a very high value on his freedom and had always moved on from one affair to the next with a light heart. But this woman was different from all her many predecessors in one crucial field, he conceded grimly. She carried his baby in her womb. But did that give her the right to hold him to ransom and make such a far-reaching demand? Most women would have been honoured to be invited to live in his home and share his bed, but she had transformed his invitation into some kind of backhanded affront. His lean, compellingly attractive features stubbornly taut, he thought she was demanding too much and he dug his heels in with every atom of his stubborn strength of will.

'I think that the children deserve something more from us than us just *trying* to live together. You would have to be more committed to the relationship than you obviously are prepared to be. I'm not interested in your money. Although I have no intention of becoming your temporary mistress, I don't think that you see me as anything more than that. Let's not discuss it any more,' Flora urged with a forced and strained smile, keen as she was to sidestep further debate on the thorny topic. 'It's not doing us any good to argue about it.'

Usually more than willing to sidestep female aggression and disagreement, Angelo was taken aback by the furious flash of dissatisfaction and sense of injustice that gripped him when she chose to bring their dialogue to what he saw as a premature conclusion. Clearly it was a matter of her way or the highway… *How dared she* lay down the law to him in such a manner?

'How do you propose to continue your relationship with Mariska?' Angelo enquired with scantily leashed contempt.

Flora lifted her chin. 'I'll fly over and visit as often as I can.'

'It won't be an adequate substitute for you being on the spot.'

Flora lost colour, guilt and more than a touch of doubt assailing her. 'It would be much harder for Mariska if I was there for her for a few weeks and then gone again.'

Angelo dealt her a grim appraisal. 'It's not that straightforward.'

'Oh, I think it would be with a guy like you—used to having his options and enjoying them no matter what the cost,' Flora returned without hesitation, as she knew all too well that a sexually predatory man got bored with just one woman and preferred variety in the bedroom. Her father had never hesitated to indulge himself with an attractive woman and, regardless of his marriage or his children, had always put his own desires of the moment first.

Outrage at that rejoinder cut through Angelo in a boiling hot swathe, since he was neither self-indulgent nor destructive with women. Female companionship and sex were essential to him and it had never been a challenge for him to fulfil his needs with like-minded partners. It was rare for his affairs to end on a sour note because his lovers understood from the outset that he was not promising either everlasting love or fidelity. Did Flora really expect to dictate rules to him? What sort of men was she accustomed to dealing with?

'I only visit the UK about once or twice a month,' Angelo intoned curtly. 'It will be difficult for me to offer you the level of support that you deserve.'

'I'll manage just fine on my own,' Flora asserted, lifting her head high and watching anger flare in his bright blue eyes as he translated her response as yet another offensive rejection.

'I will at least accompany you to your medical appointments,' Angelo declared on a decided note of challenge.

'That's unnecessary...'

'Clearly you intend to shut me out completely!' Angelo growled in a driven undertone.

'Not at all,' Flora fielded uncomfortably. She was already moving back to the hall to take her leave, keen to evade the stab of conscience beginning to gnaw at her. After all, lots of men evaded their responsibility when a woman fell pregnant and Angelo did deserve her respect for his determination to give her his support. 'But I do think that once the baby is born we'll have more to talk about.'

Infuriated by her determination to keep him at arm's length until that stage, Angelo strode after her. 'My driver will take you home and I'll stay in touch. Please don't tell me that that's not necessary either!'

Those words literally bubbling on the tip of her ready tongue, Flora reddened and sealed her soft lips closed again. They were at daggers drawn and she had not intended that but she did not see how she could change the situation. He had expected certain responses from her and he had lost patience with her when she failed to deliver those responses. He was a very powerful personality and he was accustomed to women falling in with his wishes. Flora, however, believed that it would be downright dangerous to get more deeply involved with Angelo van Zaal when the relationship would clearly be of short duration. The eventual breakdown of a relationship between them would only create bad feeling that might well jeopardise her ongoing ties with Mariska, as well as his with their unborn child. As someone whose own childhood had been deeply scarred by quarrelling, unhappy parents, Flora was keen not to inflict that lost sense of pain, fear and bewilderment on any other child.

Lean, dark face sardonic, Angelo felt bitter as he watched Flora leave his apartment. It was many years—indeed not since his stepmother had died—since Angelo had felt so angry with and exasperated by a woman. Once again, Flora Bennett had taken him by surprise. He had assumed she would grab at the opportunity to move in with him and not only for mercenary reasons either. The sexual heat between them was mutual and strong and in his opinion more than sufficient to sustain a relationship, yet she was refusing to take account of it. It was very hard for him to accept that although his first baby was on the way its mother wanted nothing to do with him. If that was her attitude now, how much was he likely to see of his child once it was born? His handsome mouth twisted. And all because she had deemed him unworthy for refusing to declare that there would never be another woman in his life.

FLORA SETTLED INTO her bed that night and fought off a powerful desire to picture what life might have been like living with Angelo in Amsterdam. It wouldn't have lasted five minutes, she told herself staunchly. She would get hurt and humiliated when he became bored with her and then sought out other females for variety. After all, she was no sex goddess and he was a very good-looking, very rich tycoon. He was the sort of guy who would always be spoilt for choice and subject to temptation when it came to women. Besides, a brief and ultimately unsuccessful live-in arrangement would only have confused and upset Mariska; the little girl deserved better from the adults she had to depend on in her life.

But what, a little voice dared to ask, if it worked out between her and Angelo? What if Angelo was prepared to agree that she would be the only woman in his life for the duration of their relationship? In the darkness, Flora's eyes shone at that unlikely but energising image of life as it might be in a perfect world. What if she was letting her fears rule her too far? What if she was wrong not to even give Angelo a chance?

At that point, Flora turned over and punched her pillow with unnecessary force. Next she would be believing that a fairy ready to grant her three wishes might be living at the foot of the garden, she scolded herself in exasperation. Angelo was not in love with her, so why would he give up other women for her benefit? He only saw her as a temporary aberration, a short-term affair, and nothing lasting was likely to come from such a weak foundation.

Her mother's experience had taught Flora the lesson that it very often was women who took the greatest responsibility for their children and made the biggest sacrifices. Her childhood had been deeply scarred by her quarrelling, ill-suited parents. Although being a single parent was not the lifestyle she had foreseen for herself, she soon convinced herself that she had made the *right* choice in opting to pretty much go it alone with her pregnancy...

CHAPTER SIX

ANGELO SLID LITHELY out of his limousine and studied the ivy-clad prettiness of Flora's detached village home. There were three cars parked in the driveway. He frowned, wondering how many guests she had staying and how she was coping.

But then, such matters were none of his business according to Flora, he reflected with a grim light clouding his vivid blue eyes. Over the past two months it had become increasingly plain to him that Flora intended to keep him at a distance where he could neither interfere nor offer his assistance. His phone calls had met with stilted impersonal responses from her that told him virtually nothing. His attempt to pay her a monthly allowance to enable her to take life a little easier had been roundly rejected as well.

Angelo was bewildered by her attitude. Nothing about Flora Bennett added up and Angelo hated mysteries. If the private investigator's report he had received on Flora and her sister two years ago had been on target, cold hard cash should have paved an easy path to Flora's heart. She should have been eager to fit in with his plans and reap the generous rewards of pleasing him. That she was not eager or even willing told him that either the report had got her wrong or she was playing a much more clever game of deception than he had so far had cause to suspect. Yet would a materialistic woman turn down the opportunity to move in with a billionaire and live in the lap of luxury? And why would she refuse his financial help? Or was that a ruse to come back later through the offices of a court of law and sue him for a final settlement amounting to many, many thousands of pounds? That was perfectly possible, he acknowledged grimly.

His suspicions about Flora's motives did not make it any easier for him to handle the mother of his future child. Furthermore, for the first time in his adult life, Angelo was dealing with a tricky relationship with a woman instead of turning his back and walking away, deeming her too much trouble to be worthy of his time and patience. He was not enjoying the process either, for her every rebuff infuriated him.

Indeed the problems created by Flora's continuing hostility were matched by the widespread disruption of Angelo's once regimented and perfectly composed mind. Angelo was uneasy with the unfamiliar feelings of frustration and anger regularly assailing him. His concentration was no longer what it was, nor was his famously single-minded focus zeroed in on business goals alone. All of a sudden, he was suffering from moments of abstraction. He was also noticing every pregnant woman and every redhead in his vicinity. He was even more disturbed by the fact that he had not slept with a single woman since Flora. Celibacy agreed with Angelo even less than mental turmoil. Sex had always been his foolproof means of unwinding from his demanding schedule. Sex had never been any more complicated for him than a good workout at the gym. But Angelo had recently become worryingly impervious to the sexually sophisticated women who had once entertained him most effectively outside working hours. His highly active libido had taken a hike and he had no idea why or what to do about it.

He hit Flora's doorbell, knowing in advance that his uninvited visit would be as welcome as a snow shower in summer. In an unusually disorganised and last minute decision the night before, Angelo had reached the end of his patience and he had flown over to England too late at night even to call Flora. The door of her home was opened by a stranger and the hall was confusingly awash with more strangers. He counted three middle-aged couples, presumably Flora's current boarders.

'Where's Flora?' he asked.

'Upstairs in the bathroom…she's not well,' one of the women informed him. 'We're getting ready to leave.'

'*Without* our breakfast,' a disgruntled older man pronounced.

'If you'll give me a few minutes to check on Flora, I'll sort that out for you,' Angelo declared, his concern at the news that Flora was unwell prompting him to take the stairs two at a time. It took him a minute or two to establish which door led to the bathroom.

That achieved, he rapped loudly on the solid wood. 'Flora? It's Angelo. Are you all right?' he asked urgently.

Flora was very far from being all right. White and shaking, she clung to the edge of the sink to steady her wobbly lower limbs. She felt like death warmed up and her brain was woozy, thoughts coming only slowly. Why on earth had Angelo come to see her again? She felt too sick to protest as she usually would have done. Sickness had a way of making one concentrate only on the immediate. In any case, Angelo was so determined that protest would have been a waste of time and energy. Like a steamroller chugging unstoppably downhill Angelo just kept on rolling no matter what she said or did.

Flora opened the door a crack and clung to the handle for support. Angelo pressed the door wider open and she stepped back awkwardly. She was so much more colourful and somehow *real* than other women, he thought helplessly, immediately admiring the flame colour of her bright hair against her creamy skin and the sheer leggy elegance of her tall, slender figure. And his libido, which had steadfastly refused to react to a single one of the nubile models whose numbers were stored in his mobile phone, suddenly took high-voltage flight. That surge of intense sexual arousal froze Angelo in place and the source of it so much took him aback that he then viewed Flora with instantly cooler and more critical eyes. Just as quickly he saw the change in her and consternation took hold of him instead.

'I'm fine…I'm just suffering from nausea,' she told him wryly. 'Welcome to the reality of being pregnant.'

But Angelo was shocked by her shadowed eyes and pallor and he recognised from the sharpness of her cheekbones and the loose fit of her clothing that she had lost a good deal of weight since he had last seen her. '*Dios mio*, you look terrible,' he breathed, backtracking from his opinion a mere sixty seconds earlier when just a welcome glimpse of her warm familiar colouring had instantly convinced him that she looked terrific.

Pain pierced Flora as she still secretly cherished the memory of him calling her beautiful. This revised opinion hit her hard, even though she was aware that she looked less than her best in jeans and a shirt with not even a dash of make-up to brighten her up. Angelo, on the other hand, looked absolutely effortlessly gorgeous. The breeze had tousled his thick black cropped hair and scored colour along the splendid line of his high cheekbones, accentuating his superb bone structure. Even this early in the day his golden skin was beginning to shadow with dark stubble across his stubborn jaw line and round his wide sensual mouth. He was more casually dressed than she was accustomed to seeing him in jeans and a fine expensive sweater worn with a very masculine jacket. Her mouth running dry, she was quite overpowered by his magnetic presence for a couple of minutes.

'You should lie down for a while,' Angelo instructed.

'I can't,' Flora groaned. 'I have guests waiting for their breakfast downstairs…' And she was dreading the prospect, having already learned that certain cooking smells could make her feel horribly nauseous.

'I will deal with them. Go to your bed,' Angelo urged with impressive assurance.

Flora had never seen Angelo as a guy likely to be handy in the kitchen and she hovered uncertainly. *'But…'*

'Go and lie down,' he said again, stepping to one side to thrust open the door to the room he had already identified as hers.

The sight of her comfortable bed was all the pressure Flora needed at that moment and she crossed the corridor to gratefully collapse in a heap on top of the duvet. Her weary limbs were heavy as iron. She was so tired, indeed she was convinced that she had never been so tired in her whole life. The bouts of constant sickness that seized hold of her at all times of day and the exhaustion of continually feeling unwell had conquered her stubborn spirit as nothing else could have done.

Angelo closed the door on her and rang the country hotel he had checked into late the night before. Within minutes he was ushering Flora's paying guests out to his limousine and instructing his driver to take them to the hotel for their breakfast. Everybody more than happy with that new arrangement, he returned to Flora and explained what he had done.

Flora studied him with thoughtful green eyes, reluctantly impressed by his adroit handling of the situation. She would have enjoyed seeing him wielding a frying pan in her kitchen, but the shrewd organisational and negotiating skills he had just displayed were in all probability basic van Zaal business traits.

'I appreciate that I know very little about pregnant

women,' Angelo said with enormous tact, keeping quiet
about his current bedside reading, which would in fact
have proved that he knew much more about being pregnant than Flora did. 'And naturally I've heard of morning
sickness, but I really don't think it's normal for you to be
feeling this ill. You should see a doctor.'

'I already have,' Flora sighed wearily, turning over and
tucking her hand below her cheek as she made herself as
comfortable as possible. 'My GP says that some women
suffer like this and that hopefully it will slacken off soon.'

'I would still like you to agree to see Natalie again,'
Angelo imparted.

Already drifting off to sleep, Flora gave him a rare nod
of assent, pathetically willing to consult anyone who might
have the power to make her condition a little more bear-
able. Right at that moment, she felt as though her pregnancy had taken over her entire life, sapping the energy
and confidence that she had always taken for granted.

His big powerful frame alive with brooding tension,
Angelo watched her sleep, his lean dark features set in
tough lines and his jaw at an aggressive angle. He lifted
a throw lying folded on a chair and shook it out to cover
her up. Then he stepped out again to contact Natalie on his
mobile phone and share his concerns. Nothing his friend
said soothed his apprehension on Flora's behalf.

Flora wakened when Angelo touched her shoulder and
gazed straight up into azure-blue eyes surrounded by
swirling ebony lashes. Her heart skipped a whole beat inside her chest. 'How long have I been asleep?'

'About two hours. I'm only waking you now because
Natalie wants to see you this afternoon,' he explained.

'Have I got time for a shower?' Flora sat up very slowly,
too well aware that sudden movements were likely to bring
on dizziness and nausea.

Freshening up with a shower lifted Flora's spirits. As

she got dressed she reflected that, although she had lost weight in recent weeks, her shape had changed and not for the better. With her trousers already refusing to button at her waist, she donned recent purchases, a skirt with a partially elasticated waist and a top in a larger size than she usually wore. Even though it was early in her pregnancy, her breasts had already swelled by a couple of cup sizes and her waist seemed to be vanishing even faster. Reflecting on those unwelcome alterations to her body, Flora grimaced, deciding that what attraction she had possessed was now very much on the wane. Praying that the sickness would remain at bay, she joined Angelo in the limousine.

'Why were you trying to cater to so many people without help?' Angelo asked her then.

A few weeks earlier, Sharon Martin, Flora's part-time employee, had been diagnosed with cancer and the older woman was currently undergoing treatment. Flora had not managed to find a replacement for Sharon and, reluctant to cancel bookings at short notice, she had contrived as best she could to manage alone.

'It's been a struggle,' she admitted reluctantly.

'Yet you still found the time to spend several days in Amsterdam with Mariska,' Angelo remarked.

'She's so young. If I don't make the effort to see Mariska regularly, she'll forget who I am,' Flora pointed out ruefully.

Angelo answered a phone call and while he was talking Flora kicked off her shoes and curled up into a comfortable position, resting her cheek down on the cool leather back of the passenger seat. A blink of an eye later she was fast asleep again and he had to shake her awake at the end of their journey.

'Sorry,' Flora framed, politely shielding a yawn before finger combing her tumbled coppery hair back from her brow in some embarrassment. 'I've a lot of sleep to catch up on.'

In the waiting room she watched Angelo, only to redden uncomfortably when she realised that he was watching her. On their previous visit to Dr Ellwood's surgery, Angelo had very effectively tuned out of the proceedings and done as much business as if he were still at the office. Now his obvious disquiet touched her and stirred her conscience because she knew she had made things difficult when he had tried to stay in touch with her. If he had asked her why she would not have had a ready answer for him, because even she did not fully understand her often hostile attitude to him. What she did know was that when she focused on Angelo van Zaal's darkly handsome features she felt intensely vulnerable and scared and that was more than sufficient to ensure she stayed away from him and avoided his influence.

Natalie called Flora into her surgery and discussed her symptoms before giving her an examination and a blood test. After that the nurse showed Flora into the small room where the ultrasound scanning machine was kept and helped her get up onto the couch in readiness.

'Angelo wants to know if he can join us,' Natalie told her, popping her head round the door.

Startled by that request, Flora started to sit up. 'Er…'

But Angelo appeared in the brunette's wake, and to object struck Flora as petty, particularly when she was about to receive her very first view of the baby in whom Angelo appeared to have an equal interest. She lay back down again while Angelo stationed his tall, powerful frame in a discreet location by the wall, his keen gaze welded to the screen while Natalie talked about what they could hope to see at this stage of Flora's pregnancy.

'Ah, yes, this is what I suspected,' Natalie remarked with satisfaction as she moved the transducer over the gel slicked across Flora's stomach. 'There to the left, is the first baby…see the heartbeat…and there is the second baby…' for an instant the doctor paused and then drew in an audible breath before continuing '…and tucked in behind that one, is the *third* baby! My word, I already suspected that you might be expecting twins, but you're carrying triplets, Flora. That's probably why you've been feeling so very sick. Your hormones are in override.'

'*Triplets?*' Flora parrotted, her voice sounding as squeezed as if someone were bouncing up and down on her lungs. 'You mean that there's three of them?'

A large hand closed over her nervously clenching fingers. 'That's amazing news,' Angelo pronounced with admirable conviction.

Astonished, Flora tipped back her head to look up at him and noted that he was unusually pale. She reckoned that he too was shocked by Natalie's revelation but simply better at hiding his reactions than Flora was. Flora was stunned and totally overwhelmed by the prospect of three babies rather than one. She had naturally imagined how she might cope if she won custody of Mariska but had calculated her niece would be a toddler at a different stage of development by the time she gave birth.

The news that she was carrying triplets turned all her careful plans for the future upside down. It would be a challenge to continue her bed-and-breakfast business and even part-time childcare costs would be *huge*. For the first few months of motherhood she would definitely have to live off the money in her bank account. On the other hand, that cash bonus was her only nest egg and with the needs of at least three children to meet in the future she realised that it would probably be wiser to try and work and save the money she currently had in the bank.

'I can't tell you the sex of the babies yet. It's too early,'

Natalie Ellwood informed them cheerfully. 'Are there any multiple pregnancies in either family?'

As Flora shook her head in a negative motion Angelo opened his mouth and then closed it again, deeming what he had been about to say concerning his own early history inappropriate. He knew that a multiple pregnancy carried greater risks and it worried him that Flora was already far from well. Registering that the news about their triplets had struck her dumb, he lifted her down off the couch with care and accompanied her back into Natalie's surgery. Flora, still in complete shock from what she had learned, was urged to avoid stress, rest more and eat little and often in an effort to regain the weight she had lost. If the sickness continued at the same rate, Natalie said she would need to go into hospital to receive treatment. Flora was shaken by that last warning because it had not once occurred to her that her health and that of her unborn baby might be at risk. Unborn *babies*, her mind adjusted, while she recognised that she would need all her health and strength to carry three babies as close to term as possible.

'I would like to take you back to Amsterdam with me,' Angelo pronounced before they had even left the building. 'No, don't argue with me...think of the advantages. You can stay in bed all day if you like. You won't have to cook for yourself and everything will be done for you. You'll have Mariska to fill your days instead of demanding guests.'

'And Mariska will never ask me to cook a fried egg,' Flora mumbled, striving not to get caught up in the lazy blissful imagery of the dream world he was describing. 'I'm used to working and keeping busy, Angelo.'

'But right now you need some time out to regain your health.'

It was true; there was no arguing with that reminder. Natalie had emphasised that tiredness and stress were very probably only making the sickness Flora was suffering from worse. And she knew she had lost more weight than was good for her. She would also have Mariska to keep her occupied. At that moment, the proverbial *weak* moment, an image of the picturesque streets and canals of Amsterdam and having meals cooked for her carried considerable appeal for Flora.

Angelo tucked her into the limousine. Although he had said and done nothing to reveal the fact, the prospect of becoming the father of four children had knocked him sideways. Only three months earlier he'd had no plans to have any children of his own. But now, he gazed down at Flora and, in one of those inexplicable moments of flawed concentration that currently afflicted him, he was immediately sidetracked by the view. From that angle the newly full rounded globes of her breasts and her shadowy cleavage were visible below the modest neckline of her cotton top. There was something incredibly powerfully erotic about that illicit glimpse and he remembered the taste of her and the fresh scent of her skin. That fast lust ran through Angelo like a river of lava and the swelling hardness at his groin became a greedy ache. A muscle at the corner of his handsome mouth pulling taut, he swung in beside her.

Brilliant sapphire-blue eyes sought out hers in a sudden assault. 'I still want you in my bed, *enamorada mia.*'

In the aftermath of what they had just found out, Flora was startled by his candour. That bold husky reiteration sent tiny quivers of awareness darting through her tense body. His potent emphasis shook her as, removed from his radius, Flora had once again stopped seeing herself as a sexual being. Soft pink mouth opening, her tongue slid out to moisten her dry lower lip.

'You are *so* hot,' Angelo growled thickly, and he bent his proud dark head to crush her lips under his, his tongue delving into the moist and tender interior with a darting erotic finesse that sent the blood drumming madly through her veins and brought her hands up to clutch at his arms.

Responses that had bothered Flora in uneasy dreams that even she could not control leapt straight back to life. A squirming, curling heat shimmered low in her pelvis, dispatching tingling warmth to private places. Her nipples pinched into stiff straining crests and the tender flesh at the heart of her dampened while she held her body taut in defiance of that response.

'I want you,' Angelo husked, running his sensual mouth down her slender neck in a way that made her shiver violently, while his hand reached below her top to toy with the engorged peak of one breast.

In one urgent motion Flora jerked free and contrived to move a good two feet from him. Wide-eyed and flushed, she muttered hurriedly, 'No!'

His ebony lashes dipped low over his extraordinary jewel-bright eyes. 'I'm sorry. You excite me so much that I even contrived to forget that you aren't well.'

'That's okay,' Flora framed before she could think better of it, wanting to shut the door, as it were, but not bar and lock it for ever. Even with all her hormones leaping and bounding like spring rabbits through her rebellious body, she would not have confessed why she had drawn back from him. Being ill or unwilling had nothing to do with it. As she smoothed down her top wild horses would not have forced her to admit that she had had to put some space between them before he discovered that she was wearing an industrial-strength bra with a line of hooks and thick straps. *You excite me?* Well, he would not have retained that impression for long, she reflected with a shrinking quiver of embarrassment. At the same time she was helplessly thrilled that he still appeared to find her sexually attractive.

'Just not now,' she added, striving to add a discreet hint

of encouragement for the future while her face burned hotter than a fire. 'In Amsterdam.'

'So, you'll come back with me,' Angelo breathed with intense satisfaction.

And Flora could not meet his questioning gaze, because there was something about him that made her so ridiculously impulsive and, incredibly, unbelievably, she had just agreed to move in with him without thinking it through in triplicate and over the space of at least a week of sleepless nights. And now, if she immediately took the declaration back, he would think she was a total airhead who didn't know what she was doing or saying. Dismayed by a recklessness that ran contrary to her usual nature, however, she could not withstand the urge to try and backtrack. 'My pets would have to come with me as well and I would have an enormous amount of packing to do even for a short stay.'

'I'll organise everything for you. I don't want you tiring yourself out.'

'I don't know if I can live with you…'

Long brown fingers tilted up her chin so that she collided with his cerulean-blue gaze in which ferocious determination was writ large. 'But it costs nothing to *try…*'

Flora disagreed but she kept the thought to herself. She didn't want to get used to him being around if he wasn't going to stay with her. She didn't want to fall for him. She didn't want to get hurt. She had put all her eggs in one basket with Peter and at the end of the day had turned out to be anything but his ideal woman. Would she ever be any man's ideal woman? If she had not fallen pregnant, would Angelo be inviting her to move in with him? Would she even have heard from him again? Worrying along those mortifying lines sent a cold chill through her and severely wounded her pride.

'You do way too much agonising over things,' Angelo informed her abruptly, one hand closing over hers, his vivid azure gaze narrowed and intense on her expressive face. 'We have *four* children to consider now,' he stressed. 'If you can't be optimistic, at least attempt to be practical.'

His advice engulfed her like a landslide and was even less welcome. Practical was a very dirty word to Flora at that instant. She did not want Angelo van Zaal to settle for her because she was carrying his triplets and also happened to be Mariska's aunt. She needed more; she desperately longed to be wanted for herself.

'I don't want to be practical…I want to be loved,' Flora admitted gruffly before she could lose her nerve and duck making that very personal admission.

Angelo gave her a look of complete exasperation as if she had suggested something utterly outrageous. 'I've never been in love in my life!'

It was Flora's turn to raise her brows. *'Never?'* she pressed in disbelief.

'Not since I succumbed to an infatuation as a teenager,' Angelo derided, his wide sensual mouth curling.

It was depressing news but it also gave Flora a very strong desire to slap him. 'I suppose you don't believe in love?'

'I believe in lust.'

Flora flattened her lips into an unimpressed line and lifted her chin in silent challenge.

'Go on, confess,' Angelo murmured with silken scorn. 'You fell madly in love with me that day on the houseboat and that's the only reason you slept with me!'

In receipt of that sardonic crack, Flora was so desperate to slap him and working so hard to restrain that urge that she trembled. 'I'm afraid I still can't explain *why* I slept with you.'

'Lust,' Angelo told her with immense assurance.

Flora's self-control snapped clean through as if he had jumped on it. 'Well, if that's all we've got together, I'm not coming to Amsterdam. I can find lust anywhere with a one-night stand and I don't need to leave the country to do it!'

Angelo shot her a blistering look of dazzling blue fury and frustration. 'You're being totally unreasonable—I can't give you love. I can respect you, care for you, like you and lust after you, but don't make a demand I can't hope to meet!'

Respect, care, like, lust, she enumerated and her chin came up even higher. 'Why not? What's wrong with me?' she shot back at him baldly.

Her obstinacy in sticking to her point sent Angelo's temper shooting up the scale. 'Nothing is wrong with you. I just don't *do* love and romance!'

Flora lifted and dropped her slim shoulders in a shrug of finality. 'Well, I feel too young and lively to settle for respect and liking!'

Angelo ground his even white teeth together and mentally counted to ten. It didn't help him overcome the suspicion that she kept on raising the bar he had to reach to heights he had no desire to aspire to. 'No matter what I offer you, it's never enough!'

'Be warned: our differences cut both ways. I might come and live with you and then fall madly in love with some other guy,' Flora pointed out dulcetly.

'No, you won't, *enamorada mia,*' Angelo told her with ferocious cool. 'I won't give you that kind of freedom.'

Her eyes danced with provocation. 'You work long hours. Are you planning to lock me up every night in the cellar?'

'No. I plan to keep you far too busy in bed!' Angelo ground out. 'You won't have the energy to chase other men.'

'How do I know you're not all talk and no action?' Flora tossed back before she could think better of it.

His mouth closed over hers again with passionate punitive force. He crushed her to his lean, powerful body and her every skin cell leapt with sensual energy, sensation swelling her breasts and sentencing her to a bone-deep ache between her thighs. He kissed her until she was breathless and trembling and strung high on a hunger more powerful than any she had ever known. To catch her breath she had to tear her mouth from his and she was so weak in the aftermath with the lust she had decried that she bowed her brow down on his shoulder while she fought to get a hold on herself again. He had the power to turn her inside out with a single kiss and the awareness shocked her.

'I'm just warning you,' she contrived to trade in a final assault. 'Lust isn't enough for me and if I meet someone else who—'

Angelo rested a long brown finger against her parted lips to silence her, his narrowed gaze bright and fierce. 'I will make it enough, *enamorada mia*,' he told her rawly…

CHAPTER SEVEN

LITTLE MORE THAN a week after having that conversation, Flora received a visit from her friend, Jemima, whom she had not seen for several months. Jemima was married to Alejandro, a Spanish aristocrat, with whom she had two children, Alfie and Candida. Flora had got into the habit of visiting the family at their castle in Spain until Mariska had become an orphan, from which time Flora's trips abroad had taken her to see her niece in the Netherlands instead.

Before she arrived, Jemima, a tiny beautiful strawberry-blonde with violet blue eyes, was already aware that Flora had fallen pregnant. Brought up to speed on the latest developments, Jemima was quick to offer her opinion. 'Of course you should move to Amsterdam and give the relationship a chance. If everything works out between you and Angelo it will be wonderful for your niece and for those babies you're carrying.'

At that advice, Flora grimaced. 'But what if it doesn't work out?'

'That's a risk you have to take. When Alejandro and I reconciled I didn't want to take that risk either,' Jemima admitted to her friend, referring to the reality that she and her husband had lived apart for a couple of years before having a second go at making their marriage work for the sake of their son, Alfie. 'You're scared of being hurt. You're afraid to let your life go here in England, but you have to take those chances before you can find out if you and Angelo are meant to be together.'

'What happened between us was just an accident,' Flora argued ruefully. 'I don't think Angelo and I *are* meant to be together.'

'Flora, you haven't trusted a man since your engagement to Peter bit the dust,' Jemima remarked ruefully.

Flora sighed. 'It's probably been even longer than that. My father being a womaniser predates Peter, and that's the problem with Angelo—'

'He's a womaniser too?' Jemima interrupted with a frown of dismay.

'I don't know about that.' Flora groaned and pulled a face. 'He's a gorgeous-looking guy and he's single and rich, so of course he's had a lot of women in his life. But he doesn't believe in love or romance. Strikes me he's a commitment-phobe.'

'Yet he clearly loves Mariska, or he wouldn't be so determined to bring her up, so I wouldn't give up hope on him yet. A child is a very big commitment for a single man to take on,' Jemima pointed out thoughtfully. 'He's also doing everything he can to support you and he clearly wants the triplets as well. Full marks for him on that score.'

'I'm not saying that he doesn't have an admirable side to his nature. I mean, it's obvious that he really likes kids,' Flora conceded grudgingly.

'And fancies the socks off you,' Jemima chipped in. 'Or you wouldn't be in the condition you're in now. He'd be keeping more distance between you if he didn't want a relationship with you. I think his inviting you to share his home with him is quite a statement for a so-called commitment-phobe.'

Encouraged by her friend to look at the more positive side of Angelo's invitation, Flora began to come to terms with her seemingly impulsive decision. She was starting to appreciate that something a good deal stronger than impulse had prompted her to accept Angelo's proposition. In her heart of hearts she recognised that, in spite of her fears, she did truly want to have the courage to take a chance on Angelo. He might often infuriate her but she did find him hugely attractive and stimulating company. He was the first man since Peter to make her feel that sense of connection and she wanted and needed to explore that in greater depth.

Three days after Jemima's departure, a professional firm arrived to pack and transport her most cherished belongings to Amsterdam, while special travelling arrangements were made for her dog and cat. Angelo rang most days but since he was very busy and often between meetings they would only have time to speak for the space of a minute so it was never a challenge to maintain a conversation. Flora was already feeling a good deal stronger since she had cancelled her remaining guest bookings and had spoiled herself with early nights and relaxing days. She was relieved when the worst attacks of nausea almost immediately receded and her appetite began to slowly recover.

Only three weeks after she had learned that she was carrying triplets, Flora arrived at Angelo's Amsterdam home.

Skipper, who had travelled over two days earlier, raced to greet her with boisterous enthusiasm and she clutched his little squirming body below one arm while the driver who had collected her off her flight brought in her suitcase. Mango the cat, Angelo's housekeeper, Therese, informed Flora, was sleeping in his basket by the stove in the basement kitchen.

'He is being spoiled a lot. Therese adores cats,' Anke shared laughingly as she came downstairs holding Mariska.

The little girl held out her arms to her aunt in immediate happy recognition. Flora scooped the child into a loving embrace. All the agonies of insecurity and the misgivings that had tormented Flora since she had first agreed to move to Amsterdam fell away with her niece's first hug. As she held Mariska's solid weight to her and felt the warmth of her smooth baby cheek against her own, Flora finally believed that she had made the right decision.

A couple of hours later, comfortably clad in casual togs, Flora was happily sitting on a rug in the nursery building up brick towers with Mariska and toppling them again when she received an unexpected visitor.

An elegant platinum blonde, wearing a beautiful flowing top and trousers in a shade of grey that lent an even more flattering silvery hue to her hair and porcelain complexion, rapped lightly on the ajar door to attract Flora's attention and gave her a wide smile that showed off perfect teeth. 'I hope you don't mind me dropping in. I asked Therese if I could come up. When Angelo mentioned that you were arriving today I wanted to be the first to welcome you to our city,' she said brightly.

It was Bregitta Etten, whom she had first met in Angelo's house on the evening of the same day that she had conceived her triplets. Angelo and Bregitta had been on the brink of going out somewhere that night but Flora had never had the courage to ask what the beautiful blonde's exact relationship to Angelo was, and just at that moment not knowing made her feel distinctly uncomfortable. She scrambled upright while Mariska crawled round her feet and grabbed her aunt's trouser leg to haul herself into standing position on sturdy little legs. 'Thank you,' Flora responded a little awkwardly, while reaching down to pat the little girl's head soothingly.

'It's wonderful to see you with Willem's daughter…poor little girl, such a tragedy to lose *both* parents at once,' Bregitta sighed with rich sympathy. 'Of course, when Mariska has grown up she'll have a very large inheritance to help her come to terms with that tragic loss.'

Taken aback by that remark and its rather mercenary tenor, Flora frowned. 'Mariska…has an inheritance?'

A look of surprise flared in Bregitta's bright dark eyes. 'Mariska will come into her father's trust fund once she's an adult. Didn't you know that?'

Rosy colour warmed Flora's cheeks because she was embarrassed that it had not occurred to her that her niece would inherit and she also wondered why Angelo had neglected to mention it to her. Evidently Bregitta was much more informed about the van Zaal family's private financial affairs than Flora was and in the circumstances it was a slap in the face for Flora to be confronted head-on with that reality.

'Of course, had he had the opportunity Willem would have wasted his inheritance, and Mariska, just like her father before her, is a heavy responsibility for Angelo to take on.'

Flora lifted her chin. 'I realise that Willem had his problems,' she commented, choosing her words with care. 'But he was kind, he loved my sister and I liked him.'

'I didn't intend to offend you,' Bregitta responded ruefully. 'We Dutch simply like to be frank.'

'Oh, no, you didn't offend me!' Flora proclaimed in haste, wondering why it was that she was finding it so hard to warm to the other woman's apparent friendliness.

Bregitta shook her silver-blonde head, her expression wry. 'I shouldn't have commented but Angelo already has so many weighty commitments in his life.'

'I wouldn't really know about that,' Flora admitted uneasily, wondering if she with her expected progeny fell into that demeaning category as well.

'Angelo just accepts it—his life has always been that way. When his father made such a disastrous second marriage, Angelo had to grow up fast, and then, of course, Katja's accident only made it worse.'

Katja? Who was Katja? Flora was hanging on her companion's every word and eaten alive by curiosity, for An-

gelo revealed few personal facts. The marriage between
Angelo's father and Willem's mother had been a disaster?
Why? And what on earth had happened to this Katja? It
did, however, set Flora's teeth on edge that she should
know so little while Bregitta evidently knew so much.

'Mariska is very lucky to have you and I'm sure Angelo is extremely grateful for your assistance with her,'
Bregitta commented, frustratingly moving the dialogue
on in another direction after having whetted Flora's appetite for more information. 'Of course, a lot of women
have recently offered Angelo help and advice with childcare. There is something so touching about a man trying
to raise a little girl alone, isn't there?'

'I wouldn't know.' Flora could feel her face assuming a
more and more wooden lack of expression. 'Angelo's the
only male single parent I've ever met.'

'He's been positively *swamped* with offers of assistance. But then women have always found Angelo irresistible!' Bregitta pronounced with a rather pitying giggle.
'My husband used to tell me stories about when he and
Angelo were boys together and even then Angelo was a
total babe magnet!'

Suddenly Flora's tension ebbed and she began to smile.
'Your husband and Angelo are close friends?'

'The very best of friends…until Henk died last year,'
Bregitta replied with a slight grimace.

'I'm sorry. I didn't know,' Flora responded, scolding
herself for instantly wondering if the lovely outspoken
blonde was of the merry widow variety.

'Henk was ill for a long time. Angelo was a wonderful
friend to both of us.'

Relieved to establish that Bregitta was a friend rather
than a more intimate connection, Flora nodded her understanding.

'Angelo said that you had been ill and needed rest and

recuperation. How are you feeling?' Bregitta enquired with a sharply assessing appraisal.

'I'm feeling fine now.'

Unable to conceal her curiosity, Bregitta continued to study Flora closely. 'I hope it was nothing serious. Looking after a young child is very hard work.'

It dawned on Flora that, while Bregitta might have known about Mariska's inheritance, she was not aware that Flora was pregnant by Angelo. Her cheeks colouring again in a hot rush at that awareness, Flora shrugged off the comment and said nothing more while she wondered why she would have preferred to hear that Angelo had been more open about her condition. Was she afraid that his silence on that score meant that she was an embarrassment to him? Or that her moving in with him was such a casual arrangement on his terms that he had seen no reason to mention it to his acquaintances?

Shortly after Bregitta's departure, Angelo phoned Flora.

After asking her how she was settling in, his dark drawl sending little tingles of awareness down her taut spinal cord, he said casually, 'At this time of year I usually spend weekends at my country house. I'll understand if you prefer to remain in Amsterdam though because you've only just arrived.'

'I would love to see the house,' Flora broke in impulsively.

'Good. I'll make the arrangements and I'll join you there for dinner. I did intend to meet you at the airport but I'm afraid a crisis arose at one of the plants in India.'

Minutes later he had rung off, and Flora lifted Mariska and went off to pack a weekend bag. Anke packed for Mariska with the ease of long practice and mentioned how much she enjoyed the relaxed atmosphere at Huis van Zaal. In turn Flora wryly recalled her late sister's vehement complaints about how bored she had been when Willem had

insisted that they visit his brother's country home the previous summer. Of course, Julie, she reflected wryly, had
always been very much a city girl.

Flora enjoyed the drive out into the pretty countryside
where herds of black and white Friesian cows grazed the
meadows and windmills presided over the ever-present
stretches of water. Her first view of Angelo's red-brick
country seat through a line of espaliered lime trees took
her breath away, for, in spite of its name, Huis van Zaal
was a small castle complete with a pair of enchanting tur-
rets and a wide moat studded with water lilies.

'I didn't realise that it was a castle!' Flora commented
in surprise.

'It has been in the van Zaal family for over two hundred
years,' Anke told her. 'My parents farm nearby.'

It was not a huge building and was less a fortress than a
home, for, although it might have battlements, it also had
shutters on the windows and sat in a lush green oasis of
lawns and box-edged borders.

Skipper raced out of the car and had to be sternly recalled before his investigations took him for a dip in the
moat. Greeted by a smiling older man called Franz, Flora
was shown upstairs to a light-filled bedroom furnished
with a magnificent four-poster bed rejoicing in sunflower-
yellow damask drapes. Her face warmed as she wondered
if she would be sharing the room with Angelo, but she
soon discovered that there was no male apparel stored in
the antique furniture. By the time she had applied a little
make-up and put on a leaf-green dress that swirled round
her knees, Anke had Mariska in the old-fashioned bath
adjoining the nursery at the end of the corridor.

Flora was finishing off Mariska's bedtime story when
Angelo arrived and as her niece vented a little shriek of
excitement Flora fell silent at the sight of the tall, darkly
handsome male in the doorway. His brilliant smile lit up

his lean dark features and made her heart thunder in her ears. She watched him lift Mariska out of her cot and saw the delight on the little girl's face, recognising the bonds that had already formed between Angelo and her niece.

But while Mariska's attention was all for Angelo, his sapphire-blue eyes immediately sought out Flora. She was smiling, her vivid colouring and blooming silhouette accentuated by the backdrop of the pale curtains. She could not drag her attention from his tall, powerful physique. Angelo looked amazing in a dark, well-cut suit and a blue tie that picked up the stunning hue of his eyes. He really was gorgeous, she savoured helplessly, in thrall to the wicked hormones rampaging through her body in a floodtide of reaction.

'I'm afraid I'm much later than I hoped to be,' he confided in his husky, sexy drawl before bending his head to address Mariska in Dutch for a couple of minutes. Then he turned back to give Flora his full attention. 'I'm glad you're here. Very often I only see Mariska first thing in the morning and last thing at night.'

'Yet, even though I had much more time to offer her you were still determined to adopt her,' Flora could not resist reminding him.

His brilliant gaze cooled and his handsome mouth tightened. 'Now she has both of us and hopefully the best of what we can both offer her,' he countered smoothly.

Made to feel mean for having made her less than gracious reminder, Flora reddened uncomfortably. But she could not forget that, even though in terms of time and attention she had much more to offer Mariska, Angelo had demonstrated very strong resolve in continuing to battle to become Mariska's sole legal guardian. For the first time she wondered if that resolve had been driven purely by his fondness for Willem's daughter. Or by the conviction that he, rather than Flora, would make the better parent.

A pang of hurt cut through Flora at the thought that she might have been tried and found wanting by him without ever being aware of the fact and she hastily suppressed the feeling, irritated that she was so sensitive where Angelo was concerned. Why hadn't he made her aware that her niece was to inherit her father's substantial trust fund? That mysterious oversight on his part niggled at her, for she could think of no good reason for his silence on that issue.

While Angelo excused himself to go for a shower, Flora descended the gracious carved staircase alone. Franz showed her into an elegant drawing room and offered her a drink, which she refused. She stood at the French windows, which overlooked the charmingly picturesque gardens.

'What do you think of Huis van Zaal?' Angelo asked as he came through the door to join her.

'It's got wonderful warmth and character,' Flora responded and her voice shook a little when she focused on his tall, well-built figure. With his black hair damp and spiky, and clean-shaven, he had the sleek bronzed face of a fallen angel and the level of his charisma just took her breath away.

'I'm glad you like it here. It's my childhood home and I'm very attached to it.' His dazzlingly blue eyes flared, his handsome mouth tautening as her attention lingered on him. 'Don't look at me like that.'

Warm colour swam into Flora's cheeks but still she couldn't look away from him and the heat of desire simmered in the pit of her stomach like a taunt, because she had believed that she was stronger than that, stronger and fully in control. Only now was she learning her mistake. 'Why not?'

'It ties me in knots and I'm struggling to be a civilised host and follow the accepted script,' Angelo murmured huskily. 'And we're about to have dinner to celebrate your arrival.'

'I'm not hungry right now,' she heard herself object, as she was infinitely more eager for physical contact and the strength of her own longing shook her.

'*Dios mio*, you're tempting me, *enamorada mia*.' To drive home that point, Angelo crossed the room in a couple of strides and reached out to haul her unresisting body up against his lean, hard physique.

Behind her breastbone her heart started to crash like cymbals being banged together and a dark insidious excitement began to build, along with a wild sense of anticipation. Without further ado, he brought his mouth down hungrily on hers and her hands closed over his wide shoulders to keep her upright. That first kiss was nothing short of glorious. His raw masculine passion smashed down her barriers and desire sweet and painful and all pervasive engulfed her in a floodtide of reaction. But she wanted more, much more, and it was terrifying and exhilarating at one and the same time.

'You use a lot of Spanish in your speech,' she mumbled abstractedly when he finally released her reddened lips and allowed her to breathe again.

'It was my first language.'

'Not Dutch?' she queried, surprised by the information.

'My Spanish mother never learned to speak Dutch fluently, which was why we used her language within the family,' Angelo told her before returning to pry her lips apart with the seeking thrust of his tongue and then delve deep when she opened to him, with a raw groan of appreciation rasping low in his throat.

And that was the magical moment when she discovered that even a second kiss from Angelo could make her tremble and yearn with a force of desire she had not known possible. Every kiss set her on fire for the next so that she squirmed against him, desperate with the driving need for closer contact.

'Feel what you do to me, *querida mia*,' Angelo husked, a hand on her hip crushing her to him so that she could feel the urgency of his erection even through their clothes. 'I want you so much it hurts to exercise restraint.'

'Don't be restrained—why should you be?' Flora broke in helplessly, loving the way he shuddered against her with an arousal he could neither hide nor deny, for in that field at least it seemed that they were equals.

His bright eyes had the crystalline glitter of diamonds. 'I need you,' he growled.

And that admission was like the magic talisman that unlocked the gate to the treasure house of trust inside Flora. The word 'need' meant so much more than mere wanting to her. It had depth, hinted at staying power, suggested closeness on other levels, in short was everything she had dreamt of receiving from a man. She found his wide, sensual mouth again for herself and revelled in his unashamed passion for her.

Angelo bent down and swept her up into his arms to carry her out to the stairs.

'We *can't*!' Flora gasped, torn between horror and laughter at his single-minded audacity.

'We can do whatever we want to do, *enamorada mia*. There are no restrictions and there is no right or wrong way for us to be together.' As he spoke his carnal mouth nudged against the sensitive cord of her slender neck and followed it down. She quivered helplessly as he teased and nuzzled the nerve endings below her smooth skin. He knew things about her body that she didn't know and she rejoiced in his carnal skill and confidence.

He laid her down on the four-poster bed in her room and slipped off her shoes.

'You know I'm not made of glass,' Flora told him awkwardly, conscious that he was holding back. 'I won't crack or break.'

'I know.' Angelo flung her a hooded look of dark sexual promise, his jewelled eyes a bright gleam behind the thick black frosting of his lashes. 'But going slow is sexier and I've waited a long time to get you back. I want to enjoy you and I want you to enjoy me, *querida mia*.'

Suddenly Flora was breathless and wreathed in blushes as self-consciousness threatened to eat her alive. That day on the houseboat there had been little time to think about what they were doing; they had succumbed to a mad, impetuous bout of passion. It was a little different from lying back on a bed watching Angelo unbutton his shirt. The edges parted on the corrugated muscularity of his washboard-flat stomach and just as quickly watching became a sweet seductive pleasure. He strolled back to the bedside and gently turned her to access the zip on her dress, stringing a line of kisses across her shoulders as he eased the dress down to her waist.

I've waited a long time to get you back. She tasted that admission afresh, loving it, for it suggested she was special and that he would have wanted her even though she had not fallen pregnant. She was stunned by how much that idea meant to her and finally appreciated that by some insidious means Angelo had long since succeeded in getting below her skin. For the first time in a very long time the prospect of caring for a man didn't frighten her.

Angelo lowered her to the pillows and removed the dress, pausing to run boldly appreciative eyes over her full breasts cupped in a pretty white and blue polka dot bra. Before the packing was done, she had binned her sensible pregnancy bras with the thick straps and popped out to go shopping for new lingerie. From his reaction, it appeared to have paid off handsome dividends. But within the space of a minute the bra was gone and the ample bounty of her curves was spilling into his hands instead. A startled gasp parted her lips as he stroked the soft mounds and rolled the distended pink nipples between his fingers before lowering his handsome dark head to suckle the stiff crests. She was so sensitive there that she moaned helplessly, her breathing shallow and erratic as the pulse of heat between her thighs burned hotter than ever.

He peeled off her remaining garments and touched her where she could almost not bear to be touched. He teased the exquisitely tender flesh with erotic skill and she shuddered in his embrace, so hot and wet and eager she couldn't find words for the intensity of the hunger that possessed her. He tugged her to the side of the bed so that her legs dangled free. He spread her thighs and she felt shockingly exposed and she shivered, fingers knotting nervously into the silk spread below her hands.

'You shouldn't,' she told him shakily between gritting teeth, for every natural instinct and modest fibre was urging her to push him away and reject such intimacy.

Angelo surveyed her with fierce intensity and it was a look that brimmed with ravenous desire. 'I *must*,' he contradicted. 'I love your body, *querida mia.*'

He slid upright and dispensed with his trousers and boxers in one impatient movement. The hard thick contours of his erect manhood bore witness to his declaration and at the sight of his arousal Flora felt absolutely weak. He came back to her, pushing her knees to her chest to explore the slick damp pink folds she would have hidden from him, had she not been limp with the desire he had already awakened. He slid a finger into her tight passage while he used his tongue on the little pearl at the heart of her. As the sweet, tormenting pleasure began to build, she moaned out loud and jerked, her hips giving way to a feverish twisting motion. She had never reached such a high of sensation and when she could no longer withstand that sensual assault she went spinning over the edge of it with a keening cry and fell into the depths of writhing ecstasy, her every fantasy fulfilled.

'Oh…Angelo.' Struggling even to speak, Flora gasped as Angelo kissed her and rearranged her limp body on the bed before returning to her with urgent intent.

His bold shaft nudged at her damp entrance and then sank deep. He groaned out loud in satisfaction. 'You're so tight, *querida mia*…so wonderfully tight.'

'I've not had a lot of practice at this,' she admitted, exulting in the sensation of her inner muscles stretching to accommodate him while wondering if it was humanly possible to die from an overload of pleasure.

Briefly, Angelo frowned down at her as if he was seeking her meaning, but her eyes had closed and at that instant she was in the mood to say no more. Her head rolled back as he gripped her hips to surge deeper into her tender channel, answering her need with the long sure strokes of his urgent possession. Quivering with delirious delight, she arched up to him, catching his rhythm and ready to reach for the stars again.

The sensations were getting sharper, the fiery ache in her pelvis stronger, and then her body jerked and flew into orgasm and she was crying out and shaking in receipt of the indescribably intense waves of devouring pleasure. For a minute or two she lay with her skin hot and damp with perspiration, cradled in the warmth of his embrace.

'You were more than worth waiting for, *querida mia*,' Angelo declared, smoothing her hair back from her flushed face with gentle fingers.

Her lashes lifted and she focused dreamily on the lean, darkly handsome face so near to hers. She shifted closer still and hugged him, all the deep affection of her nature surging to the fore in the aftermath of that powerful physical release. She wondered when it had happened, when exactly she had fallen head over heels in love with a guy she had continually told herself she felt nothing for. That day on the houseboat? The weeks afterwards when she had denied herself even the pleasure of speaking to him on the phone for longer than thirty seconds? The afternoon she had learned she was pregnant and he had responded with laudable cool and the immediate offer of his support? In truth Flora didn't know when or even how she had fallen for Angelo van Zaal, only that just then it felt good to have taken that leap of faith and for once not to expect the worst from a man.

'You said I was worth waiting for. How long is it since you've had someone else in your life?' Flora asked boldly, already seeking to establish boundaries and know where she stood.

Angelo vented a roughened laugh and dark colour demarcated his superb cheekbones. 'I haven't been with anyone else since I was with you.'

Flora gave him a dazzling smile in reward and thought that he was showing great promise in the relationship stakes.

As if wary of having made that admission, Angelo added with a frown that drew his ebony brows together, 'I don't know why. Other women have seemed less appealing...somehow. Perhaps it's because—'

'No, don't spoil it by trying to explain it!' Flora urged, laying her forefinger against his wide mobile lips in a silencing gesture.

'I don't think I could explain my recent weakness for a particular tall, spirited redhead but it does seem to be working out very well indeed, *enamorada mia*,' Angelo murmured with satisfaction, and he sucked her finger into his mouth and laved it with his tongue while watching her with slumberous shimmering blue eyes awash with hot expectation.

Heat swept through Flora even before he kissed her

again and she responded with a fervour she could not restrain. Everything had fallen into place when she was least expecting it to do so and they had shifted into the role of lovers quite naturally. No longer was she holding back, checking out every word she spoke in advance and searching for double meanings in everything he said. She had abandoned the intense caution that had guided her and kept her heart whole and safe for several years and without that defensive barrier she did feel vulnerable. Yet turning her back on the uniformly low expectations she had of the male sex and putting Angelo into a category all of his own also left her free to enjoy being happy for a change.

And, in the aftermath of yet another bout of passionate lovemaking, Flora was on a high such as she had never experienced with a man before. Within the hour they sat down to eat in the panelled dining room, the home of a wonderfully colourful collection of Chinese porcelain, stored in elegant white cabinets that kept the room looking airy and light. Undaunted by their earlier non-appearance, Franz had put together a chicken salad and an array of mouth-watering desserts for their enjoyment. Skipper, who snored like a little steam train, was noisily asleep beneath the table, though once the food was served he stirred a little to maintain a mistrustful if drowsy watch on Angelo's every move.

It was only while Flora was toying with a dessert that was a little too sweet for her taste buds that she remembered what she had meant to ask Angelo to explain earlier. Glancing up from her plate, she casually tucked a straying strand of coppery hair back behind her ear. 'I have something I've been meaning to ask you…'

Angelo studied her with a lazy smile. 'Ask away.'

Flora straightened her slim shoulders. 'Why didn't you tell me that Mariska was going to inherit your stepbrother's trust fund?'

And the instant she asked, she knew she had strayed
into dangerous territory, for Angelo perceptibly tensed,
his brilliant eyes veiling to sharp arrows of blue while
his lean strong face shuttered. 'Who told you about that?'

'Bregitta Etten called in to wish me well this afternoon
and she mentioned it,' Flora explained in a rush of nervous
energy. 'Naturally it felt a little weird that I had no idea
that my niece was in line to come into Willem's money!
Why was I the last to be told?'

A heavy laden silence stretched between them like a
treacherous sheet of ice that could not be crossed and mentally she told herself off for being so fanciful...

CHAPTER EIGHT

'I SAW NO reason TO discuss the matter with you,' Angelo
fielded with measured cool. 'After all, surely it was fairly
obvious that my stepbrother's trust fund would go to his
only child?'

'Yes, I suppose, if you think about it from that angle
perhaps it was rather obvious. But it didn't occur to me
because while Willem was alive he didn't have access to
that money,' Flora pointed out, unimpressed by his explanation, indeed smelling a rat and a cover-up in his guarded
response. 'I didn't consider it... I genuinely had no idea.'

'It is a private matter. Bregitta shouldn't have broached
the subject with you,' Angelo remarked flatly.

'But she did and it made me feel rather foolish—why
was I kept in the dark?' Flora enquired a little more forcefully, for, unless it was her imagination, Angelo's handsome mouth had curled with a hint of scorn when she had
contended that she had had no idea that her niece was
an heiress. '*Why*, Angelo?' she repeated with greater emphasis.

Angelo expelled his breath in an impatient hiss and
sprang upright to his full intimidating height, forcing her
to tilt her head back to look up at him. His brilliant blue
eyes collided with hers and held her gaze stubbornly fast.
'I didn't know for sure whether you knew about her inheritance or not, but I was concerned that your desire to
adopt Mariska could be influenced by the reality that she
will one day be a rich young woman. What's more, were

you now to win custody of her you would be legally able
to apply to the trust fund for a sizeable income with which
to raise her.'

Flora was stunned into silence by those twin admis-
sions. She wanted to believe that she had misheard him or
taken his words up wrong, but he had left her no margin to
dream of error. As always, Angelo had spoken with con-
cise crystal clarity. Incredibly, the man she had just spent
most of the evening in bed with, the man whose babies
she carried in her womb, saw no shame in admitting that
he thought that she might be a gold-digger. And not only
that, a calculating gold-digger so shameless and hard of
heart that she might be willing to use an innocent child's
birthright to enrich herself. It was equally apparent that
he would not have trusted her with access to Mariska's
inheritance. Flora was absolutely horrified that he could
see her in such an appalling light.

She thrust back her own chair and stood up, the oval
of her flushed and taut face reflecting her sense of angry
disbelief. 'What on earth gave you the impression that I
might only want my niece because she stands to come
into a substantial bequest? What did I ever do to leave you
with that idea? What did I say?' she demanded emotively.

Angelo spread fluid brown hands in a wry gesture.
'You didn't need to do or say anything, Flora. Before Willem even married your sister, I was acquainted with, not
only her past history, but also yours,' he confessed grimly.

Her brow indented. 'You're talking about that private
investigator's report that you mentioned you'd commis-
sioned,' she guessed, and her heart began to sink as she
immediately deduced the most likely source of his reservations about her character.

'I'm aware that you slept with your married boss three
years ago and tried to blackmail him to gain a lucrative
bonus,' Angelo informed her flatly.

Flora reeled back a step as though he had slapped her, but what he had just thrown in her teeth was much worse than a slap, for he had resurrected a distressing episode that she had believed had long since been laid to rest, even though it had not had a satisfactory conclusion from her point of view. To be confronted by that same episode again years later, and by someone she cared about, was an agonisingly humiliating and painful blow for her to withstand.

'That is not what happened, Angelo,' she pronounced with quiet dignity as Skipper emerged from below the table and stationed his little black and white body protectively by her feet. 'Those malicious allegations against me were made in an employment tribunal hearing, not in a court of law, and they were not proved either. I did not sleep with my boss, nor did I try to blackmail him!'

His lean hawkish features stamped with unhidden distaste, Angelo made a decisive movement that dismissed the thorny subject with one lean brown hand. 'It was some years ago, Flora. I'm well aware that what is past is past and that young people in particular can and do learn from their mistakes and change…'

The target of that extremely patronising response, Flora experienced a shot of adrenalin-charged rage, which coursed through her with such powerful effect that she was surprised that she didn't levitate off the floor. She ground her teeth together in an effort to think before she spoke but it was hopeless. She felt both betrayed and gutted. The most traumatic episode of her life had been dug up by the guy she believed she loved and she felt cheated by his distrust and gutted by his low opinion of her as a person.

'I will never ever forgive you for this, Angelo,' she said shakily, targeting him with tempestuous emerald-green eyes that shone as bright as stars in her pale face. 'How dare you stand in judgement over me for something that I didn't do? How dare you condescend to suggest that people change? I've got older but I haven't changed one little bit. All I learned from that tribunal was not to trust people, and that when things get really *really* tough you're very probably going to be left standing alone!'

'I don't think we should try to discuss this when you're so upset,' Angelo breathed deflatingly, registering that Skipper, a perfect illustration of Flora's mood, was now growling and baring its teeth at him.

'*You* brought it up, *you* threw it at me!' Flora reminded him with spirit. 'You can't deny me the right to defend myself.'

'I had to explain why I was reluctant to be more frank about Mariska's financial status. I am not denying you the right to defend—'

'Of course, it's none of your business. My past is none of your business either and I can only wish that I had kept my present in the same category!' Flora flung in furious rejection of the choices she had recently made and Skipper, picking up on his owner's increasing tension, started to bark noisily. 'But when you had such a poor opinion of me, why didn't you mention it before now? How dare you lure me over to Amsterdam to live when you think so little of me? You deceived me by staying silent...'

'Tell the dog to stay out of this,' Angelo urged with a sardonic look down at the small canine bouncing excitably round her feet and barking so loudly that Flora was now virtually shouting to be heard. 'I had no deceptive intent.'

'Well, isn't that a surprise? Once again you try to take the moral high ground. But it doesn't matter what you think this time. I firmly believe that I was lulled into a false sense of security and deceived by you!' Flora slammed back at him in wrathful condemnation.

Angelo studied her with hard blue eyes, every inch the global steel magnate whose ruthlessness had earned him substantial achievements. 'I had no choice but to remain silent. How could you expect me to challenge you about your unsavoury past while you were carrying my children and you were unwell?'

Flora was trembling. Even his choice of words was revealing. Her *unsavoury* past. Without any input from her on that issue, he had clearly tried her, judged her and condemned her as guilty. At least she now knew why she had always suspected that he disapproved of her and disliked her. Angelo van Zaal had decided that she was not to be trusted even before he first met her. She need not have worried about trusting him when it was clear that he had never trusted or in fact respected her. Indeed the very existence of her pregnancy had forced him to swallow his misgivings about her character and attempt to form a relationship with her. Was it any wonder that he had decided that the most he could offer to share with her was a bed? No doubt had he been in a position to do so, he would have happily kept his distance from her and her sleazy past, she conceded wretchedly.

'I hate you,' Flora breathed thickly, struggling to enunciate the harsh words of rejection and alienation that seemed to come from the very depths of her being. 'And I'm leaving!'

As Flora made her way towards the door Angelo was suddenly there in front of her, blocking her exit like a massive stone wall. 'I won't let you leave—'

'I'm not giving you a choice!'

Angelo stared down at her with brooding force, jewelled blue eyes shimmering like a heat haze over her defiant and resolute face. He took a step closer as if to dare her to do her worst. 'I won't allow it!'

'Newsflash, Angelo—I don't need your permission to leave you!' Flora flung wrathfully. 'So, get out of my way and stop trying to crowd me!'

'*Por Dios*, I insist that you calm yourself down,' Angelo instructed in a low growl of explicit warning.

And Flora just lost her temper at that ringing admonition, for she fiercely resented being treated like a misbehaving child when it was very much his fault that she had found herself in such an untenable situation. Did he honestly believe that they could simply continue as though nothing had happened? That she could just live with the news that he believed that she was greedy and untrustworthy with money?

Her hurt and her anger combined in an explosive melding of emotion. She flung herself at him with knotted fists and thumped his big wide shoulders to fully illustrate her point. '*Move!*' she yelled at the top of her voice.

'*Madre mia!*' Angelo vented in a savage undertone as he shifted before the overexcited Skipper could bite his ankle. 'What the hell are you playing at?'

In the hail of her dog's frantic bout of barking, Flora froze, her balled fists dropping back down to her sides, because somehow she had never envisaged Angelo losing his renowned cool. But Angelo's jaw line had taken on an aggressive angle and his electrifyingly blue eyes were luminous with outrage. All of a sudden, a silent Angelo was channelling anger like an intimidating force field.

'You provoked me beyond bearing,' Flora slammed back at him in her own defence because an apology of any kind would have choked her. 'And you're still in my path!'

'Where I will be staying until you have got a grip on your temper…or should I say tantrum?' Angelo derided in a cutting undertone.

'Get out of my way!' Flora launched at him afresh, any desire to be reasonable crushed at source by that crack, although she did admonish Skipper for the racket he was making and the little dog finally fell silent.

Lean, darkly handsome face rigid with displeasure,

Angelo stepped back with infuriating reluctance. Flora flashed past him to head for the stairs. Halfway up, she almost tripped over Skipper as her anxious pet got below her feet and that instant of hesitation almost unbalanced her into a fall. As she clutched at the balustrade with a hissing gasp of fright Angelo braced his hands on her shoulders from behind and steadied her.

'You're okay. I've got you,' he said fiercely.

Unable to tolerate even that throwaway remark, Flora twisted her head round. 'But that's just it! You haven't got me and you never will again! You actually believe I'm after your money, even though I've flatly refused to touch a penny of it!' she reminded him doggedly. 'I was totally independent until you pushed your way into my life and insisted on interfering—what was that all about? Why didn't you just leave me alone?'

'Lower your voice,' Angelo growled.

No!' Flora fired back her refusal without hesitation because shouting at him was making her feel better by giving her an outlet for the emotions dammed up inside her. She didn't want to stop fighting with him either because she dimly recognised that when the argument was over she would find herself standing amid the debris of a wrecked relationship and she was in no hurry to reach that sobering point.

'You've screwed up my life!' Flora continued between gritted teeth as she stalked back to her bedroom where Skipper shot below the bed and whined, disturbed by the raised bite of their voices and the furious tension still in the air.

'Dios mio, my life has been turned upside down as well,' Angelo retaliated.

Flora's head spun, for she had not expected a response to her accusation. 'Try carrying triplets and see how much worse you feel!' she stabbed back, determined to have the last word.

Incensed by her complete obstinacy, Angelo watched Flora throw herself down in a heap on the still disordered bed. 'You're very pale. You need to be resting, not fighting with me,' he told her grimly.

Flora reared up again on both elbows, green eyes full of rancour. 'Were you expecting me to jump up and down with glee when you told me you thought I was a gold-digger, ready to fleece my baby niece?'

'I refuse to lie and pretend that I wasn't suspicious of your motives when you first applied to adopt Mariska,' Angelo declared, standing his ground.

'But even so, in spite of your suspicions you *slept* with me!' Flora raked back at him with a look of fuming feminine censure and incomprehension.

A flare of colour scored the sculpted line of his high cheekbones, but he stared her down, refusing to admit fault on that score. 'When did I say that I was perfect?' Angelo traded in his dark deep drawl.

Flora looked daggers at him and then rolled over to push her face into the welcome coolness of a pillow. What a mess, what a gigantic mess it all was! She wanted to cry and scream but she would do neither in front of him, so she pummelled the pillows with her fists instead. She was here in his home, she was available and because she was pregnant he was currently stuck with her, so that was probably why he had insisted that he still wanted her and that their relationship should be an intimate one. But their ties were the result of happenstance rather than planning. He might still desire her body, might want to have sex with her, but that was *all*. There was nothing deeper to his feelings for her. What an idiot she had been to lower her guard, let herself soften and fall in love with him! When had she forgotten that she knew next to nothing about men and invariably got it wrong with them? How had she over-looked the fact that she was dealing with a very rich, very handsome womaniser more used to taking than giving?

'Just leave me alone,' Flora urged from the muffling depths of the pillow. *'Please...'*

Angelo clenched his even white teeth and closed strong brown hands over the footboard of the bed where he flexed his fingers impatiently on the solid wood. 'Women usu-ally prefer honesty...'

Flora rested her hot cheek on her hand and half turned her head to squint at him, tousled copper hair settling in a glorious silken tangle round her shoulders. 'Oh, we just say that because it sounds good...but we don't want hon-esty unless it's the kind of stuff we want to hear,' she told him tartly.

Angelo breathed in deep and slow and then swore below his breath anyway, while his knuckles showed white on the footboard as he held it too tightly for comfort. 'I didn't intend to hurt or upset you—'

'Oh, shut up,' Flora interrupted. 'What you intended has nothing to do with this. There's no wriggling out of it ei-ther. You had serious reservations about my character and you concealed them from me. In the circumstances that was very unfair. Do you honestly think I would have come here to live if I'd known what you really thought of me?'

'The jury's still out on what I really think about you.'

Flora shrugged her slim shoulders in a gesture of sub-lime disinterest on that score. *'So?* You think I'm about to tie myself up in knots struggling to win your good opinion? I couldn't care less,' she claimed defiantly, flipping over onto her back to study him with accusing green eyes. 'But there's one fact which you ought to know. I was a virgin when you slept with me that day on the houseboat. You didn't notice but that fact does make it impossible for me to have staged a sleazy affair with my boss three years ago.'

'A virgin?' Angelo repeated in a seriously shocked undertone, his strong black brows pleating into a brooding frown as he stared searchingly down at the composed oval of her face. 'I was your *first* lover?'

'Virgins don't all go round wearing helpful labels to warn off predatory men,' she said flippantly, annoyed by his scepticism over her confession and deciding there and then to tell him no further secrets when he was clearly such an undeserving cause.

'I'm not a predator. I had no reason to think that you might be that innocent. I was also aware that you were engaged at one time,' he reminded her, clearly still reluctant to accept that she might have been as inexperienced as she had claimed.

Flora grimaced and compressed her lips. 'Peter respected me,' she fielded.

At that response, Angelo studied her with scantily veiled incredulity.

'Well, that was his excuse.' Her grimace had acquired a pained edge and she screened her gaze from his keen appraisal, for the dialogue had become too personal for comfort. The hurt that her one-time fiancé and former best friend had inflicted had left a wound that had still not fully healed. As she had her selfish father before him, she had trusted Peter and where had that got her? He had let her down when she most needed him. And in spite of the fact that Peter had been a big part of her life for several years she had not heard a word from him since they had parted.

Angelo was studying her troubled expression fixedly, his strong jaw line clenching hard as her gaze continued to evade his. 'You still care for your ex-fiancé, don't you?'

'We were good friends until we broke up.'

'That's not an answer.'

'You don't do romance or commitment. You're not entitled to any more of an explanation,' Flora told him loftily.

Angelo gave her a look that had the pure cutting edge of a steel blade. 'I'll see you in the morning. You must see that you can't leave. What about Mariska? And your health?'

Her brain suffered from overload when he mentioned the little girl that she loved and her pregnant state in one loaded and unnecessary reminder. Turning her back and leaving Angelo might feel doable in the rawness and pain of being confronted by his true opinion of her, but the concept of walking away from Mariska straight away threatened to tear Flora apart. She closed her eyes tightly, shutting him out completely, and she didn't move again until she heard the door close on his departure.

Angelo might be a whizz at the realistic stuff, but there was nothing practical about the powerful emotions engulfing Flora. She had fallen head over heels in love with Angelo and now she had to get over him again, detaching herself from both love and sexual hunger. And, as even looking at Angelo's lean bronzed darkly handsome features sent a dizzy jolt of craving through her that she despised, recovering from that weakness promised to be a big challenge. The bottom line was that Angelo van Zaal had hurt her badly and inside she felt deeply hurt and foolish.

What sort of a man had chosen to believe a tabloid scandal about her rather than seek out the truth? Of course, how had the investigator chosen to represent that particular episode? Probably with his own assumptions wrapped up as facts. And hadn't Peter, who had supposedly loved and known her through and through, chosen to disbelieve her side of the story as well? That old 'no smoke without fire' cliché had certainly not worked in her favour. Peter and his family had been appalled by the sleazy tabloid stories depicting her as a woman scorned out for revenge and their engagement had died on that funeral pyre of suspicion and embarrassment. Although, if she was honest, Flora ruminated wryly, her relationship with Peter had been under strain even before that.

When they had first met at university Flora had been firmly set against premarital sex and live-in relationships and determined to protect herself from that kind of potential disillusionment. Her mother, after all, had lived with her father for years before he reluctantly deigned to marry her and his unwillingness to be bound by one woman had enabled her father to cause havoc in many female lives.

Peter, who had studied accountancy while Flora had studied business at university, had come from an old-fashioned family and her uncompromising views had impressed him. His loyalty was soon stretched thin, however, when Flora won a job that paid more than twice what he was earning as well as offering the prospect of substantial bonuses. His mother and sisters had made snide comments about what a career woman Flora was turning out to be.

Unhappily for Flora, that high-flying job had swiftly turned into a nightmare. The only woman on an all-male team, Flora had found herself working for a despotic boss, who demanded that she work impossible hours and who cracked smutty jokes and made continual embarrassing comments about her figure. She had tried hard to be one of the boys and laugh his behaviour off, but the comments had ultimately led to inappropriate touching and sexual suggestions. A married man in his thirties, Marvin Henshall had had considerable success with such tactics with other female staff and Flora's resistance had only made her a more desirable target.

When the pressure Henshall was putting her under became unbearable, Susan, one of the women in the administration office, had confided that she had been subjected to a similar campaign. Together the two women had made a complaint about Marvin to Human Resources and, from that moment on as their grievances gathered pace through official channels, Flora's life in the office had become intolerable, with the other male staff ignoring her while Marvin ensured that her most successful client accounts were gradually parcelled out to her colleagues.

Peter had pleaded with her to find another job, but there had been nothing offering a commensurate salary and Flora's pride had refused to allow Marvin Henshall's victimisation, bullying and sexual harassment to go unpunished. Unhappily, however, her tribunal case had come badly unstuck when Susan backed out on her at the last possible moment and Marvin made up a sordid if credible story that was difficult to disprove. Humiliatingly, Flora had lost the case.

Her reputation destroyed by the amount of mud flung at her in the newspapers, Flora had bitterly regretted not just leaving her employment and seeking out another job. That Angelo should tax her with that tribunal case and the ludicrous accusations laid against her outraged her sense of justice and resurrected her need to be independent. She would never look at another man again, she promised herself fiercely, for sooner rather than later every man she let into her life let her down.

The following morning, Flora's breakfast was served to her in bed. She had suffered a restless night and just to remind her that she was still not back in full control of her pregnant body she was horribly sick. What remained of her strength was sapped from her by the shower she took. Fully dressed, but weak of limb and bathed in perspiration, she lay back down on the bed to recover. Her spirit as feisty as ever, though, she used the opportunity to rearrange her thoughts and fine-tune them, because she was determined to resolve her situation with Angelo and find a viable alternative to their current living situation.

She found Angelo much more easily than she had expected in so spacious a household. With Mariska tucked

comfortably below one arm, he was standing in front of a
portrait on the wide galleried landing and talking in Dutch
to the little girl.

'Flora...' Breathtakingly handsome in well-worn denim
jeans and an open necked shirt, Angelo swung round to
settle azure-blue eyes fringed by luxuriant black lashes
on her.

As heat formed low in Flora's pelvis and her nipples
pinched to tingling tightness, warm colour blossomed in
her cheeks. In spite of the fact that she was still angry with
him, that rush of sexual response was unnervingly strong.
Her niece beamed at her but continued to cling to Angelo
and Flora tried to be a bigger person and not mind the fact.
She joined them in front of a large gilt-framed picture of
an elegant lady. 'Who is she?'

'My late mother. I can't show Mariska a portrait of Willem's mother because my father didn't commission one.'
His wide sensual mouth quirked. 'And even if he had, I
wouldn't have given it wall-space!'

Flora glanced at him. 'You didn't get on with your stepmother?'

'She was a shrew, always picking fights with friends
and family. She bullied poor Willem unmercifully. People avoided her. Sadly my father didn't have that power.'

'Why on earth did he marry her?' she asked on their
passage down the gracious staircase.

'He was very happily married to my mother, who died
when I was ten. He assumed that he would be equally
happy in a second union and remarried hastily without
truly knowing Myrna. He was very unhappy with her,'
Angelo confided grimly. 'I still believe that the stress of
living with that woman brought on the heart attack that
killed him.'

'Bad marriages can damage and hurt the children involved,' Flora conceded, entering the drawing room, which

overlooked the lush gardens and rejoiced in an array of inviting seating. 'I've told you about my history and Julie's.'

'*Sí*, her mother was your father's girlfriend.'

'But only one of them. Dad spread his favours far and wide,' Flora admitted wryly and she reached out to accept Mariska, who was by now holding out her arms in welcome to her aunt. She smiled as she received an enthusiastic hug and stroked the little girl's soft cheek with warm affection as she settled down on a sofa with her.

Angelo viewed them with veiled eyes. 'I was planning to offer you a tour of the local sights today.'

Flora froze, thinking that only Angelo would dare to try and ignore their explosive and bitter argument the night before and move on so smoothly. 'Not just at the minute. I think I should take it easy after all the travelling I did yesterday.' Seeing renewed tension enter his lean masculine features at that refusal, Flora continued awkwardly, 'About last night…'

'Lying doesn't come naturally to me,' Angelo remarked drily. 'I'm too accustomed to the freedom of speaking my mind.'

Flora stiffened, for it was clear that he had no regrets about having admitted his reservations about her as a person. But then, who would ever have dared to call him to account over his bluntness? She could well imagine that women eager to please the very rich and very handsome billionaire had let even the most wounding candour slide past without protest. Being labelled a gold-digger had, however, left Flora in an unforgiving mood and she had no desire to placate him. 'I now know where I stand with you and I can't regret that. I think I know how we can work this out.'

For a big powerful male Angelo moved with extraordinary grace, but at that assurance he stilled by the window, his simmering tension obvious in his stance. His dazzling

blue eyes were bright as peacock feathers between the
ebony fringes of his lush lashes. *'How?'*

'Well, obviously we don't go on trying to live together
as we started out last night. The words "frying pan" and
"fire" come to mind. We just forget that angle,' Flora proposed in a clipped undertone, stress and concern at how he
might react to her proposition tightening her facial muscles. 'You seem to own very large houses, so living sepa-
rately below the same roof shouldn't be a problem in the
short term.'

It might well have been her imagination but the healthy
glow of vitality that Angelo's vibrant skin tone usually lent
him suddenly seemed strangely dull and absent. 'Is that
truthfully what you want?'

Flora released her breath in a slow sigh. 'Right now I
don't want any complications or stress. I want to concentrate on Mariska and these babies I'm carrying.'

Angelo jerked a shoulder in an eloquent shrug. 'I can't
fault you for that, but I had hoped that we could *discuss…*'

Flora's green eyes were suddenly as flat and hard as
green jade and her chin came up. 'I don't want to discuss
anything with you. I know what you think of me and that
made it clear to me that there was no future for us as a
couple,' she framed doggedly. 'I may need your support
right now because I'm carrying triplets but I would prefer you to treat me only as a friend or…er…housemate
from now on.'

Angelo was frowning. 'If that is honestly what you
want?'

Her teeth ground together because he was making it
very obvious that he had little experience of a woman saying no to him and that he could not quite credit that she
might know what she was doing.

'It has to be what you want as well!' Flora snapped
back, her temper leaping because even though he had not

opposed her his whole attitude seemed to imply that she was being somehow unreasonable. 'You admitted that my pregnancy had turned your life upside down.'

His very blue eyes burned like sapphire jewels above his hard cheekbones. 'But it doesn't necessarily follow that that is a bad thing.'

Flora dragged her attention from his all too charismatic appeal and folded into a bristling ball, with Mariska cradled sleepily on what lap she still had to offer. 'Oh, come on, you had it *all* before that day your luck ran out on the houseboat,' she muttered with a snide edge that she could not suppress. 'The beautiful women, the choices, the lack of ties or commitment. That kind of relationship was never ever going to suit me and it's better to recognise our differences now *before* the babies are born.'

A muscle pulling tight at the corner of his unsmiling mouth and his bright eyes veiled, Angelo inclined his arrogant dark head in grudging acceptance. 'It's very important that you can feel happy and secure here. I will respect your wishes. But, for the record, I think you're making a major mistake for both of us.'

Mistake or not, Flora had all the painful satisfaction of knowing at that instant that she had hoped he would fight with her and *for* her, wanting and demanding more than she thought it sensible to give. Of course his ready agreement merely pointed out what intelligence had already tried to tell her. He cared about what might happen to her but his feelings ran little deeper than ensuring she stayed strong and healthy for the sake of the babies she carried. *His* babies and, for a male as fond as he was of children, that was always likely to be a very big deal.

Hot prickling tears stung Flora's eyes and she lowered her lashes so that he would not see and she hugged Mariska in consolation. She might have fallen hard for Angelo van Zaal, but she had no intention of giving him cause ever to suspect that mortifying truth. From now on, she would be brisk, businesslike and as cool as a cucumber in his radius...

CHAPTER NINE

'YOU LOOK MARVELLOUS,' Bregitta Etten chorused with her usual girlish enthusiasm. 'The expression "blooming" comes to mind.'

Flora resisted an uncomfortable urge to smooth her lilac dress down over her sizeable bump; she was almost seven months pregnant and pretty large in the tummy stakes and standing for long periods was a strain for her. Unhappily, Bregitta always made Flora feel ill at ease. 'Do you mind if I sit down?'

'Of course not. I can see you need to. It must be exhausting carrying all that extra weight around,' the beautiful blonde carolled, planting her reed-slender body down beside Flora on a hard gilded sofa. Both were attending an event that was being staged in a grand public building offering more splendour than comfort. 'It is so unfortunate that Henk and I were not blessed with children.'

'That is sad.' While striving to remain pleasant in the face of Bregitta's fake friendliness, Flora endeavoured not to look around to see where Angelo was. The benefit was being held in aid of one of the charities that Angelo headed up, an organisation that raised funds for brain-damaged children. As Angelo knew virtually all the guests present and had given a rousing speech he was very much in demand. He had asked her to attend as his partner and since he rarely asked her to accompany him anywhere she was determined not to be clingy or needy.

'I'm an old-fashioned girl,' Bregitta murmured sweetly,

eyes as cast down as a dewy teenager's in her show of modesty. 'I would have to be married before I could take the risk of having three children at once.'

'Would you?' Flora simply laughed, too used to the blonde's needling little digs to even react. She had long since worked out that Bregitta cherished very personal designs on Angelo and would have been deeply resentful of any woman sharing his home. The news a couple of months earlier that Flora was also carrying triplets had shocked Bregitta rigid and left her as aggrieved as though Angelo had been stolen from her.

That rather amusing recollection made Flora's soft full mouth quirk, for she was convinced that Angelo did not share Bregitta's intimate aspirations with regard to their friendship. Furthermore, while Angelo might not have told his friends that he was to become a father *before* Flora's arrival, he had positively bragged about the fact since then. Although he had failed to be equally frank about the fact that they were only living together now for the sake of convenience, she cherished no doubts about his enthusiasm for his impending fatherhood. And as a daily witness of his relationship with her niece, Flora had come to accept that Angelo was one of those special men who truly loved children and enjoyed their company.

During the past four months, Flora had regained her health but as her pregnancy progressed she had become more physically restricted in terms of what she could do. She got tired much more easily and her back and hips ached if she walked too far. Getting down on the floor to play with Mariska was impossible now, as was sleeping the night through with three very active babies moving about inside her. Yet she was always aware that the closer her triplets got to term before she brought them into the world, the safer they would be.

Natalie had put her in touch with a consultant obstetrician in Amsterdam, who maintained a careful weekly check on her condition. Jemima also rang her friend regularly to be reassured that she was all right. But Angelo, more than anyone, had provided Flora with unparalleled support. Ironically, that acknowledgement made Flora feel almost unbearably sad, for the more she learned about Angelo van Zaal, the more she knew why she loved him. She might have initially been attracted to him because he was downright gorgeous and very sexy, but he was also courteous, considerate and always ready to listen if she was worried about anything. Indeed she had no grounds for complaint whatsoever because Angelo had given her exactly what she had asked him for: her privacy.

Usually they only mixed when Mariska was present and, with the single exception of tonight's charity benefit, the several outings they had shared had included the little girl. In every way that mattered, Flora and Angelo currently led separate lives. Angelo spent most of the day at his office and about one week in four travelling abroad. When he was at home they occupied separate rooms and often ate at different times as well. As the weeks wore on Flora began to wonder if she had made a drastic misstep in her overwhelming eagerness to save face. Angelo was leaving her alone just as she had requested and she had to assume that there were now other women in his life. She could hardly expect a male with a high-voltage libido to abstain from sex and live like a monk. He was, however, being admirably discreet about any other interests. Even so, his discretion was not a comfort for her because jealousy was eating Flora alive if he so much as looked at another woman.

And although Angelo appeared content, Flora was very much aware that she was feeling lonely, unhappy and insecure. Her pride had certainly come before her fall, she acknowledged ruefully. She recognised that her refusal to challenge his belief that she was a gold-digger head-on had put a wall of misunderstanding between them, which he was understandably reluctant to tackle in the current climate. Naturally he did not want to distress her or make her more hostile to him. He could scarcely be expected to understand that as she had got the chance to know him without the unsettling influence of sexual attraction always taking front-row billing he had finally earned her trust. With Angelo, she had come to accept, what you saw was what you got. There was nothing false, nothing hidden, no polite pretences or lies. He was as far removed from a lying, cheating philanderer of her late father's ilk as any man could be and had a much stronger character than Peter had ever had.

'You are so brave, Flora. How can you be so calm?' Bregitta asked in measured disbelief, lifting her pencilled brows in emphasis of the point. 'In a few months you'll have four children under two years old and Mariska is already running around and creating havoc as toddlers do. I'm afraid I cannot picture Angelo in so domestic a role.'

'He's crazy about kids,' Flora fielded confidently.

'Any man in my life would have to want me more than any children I might have,' Bregitta informed her without hesitation, 'but with Angelo that could be a problem for you.'

Stung by that all too perceptive comment, Flora made no response for on that score she had no comment to make. Angelo was only with her, after all, because she was pregnant, and once her babies were born they would have to come to some other convenient arrangement, which was highly unlikely to be one in which they continued to live below the same roof. Soon, she recognised painfully, even living within easy reach of Angelo on a daily basis would just be a fond memory. Then wasn't it time for her to speak up in her own defence? Was he content with the way things were? And if he wasn't content, why hadn't he said anything?

'If you ask me, the only woman who ever held Angelo's heart was Katja.' Bregitta sighed. 'And as she's the one who got away, metaphorically speaking, who else is likely to make the grade?'

Flora was confounded by the idea that Angelo might once have loved and lost a woman, or might even have been rejected, but she was too proud to question Bregitta, who she was well aware was a troublemaker. Instead Flora looked across the room to where Angelo was laughing with another gorgeous blonde in a skimpy red cocktail frock that showed off her pert breasts and slender thighs. A sharp and painful pang darted through Flora because her own once shapely figure had vanished. Were Angelo and the blonde sharing an innocent joke? A flirtation? Or was Flora, in fact, seeing lovers using the opportunity to enjoy a brief moment of intimacy in public? That she had no idea of what she was seeing or indeed what was happening in that part of Angelo's life hurt her and underlined the gulf she had opened up between herself and the man she loved. For, in spite of all her efforts to the contrary, she loved him more than ever, she conceded ruefully.

Angelo joined her ten minutes later. 'You look sleepy,' he murmured softly.

Lie, she wanted to shout at him. Tell me I look sexy or beautiful or anything other than tired even if it is a barefaced lie! But she swallowed back her discomfiture over her excessively sensitive reaction while he stretched down a hand to help her upright with as much care and concern as if she were an ailing and elderly lady. Suddenly she hated being pregnant and longed to be small and blonde with pert breasts and a tiny waist! I'm so shallow and superficial to feel that way when I'm pregnant, she thought shamefacedly, but with all her heart she was longing for the smallest sign that Angelo could still find her attractive.

Jolted by the strength of that craving, Flora was furious with herself and she went straight up to bed, turning down the offer of the supper that Angelo suggested they share. She was cutting off her nose to spite her face, she reflected ruefully as she settled heavily under the covers. In spite of the uneasy mood she was in she slept for a couple of hours, though only to waken to the sensation of what felt like a game of football being played inside her womb. She lay still for a few moments, her palm lightly covering her swollen abdomen and the little movements she could feel with a tenderness she couldn't help. A pang of hunger assailed her about then and although she tried to ward it off, she failed and her mind was soon awash with images that merely revved up her taste buds. Minutes later, she finally climbed out of bed and reached for her robe.

In the basement kitchen Mango purred continuously and wound himself round her legs while Skipper continued to snore in his basket. The big traditional kitchen in the Amsterdam house was a wonderfully warm and inviting place. Delft tiles covered the massive chimneypiece while cream-ware crockery was displayed on the painted dresser and polished copper utensils on the walls. In one corner an antique walnut grandfather clock slowly ticked out the time.

'*Dios mio*…I thought I heard someone…'

At the sound of Angelo's voice Flora turned her bright head and saw him framed in the doorway. Skipper loosed a sleepy bark and then scrambled out of his bed to go and welcome Angelo while his mistress watched with jaundiced eyes. She had discovered that Skipper was very much a man's dog and prone to lying in wait at the front door waiting for Angelo to come home. How Angelo had accomplished the feat of overcoming Skipper's distrust and replacing it with downright devotion, she had no very clear idea, for she had yet to see any sign of Angelo doing anything more than giving Skipper the most cursory pat on the head.

Unlike her, Angelo was still fully dressed, although he now sported a pair of faded jeans with his ruffled white dress shirt and had removed his jacket and tie. Her cheeks reddened because she knew her hair was as tousled as a bird's nest. She indicated the salad sandwich she was in the midst of putting together. 'I should have had supper,' she admitted wryly.

'I know better than to say, "I told you so",' Angelo drawled, lounging back against the massive scrubbed pine kitchen table with his lean powerful thighs spread in a relaxed attitude.

'That doesn't always stop people saying it. Are you hungry?'

'Thanks, but I ate earlier. I stayed up to do some work.'

'Sometimes the babies move around so much they wake me up. I don't sleep very well,' Flora admitted, sinking down into Therese's rocking chair by the stove to eat her sandwich. 'I've been thinking too…'

'What about?' Angelo prompted.

Flora made herself withstand the appeal of the sandwich for another moment and breathed in. 'I think it's time I told you about that tribunal case.'

Watching her eat, Angelo frowned, a wary light in his bright blue eyes that immediately put Flora on the defensive. 'You can believe or disbelieve me—that's your choice,' she added with more than a hint of challenge.

'Naturally I would like to hear your side of the story.'

A little of her discomfiture ebbed and she began to tell him about the wonderfully well-paid job she had won within weeks of gaining her business degree from a top university.

'But why didn't you complain the instant your boss began harassing you?' Angelo was quick to enquire with a frown.

'At first I was worried that I was being over-sensitive and misinterpreting his signals. I think a lot of women feel like that in an all-male work environment when there's a lot of pressure not to make a fuss about anything,' she confided tautly. 'I was trying very hard to fit in and I didn't want to get a name for being difficult. When Henshall's approaches became more blatant I started worrying about how a complaint about him sexually harassing me—and he was *very* highly thought of in the company—would affect my career.'

Angelo was frowning. 'That is not how you should have felt…'

'I'm not talking ideals here…I'm talking about what it was like on the ground. Many of the people I was at university with hadn't even found jobs. I knew I'd been given a terrific opportunity and I was desperate not to screw it up.'

'It was your boss who was screwing it up, not you. If what you're telling me is true, how on earth did you lose the case?'

Flora grimaced. 'Two things ensured that I lost that tribunal case. The other woman making a complaint with me against Henshall got cold feet and withdrew it, so I was left without supporting evidence. The second was Henshall's claim that I'd been having an affair with him and it had turned sour because he'd stayed with his wife and refused to give me that bonus.' Flora's oval face was pale and strained. 'That provided the sleaze angle that attracted the attention of the tabloid newspapers and resulted in some very nasty headlines on my account. Many people chose to believe Henshall's story, because nobody could believe that a married man would own up to an affair when there hadn't been one—'

'Why do you think he pretended that you and he had had an affair?' Angelo asked levelly.

'Because he was afraid he would lose his job if I was able to prove that he was a sex-pest. He earned a huge salary, so lying and striving to discredit me by blackening my reputation made sense from his point of view. His wife supported his appearances at the tribunal every day for the same reasons. He'd had at least half a dozen work affairs and she must have known what he was like.'

'Your engagement broke up around the same time,' Angelo recalled.

'After the newspapers got involved, Peter and his family felt that being associated with me was too much of an embarrassment. But I did get that wretched bonus in the end,' she completed ruefully.

Angelo could not hide his surprise on that score. 'You *did*?'

'I had earned it fair and square on performance and the company knew it and paid up, but only after the publicity had died down. I still have it in the bank…untouched,' Flora admitted.

'Not much of a consolation in the circumstances, I imagine,' Angelo remarked, helping her upright as she began to rise slowly from the chair.

'It wasn't,' she agreed.

'I'll see you up to bed,' Angelo murmured.

Flora buttoned her lips on an immediate urge to tell him that she would manage fine on her own. Fiery independence was all very well but keeping Angelo at arm's length was no longer what she wanted. As he drew close a whiff of the exclusive citrus-based cologne he used wafted over her and unleashed an intimate tide of images. She remembered the hot passion of that wide sensual mouth on hers, the sure tantalising touch of those lean brown hands, and a knot of pure sexual tension tightened between her legs. Distracted by her embarrassing thoughts, she tripped over her feet in her haste to enter her bedroom and Angelo closed his arms round her from behind to steady her.

'Take your time,' he urged softly.

But there was hardly any time left for them to be together, she thought painfully. She knew that her obstetrician was wavering on the brink of instructing her to take bed rest for the remainder of her pregnancy. Once the freedom to move around was taken from her, she would be even more isolated and separate from Angelo than she already was.

Angelo slid her robe off her shoulders with an ease that reminded her just how at home he was with a woman in a bedroom and her cheeks burned. As jumpy as the proverbial cat on hot bricks, she lay down on the bed and as he began to move away she found herself reaching for his hand in a movement that took her as much by surprise as it appeared to take him. He swung back, his dark lashed gaze positively welded to the sight of her hand on his, the tension in his lean sculpted features palpable. 'Don't go…' she framed without even being aware that the plea was brimming on her lips. 'Yet,' she threw in stilted addition.

Angelo glanced at her. His brilliant blue eyes had a crystalline glitter behind his lashes and he settled his long powerful body down on the edge of the bed. 'Are you feeling all right?'

Her teeth gritted. She had that familiar feeling of inadequacy she often got in his radius of late: a near overpowering urge to sob and scream in frustration. She asked him to stay with her and the only reason he could come up with was that she might be ill or in the grip of her nerves. Of course, she was hardly a beguilingly sexy proposition just at present, she reasoned ruefully, striving to be fair to him.

'I'm all…r-right,' she started to say, only a kick from one of the babies stole her breath and made her stammer.

'Just a kick,' she explained, pressing the heel of her hand against her stomach.

'Would you mind?' His interest clearly caught, Angelo rested his palm down very close to hers, evidently in the hope of feeling one of the babies move again.

'Of course I don't mind,' Flora lied because, in truth, she was now even closer to sobbing in frustration. Lying very still, she stared down at the rising mound of her stomach and wondered what on earth she had been playing at in even dreaming of acting the temptress. Once again the triplets had effortlessly contrived to take centre stage.

As Angelo felt a baby kick a look of wonderment transformed his lean, darkly handsome features. She saw his pleasure and felt mean for minding that she was simply a human incubator for the babies Angelo could hardly wait for her to have. Had she tried, she could not have found a keener father-to-be. It was a wonder he hadn't got married years ago and already fathered a little tribe of offspring, she thought ruefully. Of course, no doubt he had learned the lesson of being cautious when his father had got badly burned in his rushed second marriage. Furthermore, there was no denying the fact that Angelo valued his freedom and had fought to preserve it from the outset of their acquaintance. Had he felt differently about the mysterious Katja, whom Bregitta liked to hold up as an unassailable rival? Flora only wished that she had not chosen to overlook his love of his freedom at the outset of their relationship, for caution might have saved her from heartbreak.

'You're amazing,' Angelo murmured in a tone of husky admiration, looking right down into her eyes with those dazzlingly blue eyes that made her mouth run dry and her shameless heart thunder in her ears.

She wanted so badly to touch him that she had to curl her fingers into her palm to stop herself from stretching out her fingers. Her breathing grew shallower and more audible, her breasts swelling until the tender tips were prominent while heat and moisture pooled in her pelvis. He held her gaze and the atmosphere buzzed with electric tension. For several taut moments she was unable to reason because she was wholly in the control of her rebellious hormones and the hunger he could ignite.

Angelo removed his hand from her stomach and tugged up the linen sheet to cover her. 'It's late. I mustn't keep you awake,' he said with precision, his voice deep and rough-edged, and he straightened and switched out the bedside light. 'Don't forget that you have an appointment with the obstetrician tomorrow afternoon.'

Moonlight was spilling welcome clarity round the edges of the curtains. Her heart in her mouth, Flora watched Angelo walk to the door and her sense of mortification was so intense she could think of nothing to say in return. What had she thought or even hoped? That he might kiss her? Show some hint of sexual interest or even regret at the distance between them? What a foolish dream that was to cherish when she was about as fanciable as a stuffed turkey!

Tears stung Flora's wide open eyes in a hot burning surge and inched slowly down her cheeks. She blinked furiously and one of the babies kicked and she just burst out crying then, pushing her face into the pillow to muffle the noise that she was making while reflecting that she would look even worse in the morning with reddened swollen eyes.

When she awoke late the following morning after a restless night, it was to the beep and flash of a text on her phone and she stretched out a drowsy hand to lift it from the bedside table. Once she realised with astonishment that the text was actually from her former fiancé, Peter Davies, she sat up in surprise and curiosity to read it immediately. Having bumped into a mutual friend, Peter texted that he was shocked at the news that Julie had died and that Flora was currently living in Amsterdam with her niece. Flora was equally taken aback to learn, when she responded, that Peter now worked for a Rotterdam-based shipping company in London, was currently in the Netherlands at a conference and was keen to meet up with her before he returned home.

Consumed by curiosity over why he should have chosen to contact her after so long, Flora discovered that Peter would be heading back to London that very evening and she agreed to meet him for coffee before he left for the airport…

CHAPTER TEN

ANGELO ACCOMPANIED FLORA to her appointment with the obstetrician. Her face fell when the doctor told her that he thought she would benefit from bed rest for what remained of her pregnancy.

'You're doing very well but, at this stage, every extra day that your triplets remain unborn is another day for them to develop into bigger and healthier babies,' Mr Wintershoven pointed out with sympathy. 'I would have advised you to come into hospital now, but with the care Mr van Zaal is able to provide you can safely remain at home.'

'It'll be so boring lying there,' Flora sighed as she and Angelo left the exclusive hospital where Mr Wintershoven had his consulting rooms. She felt guilty for even voicing that complaint because she knew that the obstetrician's advice was sensible for a woman in her condition.

Angelo looked down at her, blue eyes bright as sapphires in his lean bronzed face. 'I will keep you entertained. We'll go from here straight to your favourite bookshop and we'll buy films as well...'

'I can't—I meant to tell you earlier but I forgot to mention it. I'm meeting someone this afternoon,' Flora told him.

'Who?' Angelo enquired baldly.

Slight colour tinged her cheeks. 'Peter texted me. Apparently he was attending a conference in Rotterdam this week and we're going to meet for coffee before he travels home.'

'*Peter?*' Angelo repeated in a startled undertone that made her glance up at him and notice the tautness of his strong jaw line. 'Peter Davies? Your ex-fiancé? He was in Rotterdam this week?'

Flora smiled. 'Yes, he's an accountant with a shipping company that has its head office based there. Isn't that an amazing coincidence?'

'It is. I wasn't aware that you were still in contact with him.'

'I wasn't. Once I left London we lost touch with each other. He texted me right out of the blue after running into a mutual friend who told him about Julie's death,' Flora told him with a grimace.

Angelo was standing very still by the limousine. 'Of course, he would have known your sister.'

'Yes, but to be truthful they never got on that well,' Flora recalled wryly; Peter had resented the time and attention she gave her sister.

Angelo watched her climb into the car and smooth her trousers over her knees. 'I'll come with you.'

Flora gave him a startled look. 'Why would you do that?'

Angelo compressed his handsome mouth into a line, a tiny muscle tugging at the corner of his perfectly moulded masculine lips. 'I don't like you going anywhere alone at present. I would be happier if I went with you.'

'That's ridiculous. All I'll be doing is walking into a coffee shop to sit down and then coming back out again when I'm finished,' Flora pointed out drily.

'I'd still prefer to accompany you,' Angelo told her stubbornly, evidently impervious to gentle courteous hints.

'Well, you *can't* come! You won't be welcome,' Flora told him bluntly. 'Peter and I couldn't discuss anything personal if we wanted to with you present.'

Clearly far from reassured by that statement, Angelo

stared broodingly down into her resolute face. 'You really do want to meet up with him, don't you?'

Flora nodded unembarrassed affirmation. Curiosity motivated her more than any other reason, but she didn't see why she should share that fact with Angelo. After all, what was it to him if she met up with her ex-fiancé for a friendly coffee and a chat? Hadn't he enjoyed complete freedom to see other women for months on end? And difficult and painful though it had been to remain silent and not interfere in his life, Flora had not once weakened in her stance, or asked him a single nosy question.

The conversation over, she emerged from the limo outside the designated coffee shop and, uneasily aware of Angelo's annoyance at the novel sensation of having his wishes utterly ignored, Flora gave him a warm reassuring smile. But his brilliant eyes remained grim and his handsome mouth and strong jaw line stayed rigid. Feeling like a ship in full sail in the blue maternity top she wore, Flora headed into the café.

Peter was already there waiting for her. Although she immediately recognised him, she also noticed that his hairline had begun to recede and he had put on weight. The instant he saw her he leapt to his feet and began telling her how sorry he had been to hear about what had happened to her sister.

'I knew you would be very upset. You and Julie were so close,' Peter declared. 'And when I heard about it and found out you were living in Amsterdam, I just *had* to see you! The way we parted is still on my conscience...'

'It's a long time ago now,' Flora commented mildly, relieved to discover that even the sight of a wedding ring on Peter's rather podgy hand didn't move her to regret the past in the slightest.

As Flora turned to choose her seat Peter's attention

dropped to her bump and he looked at her in flagrant surprise. 'You're pregnant?'

Flora could not help laughing at his expression. 'Why not?'

'You're not married.' Peter dropped his voice to make that comment as if afraid others might be embarrassed by that statement of fact.

'And you are. We've both changed and moved on,' Flora declared comfortably, pausing to order her coffee. 'When did you get married?'

Peter turned brick-red. 'A few months after we split up,' he admitted. 'Her name's Sandy; we worked together.'

Flora smiled. 'And yet you never mentioned her to me.'

'I know. I felt very guilty about keeping quiet but what would have been the point of telling you?'

'If I'd known there was someone else, I wouldn't have felt our broken engagement was my fault,' Flora responded with wry assurance. 'I felt guilty about all the bad publicity my tribunal case had attracted and the effect it had on you and your family.'

Peter winced. 'I was the one in the wrong, Flora. I'm sorry. I didn't have the courage to tell you how I really felt and I used that tribunal fiasco as an excuse to break off the engagement. I'll always be ashamed of that.'

'Never mind,' Flora said generously and she sipped tranquilly at her coffee.

'I let you down and I'll always regret that but we weren't right together. I felt more like your brother than your boyfriend,' Peter confided with a look of discomfiture. 'Somewhere along the line we lost that essential spark and I handled it very clumsily.'

It was as though a little cloud had cleared away from Flora's view of the past. She saw the truth of what he had just said. Their relationship had been based more on friendship than passion and, as time had gone on, the attraction between them had waned rather than deepened. Peter had first recognised the problem because he was attracted to Sandy, whom she also noted he had wasted little time in marrying. She wished he had been more honest because she did not think she would have felt quite as rejected had Peter simply admitted that he had fallen for another woman.

'We weren't suited,' she told him, striving not to wonder if too much exposure to her was a turn-off for men in general. Was that what was amiss with Angelo? Was he indifferent to her now? Had familiarity while she lived in the same household simply led to contempt?

'You were always too headstrong and ambitious for me.' Peter shook his head. 'Sandy makes me feel good about myself—'

'Let's leave it there,' Flora advised drily before he could make any more less than tactful comparisons.

Peter asked her about the father of her children and confided that he was already the father of a year-old son. She enjoyed his surprise when she mentioned her triplets and thirty or so minutes wound up pleasantly enough before they went their separate ways. She travelled back to Angelo's mansion in a taxi and wondered why she had beaten herself up over Peter's defection for so long. By the time they had left university they had outgrown each other and become more of a habit than a couple in love, but she had been so bound up in her challenging new job that she had failed to appreciate that truth.

The baby bag already sitting packed in the hall reminded Flora that it was the weekend and time to head to Huis van Zaal again. She hoped that Angelo was not expecting her to take to her bed that very day and stay on in Amsterdam because she loved the relaxing pace of the weekends. If Angelo was free to come down to his country house, business was never allowed to act as a distraction within those ancient walls. But sadness touched her too, for although the weather was still bright and sunny the cooler temperatures of autumn were already in the air and now Angelo was a less frequent visitor to his country home.

'Where's Angelo?' she asked Anke in the nursery.

'I think he went to see Katja so he shouldn't be too long,' the nanny informed her cheerfully as Mariska toddled over to Flora to show off the new dress she was wearing. A happy confident child, Flora's niece seemed to have suffered no lasting harm from her less-than-ideal early months with her troubled parents.

And there and then, Flora almost asked Anke who Katja was, because she knew the young nanny would satisfy her curiosity without making a production out of it. But it also occurred to her that Bregitta had deliberately made a point of twice mentioning Katja, which very likely meant that there was nothing at all questionable in the relationship. Katja might well be ninety-five years old and perfectly respectable. Bregitta, after all, enjoyed making Flora feel insecure and would have been even happier to know that she had contrived to cause trouble between Angelo and the mother of his unborn children.

An hour later Flora was paying lip service to bed rest by lying on a padded lounger enjoying a glass of home-made lemonade while she basked in the early autumn sunshine. Mariska and Skipper were happily engaged in chasing the same ball tirelessly round the garden. Flora, however, was painstakingly counting her blessings. Angelo might not be in love with her, but he would be a very good father to their children and no doubt in time she would get over her constant wish and need for him to be something more than that. Four children, she thought, just a little daunted by the prospect as she registered the amount of noise that Mariska could make without any backup at all. When Anke asked if she could take the little girl to visit

her parents' farm with her that afternoon, Flora agreed
and let her weary eyes slide shut.

'Flora…?'

Flora lifted her lashes and focused dreamily on Angelo,
her green eyes unusually soft. Tall, dark and gorgeous, he
was poised only a few feet away, casually clad in well-cut
trousers and a pale shirt that made a perfect frame for his
bronzed skin and black-as-jet hair. She tilted her head to
one side while she studied him, admiring the sleek planes
of his high cheekbones, the classic patrician set of his nose
and the beautifully modelled perfection of his wide masculine mouth.

'You're staring at me,' Angelo said softly.

Her cheeks flared with colour and as she met those very
blue eyes of his her mouth ran dry. Blinking rapidly, she
began to sit up, a process that was as slow and difficult for
her with her cumbersome body as standing up in a hurry.
Within seconds, Angelo was by her side and rearranging
her more comfortably.

'How was Peter?' Angelo enquired coolly.

'He hadn't changed much.' Reluctant to run her former
fiancé down or discuss what he had shared with her, Flora
fell uncomfortably silent.

Angelo surveyed her with an odd intensity that she
could almost feel like a touch on her skin. 'I have a question to ask you,' he imparted tautly.

'Go ahead,' Flora advised, hoping it didn't relate to
Peter and taking a sip at her lemonade in an effort to seem
composed.

'Will you do me the honour of becoming my wife?'
Angelo asked levelly.

Flora glanced up at him in shaken disbelief and somehow contrived to choke on her drink, breaking down into
a fit of coughing that led to him banging her on the back
to aid her recovery. Eyes still streaming in the aftermath,

she mopped them with a tissue and tried frantically to work out where the marriage proposal had come from. He was asking her to marry him! *He was actually asking her to marry him.* After weeks and weeks of sharing the same roof without the smallest intimate contact, he was suddenly asking her to be his wife and she could not credit it. Stunned, she focused on his heartbreakingly handsome and very serious features and registered that he was definitely not joking. 'I…I…er…'

'I appear to have taken you by surprise,' Angelo breathed tensely.

'You've really shocked me… I mean, I definitely didn't see this coming over the horizon,' she mumbled unevenly, scarcely knowing whether she was on her head or her heels.

Angelo dropped down on the chair beside hers and reached for her hand. Brilliant blue eyes sought out hers. 'I would be proud to call you my wife.'

Flora tugged her fingers reluctantly free. 'Even though you think I'm a gold-digger?'

'Only a stupid man would get to know you as well as I know you now and still think you capable of such a motivation…I am *not* a stupid man, *tesora mia.*'

Flora was not so easily soothed. 'It's all very well saying now that you've changed your mind about that, but why has it taken you so long to tell me so?'

His lush black lashes semi-screened his gaze from her keen scrutiny. 'I had made you so hostile that I was reluctant to open the subject again in case I made matters worse. I'm not very good at eating humble pie either,' he admitted with gritty reluctance.

'You're as stubborn as a rock,' Flora pronounced without apology, studying the fierce tension etched into his hard masculine features.

'I should have had that tribunal experience of yours checked out again. Unfortunately it wasn't important enough to me when I first met you, but it was a mistake to accept what proved to be speculation as fact and to allow it to colour my judgement to such an extent.'

'I was very upset when I realised that you had always had a low opinion of me and why,' Flora admitted ruefully.

'I did finally have further enquiries made,' Angelo confided with gravity. 'It may be a consolation for you to learn that eighteen months after your departure from that company where you worked, Marvin Henshall was sacked for gross misconduct. There were fresh allegations of sexual harassment laid against him by a new employee.'

Flora was disgusted to hear that her former boss had found yet another victim but relieved that allegations against him had finally been made to stick and that he had paid the price for his behaviour. 'I'm glad that no other woman will have to go through what I went through again,' she murmured with heartfelt sincerity.

'I'm sorry that you had to suffer that way and that I took so long to admit what I believed I knew about you. You were right,' Angelo declared, his lean, strong face serious as he made the admission. 'It was unfair of me not to give you the chance to speak up in your own defence. My only excuse is that our relationship was already tense and I was afraid to put it under more strain.'

'You mean, I was pregnant,' Flora translated heavily.

'That only influenced me after I realised you were pregnant and unwell,' Angelo countered levelly. 'Prior to that point my only interest was in you and, right from the start, I didn't want to accept that our stolen afternoon on the houseboat was the most we would ever share.'

Her lashes lifted, her interest ensnared by that declaration, and she studied him with questioning cool. 'You wanted more?'

'*Dios mio!* Didn't I immediately ask you to spend the weekend with me here? Of course I wanted more. I lived my whole life through and I never once felt as alive as I did with you on that boat!' Angelo delivered in an undertone raw with the strength of his conviction. 'It was different; together *we* were different, even when we were arguing, and I'd never experienced a connection like that with a woman before.'

For the first time, Flora appreciated that she might have allowed the very fact that she was pregnant to get in the way of a closer understanding between them. In fact she too had been guilty of making far-reaching assumptions. 'I thought you were only interested because I fell pregnant.'

'How could I fake being interested and why would I do that anyway?' Angelo dealt her a bewildered look as Skipper dropped his ball at his feet.

'Because you felt it was the right thing to do when I was carrying your children...'

'I would never have invited you to share my life if I hadn't wanted you for yourself. To do otherwise would have involved us both in a relationship that could only have come to a painful conclusion.'

Pushing her hands down on the arms of the lounger, Flora got up and slid her feet back into her shoes to walk away a few steps. She had found it hard to believe that he truly wanted her and her pride had not allowed her to accept support from a man only offering it out of a sense of duty.

'When I first fell pregnant I wouldn't let you help me. I honestly thought that you only wanted to help because you felt you *had* to,' Flora told him in a troubled admission.

'I needed and wanted to help you but you made it so difficult. Sometimes it annoys me that you're so proud and so determined to be independent,' Angelo confided levelly.

'I'm a freeloader who's been living off you for months!' Flora proclaimed with spirit. 'Where's the independence in that?'

'You're no freeloader. You may live in my home but when have you ever even gone shopping at my expense?' Angelo prompted in frank exasperation as Skipper nudged his shoe with the ball. 'You won't spend my money—what am I going to do with you?'

Flora studied him warily from below her feathery lashes. 'Why have you asked me to marry you, Angelo?'

His jaw line squared. 'Believe me when I say that it is for all the right reasons.'

'Because we're going to have four children between us in another few weeks?' Flora shot at him.

Angelo laughed out loud, his irreverent grin chasing the serious aspect from his bronzed features. 'No, oddly enough that hasn't once entered my thoughts.'

Her brow pleated because she was baffled by that claim. 'It...*hasn't*?'

'Should I be ashamed to admit that the only two people in my thoughts are you and I?'

'No, not ashamed, but you're still not answering my question.'

Angelo bent down and lifted Skipper's ball to throw it. The little terrier went racing madly across the lawn and bounced across a box-edged border. Angelo studied Flora with narrowed blue eyes and a rueful expression that tugged at her heartstrings. 'I'm asking you to marry me today because I panicked when you went off to meet Peter. I was planning to wait until after our children were born before I proposed—'

'You panicked about Peter?' Flora cut in blankly. 'What's that supposed to mean?'

'The obvious. I was afraid that you still had feelings for your former fiancé and I didn't want you meeting up with him again.' Angelo compressed his handsome mouth. 'I was jealous. Okay?'

'Of...Peter?' Flora gasped incredulously, barely able

to compute the concept that he could be jealous when she was so heavily pregnant. 'You were jealous of Peter...even with me looking as I do now?'

'You still light my fire, *tesora mia*,' Angelo intoned huskily, reaching for her hands and tugging her towards him. 'Why not his?'

'Because, for one thing...' Flora hesitated before continuing '...Peter and I never managed to light a fire in the first place and that was why we broke up. Are you serious? You still find me attractive looking like this?'

'*Por Dios*...very much,' Angelo asserted in a low-pitched growl of confirmation that sent a shimmy of desire dancing down her taut spinal cord.

Her eyes had opened to their fullest extent. 'But you haven't even kissed me—'

'You asked me to treat you like a housemate,' he groaned.

'You were supposed to argue with me when I said that but you didn't, so I assumed it didn't matter to you.'

'Of course it mattered. I'm not a block of wood!' Angelo exclaimed feelingly, releasing her fingers to cup her cheekbones and then lift his hands to run his fingers lightly through the fall of her hair. 'Have you any idea how hard it's been for me not to touch you?'

'No...'

And then he kissed her and the amount of pent-up passion and longing he contrived to put into that single kiss almost blew Flora away. Reeling from the effect of it, she leant up against his lean, powerfully aroused body and smiled secretly against his shoulder. Now she believed him. Now she knew that she had been blind and it was one of those rare occasions when she was happy to have been proved wrong.

'Even sharing the same bed with you would be an incredible thrill,' Angelo confessed raggedly. 'Nothing else is possible right now but that doesn't matter.'

'I thought "amazingly good sex" was my main attraction?'

'I've gone way beyond anything that basic. If I had realised that I was your first lover, I would have been a lot more diplomatic. Unfortunately I was trying too hard to be cool,' Angelo confessed with an almost shamefaced expression, pressing her in the direction of the house. 'Are we getting married?'

'Give me one good reason why,' she urged, her lips still tingling from that passionate kiss. She was very much open to persuasion.

'I love you. I love you so much that I can't imagine my life without you,' Angelo informed her as naturally as if he had already told her that every day for a year.

Flora turned shaken eyes on him. 'You told me that you don't do romance or commitment.'

'Well, I should have added the proviso…at least not until the right woman comes along,' Angelo incised silkily, closing an arm round her narrow spine. 'And you are, without a doubt, my perfect match. I'm a strong personality but so are you. I don't intimidate you.'

'You do annoy me though,' she muttered helplessly while trying to come to terms with the heady idea that he might love her.

'We bring out the best and the worst in each other. We're both stubborn, proud, impatient…'

Flora touched the arm he had curved round her. 'Get back to the love bit!'

'Equally bossy and we both like our own way.' Angelo slung her a wolfish smile. 'When are you going to answer me? I'm offering you everything you said you wanted.'

Flora came over all shy. 'I'm thinking it over.'

Angelo dug into his pocket and produced a small jewellery box, which he flipped open. 'Engagement ring…'

'Wow!' Flora exclaimed, watching the sunlight ignite a river of fire in the emerald and diamond cluster. 'I love it!'

He came to a halt in the hall and lifted her hand.

'It won't fit!' she wailed. 'My fingers are swollen!'

With an air of solemnity, Angelo discovered that for himself and slid it onto her little finger instead. 'I'd like to get married in the local church where my parents took their vows.'

'When?' Flora stretched up and pressed a kiss against the corner of his mouth before falling back from him again, prevented from staying close by the size of her stomach.

'As soon as possible.' His sapphire-blue eyes stared down into hers with flagrant anticipation. 'I love you… I can't wait to marry you.'

'But I'm…*huge*!' she lamented.

'And supposed to be lying down and resting,' he reminded her in a tone of suppressed urgency, angling her in the direction of the stairs.

Still in shock from having all her dreams come true at one and the same time, Flora allowed him to help her onto the bed and slip off her shoes. She admired her gorgeous ring. She admired Angelo and she smiled sunnily up at him. 'I love you too,' she said belatedly. 'I've been madly in love with you for months.'

'A fine way you have of showing it, *querida mia*!' Angelo teased, folding down on the bed behind her and easing her into the possessive circle of his arms. 'I was terrified you were going to move out as soon as the babies were born.'

'While I was terrified of moving out because I wouldn't have been able to see you every day any more,' Flora confided. 'I also assumed that you were seeing other women.'

She twisted her copper head round to squint at him, her anxiety palpable. *'Did you?'*

'No, I'm yours lock, stock and barrel, *enamorada mia*. I'm definitely a one-woman man,' Angelo confided, his eyes bright with tenderness as he spread big gentle hands across the proud swell of her stomach. 'There's been no-body else in my life and there never will be now.'

His quiet confidence on that score touched her deep. Happiness engulfed her and she covered his hands with hers, looking forward to the day when they could make love again and experience that very special intimacy and pleasure. But the amount of love she could feel in him was sufficient to warm and inspire her.

'I'll marry you as soon as it can be arranged,' she told him softly, stroking the strong male fingers beneath her own. 'Because I can't imagine my life without you, either.'

'And from now on,' Angelo murmured with rich satisfaction, 'I sleep in here with you wrapped in my arms. Do you realise that we've never slept the night through together?'

'Hmm…' Flora framed sleepily, finding that happiness and the amount of heat his big powerful body put out were combining to make her feel incredibly drowsy. That was one wish she could grant him right there and then.

Two YEARS AFTER that night, Flora scanned her reflection critically in the cheval mirror. The green evening dress with the hand-embroidered and beaded bodice had cost a fortune, but that particular colour did seem to give her a positive glow. The figure-fitting contours also made the most of the sleek toned curves that she had worked hard in the gym to recapture after she had given birth.

For the occasion of the charity ball Angelo held in his home every year, her husband had got the family jewels out to deck her from head to toe. She wore the magnificent diamond tiara, necklace and earrings that had once belonged to his mother and the flash of fire that accompanied her every move as the fine jewels caught the light made her feel wonderfully opulent.

'You look breathtaking...'

Flora spun round, her dress rustling with the movement, to focus on the male who had just entered. Her heart in her eyes, she smiled warmly. 'Are they all asleep?'

'Of course,' Angelo countered with more than a little self-satisfaction.

'I don't believe you. I bet they're climbing out of their cots right this minute,' Flora contended with maternal pessimism.

She adored her sons, but Joris, Rip and Hendrik were very lively little boys and getting them to sleep at night was a challenge. Their sister, Mariska, whom Angelo and Flora had officially adopted the previous year, did what she could to keep her brothers in line, but when the three twenty-two-month-old toddlers worked as a team they could be a real headache to keep under control.

'The boys are tired out tonight. Anke and Berna did a great job using up their surplus energy today. Señora van Zaal, you *do* look breathtaking.' Angelo repeated the compliment in a low husky growl and matched it by closing a hand to her wrist to tug her to him.

Flora pulled free again and raised her hands. 'Mind the make-up and the hair!'

'I don't want you so fancy that I can't touch you, *enamorada mia*,' Angelo confessed.

'Well, you will keep on throwing these swanky charity dos,' Flora teased, revelling in the electric-blue heat of his hungry possessive gaze.

She sidestepped her husband to speed down the corridor and go into Mariska's bedroom, where she removed the story books piled up on the bed so that they wouldn't fall during the night and wake the little girl. Julie's daughter was a happy, intelligent child with a lovely gentleness to her nature. She had welcomed the arrival of her three boisterous little brothers and loved being a big sister.

Joris, Rip and Hendrik had been born by C-section when Flora was thirty-three weeks along and the newborns had spent their earliest days in hospital. Rip, the smallest of three, had suffered some breathing difficulties at first but had surmounted his problems and was now the same size as his brothers. Anke had gained a backup in Berna, a second nanny to lighten her load, although Flora spent a great deal of time with her children. In truth, with four young and lively children in need of care and attention there was always plenty of work to be done.

That night's benefit was again in aid of brain-damaged children, the charity which lay closest to Angelo's heart. When Flora had finally got around to asking Angelo who Katja was, she had uncovered a tragic story. Katja had been one of Angelo's schoolmates. At the age of sixteen she had been knocked down by a car and ever since then had lived in a care home because she now had the mental capacities of a young child. After Katja's parents died, it was Angelo who had taken overall responsibility for her continuing care. Angelo visited Katja most weeks, often bringing her one of the animal jigsaws she enjoyed. Having accompanied him on several of those visits, Flora loved Angelo all the more for his generous heart.

The past two years had been action-packed and very happy for Flora, who had gained a good deal of confidence since her marriage. She had fond memories of their small private wedding at the old church that lay only a kilometre from Huis van Zaal. It hadn't mattered to her that she had worn an ivory lace maternity frock or that she'd had to return to bed to rest soon after the ceremony. What had really mattered was the love and tenderness she'd recognised in Angelo's eyes when he'd made his vows. When the boys were three months old, they had flown to the Caribbean to enjoy an extended honeymoon. Bleakly aware that she had not resonated with Angelo, Bregitta Etten had ceased her visits and was not missed.

Flora paused in the doorway of the nursery where her sons were fast asleep. Unusually, there wasn't a sound from the line of cots. She could see the three little dark heads, which were so rarely still during the day, unless they were plotting some mischief. She called Skipper out from below the nearest cot where he would happily have remained for the night had he been allowed to do so, for he adored the boys.

'I have a very beautiful wife and four wonderful kids,' Angelo pronounced from behind her, closing his arms round his wife to slowly turn her round to face him. 'I'm a very lucky man.'

Flora gazed up into his sapphire-blue eyes and her heart raced in reaction. He never got any less gorgeous, she savoured, and she began to stretch up.

'Make-up…hair, *enamorada mia*,' Angelo reminded her teasingly before her cherry-tinted lips could connect with his and wreak havoc with her carefully groomed appearance.

Her eyes glinted at the crack for, as he had once accurately remarked, they were both equally fond of having the last word. 'Later…' she whispered in a tone of feminine promise and had the very great pleasure of seeing sensuality meld with impatience in the lean, darkly handsome face that she could read so much better now.

'Later…' Angelo husked in sexy agreement, running a playful forefinger down from the pulse flickering at her collarbone to the tiny shadowy valley showing between her small high breasts. Her mouth running dry, she had to gasp for breath.

Angelo curved a hand to her spine to guide her downstairs in readiness to greet their guests. 'I suppose you know I'm crazy about you.'

'But I like it when you tell me.' Flora dealt him a provocative smile from below her lashes. 'After all, I'm totally in love with you.'

'Maybe just one kiss,' Angelo muttered thickly at the head of the stairs.

A wicked glint in her green eyes, Flora pulled away with a victorious giggle and raced downstairs with the full skirt of her dress flying like an emerald banner and Skipper tagging her heels...

* * * * *

We hope you enjoyed the
THE BILLIONAIRES
COLLECTION!

If you liked reading these stories, then you
will love **Harlequin® Presents®**.

You want alpha males, decadent glamour and
jet-set lifestyles. Step into the sensational,
sophisticated world of **Harlequin® Presents®**,
where sinfully tempting heroes ignite a fierce and
wickedly irresistible passion!

Enjoy eight new stories from
Harlequin Presents every month!

Available wherever books and ebooks are sold.

"AND what about us? Where are we supposed to go?" Belle
demanded heatedly, her temper rising. "It takes time to
relocate."

"You'll have at least a month to find somewhere else,"
Cristo fielded without perceptible sympathy while he watched
the breeze push the soft clinging cotton of her top against
her breasts. He clenched his teeth together, willing back his
arousal.

"That's not very long. Five children take up a lot of
space…they're your brothers and sisters, too, so you should
care about what happens to them!" Belle launched back at
him in furious condemnation.

"Which is why I'm here to suggest that we get married and
make a home for them together," Cristo countered with harsh
emphasis as he wondered for possibly the very first time in his
life whether he really did know what he was doing.

"*Married?*" Belle repeated, aghast, wondering if she'd

missed a line or two in the conversation. "What on earth are you talking about?"

"You said that you wanted your siblings to enjoy the Ravelli name and lifestyle. I can only make that happen by marrying you and adopting them."

Frowning in confusion, Belle fell back a step, in too much shock to immediately respond. "Is this a joke?" she asked when she had finally found her voice again.

"It is not," Cristo replied levelly, a stray shard of sunlight breaking through the clouds to slant across his lean, strong face.

All over again, Belle studied him in wonder, because he had the smoldering dark beauty of a fallen angel. His brilliant dark eyes were nothing short of stunning below the thick screen of his lashes, and suddenly she felt breathless.

* * *

The Legacies of Powerful Men

Three tenets to live by: money, power and the ruthless pursuit of passion!

*Available in June 2014,
wherever books and ebooks are sold!*

THE guest elevators at The Chatsfield hotel in London were spacious by any definition, but the confined area *felt* small to Aaliyah Amari.

"You're not very Western in your outlook," she said, trying to ignore the unfamiliar desires and emotions roiling through her.

"I am the heart of Zeena Sahra—should my people and their ways not be the center of mine?"

She didn't like how much his answer touched her. To cover her reaction she waved her hand between the two of them and said, "This isn't the way of Zeena Sahra."

"You are so sure?" he asked.

"Yes."

He laughed, the honest sound of genuine amusement more compelling than even the uninterrupted regard of the extremely handsome man. "You are not like other women."

"You're the emir."

"You are saying other women are awed by me."

She gave him a wry look and said drily, "You're not conceited at all, are you?"

"Is it conceit to recognize the truth?"

She shook her head. Even arrogant, she found this man irresistible, and she had the terrible suspicion he knew it, too.

Unsure how she'd got there, she felt the wall of the elevator at her back. Sayed's body was so close his outer robes brushed her. Her breath came out on a shocked gasp.

He brushed her lower lip with his fingertip. "Your mouth is luscious."

"This is a bad idea."

"Is it?" he asked, his head dipping toward hers.

"Yes. I'm not part of the amenities."

"I know." His tone rang with sincerity.

"I don't do elevator romps," she clarified, just in case he didn't get it.

Something flared in his dark gaze and Sayed stepped back, shaking his head. "I apologize, Miss Amari. I do not know what came over me."

"I'm sure you're used to women falling all over you," she offered by way of an explanation.

He frowned. "Is that meant to be a sop to my ego or a slam against it?"

"Neither?"

He shook his head again, as if trying to clear it.

She wondered if it worked. She would be grateful for a technique that brought back her own usual way of thinking, unobscured by this unwelcome and unfamiliar desire.

* * *

Step into the gilded world of THE CHATSFIELD!
Where secrets and scandal lurk behind every door…

Reserve your room in May 2014!